MW00638229

The God Thief

By Ben Hale

Text Copyright © 2016 Ben Hale

All Rights Reserved

To my family and friends,

who believed

And to my wife,

who is perfect

The Chronicles of Lumineia

By Ben Hale

—The Master Thief—

Jack of Thieves

Thief in the Myst

The God Thief

—The Second Draeken War—

Elseerian

The Gathering

Seven Days

The List Unseen

—The Warsworn—

The Flesh of War

The Age of War

The Heart of War

—The White Mage Saga—

Assassin's Blade (Short story prequel)

The Last Oracle

The Sword of Elseerian

Descent Unto Dark

Impact of the Fallen

The Forge of Light

Table of Contents

Table of Contents 5

Map of Lumineia 8

Prologue: The God of Light 10

Chapter 1: Caged 15

Chapter 2: Thorne...24

Chapter 3: The Assassin's Heir 30

Chapter 4: A Thief Unbound.......................................38

Chapter 5: Hunted...46

Chapter 6: Assassin of the Deep.................................53

Chapter 7: Kulldye Dreg 61

Chapter 8: Pyron's Folly 69

Chapter 9: Wart 76

Chapter 10: The *Hullbreaker*....................................84

Chapter 11: Imposter 93

Chapter 12: Ero's Gambit..100

Chapter 13: A Woman Scorned.................................106

Chapter 14: Thinning the Herd..................................113

Chapter 15: Loyalty 121

Chapter 16: Talinorian Mercenaries..........................130

Chapter 17: Talinorian Fury 136

Chapter 18: Reunion 142

Chapter 19: Wedge 150

Chapter 20: Sirani 157

Chapter 21: Thief's Flight 164

Chapter 22: The Exiled 172

Chapter 23: Betrayer 179

Chapter 24: Ero's Staff 186

Chapter 25: The Guildmaster's Mantle 193

Chapter 26: The Sea Dancer 202

Chapter 27: Humbled 206

Chapter 28: The Shattered Isle 213

Chapter 29: The City of Dawn 221

Chapter 30: Ancient Secrets 228

Chapter 31: The Vault Guardian 235

Chapter 32: A Daring Plan 242

Chapter 33: Stealing a Dragon 250

Chapter 34: The Mind Vault 256

Chapter 35: Ero's Intrigue 263

Chapter 36: Ancient Enmity 271

Chapter 37: Jack's Secret 279

Chapter 38: Last Assignments................................287

Chapter 39: To War 295

Chapter 40: The Necrolith 303

Chapter 41: Seastone 310

Chapter 42: A Thief's Army................................317

Chapter 43: Trapped 324

Chapter 44: The God Thief.................................332

Chapter 45: Crumbling.....................................339

Chapter 46: Jack's Truth 346

Chapter 47: Parting..354

Epilogue: The Living Gate 358

The Chronicles of Lumineia................................364

Author Bio 365

Map of Lumineia

Prologue: The God of Light

High Abbot Alidon donned his robe and stepped in front of the mirror. The gold and white material flowed over his gut, obscuring his tendency for excess. Elves were not prone to gluttony, but he believed one of his position deserved to partake. He licked his lips and reached for the elderberry ale.

"Drinking before dawn?" Paro asked, her voice tinged with scorn.

Alidon turned on her. "I tire of punishing you. How many scars will it take before you are obedient?"

The woman scowled, her fingers stroking the faint lines on the back of her arm. Paro had served in the Talinorian army for two decades before devoting herself to Ero. But her rise in the ranks of the Church of Light had been stunted by her vocal opposition to the church's practices.

"Have you considered my proposal?" Paro asked. "Today would be the day for an announcement."

Alidon smiled. "Ero has rejected it."

Paro glared at him. "Ero rejected a plan to close the donation wells for *one day*?"

"Careful, acolyte," Alidon said. "You may have attained the eighth circle, but blasphemy is still punishable by expulsion from the church."

Paro's lips curled with hatred before she lowered her gaze and stepped to the door. "It's almost time," she cast over her shoulder.

Alidon's smile turned smug as she departed. He loved watching a woman's eyes drop to the floor. He turned back to the mirror and added the rings to his fingers. The greatest he saved for last, the one bearing the insignia of the god Ero.

"The people call you the deity of light," he said to himself, and then a chuckle shook his jowls. "But if you exist, you are most certainly the god of gold."

He turned away from the mirror and exited his private quarters. The elven guards fell into step behind him in a whisper of cloth. They wore cloaks like his, but instead of gold and white the cloth was blue with white accents, the colors of a third circle acolyte.

He resisted the urge to smirk at them. Of the nine levels in church, everyone wanted to reach the seventh, the circle where peace in the afterlife was supposedly assured. Only the high abbot attained level nine, and the walls around him reflected the white and gold of his rank.

Banners hung from golden rods, the cloth rippling with magic. One showed a final winter storm drifting white flakes onto a mountain in Griffin, while another displayed a river in Talinor, its banks swollen with spring runoff. The adornments had been purchased from donations dropped into the wells placed throughout the temples of the church.

Although all the temples were star-shaped, the structure in Azertorn dwarfed them all. It stood a hundred feet high and contained a series of offices above the worship hall. The floor was segmented into nine circular levels, each reflecting the colors of the respective level of enlightenment. The center circle was reserved for Alidon, and contained his office, bedchamber, receiving room, library, and private worship hall.

Outside Alidon's circle, the subsequent rings represented the nine levels an acolyte must ascend to join Ero in the afterlife. Eighth-circle abbots served as heads for each of the levels, with Paro relegated to serving at the lowest.

Alidon reached the end of the curve and descended the stairs, passing a sphere hanging in an alcove. Shimmering rings reflected the nine circles, each shining brighter as they approached the center, the Heart of Ero. It was proximity to the god that everyone wanted, and their desire drove many to pour coin into the wells—and Alidon's pockets.

"High Abbot," one of his guards spoke, drawing his attention. "If I may . . ."

The curve of the staircase brushed against the exterior of the temple, and Alidon glanced out the window to see a predawn light above the edge of the city. It was still a few minutes until the ceremony so he turned to the acolyte.

"What is your request, acolyte?"

"My son is unwell, and the healers cannot help."

Alidon smiled sympathetically. "Man cannot heal what Ero wills."

The elf bowed his head. "Will you beseech him on my behalf?"

"Do you show your devotion?"

"I donate every day," the elf said.

"It is not a true sacrifice unless it cuts," Alidon admonished.

"I'll double it," the acolyte said.

Alidon reached out and touched his shoulder. "Then Ero's light will be upon you."

The acolyte smiled and bowed. As Alidon turned away he smiled as well, imagining what he would buy with the coin. At the very least his bedchamber needed an upgrade. The last acolyte he'd attempted to entice had ripped the sheets as she'd fled.

He turned a corner and descended the final steps until he reached an arched doorway. Bound by dwarven granite and inlaid with gold, the doors were hand carved from Amazonian teak. The guards at the door nodded to him and grasped the handles. Alidon readied himself and pasted a smile on his face before nodding to them.

The door swung open and he entered the great hall, advancing through the massive crowd. Shaped in a great star, the room contained thousands of elves, humans, and a smattering of the other races. The

12

pews all pointed to the stage at the center and its statue, an enlarged effigy of the god Ero. A hole in the ceiling allowed sunlight to beam upon the statue, bathing it in glory. The sun had yet to crest the horizon, but faint light illuminated Ero's marble features.

The temple in Azertorn was the head of the church, and the first dawn of each spring brought acolytes in droves for the Dawnlight ceremony. They came for blessings and to show their devotion to Ero— and they brought endless bags of coin.

Four eighth-circle abbots entered at the other points of the star, and together they approached the stage at the center of the hall. A hush swept the acolytes as Alidon stepped onto the stage and raised his hands to the great statue of Ero. Conscious of the attention, he spoke the customary prayer.

"Ero, God of light and living, grace us with your presence and fill our souls with truth."

He bowed deep and the crowd murmured the invocation, the voices melding into a hum of excitement. Then he rose and turned to the gathering, pleased to see that people lined the walls, unable to find a seat in the press of bodies.

"We gather for the first dawn of a new spring," he said, the charms on the stage amplifying his voice to fill the hall, "and I welcome you to the Dawnlight. As with every year, we gather to beseech Ero's light to be upon us . . ."

He launched into his sermon, stoking the crowd. His greatest talent was with the spoken word, and his gift had led to his rise within the church. His oration brought the believers to their feet, and even the skeptics in the room stood. Avowals of worship echoed off the walls, rising in fervor as Alidon filled their souls with hope. As the spirit of worship reached a fever pitch, he glanced to the side, and the acolyte guards slipped from the room, moving to activate their respective levers. A moment later a great thunder echoed, and the roof began to tremble.

The points on the star-shaped ceiling turned translucent, allowing a view of the predawn sky. Clouds drifted above the city, their cottony surfaces glowing red in the east. The edges of the roof reflected the light, slanting it toward the statue of Ero. Many in the crowd raised their hands to the brightening effigy. Alidon allowed the grandeur of the moment to build, relishing the sound of coins filling hands. Dawn touched the horizon and the light brightened on Ero, wreathing the statue in an ethereal glow.

"We beseech you, Ero!" Alidon called. "Grant us the light of your presence!"

To his shock the light continued to brighten. He cast about for an explanation, but the other abbots were equally as confused. They shielded their gaze as the light became blinding, exceeding the enchantment and sending cries of shock throughout the congregation.

The heavens twisted, the clouds spinning into a tornado that descended upon the temple. It passed through the hole in the roof and fell upon Ero, churning around the stone. Alidon stumbled off the stage, wind whipping his robes. The crowd surged back, recoiling as the abbots hastily retreated. But the tornado tightened, the wind slicing into the statue's fine granite, shredding it to dust.

Men and women cried out, shouting for direction, but Alidon stood frozen in shock. He watched helplessly as the tornado decimated the statue. Then the light brightened further, and amid the raging cyclone a figure descended. Wreathed in light and glory, he came to rest in the rubble and swept his hands wide. The sudden storm evaporated and the dawn returned to normal.

"You have called," Ero spoke. A smile appeared on his divine features as his startlingly blue eyes settled on Alidon. "And I have come."

Chapter 1: Caged

Jack Myst stared at the parchment on his desk. It was an assignment request by a duke in Griffin to steal the daughter of a rival lord for his son. Unfortunately, Jack knew the duke and his penchant for cruelty among his servants, and family. Dipping his pen into the inkwell, Jack scrawled *'DENIED'* across the request.

"You can't deny them all," Forlana said.

He glanced at her. Forlana was a class three thief skilled in deception and combat. She could don a persona as easily as a cloak for a winter stroll. She was a generation removed from Jack and her skewering look reminded him of his mother.

"I'm the guildmaster," Jack said, trying not to sound like a petulant child. "I can deny requests I don't like."

Forlana placed a hand on the stack of parchment. "The Thieves Guild cannot survive on just the contracts that seem 'interesting'."

He sighed and gestured for the next. "As you order."

Forlana pursed her lips as she handed it to him. He pretended to look it over but let his eyes wander. He'd changed the office when he'd accepted the rank. Spacious and open, the rectangular office contained the traditional darkwood desk at the center. Instead of blades and banners, Jack had placed memories on the walls of his office. Pedestals lined the exterior and displayed items he'd stolen in his time as a guild thief. Most were cast from light magic to represent real objects, and depicted everything from a dark necklace to an entire ship.

Jack's private bedchamber sat adjacent, while a door on the opposite side led to the top of the Machine, the testing wall for the thieves. At the rear of the room a strongdoor led to the guild's vault, the first place Jack had entered upon becoming guildmaster. What he'd found had been shocking and disturbing, but he still enjoyed exploring the myriad of hidden alcoves within the vault.

"Jack . . ." Forlana said.

"I know," he said, browsing the parchment before absently signing.

"They should be back any day," Forlana said.

He grinned and leaned back in his seat. "Ero was supposed to arrive in Azertorn a fortnight ago. Beauty should have been back by now."

"We need to finish this," Forlana said, gathering up the parchment.

Jack folded his arms. "It's time for a break."

Forlana skewered him with a look before relenting. "As you order, Guildmaster."

Jack stretched, grateful for a reprieve from paperwork. Then a commotion outside his office drew his gaze, and a moment later the door swung open. A raven-haired woman strode in, smiling as her eyes met Jack's.

"You should have been there," Beauty said.

"Forlana insisted I had paperwork to accomplish," he said sourly.

Forlana grinned at his side. "*I* do all the paperwork."

Jack laughed and didn't argue. Forlana really did most of the records, but he didn't want to admit his real reason for not attending Ero's arrival. He leaned back in his seat and tossed the quill onto the stack of records he was supposed to sign.

"Can we finish this later?" he asked Forlana.

"All you have to do is sign them," she said. "I completed the assignment records days ago."

16

"Tomorrow," Jack said. "I swear it."

Forlana's eyes sparkled with humor and she gathered the requests up. "Tomorrow, first thing."

"As you order," Jack said with a sigh, already wondering how he could get out of it.

Beauty laughed when the door shut. "You've been guildmaster for a few months, yet act like you are shackled to this desk."

He groaned and rose to his feet. "Lorelia made it look easy," he said, and strode to the row of trophies set against the wall. He came to a halt before the empty pedestal where he'd planned on placing his first conquest after becoming guildmaster. It had been months, but it was still empty.

"I used to enjoy my occupation," he said.

"Your job is to lead the guild," Beauty reminded him. "Not steal for it. Besides, you know the bounty on your head."

Jack scowled at the reminder. Skorn had stayed true to his word, and put a thousand-gold bounty on Jack's head—if it came detached from his body. Jack had thought they'd defeated Skorn at the battle of Margauth, but apparently he'd simply withdrawn to lick his wounds.

"I thought he wanted to kill me himself," Jack said.

"You sound disappointed," Beauty said.

He turned to find her smiling. "Does this *amuse* you?"

"Let's see. First Skorn was imprisoned by his brother for forty thousand years—where he spent his time plotting revenge. When he finally escaped, he became guildmaster of the Thieves Guild—using his position to hunt for a master thief that would help him reclaim his power. I'm fairly certain that was supposed to be you. But you went and opposed him, didn't you?"

"So?" Jack asked.

"You destroyed his map, his beacon, and his fortress," she said, and her eyes sparkled with amusement, "and you did it because you thought it would be fun."

"It *was* fun."

"Perhaps," she said, "but it's the reason he wants you dead."

"My safety is not worth being trapped here, scratching judgments on parchment."

Her smile faded. "Avoiding boredom is not worth getting yourself killed. Assassins are combing the five kingdoms for you. If you take an assignment outside this guildhall, you'll wake up without your head."

"Worried about me?" he asked, stepping to her.

"Yes," she said.

He sensed her desire to close the gap but hesitation bound her body. Unwilling to give a chance for her to withdraw, he returned to his desk and sank into his chair, leaning back to put his boots on the desk.

"Tell me about Ero," he said.

He motioned her to the seat across from him. Although he retained the smile, he wondered about her reaction. Jack and Beauty shared a mutual attraction, but Beauty avoided anything beyond an occasional kiss, and rarely spoke of it. Rather than discouraging, her reluctance made her more appealing, but he wondered if she would ever yield to him.

"He showed up exactly as you predicted," Beauty said briskly. "And you should have seen the high abbot's face."

Jack snorted. "I suspect most of the clergy in the Church of Light know it's all about the coin. To have their god show up probably made them empty their bowels—especially Alidon."

"I must admit," Beauty said, "Ero actually looks like a god."

"I know," Jack said, recalling the first time he'd met the ancient being in the Vault of the Eternals.

"When is Ero going after Skorn?" Beauty asked.

"You think Ero knows where Skorn is hiding?" Jack asked.

"*We* can't find him," she said. "And we've used every contact the guild has."

"It doesn't matter," Jack said. "Skorn will come to Ero."

"How do you know?"

"He won't be able to resist," Jack replied. "Like you said, Skorn was in prison for longer than we can imagine. He'll want to kill his warden, brother or not."

"I hope you're right," she said. "Because Skorn is not sitting idle, and the more time he has, the more damage he can do."

"Like you said," Jack said. "I destroyed his beacon. What can he do without it?"

"He's Skorn," she said, her expression darkening. "A member of the ancient race—one that many believe is the devil of our world. He always has a plan."

"This time we have Ero," Jack said. "And he's a powerful ally."

"Are you certain we can trust him?"

Jack thought back to the first time he'd met Ero, his eyes drawn to the small pyramid displayed on one of his pedestals. He'd stolen the beacon from the Vault of the Eternals, where he'd encountered Ero and learned of Skorn's imprisonment. Most of the world believed Ero and Skorn were gods, but they were merely survivors of the ancient race.

"We can trust his hatred for Skorn," Jack said.

"You never told me how you persuaded him to help," she said, leaning against the desk.

Jack grinned. It was a question she had asked before, but he'd been evasive with his answers. When he'd stolen from the Vault of the Eternals Jack had asked Ero if he intended on dealing with his brother, but Ero had refused. After returning from the battle at Margauth Jack had departed for the Vault a second time to enlist his aid.

"Ero did not wish to come," Jack admitted, "but I took a page from Skorn's book and used manipulation."

"You made him angry," she said, and then laughed. "I guess I should not be surprised. Skorn may have a way with manipulation, but you have a talent for inciting rage."

"Not anymore," Jack said sourly. "I've been cooped up for six months with no one to talk to but thieves."

"We're not all bad," Thalidon said, hearing Jack's comment as he stepped through the door.

Jack smirked at the dwarf. As the primary smith for the guild, Thalidon crafted gear and weapons. Now that his brother worked with him, they had managed to forge even better gear for the thieves—gear he had yet to use. He insisted on arming himself with all the new items, even though he knew he wouldn't be using them.

"Are the hopefuls ready?" Jack asked.

The dwarf nodded. "Slyver brought them in, and they are in the Machine chamber now."

"Let's get this done," Jack said. Beauty and Thalidon fell into step beside him as he left the office.

"Be nice," Beauty said. "The hopefuls don't deserve grouchy Jack."

Thalidon laughed. "Is that his persona now?"

"*No*," Jack said.

Beauty and Thalidon shared a laugh and they descended the stairs of the fortress. Located in the depths of the Evermist Swamp, the thief guildhall sat on an island in a lake. The citadel had been built ages ago by the extinct Verinai. Few dared to enter the swamp, and those that did were rarely found. Only the thieves passed safely in the Evermist.

20

Jack stepped into the cavernous great hall, his eyes drawn to the climbing wall that dominated the space. The Machine had changed since Skorn had made it lethal, with Jack's predecessor removing the more deadly traps from its surface. Now failure resulted in injury and disappointment, not dismemberment and death.

Jack strode to the line of hopefuls surveying the wall. There was more than he expected, with over a score of thieves eager to join the ranks of the guild. Jack was in his early twenties, but some of the thieves were barely fifteen.

A young woman stood in the middle of the pack. She fidgeted with a knife until she caught sight of Jack, when her eyes widened and she dropped the blade. She flushed and picked it up before falling into a whispered conversation with her companion.

The woman next to her looked to be Jack's age. Her striking red hair set her apart from the group, as did her poise. She wore dark pants and a tight vest with red threading. She caught his eye and held it without fear or anger, and enough intensity to make him curious.

"Welcome, hopefuls," Jack said.

A shiver trickled down his spine. They were the same words Skorn had said to him when Jack had infiltrated the guild to find his mother's killers. His quest for vengeance resulted in Skorn's expulsion from the guild, and the enmity between them had deepened with each subsequent conflict.

"You now face the Machine," he said. He turned his thoughts from Skorn and strode to the group of hopefuls. "It may not be as lethal as it once was, but do not dismiss its dangers."

He grinned and gestured to Thalidon, who slipped out of view. The thieves in the balcony above laughed and called out as the Machine began to turn. Jack turned his attention to the Machine, wishing he was one of the hopefuls about to ascend.

Traps and spells covered the surface. Nets and barbed hooks were hidden behind handholds, ready to spring out and grasp a climber. Water traps would explode and freeze one to the wall, while light curses lay hidden, ready to cause temporary blindness. Some holds contained a

21

numbing poison, while others hid spiders. The lethal variety had been removed and a stinging Grey Hollow spider had taken its place. Many of the handholds held banshee curses.

Although dangerous, the traps were nothing compared to the blades, curses, and arachnids that had littered the Machine when Jack had made his first ascent. Still, Thalidon and his brother Roarthin had made the climb a daunting affair, and few hopefuls made it past level one. Without the threat of death, the hopefuls could push their skills without fear. Much of what they might encounter on assignment could be found on the Machine, and it was an adequate measure of a thief's skills.

"Slyver," Jack said, gesturing to him. "You may begin."

The thief inclined his head and took the lead. "This is where you prove yourself," he said, gesturing to the wall. "Fail to pass the first level and you will be returned to Talinor. Attempt to return to the guildhall on your own and you will likely die in the Evermist."

He strode among the hopefuls. "Those of you to pass the first level will become first-level thieves and gain . . ."

Jack tuned out the rest of the speech. He'd heard it before and was already bored—and he was tired of being bored. When he'd agreed to be guildmaster he'd never thought it would be so stifling.

"I like the new wall," Beauty said.

"I miss the old one," Jack said.

"The one *designed* to kill you?"

"It was exciting," he said, watching the first hopeful get trapped in an explosion of ropes.

"I'm sure the rest of your week will be better," Beauty said.

Thalidon stepped to their side and nodded. "She's right," he said. "We have a lot planned for you."

Beauty threw Thalidon a sharp look. Jack realized the dwarf's meaning and rotated to face him, anger sparking in his blood. He grabbed Beauty's arm and spun her about, stepping so close he could see the flakes of grey in her blue eyes.

"What does he mean, *we*?"

She shrugged him off. "You're missing the hopefuls."

The evasion confirmed his suspicions. "*Thera.*"

The use of her real name caused her to finally meet his gaze. "We knew you wanted to go out," she admitted, "so we filled your time to keep you inside."

"How many are involved?"

Even Thalidon flinched at his voice. "Everyone that knows you," Thalidon said. "Forlana, Gordon, Ursana, Slyver—"

"Enough," Jack snapped. "You think to manipulate me? You're just like Skorn."

The heat to his words drew the gaze of Slyver, who drifted close. "Is something amiss?"

"Everything," Jack growled.

He shoved through them and strode across the chamber. Beauty made to follow but Jack cast her a scathing look, freezing her in her tracks. He passed through the other thieves, pushing past the hopefuls.

They called out to him but he ignored them. The hopeful on the end stepped into his path, closing off his exit. Jack veered around him, a growl on his lips—and then noticed the dagger. Serrated and long, it slipped from its sheath and pointed at Jack. He looked up as the man yanked the amulet from his neck, removing the magic that hid his features.

Jack came to an abrupt halt. "Thorne," he said.

The assassin inclined his head but did not advance. "Jack."

Jack snatched the dagger from his back and dropped his crossbow into his palm. "I suppose Skorn sent you?"

23

"Sorry Jack," the assassin said. "I really did like you." Then he lunged forward, driving his dagger toward Jack's chest.

Chapter 2: Thorne

Jack slipped to the side, narrowly missing the blade as it sliced across his tunic. Thorne rotated and came again, driving for his throat. Jack swiveled and caught the assassin's dagger on his own blade, the impact driving him back. Fighting for space, Jack parried another strike and backtracked.

"You should have waited until I was alone," Jack said.

"It wouldn't matter anyway," Thorne said with a shrug. "No one here can stop me."

Hopefuls retreated as thief guards rushed forward. Beauty beat them to it. Her body enhanced by her magic, she streaked across the space and struck at the assassin. The man anticipated the strike and caught her wrist. With a twist he redirected her motion and launched her toward the Machine. She crashed into its surface and dropped to the floor.

Thorne sniffed in disapproval. "Barbarians," he said. "Their speed charms always make them overcommit."

Beauty wiped the blood from the cut on her forehead and rose to her feet. She snarled and picked up her sword, darting to the assassin. Jack came from the opposite flank as Thalidon and Slyver struck from behind.

Thorne spun in a circle, his cloak billowing outward. His person fractured into a dozen matching assassins that scattered to engage the thieves. One leapt to Thalidon and struck, his dagger battering

Thalidon's axe. Another intercepted Beauty and drove his dagger toward her stomach. The rest engaged the thief guards, who howled in dismay as they were driven back by the sudden army.

Beauty parried a blade and drove her own weapon into the man's stomach—but the blade passed through the mirage. She withdrew in confusion and the assassin struck, cutting a furrow across her arm.

"Watch out for the blades!" she cried out, and deflected her opponent in a shower of sparks.

The real Thorne strode toward Jack. "The mirage charm can do no physical harm," he said, "unless it's given a lightcast blade."

The mirages may have been nothing but light, but their blades did plenty of damage. Unable to get around them, the other thieves couldn't reach the real assassin. Sparks scorched the floor as thieves and mirages clashed in a whirlwind of battle. Jack saw the conflict out of the corner of his eye but kept his gaze on Thorne.

The man was tall and muscular, and wielded his single blade with shocking precision. He was second out of the seven members of the Assassin's Guild, and he'd earned the rank by displaying a lethality that rivaled Gallow, the assassin guildmaster.

"I never realized you were a light mage," Jack said, retreating toward the Machine.

The man shrugged as if he were bored. "Elves are known for light magic, but humans occasionally have the talent. I actually trained with Lorelia, although I doubt she would have remembered."

The assassin darted in and Jack blocked the strike. Beauty had taught Jack a great deal, but his skill in swordplay did not compare to the assassin's. Thorne struck again, testing Jack's defenses. Jack managed to parry the blow without losing his throat, but the assassin did not take advantage of the subsequent opening.

Jack smirked at the man's patience. "You think I'm feigning weakness?"

"You have a reputation," Thorne said. "You've faced threats from across Lumineia—yet remain standing. Experience requires caution."

26

Realizing the only thing keeping him alive was the man's hesitation, Jack went on the offensive. Raising his crossbow at the assassin, he sent a freezing bolt at his feet. Thorne sidestepped easily, rotating around the explosion of ice to keep Jack retreating toward the Machine. Jack used the man's motion to fire a second, and then a third.

The second bolt turned into enchanted ropes that expanded to catch the assassin, pushing the man toward the pile of ice. The third bolt went between the ice and ropes. Trapped in the middle, Thorne caught the bolt before it dug into his chest and tossed it away. It detonated on the ground, sending bits of charred stone through the army of mirages.

"Impressive," Jack said, pocketing the crossbow and ascending the Machine. "But I expect nothing less from a member of the Assassin's Guild."

Thorne began to climb behind him, his pace unhurried as he bypassed traps with ease. "You were dead the moment I was given the order, Jack. I'm just here to complete the kill."

"And it took you this long to find me?" Jack asked.

Thorne's jaw tightened. "I admit your guildhall was harder to locate than I anticipated."

"Got lost in the Evermist?"

Thorne's eyes flashed with irritation, confirming Jack's assumption. Then the assassin leapt closer to Jack, his blade slicing at Jack's ankle. Jack spun to the side and caught another hold, but the assassin cast another mirage on the other side of Jack. The secondary Thorne swung a blade at Jack and he ducked, the weapon cutting deep into the Machine.

Realizing he was trapped between the two, Jack released his hold and dropped to the base of the chamber, darting to a door. The assassin was half a step behind him, following Jack through the door before it could shut.

The sounds of the conflict faded as Jack bolted through the fortress. Drawn to the conflict, a pair of thief guards appeared and raced toward Jack. He pointed down the hall, away from the conflict.

"But sir!"

"Go!" Jack snapped. "Close off the exits."

They hesitated but Thorne cast a quartet of mirages that threw their swords, sending four searing blades spinning down the corridor. The guards were not quick enough, and the blades cut into their bodies. Jack leapt up and twisted sideways. The weapons passed above and below him before plunging into the wall. Jack landed as a mirage of Thorne appeared in his path, forcing him into the corridor leading to the hall of archives. He reached the end and glanced back to spot four Thornes racing after him, the real assassin striding behind them.

Jack slipped inside and slammed the door—and four blades pierced it. Heat from the magic seared through the wood as the blades began to carve an opening, and Jack retreated into the turret, casting about for a plan.

The turret lay open to the glass ceiling, allowing moonlight to partially illuminate the balconies. Balconies ringed the space and held curving bookshelves. Bracketed in iron, light orbs interspersed the shelves, providing illumination for the chamber.

As the door succumbed Jack raised his arm and cast his shadowhook, sending a thread of darkness upward, where it fused to the shadows beneath the third level. He yanked himself up and landed on the second, brushing the rune linked to the light orbs. The lights dimmed, hiding him in welcome shadows as Thorne stepped into view.

"You cannot hide from me, Jack," he said, striding to the center of the turret and looking upward. "No one ever hides from me."

"Do you always talk your targets to death?" Jack called.

Thorne rotated to face him but Jack slipped away before he was spotted. The assassin frowned and cast a trio of mirages that leapt to the balconies. As they hunted, Jack used a staircase to ascend higher.

"Thieves," Thorne said with a snort. "You always think the shadows are your friends."

The assassin punched his hands together and light blossomed at the top of the turret. The moonlight brightened and spread, filling the hall like it was noonday. The shadows disappeared as the magic destroyed them, leaving every corner exposed.

Thorne smiled. "You can never hide——."

Jack slammed into his back, knocking the assassin to the floor. He'd used the burst of light to shield his approach, and plunged his dagger into Thorne's cloak. Jack's weapon dug into Thorn's shoulder rather than his heart as the assassin twisted his body. Thorne growled in pain and rage, throwing Jack to the side.

Jack landed on his feet and fired his crossbow. Thorne tried to catch it but failed, and the bolt sank into his arm. The assassin yanked it free with a snarl, all trace of civility gone. The bolt clattered on the floor and he sidestepped the next bolt.

"You will pay for that."

"Don't bleed on me," Jack said, wrinkling his nose. "I really like this tunic."

Thorne snarled and spun his cloak. The moonlight dimmed as he cast a full score of mirages, filling the base of the turret with matching assassins. The Thornes were quick to flank Jack, leveling burning lightcast blades at him. Jack began to laugh, and the humor mounted into a roar.

"How can one man be so infuriating?" Thorne growled.

"Practice," Jack said.

Jack cast his shadowhook into the now darkened balconies and streaked out of the ring of death. Thornes attacked on all sides but Jack never stopped moving. He leapt and twisted, diving through the railing of a staircase and then flipping to a lower level. Mirages filled his vision, their blades nicking his flesh and cutting his clothes.

He leapt left and right, hurtling up and down the turret. The mirages were too quick, coming at him from all sides, their blades drawing closer to his throat. He caught a handful of books and threw them into the mirages, trying to identify which was real. The records passed through the Thornes and clattered on the floor. One sliced through the book, sending a burst of pages into the air, the papers floating through the mirages.

Marking the fakes, he targeted the others with his hand crossbow, and sent bolts streaking through the mirages. He cast his shadowhook and leapt to the opposite side of the turret. Bolts exploded in his wake, filling the air with paper and smoke. The mirages flickered, all except one.

Jack caught a railing and plummeted to the floor, aiming his crossbow for the last. He fired three times, the first detonating against the floor to cover Thorne in smoke, the second froze the ground, covering his feet. The third plunged into the assassin's chest—but passed through him.

Realizing he'd been tricked, Jack spun. But Thorne darted from the shadows and wrapped his arm around Jack, his serrated dagger on Jack's throat. Jack growled in irritation as he realized the assassin had *made* his mirages flicker, leaving one for Jack to target.

"Normally I let my mirages kill my targets," Thorne snarled, "But I'd like to kill you myself."

Jack twisted his hand, bringing his dagger up toward the assassin's gut. The assassin saw it coming and shifted, hurtling Jack into the wall. Before Jack could move shackles of light appeared and bound him to the stones with shimmering bolts. Jack strained to pull free but the bindings refused to budge.

The other Thornes evaporated and the real assassin stalked forward, placing the tip of his serrated dagger on Jack's throat, his hand trembling with fury. The assassin's chest heaved with exertion, his features tight with pain. Blood stained his clothes and his hair lay in disarray.

"You're getting blood on my tunic," Jack said.

"At least death will silence you," he snarled, and leaned in for the kill.

Abruptly he froze, his eyes going wide. He looked down at the tip of a knife suddenly protruding from his chest. Shock flitted across his features, his dagger tumbling from his hand as he stumbled back. He tripped and went down on his knees before collapsing to the floor.

"Impossible," he muttered. "You're just thieves . . ."

The enchantments binding Jack evaporated and he stepped away from the wall. "Even thieves can kill," he said.

The assassin finally went still and Jack turned to find his savior. To his surprise it was the redheaded hopeful, who leaned down to pull her knife free. She wiped the blade on Thorn's shirt before returning it to its sheath. Then she stood and met Jack's gaze.

"Jack Myst," she said. "I thought you'd be taller."

Chapter 3: The Assassin's Heir

"I'm tall enough," Jack said, indignant.

She flushed at his response, betraying a touch of inexperience. "I just meant your reputation is larger than you know."

"You're not here to join the guild," Jack said. "So who are you?"

"Inna," she said, "and no, I'm not here to join the guild. I came to kill him." She gestured at Thorne's body.

"You're an assassin?" Jack asked, surprised.

"I am," she said.

Her expression lacked the darkness that assassins usually had. He fleetingly wondered if she'd come to collect the bounty herself, but something in her expression put him at ease.

"Who sent you?" he asked.

"My father would have," Inna replied, and her lips tightened. "If Gallow hadn't killed him."

"Who was your father?" Jack asked.

"Joren," Inna replied, "former guildmaster of the Assassin's Guild."

Intrigued, Jack cocked his head to the side. Before he could speak the door burst open and thieves flooded the hall of records. Beauty's eyes widened when she saw the devastated hall. A page floated down on her shoulder. She brushed it off and turned to Jack, her eyes flicking to Thorne.

"I thought you'd be dead," she said.

Thalidon absently wiped blood from a cut on his forehead. "How did you kill him?"

"I didn't," Jack said, gesturing to the redhead. "It was Inna who slew the assassin."

Beauty raised an eyebrow and stepped to her. "Thera," she said, introducing herself. "But they call me Beauty."

"I can see why," Inna said. "You fared well against Thorne."

"How many did we lose?" Jack asked.

"Four," Thalidon said. "It would have been more but the copies began disappearing."

"Jack took his focus," Inna said. "He couldn't maintain that much magic."

"You could have intervened sooner," Jack said.

She shook her head. "Thorne is adept at battling multiple foes. I had to wait until he was too focused to notice. Otherwise we'd both be dead, and I could never tell you Skorn's plan."

Jack peaked an eyebrow. "You know of Skorn?"

Inna's eyes flicked to the other thieves. "Skorn has allies in every guild. What I have to say is for your ears only."

Jack saw the resolve in her eyes and grinned. He gestured to Thalidon. "Care for the dead," he said, "and make certain the wounded are tended to. Beauty, with me."

"I said it was for your ears only," Inna protested.

"She is my ears," Jack replied. He held her gaze until she scowled and looked away.

"What about him?" Slyver asked, gesturing to Thorne's body.

"Feed him to the alligators," Jack said with a shrug.

Jack turned from the archives and threaded his way back into the fortress. Ascending a spiral staircase to the top of the turret, he reached a door and stepped outside. He blinked at the bright moonlight and strode to the center of the platform.

Spanning the gap between the tallest turrets in the fortress, the circular bridge provided an unbroken view of the Evermist swamp. Steeped in green fog, the trees seemed to shift and fade, undulating in patterns of moonlight. An alligator infested lake was just visible beneath the blanket of mist, which curled up the walls of the fortress like a living beast. The mist shrouded the citadel, making its size impossible to discern.

Jack turned to Inna and Beauty. "What do you know?" he asked Inna.

Inna glanced at Beauty and then her eyes returned to Jack.

"You can trust her more than you can me," Jack said with a smile.

"It's true," Beauty said with a grin.

Inna hesitated before relenting. "My information comes with a price."

"If it's coin you seek . . ."

"No," she said hastily. "What I seek is retribution."

"And you think I can deliver it?" Jack asked, folding his arms.

"You survived against Gallow—more than once," she said. "And I want your help to kill him."

"How am I supposed to help you do that?"

"When you go after Skorn, I go with you. Gallow is nearly always at his side."

"Do you know where Skorn is?" Beauty asked.

"No," Inna said, "but I know what he's doing."

"If what you say is true," he said. "You can join me on the assignment."

"Jack," Beauty began. "You have work here."

"No," he said. "If Thorne's appearance has proven anything, it means the assassins can reach anywhere. I can't stay here." He couldn't stop the grin from spreading on his features.

"Are you *excited?*" Inna asked. "The moment you leave here you will be hunted by assassins from across the globe."

"I know," Jack said, his voice turning positively gleeful.

"Is he always like this?" Inna asked Beauty, clearly shocked to see Jack's response.

"Always," Beauty said sourly.

Jack could hardly contain himself. After being trapped in the guildhall for months, he would have faced a thousand Thornes if it meant he could leave—as himself anyway. There was no need for Beauty to know he'd slipped out of the guildhall under the guise of different personas.

Inna now seemed uncertain, and Jack saw the calculating glint in her eye. Her expression was familiar, for he'd seen it in the mirror as a youth. She'd spent years preparing to go after her father's killer. She'd been unsuccessful on her own, and decided to find an ally. The doubt in her gaze indicated she wasn't confident in her choice.

"What do you know?" Jack asked.

She hesitated, her eyes flicking between them. "I've been keeping track of Gallow for years," she finally said. "I've witnessed much of his conflict with you, and used it to eliminate members of his guild. With him serving Skorn, he hasn't had time to gather the guild and replace them. Killing Thorne cut his ranks down to three."

"You said you've witnessed Gallow's conflict with Skorn," Beauty said. "What have you seen?"

35

"For one, the destruction of Margauth."

Beauty's eyebrows rose. "You were there?"

"I was camped on a ridge overlooking the fortress," she said. "I thought to take advantage of the conflict to kill Gallow, but by the time I descended he'd fled. Then I saw Jack activate the implosion hex that decimated the citadel."

"You saw something," Jack guessed, hearing it in her voice. "Something we didn't."

"Skorn returned the night after the battle," she said. "He came back for the remains of the beacon."

Jack shook his head. "You saw the implosion hex. If anything survived, it would be bits of trash."

"The beacon was of ancient make," Beauty said. "Perhaps it was only damaged."

"He found something," Inna said. "And he's going to rebuild it."

"It's been months since that battle," Jack said. "What took you so long to get here?"

"Same reason Thorne didn't find you earlier," Inna said. She strode to the edge of the railing and swept a hand at the Evermist. "I nearly died in the swamp trying to find you. I was forced to wait until your guild invited prospective thieves to join your ranks."

"Do you think he's already completed the beacon?" Beauty asked.

Inna shook her head, making her red hair dance. "I suspect if he had, we would know about it."

"As wise as you are beautiful," Jack said.

"His cult members are spreading across Lumineia," Inna said, ignoring his comment. "Gathering material to rebuild his beacon. They board ships and then disappear. I haven't been able to find a pattern."

"We've had similar difficulty locating Skorn's new lair," Beauty said.

36

Jack strode toward Inna but she retreated. Noting the response, he came to a halt. "So we find his beacon and destroy it."

"I said I don't know the location," Inna said. "But I do have a contact on Kulldye Dreg that might know something."

"The pirate island?"

Jack had heard of the island's nefarious reputation. Said to be a hive of killers, pirates, and outcasts, it contained the refuse of society, the dregs of the five kingdoms. A faint smile crossed his lips as he thought of exploring its streets. He turned to Beauty, but she raised a hand to forestall his words.

"Don't think I'm not coming with you," Beauty said.

"You think to watch my back?"

She smirked. "I can try—but you don't listen well."

"True," he said. "Inform Forlana she can take my place while I'm gone." He grinned. "I've given myself an assignment."

"Just the three of us?" Beauty asked.

"For now," Jack said. "I'd like to keep it small until we know what we're dealing with. Get Inna some quarters she can feel safe in."

"Done," Beauty said, and motioned Inna toward the door. "I'll see you in the morning."

"One more thing," Inna said. "Betray me, and I'll kill you faster than you can draw breath."

Her tone echoed harsh and rigid, but Jack burst into a laugh.

She scowled. "You think to mock me?"

Beauty gestured toward the door as Jack continued to laugh. "You just made it more fun for him." Beauty said.

"Has he lost his mind?" Inna asked in an undertone.

"No," Beauty said, meeting his gaze. "He's just been cooped up too long."

"Beauty," Jack called, and she looked back.

"Don't manipulate me again."

All trace of his humor was gone. He relished the idea of leaving the guild, but he hadn't forgotten what Beauty had done. She was his friend, one of the few he trusted, or thought he could. But the affection they shared made her manipulation sting all the more. He held her gaze until she nodded slowly, and Jack saw the apology in her eyes.

Once they were gone he returned to his office, his previous levity returning in force. Stepping through the door, he dismissed the guards and strode to the vault at the back of the space. Then he withdrew the key from his pocket.

The vault door contained a series of levers that had to be turned in an exact sequence to open it, or the guildmaster could use his key. The night Jack had become guildmaster he'd woken to find the key on the stand beside the bed. He'd taken no thought for it, until the following night he woke to find it in his palm. Then he'd realized it was linked to the current guildmaster, and used it to open the vault for the first time.

Jack stepped to the door and placed the key against the surface. The key stuck fast and began to turn, rotating to point at each lever. The tumblers turned in response, answering the call from the key. When finished, the key leapt back into his hand and Jack swung the door open.

Technically, everything in the space belonged to him, making it less fun to steal. Fortunately, he'd found a few secrets within the vault that he doubted his predecessors had known about—one in particular that he kept to himself.

The vault had also contained a warning from Lorelia. Instead of sharing it, Jack had decided to use it as a weapon, but never anticipated the burden it would carry.

He glanced behind to ensure he was by himself and then strode between the gold, jewels, and priceless relics. Chests sat on shelves, their contents spilling onto the floor. Jack passed the coin without a glance and came to a room at the back. Small alcoves looked back at him, the items within taken from strongrooms throughout Lumineia.

He stepped to one and reached to the back, pressing the hidden trigger that opened one of the secret alcoves he'd found. He'd taken the previous item for himself, and now used the space to store a few items he wanted kept secret. Gathering them, he placed them in the hidden pouches in his thief's webbing. Then he closed the latch and exited the vault.

It shut behind him with an odd note of finality, causing him to look back and stare at the cold door. Then he shrugged and turned toward his quarters. He packed everything he would need, checking and rechecking like it was his first assignment. When he was finished he reclined on his bed.

He stared at the ceiling, a smile spreading across his features. Of the several plans he had in motion, this would undoubtedly be the most fun. After becoming guildmaster, he'd ensured Ero's arrival and then set other plans into motion.

Inna had been right, he would encounter assassins at every turn. As if that wasn't dangerous enough, he would be attempting to infiltrate Skorn's ranks, a world rife with its own threats. To top it off he faced Gallow and Skorn. Again.

The excitement he felt would not be contained, and he spent the night fidgeting. He hadn't been so ready for an assignment since he first became a thief. Like children the night before their birthdays, he slept fitfully. When the clock finally chimed in the morning he grinned.

"Time to kill a devil," he said.

Chapter 4: A Thief Unbound

Jack rose and gathered his gear. He stepped from the room and ascended to the same platform where he'd spoken to Inna. It was early, with dawn yet to break on the horizon. He breathed deep of the misty air and smiled, relishing the impending journey. When he returned to his office Forlana was already at his desk.

She raised an eyebrow at his appearance. "You never rise before me."

"Couldn't sleep," Jack said.

"Too excited?"

He grinned. "Beauty told you?"

"It appears our attempt to contain you has come to an end," she said wryly.

"You shouldn't have manipulated me."

She skewered him with a look. "Don't pretend you don't have your own secrets."

Caught, he laughed and gestured to the pile of parchment that perpetually seemed to mar the smooth wood of his desk. "I hate to leave you with everything."

"No, you don't," she said, and slid a hand across her bald head. "You are a good thief, Jack, but a terrible guildmaster."

He should have been angry, but Forlana's honesty caused him to grin. "Were you this frank with my predecessor?"

"Yes," she said. "I thought you'd be offended."

He shrugged. "We both know the truth."

She raised an eyebrow. "If it helps, I think you can improve."

"It doesn't." He grinned and turned toward the door. "You've been doing most of my job anyway. I've just been here for looks."

Her laughter followed him into the hall. He followed the stairs past Ember Hall, the chamber reserved for upper level thieves. He spotted Ursana training on the climbing walls and paused. Then he noticed Gordon on the wall with her and stepped into the room.

"Ursana got you to rise before dawn?" Jack called up to Gordon.

Gordon looked down and laughed. Then he cast his shadowhook and dropped to the floor, advancing to Jack. Ursana was a step behind. Jack smiled at them, recalling her first attempt on the Machine. The three of them had been hopefuls together, and their friendship had only cemented on subsequent assignments

"She's relentless," Gordon said, looking to Ursana.

Ursana was only a year older than she'd been at her trial, but seemed a decade more mature. The timid girl had been replaced with a determined woman with a forceful gaze. She came to a halt before him and smiled.

"Where are you off to?" she asked.

"Guildmaster duties," he said with a sigh, feigning irritation.

"Does it have to do with Thorne and that woman?" Ursana asked shrewdly.

"Actually, it does," he replied.

They exchanged a look, and Gordon said, "I'm sure Beauty can handle it. I think Kuraltus said there were some things you needed to do."

41

Jack shook his head. "I need to go to Woodhaven. Shouldn't be gone more than a month or two." He enjoyed the abject panic on their faces before stabbing a finger at them. "Unless there are other *duties* you think I need to attend to."

Caught, their expressions turned guilty. "We were just trying to keep you safe," Ursana said.

"I can handle myself," Jack said, turning away.

Ursana began to laugh, the sound echoing off the walls of Ember Hall. "You take more risks than all of us—combined. One day your luck is going to run out, Jack, and none of us wants to see that happen."

"Have you so little faith in me?" Jack asked, his humor turning to irritation.

They exchanged a look, and Gordon said, "Thorne nearly killed you, and there are many more just like him."

"Then I should apologize," Jack said.

"For what?" Ursana said.

"For mistaking you as friends."

He turned and strode away, and they did not follow. Seething, Jack wound his way through the fortress until he reached a strongroom at the base of the eastern wall. Unlocking it with a special key, he stepped through into a small courtyard.

The remains of a garden lay scattered around the rim of the courtyard. Mist shrouded the space, clinging to the walls and his cloak. Overgrown weeds found purchase in the cracks between the stones, forcing Jack to pick his way to the well at the center.

He strode to the well and stepped onto the edge. Wreathed in fog, his position was invisible from the doors, allowing him to drop into the well unseen. He landed on the floor of the secret room below.

The chamber lay empty, the walls covered in moss. Jack stepped to the north wall and touched the rune hidden beneath it, and a lock appeared. Producing a key, he opened the door leading to a second secret room.

Golden artifacts and treasures adorned the wall. Shelves on both sides of the room held golden chalices, silver and agate pendants, and ceremonial daggers. Jack stepped past them to the mirror hanging on the wall.

An innocuous as it seemed, the mirror was a Gate, a portal to other Gates in Lumineia. While he'd been guildmaster, Skorn had placed one at each of the three thief guildhalls, and kept an additional one in his private bedchamber. It allowed the thieves instant travel to Terros in Griffin, and Woodhaven in the elven kingdom. Boots landed on the floor behind him, causing him to turn and find Beauty and Thalidon entering the room.

"It won't get us to Woodhaven," Beauty said.

Jack turned to find Beauty and Thalidon standing in the doorway. "Why not?"

"Their Gate was stolen."

"Someone *stole* the Gate?" Jack demanded, turning to face her. "From *us?*"

Thalidon grunted. "Ironic, I know. One day it was there in Woodhaven, the next it was gone. Every bit of magic used to protect it had been severed."

"When were you planning on telling me?" Jack asked.

"Why do you think it took me so long to return?" Beauty asked with a trace of irritation. I was going to tell you after the hopefuls finished their attempts on the Machine, but Thorne showed up and you were busy."

Thalidon scowled. "Kuraltus said they have no idea who the perpetrator was."

"Did anyone try Gating to it and see where it is?"

Thalidon grunted in irritation. "You don't think we tried that?"

"Whoever stole it must have disabled the magic," Beauty said.

Jack clenched his fists and looked away. "We'll deal with this later. Thalidon, you take the Gate in my office to Woodhaven, and take your brother with you. We can't afford to lose access to the elven guildhall right now. Beauty, you can take over the guardianship of Ero."

"I'm not coming with you?" Beauty asked, her features tightening.

"Don't look so disappointed," Jack said, wondering if it was jealousy he'd seen. "I'll take Inna on the overland route through Talinor and catch a ship to Kulldye Dreg."

"Alone?" Thalidon asked pointedly.

"I'm capable of handling myself," he said. "Or have you forgotten that?"

Beauty folded her arms. "Is this because we contrived to keep you here?"

"Friends don't manipulate each other."

She glared at him. "Are you saying you haven't kept your own secrets? I've come to speak to you several times and couldn't find you anywhere in the castle."

"I don't know what you mean," he said, pushing past her.

She caught his arm. "You disappear at odd hours," she said. "Care to explain that?"

He smiled blithely. "Privilege of a guildmaster," he said. "I'll see you after I return from Kulldye Dreg."

"You're sending us on delivery duty," Thalidon said with a scowl.

"And guard duty," Beauty added.

"It's a Gate," Jack said, gesturing to the mirror. "You think I would let just anyone guard it? And protecting Ero is a major priority."

"It still feels like a punishment," Beauty said.

44

"Maybe it is," Jack said.

Jack stepped on the rune on the floor, and the ascender lifted him into the well above, allowing him to exit into the garden. From there he made his way to Inna's quarters. Her door opened as he reached it and she came to a halt on the threshold.

"Ready to depart?" he asked.

"Where are the others?" she asked.

"Something came up," he replied. "They'll meet us after Kulldye Dreg. Gather your things."

She reached for her pack and joined him in the hall, but chose to remain at his back rather than his side. The tactic suggested doubt but he didn't care. Unwilling to encounter any more thieves, he led her through the bowels of the fortress to the northern exit. He stepped outside and pulled a hidden lever.

Rising from the murky depths of the lake, a bridge ascended into view. Alligators swam away from the movement, splashing and hissing at each other. The bridge breached the surface and came to a halt, allowing Jack and Inna to stride across and disappear into the Evermist.

Great cypress trees reached into the clinging mist, their canopies nearly invisible. Quicksand, poison, and prowling beasts were only a fraction of the dangers in the swamp. Whole armies had been swallowed by the Evermist, their bones and blades lost to the muck and moss.

Jack bypassed a green viperhead snake without conscious thought, and avoided a silver reaver haunt out of habit. His shaden cloak had been fashioned by Thalidon and enchanted with various magics that permitted safe travel in the swamp. Inna followed him on cat's feet, her gaze on the swamp about her.

His excitement at leaving the guildhall was marred by his lingering irritation at Beauty, Gordon, and Ursana. After everything they had been through, he'd thought they were allies—especially Beauty. He could count on one hand the people he trusted, and each of them had been part of the plan to keep him in the guildhall.

45

He snorted in chagrin, his thoughts turning to himself. How did he get to this point anyway, manipulated into hiding like a sewer rat? He'd stolen from every kingdom across Lumineia, and faced reavers, rock trolls, and even gods. Was he too distracted with Skorn to notice their intrigues? He grunted, sensing the truth to that. His other plans required enormous preparation, and he'd merely gone through the motions as guildmaster. He meted out assignments, but felt a budding jealousy every time he sent them out.

"You are not what I expected," Inna said, intruding on his brooding.

"You expected me to be principled."

"How did you know?"

"Because *you* are principled," Jack said.

For a while she did not respond. Then she said, "My father trained me when I was little, taught me how to survive and how to fight. He was a killer with a creed, and used the Assassin's Guild to punish those that kings could not."

"I've heard the tales," Jack said, dropping back to walk at her side. "He was a good man."

Her green eyes flicked to him before returning to the swamp. "On occasion he took other children in, training them to master themselves. Most became soldiers of honor, never realizing their benevolent caretaker was the head of the most lethal guild on Lumineia."

"Until he chose Gallow," Jack guessed.

"Gallow learned my father's true occupation and sought to join him. He *wanted* to kill. My father saw what he was becoming and refused, turning the boy's hope to fury. Gallow began to hunt the assassins, killing them until he recruited an exiled rock troll king to aid him. With his help Gallow infiltrated the Assassin's Guildhall and killed my father."

Inna spoke in a toneless voice, as if it were merely a story of her skinning her knee as a child. But the rigidity to her features implied a seething undercurrent of hatred and anger. The expression was all too familiar.

46

"We all have our motivations," he said.

She looked to him. "What did Skorn do to you?"

"Nothing."

"Then why do you want to destroy him?" she asked, clearly confused.

"Because it's fun."

"That can't be the only reason."

He laughed. "Sorry to disappoint."

A creak of wood caused him to look up, and he casually flicked his hand. His crossbow dropped into his palm and he thumbed the detonation rune, sending a spark of magic into the bolt. She noticed the motion and her expression turned suspicious. She drifted away and caught the hilt of her sword. Jack ignored the motion and aimed into the tree, firing against the trunk.

The explosion lit up the morning, illuminating the outline of a giant cat. Startled, the rayth cat bounded away, growling at the loss of its prey. From directly beneath the cat's perch, Inna looked at Jack.

"You just saved my life."

"Won't be the last time," he said with a grin.

Her lips tightened. "I can handle myself."

"I have no doubt," he said with a laugh. "But you have no idea what you are in for." He turned and continued on the trail.

"Who *are* you," she asked.

He glanced back, his smile widening. "A master thief. Think you can keep up?"

Chapter 5: Hunted

Jack and Inna worked their way through the Evermist until they reached the Sea of Grass on the south of Talinor. Inna breathed a sigh of relief when they left the swamp behind. Lush green grass covered the rolling hills of southern Talinor, the landscape ruffling as the wind caressed the earth. As they strode into the grass Jack looked back.

"Are you going to walk beside me?" Jack asked, "Or drive a knife into my back?"

"My father taught me that caution would save my life."

"Perhaps," Jack said. "But it's rather boring."

She didn't respond, and after a moment she joined him. Jack stifled a smile and didn't comment. Although she remained at his side, the redheaded assassin kept her distance, and a hand close to her sword.

The sun rose in the east, bathing the endless grass in light. Jack sucked in a breath, relishing the scent of the grass. He'd forgotten how good it smelled. Spring was well under way and the warm breeze brushed the grass like a paintbrush on a canvas, swirling the landscape in different shades of green. He reached out as he walked, brushing the strands with his fingertips.

They worked their way north for two days until they came to the village of Bodor. Renting a pair of steeds, they took the southern road beneath the capitol, Herosian. Jack spotted the spires in the distance and grunted in irritation. It had been months since he'd visited the taverns and haunts of the city, and he longed to return.

Passing through the smaller villages, they stayed in rural inns and taverns until they reached the coast. Then they took the route to Keese. By the time they reached the city they had picked up a follower.

"Did you see him?" Jack asked.

"He's been with us since last night," she said.

As they reached the gates, Jack glanced back and caught a glimpse of a figure on a distant hilltop. It wasn't enough to make out their identity, but it was enough to recognize them as the same man from the previous evening.

"Assassin?" Jack asked.

"Can't tell," she said. "We should split up when we get inside the city. I'll hang back and see if I can identify them."

Jack shook his head. "*I'll* hang back."

She frowned but did as requested. "I'll meet you at the Crow's Nest tonight. It's a tavern on the waterfront. Watch your back, and don't forget about the bounty."

He grinned. "That's what makes it exciting."

She cast him a wary look but did not comment. When they stepped through the city gates Jack slipped away and entered an alley. Leaping to a tree, he caught a branch and launched himself to a roof. From there he crept to a gable next to a chimney and settled in to wait.

He hadn't been to Keese since before he'd joined the guild. Back then he'd just been another street rat stealing to get by. The city guard had caught him several times and he'd struggled to survive. Then he'd met a girl with skills to teach, and a problem that needed solving. He'd dealt with her stalker, and she'd taught him to be a thief.

A smile spread on his face as he looked out over the city. Warehouses and taverns dominated the waterfront, and shouts from the sailors echoed over the gulls. Ships bobbed next to the docks while sailors worked to unload salted fish from their holds.

As the westernmost port in Talinor, Keese anchored the trade route that delivered fish and goods throughout the five kingdoms. White seastone shaped the buildings and gave the city a refined look, the wealthier homes boasting gardens and enchanted light orbs to illuminate the cobblestone streets.

The Talinorian army maintained an entire legion of soldiers as city guards, ensuring order within the city. Pirates forewent the stronghold for easier prey, but wealthy pockets drew thieves in abundance. Jack had fond memories of heavy coin purses and pretty thief maidens.

Their pursuer appeared over the hill, drawing his attention. Jack crept to the edge of the roof and watched the figure approach the city. Wrapped in a cloak, the figure kept his face cowled as he threaded his way into a group of travelers from a southern village. As he neared, Jack noticed an oddity about the movement of the cloak.

The cloak rippled like liquid shadow. It swirled about the mysterious figure, obscuring him so completely that Jack could see no defining characteristics. But the familiar motion to the cloak made him frown. He'd seen someone with a matching cloak, but it was not on the surface—it was in the dark elf city of Elsurund, on an assassin.

"Aranis," he murmured her name.

As if hearing it, she came to a halt and looked up. The cowl obscured everything but the grey skin of her lower face and her thin lips. Jack eased back into the shadows, grateful he'd chosen a vantage point that provided anonymity. The woman's gaze passed over him and then she continued on her way.

A trio of guards stepped into Aranis's path and one raised a hand to her. Although Jack couldn't hear his words, the guards clearly wanted to know the assassin's purpose in the city. Aranis didn't move or answer, her body as still as cold granite. The guards began to fidget and cast uncertain glances to each other. They palmed the hilts of their blades, their demands growing more forceful. Aranis remained silent, but her stillness seemed to heighten the danger about her, causing nearby folk to drift away.

Jack shook his head and dropped his crossbow into his palm. Aiming into a nearby street, he sent an exploding bolt into an empty

50

section of the street. It detonated in a shower of stone and dirt, eliciting cries of alarm from nearby townspeople. The trio of guards facing Aranis spun and sprinted toward the conflict, clearly relieved for the excuse to abandon the silent dark elf.

Jack used the distraction to withdraw. Retreating across the roof, he dropped into an alley and entered a neighboring street. Avoiding Aranis, he strode to the waterfront and disappeared into the crowd of sailors. Then he made his way to the Crow's Nest.

Situated on the roof of a warehouse, the tavern boasted a view of the sun setting on the ocean. Light reflected across the waves, shimmering and dancing around the ships sliding into port. The tavern's walls came from a ship's railing, while the roof had been built from a salvaged ship's hull. Masts formed the beams and were lashed together with rope.

Jack spotted Inna and strode to join her. Taking a seat across from her, he gestured to the food on the table, and the plate evidently for him.

"Buying me a meal?" he asked. "What are your intentions?"

"To eat," she retorted. "Now what did you see?"

Jack dipped his bread into the bowl of stew and took a bite. As he ate he described Aranis. Inna's expression darkened at the description and she leaned back into her chair. Jack grinned at the recognition on her face.

"You know her," he said.

"Unfortunately," she replied. "And we have much to fear."

He regarded her with new eyes. "You are better informed than I gave you credit for. Your father?"

"He didn't just teach me combat," Inna said, her features turning sad. "After he died, Gallow sought to bring Aranis into the assassin's guild for years. She refused."

"An independent assassin," Jack mused. "How interesting."

51

"She's as dangerous as Gallow," Inna said. "And she's never failed on a contract. If she wants to kill you, she will."

"You think she's here for me?" Jack asked.

Inna lowered her tone. "You have a bounty on your head that would tempt a priest of Ero. Do you think her presence here is a coincidence?"

"Of course not," Jack said. "But her presence has little impact on our course."

"Are you always cavalier about your impending death?"

"Death stalks us all," he replied with a shrug, and then smirked. "I just hope it comes from someone as pretty as you."

She flushed and looked to the sunset. "I kill the ones who deserve it, the dregs of mankind who merit a painful death. Yet I deliver a swift one."

"So an assassin is an instrument of justice?" Jack asked, raising an eyebrow.

"That's why the guild was founded," she said. "My father taught me our true purpose, and how Gallow perverted it in his desire for blood."

"And you mean to redeem your guild?"

"Just like you redeemed the Thieves Guild from Skorn."

Jack laughed, drawing looks from a ship's captain nearby. "Is that what they say about me? That I redeemed the Thieves Guild?"

She scowled at his mocking tone. "Didn't you? Skorn turned the Thieves Guild into a vile and brutal place. He stole from the poor and needy, taking for those who had excess."

"Am I any different?"

She regarded him for some time. "I hope you're better than you seem," she said. "Or we'll both be dead in a week."

"How much did you study me before you came to the guild?" Jack asked.

She folded her arms. "A great deal, actually, but it's difficult to discern truth from rumor. The godship, for example, has to be false. No one could steal a ship the size of a village."

He grinned at the memory. "It handled like a waterlogged raft, but then, it was a hundred years old."

"You really stole it?" she asked, her eyes widening.

"And sank it."

She shook her head and gestured to him. "You have no magic, no training, and no significant skills, yet you have done more than any thief in the history of Lumineia. How?"

"It's good to know I still have secrets."

She frowned at the comment. "Whatever they are, they won't keep you from being killed."

"By Aranis?"

"Probably," she said. "If she wanted it, she could kill Gallow and take the guild. She's killed members of every race, including men, women, and even children. She kills without hesitation or remorse . . . and why do you not seem concerned?"

He drained his ale. "She's not the first assassin to hunt me."

"Arrogance will get you killed."

"I've heard that before," Jack said with a grin.

Inna scowled. "Your arrogance will get *me* killed."

"I haven't lost anyone yet."

"So what happened to Lorelia?" she asked.

His humor evaporated and he leaned back. "Her choice got her killed," he said.

53

"You sure it wasn't your pride?"

Jack rose to his feet and departed without a word. Inna didn't try to stop him. Jack made his way to the inn adjacent to the tavern and paid for a room. Avoiding the raucous sailors, he strode to his quarters and reclined on the bed, his thoughts turning to his last encounter with Skorn, when Skorn had killed Lorelia.

He'd first met Lorelia at the thief guildhall in Woodhaven. There she'd been lascivious and full of mischief, yet Jack had noticed a reserved identity beneath the surface. It wasn't until much later that Jack had learned the truth. Lorelia had been born with facial defects and been ostracized by the elven people. Her young peers had scarred when her secret had become known.

She had used her formidable light magic to hide her features, donning a persona that none but Jack had ever seen. Skorn had convinced her he could heal the deformities, making her whole. She'd betrayed Jack and the guild, but redeemed herself by stepping into the blade meant for Jack's heart.

Jack reached up and fingered the amulet she had given him with her last breath. She'd used it to hide herself because of fear, the same fear Skorn had preyed upon. Now Jack planned to use the amulet to destroy him.

He caressed the rune and the amulet warmed on his neck. Magic rippled across his features, changing him into an elf. Another touch made him look like a dwarf. He smiled sadly as he extinguished the magic. Lorelia had poured her magic into the amulet for over a century until it could make the wearer appear as almost anyone. In spite of its power, it could never make her whole. Without her continued magic the amulet would deteriorate, but he hoped it would last long enough.

Jack released the amulet and stared at the ceiling, wondering if Ero would succeed in drawing Skorn out. There was always the chance that Skorn would kill Ero, in which case Jack would lose everything. Still, Skorn had shown a marked desire to gloat, meaning he was far more likely to kidnap Ero and force him to witness his victory.

"Your arrogance will get you killed," Jack murmured with a grim smile.

54

He fell asleep thinking about what he would do to Skorn when he finally had him at the end of his dagger. His dreams were restless and filled with visits from Lorelia, Ero, Beauty, and Inna. Then he woke to find a ring dagger at his throat, and looked up to see Aranis.

"Hello, pet," the dark elf said.

Chapter 6: Assassin of the Deep

Jack wrinkled his nose at her words. He could barely see her eyes behind her cowl, but her lips twitched into a possessive smile. The press of the cold steel on his throat kept him still, and he pointed to it.

"Come for the bounty?"

"And other things."

Jack burst into a laugh, the motion causing the knife to scrape against his throat. The blade lay as still as marble, cold and unflinching on his flesh.

"Why am I not dead already?"

"I haven't played yet," she said.

"And when you're finished with me?"

"Maybe I'll give you to Gallow," she said. "He wants you so bad he's like a rabid dog. What's his obsession with you?"

"Can I sit up to answer?"

She regarded him for several seconds—and the dagger disappeared, gone as if it was never there. Jack kept his motions slow and smooth as he rose from the bed and reached for his tunic. Aranis's smile turned smug as she eyed his bare chest.

"Do you want to talk while we eat?" Jack asked, pulling a tunic over his body. "You can join me for breakfast."

"You are not afraid."

A trace of surprise had seeped into her voice, prompting Jack to grin as he slid his boots on his feet. "I'm still alive, aren't I?"

"Life is tenuous." Her voice was quiet, almost bored, yet the threat seeped into every syllable.

"Breakfast?" Jack asked as he wrapped his thief's webbing around his shoulders and reached for his dagger.

She rotated with him and remained relaxed, but the tension in the room mounted. Jack noticed a swirl in her shadow cloak, and a ring dagger spun into view. Aranis idly twirled it in her hand, the tip flashing crimson with a trace of blood.

His blood.

He wanted to laugh but didn't. Aranis was every bit as dangerous as Inna had said. With great care he slid his dagger into its sheath along his spine and then pulled his shaden around his shoulders. As the cloak fell to his feet he turned to face her—and found a dagger touching his heart. Aranis had not moved, but a thread extended from her cloak and held the blade.

"At least I'm dressed for the kidnapping," Jack said. "You wouldn't want others seeing the goods."

"Why does Gallow hate you?"

Jack smirked. "Still curious?"

She stared at him for several seconds, her blade digging into Jack's tunic. "I won't ask again."

"I believe you," Jack said.

In a burst of speed he turned and leapt for the window. He dived through the glass and fell three stories to the street. Rolling into a flip, he landed on his feet, grunting from the impact. He rose into a run, throwing a smile back at Aranis

"Thank you for the lovely breakfast!"

57

Aranis dived after him and caught a gable, slowing her momentum and alighting on the roof of a bread cart, eliciting cries of alarm from a woman below. She dropped into the street and raced after Jack, her shadow cloak streaming behind her. Townsfolk parted with cries of alarm but she paid them no mind.

Jack veered down an alley and leapt to the roof of a rope shop. Using the wares hanging from the sign, he scaled to the roof and raced to the adjacent building. Jumping to it, he sprinted across the rooftops, aiming for the ocean.

In spite of his enhanced ability, Aranis kept pace with him. Her cloak billowed behind her as she skipped across a gap. Jack reached a throughway and leapt onto a horse-drawn carriage, rebounding off the roof to catch a building across the street.

Aranis pointed her arm and sent a thread of her cloak outward. The shadow cloak curled around a pole that contained a light orb, and she swung across the street, shocking a group of women and eliciting a shout from a mounted man. Alighting where Jack had ascended onto the roof, she accelerated after him.

"Do you mind if I ask you something?" Jack called back.

A pair of daggers swirled into view as she closed the gap. "A final request before you concede defeat?"

"Do they call you the angel of death?"

Her eyebrows pulled together in confusion. "No."

"They will when I talk about you," he called back with a laugh. "You may be an assassin, but you look like a dark angel."

A touch of pink appeared in her grey skin and Jack smirked, pleased that he'd been able to disconcert the dark elf. Then he pulled his arms in and dropped into a narrow alley. Catching the border of an open window, he swung himself into the interior of a home. Dark and containing a single bed, the room carried the distinct scent of fish and salt, marking the owner as a sailor.

Jack swiveled to the side as Aranis followed him in. On impulse he reached out and grabbed the shadow hand that preceded her, yanking on the thread. The hand turned ethereal the moment he touched it, but the motion was sufficient to cause Aranis to trip on the window. She tumbled to the floor and Jack pointed his crossbow at her. The bolt disappeared into the shadow cloak and reached her flesh, exploding into enchanted ropes.

The impact slammed her into the wall and she fell to the floor. Her body may have been bound, but threads of darkness streaked out from her form, turning into a score of hands each wielding a ring dagger. Two went for the ropes but the bindings resisted their efforts.

Jack retreated to the hall and smiled. "I'd stay," he said, "But I have a boat to catch."

"Curiosity will not stay my hand again," Aranis said, her voice seething with anger.

"I look forward to waking up to you again," he said.

Her lips tightened. "You should kill me while you can. You will not get a second chance."

"I have three rules I follow with absolute regard," Jack said. "And killing a bound, beautiful woman would break one."

He turned and strode away, passing a shocked woman in the hall before exiting the house. Then he slipped behind a loaded cart of fish and glided into a shop. He exited out the rear entrance and disappeared into the crowd of the neighboring street. Aranis was lethal and smart, and he had no doubt that she would escape in minutes. It wouldn't take her long to find him again. He returned to the inn and stepped inside to find Inna just sitting down to a meal.

"Our boat just arrived," Jack said, coming to a halt beside her.

"It can wait until after breakfast," she said, picking up her fork.

"Aranis might disagree."

Her fork stopped halfway to her mouth. "Have you seen her?"

"She was in my bed this morning," he said wryly. "We shared a conversation before she tried to kill me."

"And you survived?" she asked, rising to her feet.

"Don't sound so surprised," he said.

Her cheeks turned a shade of pink. "That's not what I meant," she said hastily. "I'm just surprised she spared you."

"She didn't," Jack said as they strode to the door. When they stepped outside he shared what he'd done.

Inna looked at him with new eyes, and Jack couldn't resist the smug smile as he described binding the assassin. After months of being cooped up in the guildhall, Jack had relished the heat of conflict.

They made their way to the docks and to a ship at the southern end of the waterfront. Smaller than its neighbors, the ship reeked of tar and mold. Jack wrinkled his nose as he stepped onto the deck.

"Sure we can't find another?"

"It doesn't look like much," Inna replied. "But it's fast."

Bearing two masts and covered in stains, the ship nevertheless carried a sleekness beneath the grime. Most of the paint had peeled off and sun had bleached the wood to grey. The sails tied to the crossbeams were tattered and sewn with a sloppy stitch. Jack expected barnacles to cover the hull, but the crustaceans were surprisingly absent.

A man stumbled onto the deck and spotted them. He flashed a toothless grin at Inna and advanced to her, engulfing her in a hug. Jack retreated at the stench, but Inna did not seem to mind.

"Hello, Borne," she said. "It's been a few years."

He released her and leaned back, his bleary eyes turning sorrowful. "I was sorry to hear about your father."

Inna motioned to the ship. "We need to get to Kulldye Dreg."

"How soon?" Borne asked, his eyes flicking to Jack. "And who's your friend?"

Jack grinned at the hostility to his tone. "Jack Myst," he replied.

"The cheater of death?" Borne asked, and a wide grin spread on his features. "Did you really steal the Azurian godship?"

Jack smiled in turn and swept a hand at the man's boat. "Inna says your boat is fast."

"She's outrun Talinorian warships," he said, his voice tinged with affection. "What are you running from?"

"It's better if you don't know," Inna said. "Do you think we can depart soon?"

"We were supposed to take a shipment of flour to Griffin," he said, "But it hasn't arrived yet. I'm sure my supplier won't mind waiting a few days."

Jack smirked. Flour was the universal code for stolen goods, marking Borne as a smuggler. As guildmaster, Jack frequently contracted with smugglers to move guild members to and from assignments, but had predominantly worked with those on Blue Lake.

"How soon can we embark?" Inna asked.

"As soon as I wake my lout of a son."

Borne made his way to the forecastle and disappeared down the steps. A moment later Jack heard a shout, a kick, and a groan. Then a voice grunted in irritation and a few minutes later a younger version of Borne appeared on the deck. His skin was no less weathered, but there were fewer wrinkles and his hair was brown instead of white.

"Inna!" he said, a smile bursting on his youthful features. "Where have you been?"

"Training with a rock troll," Inna said.

Jack though it was a joke, but Inna's expression implied she was serious. It appeared the girl was even more interesting than Jack had originally thought, and he made a mental note to ply her for tales.

In remarkably short time Borne and his son had the ship underway. Jack watched the waterfront from the rear of the ship, his eyes sweeping the sailors and dock workers for Aranis. As the city grew small in the

61

distance he spotted a figure on the roof of a warehouse and recognized his pursuer. He smiled and raised his hand in farewell. She did not return the gesture.

"Aranis is not going to stop hunting you," Inna said, appearing at the railing beside him.

"I know," Jack said.

"How can you smile knowing a supreme assassin seeks your life?"

Jack turned to her. With the sun rising in the background the light shimmered across her red hair. The view made her even more stunning, but did little to hide the tension about her shoulders.

"They say there can be no courage without fear," he mused. "But I'd add that knowledge counteracts fear just as well."

"What sort of knowledge?"

He leaned in as if to kiss her, the motion startling her into retreating. Jack took advantage of the moment to draw a knife and put the tip against her gut. Her eyes narrowed at the ruse but she held still.

"You tricked me."

"You may be an assassin," he said, "but you are not a killer, nor do you have faith in yourself."

"And you do?"

Jack returned the knife to the sheath on his chest. "I know exactly what I'm capable of."

"You think you can defeat Aranis?" she asked. "You're more arrogant than I thought."

"I don't need to defeat her," Jack said.

"What's that supposed to mean?"

He smiled and spread his arms wide. "You'll find out in due time."

She regarded him for some time and then began to chuckle. It quickly built into a wry laugh. "I underestimated you, Jack."

"You aren't the first to do so," he replied, and strode toward the hammock waiting for him below decks. When she called out, he turned.

"It appears you are indeed as tall as they say."

He smirked and inclined his head. Then he disappeared into the cabin Borne had offered. Small and dirty, the room smelled faintly of vomit, suggesting the last passenger hadn't cared for the sea. Once inside he locked the door and put a wedge of wood beneath it for good measure. When he was certain it would not open, he removed his gauntlet and thumbed the rune, filling the space with his snoring. Leaving it on the hammock, he reached into a second pouch and withdrew a small pocket mirror. He pointed it to the wall and the glass poured to the floor before forming a Gate on the wall. Without hesitation Jack stepped through it.

His empty room continued to snore.

Chapter 7: Kulldye Dreg

They sailed southwest for four days before Kulldye Dreg appeared on the horizon. Borne's son spotted it first and called down from the helm. Jack ascended to the prow and leaned on the rail, peering into the distance. The island was the largest in a series of islands, its hills containing a motley assortment of structures. Streets wound their way in a maze of muddy avenues, culminating in dead ends and dilapidated buildings.

They pulled up to one of the docks and Borne lassoed a post. Drawing them in, he lashed them on but Jack didn't wait. Leaping onto the docks, he strode to the shore and ascended into the city. Inna kept pace with him, fingering the hilt of a blade.

Shops, taverns, and inns lay scattered about, most built from salvaged ships. They passed a tavern named *The Deep Sea* with a full brawl waging within. A sailor was launched through a window and crashed into the mud. He groaned and did not rise, even when a bottle flew after him and shattered on a post nearby.

A shop across the street contained a live manticore in a cage, the beast prowling the tiny space, eyeing the potential shoppers. A pair of mangled bodies lay outside the cage, deterring others from drawing too close. The surprisingly human features on the lion's body turned furious as gold exchanged hands, and it snarled at its new owner.

The shop adjacent to it contained an assortment of potions in the window. Jack caught a glimpse of an aged woman brewing concoctions inside a trio of cauldrons. A prominent sign hung from the door.

Fresh Corpse Poisons Available

Fresh Corpses Wanted

The island lacked government or guards, and weapons were in abundance. A band of pirates ambled by drinking from dark bottles. They leered at Inna and called out foul invitations, but her cold look kept most from approaching.

"Don't be like that," one pirate said, sidling up to her. "I'll warm you up."

Inna drew her dagger and put the tip on his outstretched hand. "I've heard a hook looks good on a pirate," she said. "Care to find out?"

The man withdrew his hand with a sullen grunt. "You should know your place, woman. You're just a—."

The crossbow bolt pierced his foot and dug into the street. The man's eyes bulged and he collapsed, grasping his foot as he shrieked. The other pirates rushed forward but Jack turned his crossbow on them.

"You mistake a shark for a fish," he said. "Wouldn't you agree?"

The leader of the group, a towering bald man with a sprawling tattoo of a sea dragon on his neck, scowled at Jack. He reached down and yanked the bolt from his companion's foot, eliciting a renewed shout.

"You'll pay for this," the bald man growled.

"I know," Jack said, unable to keep the glee from his voice.

The men dragged their companion away and Inna turned to Jack.

"He would have departed without a vendetta," she said, her tone one of disapproval. "Now he'll come for you."

"He needs to learn respect," Jack said. "And the prospect of providing another lesson is appealing."

65

"I've never met a man who actively courts danger," she said, shaking her head.

"What would life be without it?" Jack asked. He motioned to a youth working in a stable beside a tavern, cleaning out the stall. "If you liked the mundane, why did you choose your occupation?"

She looked away and did not answer. Jack grinned at her silence and stepped around a man slumped in the street. He wondered if he were dead or just drunk. Then the man released a wild snore and rolled over.

"Where's your contact?" Jack asked.

Clearly ready for a change in topic, she turned up a hill toward a tavern on the summit. Built of mismatched beams from dozens of ships, the structure sprawled across the slope. As they climbed toward one of the entrances, Inna lowered her tone.

"We're here for Wart," she said, "a low-level bandit with a penchant for survival and information."

"You think he knows about Skorn?"

"The Cult of Skorn used him to spread the word that they were recruiting. I doubt he knows where Skorn is, but Wart will know what he's doing."

They reached one of the entrances and stepped inside. Jack wasn't surprised to see the interior as disorganized as the exterior. The look resembled four taverns that had fallen together into one.

A long bar curved around one side of the room, and a score of sailors sat along it. Instead of wood, the tables and chairs were built of sea stone, likely to prevent damage in a fight. Then he noticed that the table surfaces were not marred by scratches, chips or gouges, suggesting the tavern saw less conflict than he would have expected.

Light orbs hung from ropes stretched taught between beams, flickering as they swayed. Women made their way beneath them and brought steaming food to the packed tables. The scent of grilled fish and lemon wafted across the tavern, making Jack's mouth water.

"The food is delicious," Inna said, gesturing to a plate of sea rice and blackened fish. "The cook used to be head of the kitchens in Griffin, until she tried to poison the king."

The atmosphere of the tavern was quiet and relaxed, with the patrons surprisingly calm for such a place. Jack saw two men arguing in furious tones, their hands twitching toward their sabers. Instead they fell silent and chewed on their meal.

"What binds their natures?" Jack asked.

"The cook," she said with a smile.

"She's a fighter?"

Inna shook her head and tilted her head toward the massive woman standing behind the bar. "Brawlers are banned from her food," she said. "And it's enough to keep even this crowd in check."

"Who knew? All it takes to tame wild men is dinner."

Hearing the comment, a woman nearby frowned. "Don't mock Hillon," she said. "You'll regret it. She'll sentence you to a month without her food."

Jack laughed but did not argue, and together they wove their way to the bar. The seats were packed except for two which already had plates in front of them. Jack spotted a pair of burly men striding to them and intercepted their path, taking the seat in front of one.

"You're in our chairs," the man growled.

Jack looked at him and raised his chin in invitation. "Care to take them?"

The man growled and raised his fist but his companion caught his arm. "It's not worth it. Next week she's serving salmon with mango."

The first growled at Jack. "When you step outside, you're dead."

Jack ignored him and took a bite from his plate—and his eyes widened. Taking another, he savored the flavor before shoveling the fish into his mouth. Spotting his reaction, Hillon waddled her way over and wiped her hands on her apron.

"I can always tell a first timer," she said with a jowly grin.

"It's *amazing*," he said, his voice muffled through the mountain of food.

She leaned over the bar. "You can pay with a kiss, handsome."

Without hesitation Jack leaned over the bar and planted one on her lips, eliciting a gasp from Inna. Hillon leaned back, her expression surprised and pleased. She turned and grasped a plate from the counter behind her.

"That deserves dessert."

Jack laughed. "I thought the kiss was dessert."

Hillon burst into a hearty laugh and her eyes shifted to Inna, who had begun eating her own meal. "Where did you find him, Inna?"

"You know each other?" Jack asked.

"Hillon has a perfect memory," Inna said, and took a swig from her mug. "She remembers everyone."

"Jack," he said, introducing himself.

Hillon leaned in, her eyes dancing with amusement. "Oh I already know you. Jack Myst, guildmaster of the Thieves Guild, cheater of death, wooer of women."

"I think the last one is a bit much," Inna said.

"You forget I've kissed him," Hillon said. "And honey, you're in for a treat." Then she lowered her voice. "If he wasn't so handsome, I'd slip poison into his drink."

Jack grinned, realizing that she knew of the bounty, but was choosing not to attempt a collection. He raised his glass in gratitude and inclined his head. She returned the gesture. Then a shout drew her gaze and she ambled away.

68

"Enjoy the meal Jack. Stop by if you want more dessert."

When she was gone Inna released a snort of disgust. "Does every woman love you?"

"Usually," he said, polishing the plate with the savory sweet bread.

She ate her own meal while scanning the crowd. As she finished she leaned back. "Wart's here."

"Where?" he asked.

"Just entered," she said, "North side."

Jack swiveled in his seat and glanced about the room. Then he noticed a new patron slipping into a table beside a shabbily dressed woman. His face resembled a rat and his chin sported a wart almost as large as his nose.

"How do you want to approach him?" he asked.

"If he sees me he'll bolt," she replied.

He raised an eyebrow. "I thought you said he was your contact."

"I may have overstated our relationship," she said. "The last time I saw him, I broke his arm."

He chuckled in appreciation. "I didn't think you capable of such brutality."

"I am when someone stands between me and my target."

Jack realized he'd underestimated the redhead. She may have been young and inexperienced, but she was committed. She wanted to kill Gallow and would not let anything stop her, even a thief guildmaster.

"I'll bring him out the side door," he said, "Meet me in the alley."

"He might look harmless," she said, "but he's devious. He's killed more than one that thought he was weak."

Jack shrugged and stepped away from the bar. "I'm not a fool," he said.

Weaving his way through the crowded tables, Jack took an indirect approach toward Wart. The man saw him coming and his eyes narrowed. Unconcerned, Jack reached his table and grabbed an empty chair.

"Wart," he said.

"Jack Myst," he said with a sneer. "You're a long way from your guild."

Jack wasn't surprised that Wart recognized him. "I need information."

"Doesn't everyone?" the woman asked, and flashed a black-toothed smile.

"I want to know about Skorn."

Wart twitched, his hand shifting to a conspicuous knife-shape beneath his sleeve. "Word is he ascended from hell to lead his cult personally."

"What's he planning?" Jack asked.

Wart's gaze turned calculating. "How would this crowd react to learning about your bounty?"

Jack grinned. "If someone kills me, you don't get paid."

"What if *I* kill you?" the woman asked, a knife appearing in her hand.

Jack burst into a laugh and leaned in to her. "Is your life so empty that you would throw it away?"

She scowled when she noticed Jack's knife against her knee. "What do you know?" Jack asked, shifting back to Wart.

Wart's expression had hardened, his eyes returning to Jack. "If you're a friend of Inna, you're no friend of mine."

He rose to his feet and stepped toward the door. Jack made to follow him but the door smashed open. The bald man from earlier in the day appeared, with his crew filing in behind him, swords in hand. The

70

anticipation on his features caused the patrons around him to retreat. He pointed his blade at Jack.

"Now is when you pay, thief."

"Pyron," Hillon barked. "You're not welcome here. You still have two years on your sentence."

"With what I'm about to earn," he said. "I'll be able to buy this place and the entire Dreg."

Hillon folded her arms. "And your men are as willing to earn a ban?"

Pyron's crew shifted their feet and refused to meet her gaze. Realizing they would not be dissuaded, Jack turned to Hillon.

"If I don't break anything, do I still get to eat?"

A smile spread on her face. "Of course."

Jack grinned and flicked his wrist, sending his crossbow into his hand. Then he gestured to Pyron.

"Ladies first."

Chapter 8: Pyron's Folly

Pyron charged through the tables but Jack was faster. He drew his dagger and whipped it up, blocking the pirate's slash. Reaching past the blade with his free hand, he caught Pyron's wrist and heaved. Thrown off balance, the man hurtled into the pirates behind him, knocking them to the floor.

A sword streaked for Jack's skull but he leaned to the side. The blow smashed into the table, narrowly missing a glass. Jack reached up and caught his neck, slamming him into the table and leaving him to slump to the floor.

Jack weaved through the swarming pirates, deflecting the swords in a ring of steel. One man lunged, his sword sliding past Jack's stomach as he spun up the blade. Then he wrapped his hand around the man's throat and placed a leg behind him. With a deft twist he shoved him between a pair of tables and smashed him to the floor. Rolling with the motion, he came up on the other side of a table and sliced his blade across a man's knee. The pirate cried out as he fell, and gave Jack the space to leap onto a table.

Conscious of the plates and mugs, Jack danced among them, parrying the swords reaching for his legs. He fired his crossbow and slashed his dagger in a whirlwind of destruction that managed to avoid the tavern's glassware. The pirates were not so careful and blundered about, struggling to get a hand on Jack.

Another pirate leapt onto a table in his path. His curved sword twirled and slashed, forcing Jack to come to a halt. The other pirates converged upon him, shouting in triumph. Jack aimed his crossbow at the ceiling and sent a darkbolt into the wood. The bolt pulsed once, dimming every light orb in the tavern. In the ensuing shouts Jack cast his shadowhook and leapt into the darkness above.

"You can't hide from me!" Pyron shouted, branding his sword as he searched.

"Who said I'm hiding?"

Jack's voice seemed to come from everywhere, echoing and re-echoing about the tavern. The pirates spread out and the other patrons gave way, retreating to the walls. The clink of gold exchanged hands as they began to wager. Abruptly a pirate cried out as he was yanked from view, his scream shattering the stillness.

The other pirates shouted and converged on the spot but the man dropped into their midst hanging from a rope tied to his feet. His unconscious form dangled like a dead fish and the rest of the crew retreated in fear. Before they could react, another pirate was lifted into the shadows, and another scream came before he too dropped, this time hanging by his arm.

"Swords up," Pyron barked. "Don't let him escape."

The nervous pirates swung their weapons above their heads, and one failed to notice the rope that caught his ankle. He shrieked as he was dragged away, his sword tumbling from his grip as he too was strung up.

"Thirty pirates go out to dinner," Jack's voice echoed again, "But none can say why their ranks get thinner."

In the same instant two pirates disappeared from view—on opposite sides of the room. Their screams were cut off, leaving a tense silence. The pirates banded together in knots, hacking at shadows and shouting. Then another voice overpowered them.

"Two gold on the thief!" Hillon called.

Shouts erupted as other bets were placed, the amounts escalating quickly. Another pirate disappeared, and then another. Their bodies joined those already hanging from the ceiling. Terror seeped into the pirates as Jack picked them off one by one.

When he'd whittled them down to ten, Jack took a break. He leaned against the ceiling beam and munched on a piece of bread he'd swiped in the confusion. Pirates screamed and raced about, their panic rising as they pushed through the hanging bodies.

"Fifty gold to the one who guts the thief," Pyron cried.

The betting came to an abrupt halt. Fifty gold was a fortune, especially on Kulldye Dreg, and sailors glanced about, measuring each other. Then one stood up, and another. Within seconds a dozen men and women had joined his crew.

"Where is he?" one hissed.

"Someone activate the orbs!"

"He's a devil."

Jack dribbled crumbs on the head of a man, relishing the renewed panic as the man blindly swung his sword, nearly beheading his companion. Then Jack spotted Wart attempting to slip out a door. Jack casually aimed his crossbow at the sneak and sent a bolt at his back. It struck and exploded into ropes. Wart squeaked in surprise and crashed into the floor, grunting from the impact.

"I still need answers," Jack called, the enchantment of his gauntlet casting his voice off the walls.

Some of the pirates began lighting torches, the firelight dancing between the hanging bodies to cast a sinister air upon the tavern. A burly figure threw the torch upward, briefly illuminating Jack's form. A pair of pirates swung about and fired crossbows, the bolts swallowed by the darkness.

"Did we get him?"

"Is he dead?"

Jack's laugh echoed again. Long and mocking, it caused the men to race about, struggling to gather light orbs and throw them into the ceiling. Several succeeded and launched the glowing spheres into the rafters, but the spots of light were drawn into the darkbolt and the empty glass shattered on the floor.

"Fight like a man!" Pyron roared. "Or are you a coward?"

Jack hooked another pirate with his shadowhook and yanked him up. He punched the struggling form in the jaw and then wrapped a rope around his ankle. Then he dropped him in the midst of a trio of pirates. They shrieked and scattered as the body slammed into them.

"You plunder and you pillage," Jack called, "yet prey on the weak. Who is the coward?"

Pyron swung about, shouting to his men for more light. The crew had to push through a herd of swinging bodies to reach the bar, but their demands for light orbs were denied by a laughing Hillon. Jack grinned at her reaction, and turned as Inna appeared at his side.

"I shouldn't have been worried for you," Inna murmured.

"You could have helped."

"Why?" she asked wryly. "It appears you're enjoying yourself."

Jack grinned and did not deny it. A panicked man raced for the door and Jack cut a rope holding a series of light orbs. With a deft sweep he formed a knot and tossed it over the man's neck. Then he lifted the choking man upward. A single blow sent him to sleep and Jack uncoiled the rope. Looping it around the man's feet, he let him fall.

"Where do you draw your strength?" Inna murmured. "It's greater than a normal man."

"I'll leave that for you to figure out," he teased.

She chuckled ruefully. "Care for some help?" she gestured to the seven pirates that frantically raced about below.

"Do you *want* to help?"

"I was trained from birth to fight and kill," she said, and her lips twitched into a smile. "I never learned to enjoy it."

He laughed, causing the pirates to shriek and scurry anew. "It's time you learned." He cut a rope and handed it to her.

She grinned, her eyes turning mischievous as she skipped across rafters. Coming to a stop above a pirate backed against a wall, she dropped down beside him and landed on cat's feet. He heard her arrival and spun but she wrapped an arm about his throat. He squirmed and shouted for aid but she twisted and smashed his skull into the wall. She wrapped the rope around his hands and ascended to the rafters to pull him up. Pyron arrived to find the man swinging with the others.

"I'll gut you like a fish!" he screamed. "And leave you to the gulls!"

Inna slid up next to Jack with an unrestrained smile on her face. "I've never seen a pirate so scared."

Jack used his dagger to gesture an invitation. "Care to handle the others?"

She folded her feet and dropped from view, her smile lighting the shadows. Jack leaned against a rafter and used his shadowhook to snag a loaf of bread. The serving girl squeaked in surprise when the loaf on her tray disappeared. Jack settled in to watch Inna, idly wondering what Hillon put in her bread to make it so delicious.

Inna slipped in and out of the shadows like a wraith, striking in a swirl of red hair before evaporating into darkness. Pirates dropped from view, crying out as limbs snapped. Jack tracked her movements by the whisper of her boots on the wood floor.

She was quick and precise, using the shadows and the hanging bodies to move about the room unseen. Jack admired the sweep of her cloak, the shift of her weight as she punished the pirates, snuffing out their torches until only one remained.

Alone in a sea of swinging bodies, Pyron screamed his rage and fear. He caught up a crossbow and fired indiscriminately into the rafters, one bolt sinking into an arm of a hanging pirate, rousing him in a bellow of pain and fear. Pyron ignored him and shoved his way through the unconscious forms.

76

"A hundred gold for his head!" he shouted. "A thousand!" When no one joined him, he gave in to desperation. "He's Jack Myst, guildmaster of thieves! There's a ten thousand gold bounty on his head!"

The remaining patrons avoided his gaze, either too weak or too afraid to join him. Pyron abruptly sprinted for the door but Inna stepped into his path, extending her dagger toward him. He attacked in a frenzy but she defied every strike, blocked every swing. Then she spun inside his guard and grabbed his wrist, yanking the sword free.

Pyron fled, shoving his way through the hanging bodies of his men. He tripped in the midst of them and rose surrounded by unconscious and bleeding forms. Terror robbed him of his voice and he drew a knife from his belt, spinning about.

"*I'll kill you!*" he screamed. "*I swear it!*"

The body hanging behind him reached out and placed a dagger on his throat. Pyron went still, his hands trembling.

"No you won't."

"What *are* you?"

Jack laughed in his ear. "I'm just a thief." He removed the dagger and dropped, twisting into a flip to alight next to Pyron.

"If you apologize for your gender," Jack said, "I'll let you go."

Pyron stared at him in shock. "You want me to do what?"

Muffled laughter and jeers came from the sides of the tavern. Jack thumbed a rune on his crossbow and the darkbolt disintegrated, allowing the lights to brighten. Pyron shielded his eyes at the sudden brilliance.

"Say it," Jack said.

Pyron straightened. "I'm not going to—."

Jack's dagger touched his nose. "I didn't kill the others, but I don't mind killing you."

"I . . . I'm sorry for men," Pyron stuttered.

"And how will you treat women in the future?"

"With respect," Pyron said hastily.

Jack leaned in. "If I hear that you have broken your promise, I'll come back to steal your life."

Pyron nodded vigorously, his earrings jiggling. Jack smiled, and then grabbed Pyron's neck, slamming him into the table. Pyron folded in half and dropped to the floor, and Jack wove his way through the swinging pirates to the bar. He produced a gold coin and placed it on the bar in front of Hillon.

"For the ropes," he said. "You'll need to replace them."

Hillon grinned and slid it back to him. "For the entertainment. You come back anytime, Jack."

Jack grinned and collected the coin as he turned away. He strode to Wart, who was dragging himself toward the door by his free hand. Catching the rope, Jack heaved him out the door and sent him tumbling into the dirt. Then he turned and bowed to the room.

"Feel free to come after me," he said blithely, "but do not forget where you'll end up."

The bodies of pirates continued to swing from the rafters as the door shut, and no one followed Jack into the street.

Chapter 9: Wart

Jack dragged Wart into the street and triggered the release on the bindings. The ropes collapsed into the bolt and Wart fell into the mud. Spitting it from his mouth, he rose and leveled a finger at Jack.

"I'm not letting you string me up."

"Why such fear?" Inna asked, appearing behind him. "We're just here for information."

"That's what you said the last time," Wart said, rubbing his arm.

"Do you want me to break a leg this time?" Inna asked.

Jack put his arm around the scrawny man. "Tell me what I wish to know, or I'll let her ask the question."

Wart pushed his arm away. "Skorn's been sending shipments to his new haunt."

"Where?" Jack asked.

"I don't know," Wart said.

"Inna?"

She took a step closer but he raised his hands. "I don't know, I swear it."

Jack read the truth in his fear. "Tell me about these shipments."

"I don't know what's in them," Wart said, "But rumors have it Skorn wants artifacts, powerful ones. It seems he's building something, and by the size of the shipments, it's big."

Jack exchanged a look with Inna. Then he said, "How has he kept the shipments from being noticed?"

"He pays for them," Wart said, "and pays well. Everyone involved believes they are shipments of iron ore from Griffin. They leave from Keese, Woodhaven, and Terros."

"By ship?" Inna asked, surprised. "That means he's on an island."

"I've told you everything I know," Wart said.

Jack caught his arm as he tried to slip away. "When is the next shipment?"

"I don't know," he said.

Jack smiled at the note of falseness to his voice. "I don't care for lies," he said.

Wart flinched away from Inna. "I overheard more than they meant for me to know. If the cultists learn I told you they will tear me apart."

"Do you choose pain now?" Inna asked, brandishing her knife. "Or later?"

"You can always find a hole to crawl into," Jack said. "Or Inna can break your leg right here in the street."

His eyes flicked to Inna and Wart rubbed his arm again. "There's a shipment coming through Keese in twelve day's time. The papers say its iron ore, but there are going to be five times as many guards as necessary—and they're Talinorian mercenaries"

"Well now," Jack said, surprised to hear the reference. Talinorian mercenaries were as vile as they were dangerous. "Let's go steal ourselves a caravan," Jack said.

"You've got what you came for," Wart said, "Can I go?"

"For now," Jack replied. "But if it turns out to be a trap, I'll come back for your tongue."

Jack's smile was gone, his voice as cold as wind driven snow. Wart swallowed and retreated a step, and then turned and bolted. Jack held his smile in check until the man had turned a corner.

"Would you really cut out his tongue?" Inna asked.

"Of course not," Jack said. "But I think I can use him in the future, and some relationships work best with a healthy dose of fear."

She glanced back at the tavern. "Can we depart before more of them consider the reward for killing you?"

He sighed regretfully as they made their way back toward the sea. Kulldye Dreg held more interest than he'd thought, and he abhorred departing so soon. They reached the docks and climbed back onto the boat to find Borne sleeping in a hammock strung between the masts.

"Asleep already?" Inna asked.

He jerked awake and blinked in surprise when he spotted them. "You're not supposed to be here."

"It's only been a few hours," Jack said regretfully. "Not nearly enough time to explore the island."

Borne rolled out of his hammock and made his way to the rear of the ship, looking up at the island. "What happened?"

"A few pleasant encounters and now we must go," Jack said, falling into the recently departed hammock.

"We really should embark," Inna said. "It's possible we picked up a few threats while in the Dreg."

"We can't leave yet," Borne said. "My son is stocking up on supplies."

Borne's son appeared on the dock pushing an overflowing cart. He reached the gangplank and looked up, his face beaming when he saw Inna. She stepped down and helped him hoist up the cargo.

"Borne said you wouldn't be back until tonight," he said. Then he noticed Jack and his expression turned confused. "And I thought you weren't returning with us."

"Nonsense," Borne called down, "Get the cargo loaded below and we can be underway."

Borne smiled at his son but the expression was stiff and forced. His eyes flicked to Kulldye Dreg and back to Jack. When their eyes met, Jack saw the sweat on his face that had been absent when he'd been in the hammock.

"Borne," Jack drawled. "I thought you were a friend."

"Any friend of Inna's is a friend of mine," he said, but he began to fidget with his tunic and glanced again toward the Dreg.

"What's going on?" Inna asked, her eyes darting between them.

"All is well, my dear," Borne said, and moved to the ropes on the dock.

"It's not polite to lie," Jack said, his eyes on the island.

Borne turned indignant. "I'm no liar—"

"He told Pyron who I was," Jack said, relaxing into the hammock. "That's why he came after me."

Inna rotated to face him. "Is that true?"

"Of course not!"

She advanced down the gangplank until she stood nose to nose with the trembling man. "Speak the truth."

Borne cast about for an escape but the dock was empty. Then he wilted. "I knew about the bounty, and saw a way to get a cut."

"You sent pirates to kill us?"

He flinched at her voice. "Not you," he said. "Our deal was that they'd only kill the thief."

"You're disgusting," she snapped, and turned away.

"You don't understand," Borne said. "I want a new boat, and with that much coin I would never have to work again."

"If you don't get us out of here, I'm going to slit your throat."

Borne swallowed. "We could split the bounty. You'd have enough to buy the Assassin's Guild outright."

She stood still for long enough that Jack glanced at her. He doubted she would turn on him, but people could be unpredictable. Abruptly she whirled and faced Borne again, speaking so quietly that Jack could not hear the words. Whatever she said, the man's face turned to ash and he scurried back onto the deck. In minutes they were free and the sail filled with wind. Jack took a final look at the island to see hundreds of sailors rushing to their ships.

Borne's son ascended to the deck and froze, his eyes widening as he spotted the horde sprinting toward the sea. Confusion washed across his face and he turned to Jack, but his father barked an order.

"They're coming for me," Jack said, putting his hands behind his head.

"Why?" the boy asked, moving to the ropes and unfurling the sail.

"There's a ten thousand gold bounty on my head," Jack replied.

"I'd think you'd be more concerned," Inna said, hurrying to the opposite mast to unfurl the sail.

"You said your boat was faster than a Talinorian warship," Jack said.

"It is if you help," Inna said.

Jack groaned and pulled himself from the hammock. Then he climbed into the rigging and set to work. As the ship accelerated out to sea he had a perfect vantage point of dozens of vessels pulling out of port. One crashed into another, and a volley of arrows flew between the two.

Jack leaned out from the mast as Borne's ship crashed through the waves, riding the vessel as it skipped across the sea. With the afternoon sun beating down upon him he grinned, relishing the sensation. Inna ascended to his side and he looked back to their pursuers.

"Are all your friends this reliable?" Jack asked.

She scowled. "Borne and my father were friends for years. I thought he'd value that over coin."

"You have my gratitude for not joining him."

She cast him a look. "I still need you. Besides, I don't care about coin."

"They certainly do," Jack said, gesturing to the armada. "Do you really think this boat can outrun them?"

"I don't know," she said, her voice tightening. "Some of the pirates from Kulldye Dreg have ships that make this one look like a rowboat."

Jack noticed one of the vessels outstripping the others. The three-masted ship plowed through waves, its dragon figurehead visible as it climbed into view. Even with the distance, Jack spotted the enormous ram extending from the front of the vessel.

"Like that ship?"

She followed his gaze and frowned. "That's the *Hullbreaker*, Captain Raize's ship. He's ruthless and smart, and uses what he plunders to improve his ship."

"I can see that," Jack said.

The *Hullbreaker* continued to outstrip the others, its hull knifing through the sea. Unlike Borne's ship, its sails were flawless, it's wood freshly painted. The detail bespoke a captain intelligent and controlling.

"They're gaining on us," Inna said.

"Not by much," Jack replied. "We might make it to Keese in time."

She didn't respond, and used a rope to descend to the deck. A moment later Borne's son took her place and hastily began adding more

84

sail to the mast. Noticing the boy's trembling hands, Jack moved to his side and helped.

"They want me," Jack said. "Not you."

"But you're on our ship," the boy said.

Jack laughed lightly. "Trust me."

"Why should I?" he asked. "You've brought them upon us."

"I trust you to be a sailor," Jack said. "You trust me to be a thief."

Jack held his gaze until the boy nodded. Then they set to work together. As Jack helped him add sail the boy remained tense, but he directed Jack with precision. Under his leadership Jack added a small sail at the top of the mast and a triangular sail lashed to the prow. Then he dropped to the deck and approached Borne at the helm.

"It's in Ero's hands now," Borne said.

Jack burst into a laugh at the reference to the deity, causing Inna and Borne to cast him strange looks. Unable to contain his mirth, Jack continued to laugh as Borne's son joined them. He threw Jack a confused look before speaking to his father.

"I've added every shred of sail we have onboard," he said.

His voice was cold enough that Borne scowled. "Don't speak to me like that, boy."

"Mother would never have betrayed a passenger," he said, jutting his chin out.

Borne's expression clouded with fury and he reached out to cuff the boy on the head. Jack caught the blow and cuffed him instead. Borne blinked in surprise and then recoiled from Jack's anger.

"Don't do that again."

Borne swallowed and turned back to the helm. "Raize has the best ship on the sea," he said, his voice sullen. "Even with the extra sail I can't outrun him."

"Can we make it to Keese?" Inna asked.

"Not likely," Borne said. "He likes to hit elven ships carrying water oars, and keeps a few on hand whenever Talinorian warships try to catch him."

"Water oars?" Inna asked.

Jack grinned, recalling how he'd used them to steal the godship. "Disks enchanted with water magic," he said. "One can propel a small ship for a short time, but they cost a small fortune."

"Aye," Borne said. "It would take two or three to get a ship the size of the *Hullbreaker* to accelerate. I doubt he's willing to use them on you."

"Are you certain?" Inna asked.

Jack followed her gaze to the great ship in the distance. A rumble echoed across the sea and the ship surged forward, smashing waves into explosions of white. Borne's eyes widened in fear and he gripped the helm until the wood cracked.

"We're not making it to Keese."

Chapter 10: The *Hullbreaker*

The afternoon passed in tense silence as the *Hullbreaker* gradually closed the gap. When the sun kissed the horizon, half a mile separated the hulking vessel from its prey. Once again on top of the mast, Jack frowned, considering his options.

The proximity allowed Jack to get a measure of Raize and his crew. At least a hundred pirates moved about the ship like the gears of a clock. Borne had said the man was former Talinorian military, and led his crew with the same level of discipline. They were taking no chances with Borne's small ship and were busy stockpiling crossbows and other weapons. Wearing garish tunics and pants, the men were rough and weathered, their beards lined with beads, jewels and crystals.

The ship itself was huge, with three towering masts and an abundance of sails. Training circles lined the deck. Extending from the front, a steel-tipped ram rose into view every time the ship crashed through a wave. Jack guessed they had less than an hour before the *Hullbreaker* lived up to its name.

Jack scowled and descended to the deck. Alighting close to Inna, he motioned her to the rear of the ship. When they reached the back rail he glanced at Borne's son standing at the helm, but the boy was focused ahead.

"Any ideas?" he murmured, but the boy didn't hear them.

"I may dislike Borne now," she said, "but I don't want to see him get killed."

"Will Raize take me alive?"

She shook her head. "He won't want to risk Talinor learning about your death. He also won't want others attempting to take your head before he can deliver it."

"I like my head attached to my body," he said, rubbing his throat.

"Then what do we do?" she asked, turning to him.

"Think we can defeat them?" he asked, motioning to the *Hullbreaker*.

"No," she said. "They aren't Pyron's trash. Besides, there's nowhere for us to strike from the shadows." She swept a hand at the darkening ocean.

Jack cocked his head to the side and smiled. "What if there was?"

"What do you mean?" she asked.

"They think us helpless."

"Aren't we?"

"Not if we strike first," he said with a sly smile.

Her eyes lit with curiosity. "What do you suggest?"

He pointed at the ship's wake below them. "Care for a swim?"

She looked to the charging ship in the distance. "If we fail to board the *Hullbreaker*, we'll be stuck in the middle of the ocean with no chance of rescue."

"That's what makes it interesting."

She grinned and leaned on the rail. "I'm beginning to think you always take such risks."

"I do," Jack said.

"What about them?" She pointed to Borne's son.

"Do you really want to tell them our plan?" he asked. "Or let them sail into the night and discover we disappeared?"

She snorted. "Borne will count his good fortune and go back to smuggling."

He grinned and stepped over the rail, leaning out over the water. "Then what are we waiting for?"

Inna looked at Borne's son, but the boy had not noticed their conversation. Then she sighed and climbed over the railing. Tightening the straps on her weapons, she grunted in amusement.

"You should have warned me that your recklessness is contagious."

Her green eyes met his and he grinned. "One more thing—"

She'd already jumped, and fell into the turbulent waters of the sea. She pushed her way to the surface and wiped the water from her hair. Then she spotted Jack still standing on the rear of the receding ship. Her features twisted in anger so he shrugged and jumped after.

And landed on the water.

Her eyes nearly popped from her skull as Jack landed on the sea as if it were a street in Keese. He floated up and down with the swell but walked toward her, shrugging apologetically.

"I tried to tell you," he said.

"That you could *walk on water?*" she snapped.

"They're new," Jack said, gesturing to his boots. "Do you like them?

The water beneath his boots was as still as stone, the aquaglass enchantment allowing him to stand on the ocean. It was one of the latest tools that Thalidon had come up with, and he'd used a new water mage thief to enchant them.

She flipped her hair, her features contorted in anger. "I would have liked them more if you'd mentioned them while *we were still on the boat*." She surged out of the water and caught his leg, yanking him off balance.

Jack cursed as he plunged into the sea. Tasting salt, he broke the surface and shoved water at Inna. "I brought these boots because I *didn't* want to get wet."

She laughed at his dismay. "They probably would have spotted you anyway," she said.

"I was counting on it," Jack replied. "I wanted to sow fear into their ranks before we boarded."

"That's . . . actually a good idea," she said.

"Not anymore," he said acidly.

He cursed and struck out, swimming for the approaching *Hullbreaker*. His gear and clothing dragged him down but the ship's speed brought them together. He angled for the side of the vessel and tried not to flinch as the massive ram came at his face.

They managed to get to the side and the ship barreled past. Wrapping an arm around her waist, he cast his shadowhook and sent it digging into a porthole. He braced for the jolt and it yanked them out of the water. Then he grasped the moulding and hung on.

Jack spotted an open window and climbed to it. He leaned up and peeked inside to see a bunk room. Hammocks swayed within, containing several sleeping men. A trio of trunks were bolted to the wall, their size and shape suggesting they were for personal use.

"Do you intend on killing them?" she murmured.

Jack leaned back until the light from the surface of the ship showed his face. "They're pirates," he mused, "so I wouldn't mind. That said, I'm not an assassin that murders men in their sleep."

"Then what?" she asked.

"Drop his water oars into the ocean," Jack murmured. "Then we rig the rudder to break and wait for them to close the gap. Once we're back on Borne's ship, we let the rudder take the *Hullbreaker* in another direction."

"Clever," she said. "If there was a way to break the rudder from a distance."

He grinned. "I'll handle the rudder. You find the water oars and dump them overboard. Keep one so we can get back to Borne's ship."

She agreed and clambered through the window. Once she was gone he worked his way around the exterior of the hull. The surface of the wood was wet and he was drenched, making the passage difficult as the ship bucked with the sea swells. When he reached the stern he found the giant rudder connected by wooden pins. The joints were well maintained and covered by oil. Jack reached one hand on the railing above and peeked over.

Two dozen pirates were in view, as was Raize, standing beside the helm. He seemed content to wait and spoke in undertones to the man at the wheel. Then he strode toward the forecastle and disappeared down the stairs. Jack ducked down before he was spotted and reached into a pouch to retrieve a star shaped object. He wedged it into the joint at the top of the rudder and then pressed the rune at the center. The points of the star glowed faintly before it went dark. Satisfied, Jack returned to the window and eased himself inside the ship.

He paused and stretched his fingers, before gliding to the door to peek into the hall. Lit by a line of light orbs bracketed into the ceiling, the corridor lay empty. He stepped into it and advanced until he reached a body on the floor. The man was still breathing, but the lump forming on his face implied he would be angry when he woke.

"I see you've met Inna," he said.

He patted the unconscious man and stepped over him. When he turned the corner he came to a halt. A dozen more bodies were sprawled in front of him and Jack had to pick his way through to reach the stairs at the end. Descending to the cargo hold, he found a broken strongdoor with a figure in the darkness inside. He slipped into the interior and smiled.

"My part's done," he whispered. "Did you finish yours?"

91

Inna reached up and brushed a light orb bracketed in the wall. The light blazed to life, illuminating the room and revealing it was not Inna.

"I see you found my cargo," Raize said.

Jack's eyes flicked to Inna, who was bound at his feet. She struggled in her bindings but Raize kicked her. Her head snapped back and she slumped to the floor. Raize folded his arms, putting his hands on the two scimitars on his hips.

"You're a tough bounty to track down," he said.

"Did you expect it to be easy?" Jack asked.

A clattering echoed in the wall and Jack glanced back. All the men he'd assumed were unconscious stood and closed ranks, filling the corridor. The glint of steel reflected in the light as they drew sabers and swords. Jack realized the man had anticipated his attempt to board his ship and taken measures to be ready.

"I suppose not," Raize said with a smile. "But at least now I get to collect. Bear, take him to the deck. Dump the redhead overboard."

"May I keep her?" a rumbling voice asked.

Raize inclined his head. "Don't untie her." He said. "She's as dangerous as he is."

A hulking figure stepped toward the unconscious assassin but Jack raised his hand. "Would you permit me a final request?"

"No," Raize said. "You'd just try to escape."

Jack shrugged. "It was worth a try."

He flicked his wrist and shattered his lightstone on the floor, causing a burst of daylight to explode throughout the room. With his eyes clenched shut Jack yanked a knife from the sheath on his chest and stabbed it into the floor. The blade burst into flames and cut the wood like it was warm bread. Jack spun a full circle, and the floor dropped beneath him. He caught Inna as he fell, taking her with him. The light returned to normal as he crashed into the cargo hold.

92

He rolled to absorb the impact and heaved her to his shoulder, sprinting for the door as pirates dropped down behind him. He kicked it open and raced up the stairs. A pirate stepped in front of him and shouted, reaching for the hilt of his saber.

"Catch," Jack said, tossing Inna to the man.

On instinct, the man raised his hands and caught Inna's body, the force of the impact knocking him sprawling. Jack scooped Inna up as he sprinted by, lifting her once again to his shoulder. He ducked a beam and sprinted to the deck.

Shouts echoed from below, rising to warn the sailors on the deck. Jack dodged toward the rigging before they noticed him and cast his shadowhook, ascending into the shadows as pirates exploded into view. He managed to reach the crossbeam by the time Raize appeared.

"Search the ship!" he barked. "He's here. A hundred gold to the man who kills him!"

Jack reached the crossbeam and stopped to catch his breath. As the sailors rushed about, he activated his crossbow and aimed toward the rear of the ship. The crossbow bolt disappeared into the night—and then banked to the side. Drawn to the rune at the rear of the ship, it curved through the night and pierced the beacon hex Jack had left.

Flames exploded into view as the hex detonated, shredding the top of the rudder and sending bits of sizzling wood into the water. The hull shuddered and the man at the helm stumbled, the helm spinning freely in his hands.

"He's on the back of the ship!" he shouted, drawing a dozen sailors to his side.

Raize joined them and leaned over the rail, shielding his gaze from the fire. "Get to the pumps before it spreads! And *find him!*"

Smoke and cinders drifted into the sail but the men were quick to splash water on it, drenching it before they could catch fire. Others leapt to the hand pumps, working the levers to bring seawater up to the deck. Shouting and heaving buckets, they rushed to extinguish the flames.

Jack carefully placed Inna against the mast and used a rope to tie her in place. As he did he noticed a bulge in her pack. When he opened it he spotted a quartet of circular disks. The sight of the water oars gave him an idea. He rose and cast his shadowhook at the mast and strode to the end of the beam.

"Don't go anywhere," he said to the unconscious Inna.

He slipped from the beam and dropped to the deck. A pirate cried out at his sudden appearance but Jack did not slow. He darted to the railing and leapt off, casting his shadowhook into the rigging. With the sea just feet from his boots, he soared alongside the hull and pulled the four water oars into view. Fanning them like cards, he launched them at the hull, where they stuck fast just above the waterline.

As he reached the top of the arc he glided in front of Raize. Jack grinned as he passed into his vision, their eyes connecting and Raize's eyes widening in surprise. Then Jack thumbed the runestone that activated the water oars. Water churned into the enchantments, exploding out the discs in a stream of empowered ocean. The water oars were intended to propel a ship forward, but Jack had not placed them at the stern.

They were on the starboard hull.

The ship shuddered as the discs pressed against it, forcing the *Hullbreaker* to turn like a rider had yanked on its reins. Sailors cried out and stumbled as the deck tilted. Wood groaned and creaked, protesting the shift in movement but the ship continued to accelerate. Captain Raize grabbed the helm to hold on, his face clouding with anger.

"Stop breaking my ship!"

Jack passed out of view and kicked off the wood, climbing up the rope. The ship spun faster, causing Jack to swing higher on his shadowhook. He tightened his grip to prevent being thrown into the sea and pulled himself up to the crossbeam. By the time he reached it, the ship was spinning like a child's toy, the roar of the water oars rising to a deafening wail. With the deck at a sharp angle the sailors clung to rails, unable to reach the fire at the back of the ship. Raize's shouts were all but lost in the din.

Jack reached the crossbeam and had to drag himself across it. Before he reached Inna the ropes binding her began to loosen. He strained against wood but the ropes came undone, sending Inna tumbling into air. Jack pointed his shadowhook toward her plummeting form and a thread of ink streaked to her back, catching her before she collided with a lower beam.

"Now would be a good time to wake up," he growled to Inna.

Clinging to the crossbeam, he struggled to lift her, but the force of the ship's spin was too much. He activated the magic of the bracer and the shadowhook gradually drew her in. Straining, he managed to pull her to his side, heaving her onto the crossbeam.

"I'll cut you to pieces for this, Jack!"

Raize's voice somehow managed to pierce the roar and Jack twisted his head to look down. The pirate captain clung to the helm as the ship spun like a tornado, churning the water into a fury of white in the center.

The sight of the enormous ship, on fire and spinning like a toy, brought a grin to Jack's face. He began to laugh, the sound rising to pierce the din. The boat hit a wave and shifted, swinging so Jack and Inna hung above the vortex. Pirates turned their heads up, shock twisting their features as Jack continued to laugh.

"Not every bounty is worth the reward!" Jack shouted, releasing his hold.

Jack and Inna plummeted together, falling down the center as the ship spun about them. Sailors watched helplessly as their targets fell into the churning white vortex. The next instant they disappeared into the furious sea.

Over the next hour the sailors managed to extinguish the flames and remove the spent water oars. Then they set to searching the calm water for Jack. Raize's orders echoed across the night sea, but Jack and Inna were gone.

They did not resurface.

Chapter 11: Imposter

Beauty dismounted at the eastern gate of Azertorn and stretched. After several days in the saddle she wanted a bath and a bed. She'd ridden with Thalidon and the Gate while it was en route to Woodhaven, and had arrived in Tallendale several days ago. Then she'd ridden hard for the elven capitol.

She stabled her horse and patted him on the neck. Unlike most of the thieves, she owned several steeds, and kept them in several cities. She rented a mount when she had to, but vastly preferred to ride a horse she knew. When one of the stable boys offered to care for him, Beauty shook her head.

"I'll do it myself," she said.

The boy's breath caught when she smiled at him. As the dazed boy walked away, Beauty removed the saddle and grabbed a brush, rubbing the horse's flanks until they gleamed. Then she patted his forehead.

"I'll see you in a few days, Axe," she murmured. "Don't get too distracted by the mares."

The horse tossed his head in disagreement and she grinned. She had named him Axe after her brother because the horse reminded her of Golic's weapon. He was large and powerful, his flank bearing a splash of white across the solid black.

She patted him one last time and then made her way through the stables to the stablemaster. Apparently alerted to her presence, the stable boys had congregated where they could spot her. She rewarded their efforts with a smile, and they flushed in unison. She paid the stablemaster for her horse's stay and detailed her information on a sheet of parchment. Then she exited and strode to the gate of Azertorn.

The small opening abutted the base of the Giant's Shelf, a thousand-foot cliff at the edge of a great plateau. Only elves were permitted through the main city gates, so Beauty entered through the side entrance and ascended the curving tunnel. Runes and drawings inscribed the walls in vivid detail, providing light and texture to the corridor.

The path was crowded with other travelers and the ascent to the city took time. An hour after entering she reached the end of the tunnel, and Azertorn came into view. She'd visited the elven capitol on numerous occasions, but it still elicited a sense of wonder.

Built into the massive cliff, Azertorn lay nestled between two towering waterfalls. The bowl-shaped city contained several tiers, each with homes, shops, taverns, and inns. The ruling houses and the queen's palace dominated the expansive upper levels.

Gurgling brooks trickled their way down the tiered city, flowing through gardens and under arched bridges. Small waterfalls cascaded between homes and shops, adding cool moisture to the city, a refreshing addition in the summer heat. The cadence of the streams created a subtle music that permeated the streets.

Great oaks and small fruit trees mingled with cedar and pine, lending scent and shade to the elven capitol. Vegetables lined flawless gardens, while brush and flowers were on constant display, clinging to stone walls and obscuring the sand-colored rock.

At the base of the city, Le Runtáriel grew at the center of the city gardens. At five hundred feet tall, the great tree's canopy shaded much of the city at noonday. Its massive branches provided pathways between the upper levels of the city, while smaller branches formed overlooks, spiral staircases, and graceful paths through the canopy. She was also sentient, and the elves revered her as the queen of forests.

Beauty used one of her personas to bypass the city guards and then ascended to an upper level of the city, turning toward the Temple of

Light. All the temples of Ero resembled a dome-shaped star, and the one in Azertorn was visible from miles away.

The afternoon light reflected off the gold on the structure's roof. The damage from Ero's grand entrance had been repaired, with even more gold added. Beauty wrinkled her nose at the opulence and worked her way through the crowd. The closer she got to the temple, the more people packed the streets, and she had to cast a minor strength spell to push her way through.

The people had come from every corner of Lumineia, with elves, humans, dwarves, amazons, barbarians, and even a group of gnomes filling the street outside the temple. Although many were eager, their faces lined with hope and reverence, others were skeptics. Marked by their disdain or anger, they stood rigid and muttered to their companions. They cast Beauty sullen looks when she strode to the head of the line.

"I'm here to see Ero," she said.

Flanked by a pair of guards, the abbot leered at her, his gaze sliding down her body. She endured the inspection, resisting the urge to draw a knife and teach him the right way to look at a woman.

"We are all here to see him," the man at the head of the line said, jutting his chin out.

Beauty cast him a scathing look and he flinched, instinctively withdrawing a step. Beauty would have enjoyed doing the same to the abbot, but decided to use a smile rather than a sword. The crowd rumbled its discontent as she was allowed through, but the abbot only had eyes for her. Once they were around the corner he reached out to touch her rump—and found a knife at his throat.

"I know your pig brain will have difficulty with my words," she said, "but I do not exist for your pleasure, nor does any other woman. You touch me, you lose a hand."

The man swallowed, his throat bobbing up and down as sweat beaded his forehead. She'd kept her tone calm but one of the guards poked his head into view. He scowled and approached but the abbot jerked his head.

"All is well," he said.

Beauty smiled and withdrew her knife, and the abbot recovered quickly. The rage in his eyes caused her to step to his side and gesture the way down the hall.

"Lead the way, acolyte," she said.

She was taller than him, and her looming presence caused him to hastily obey. He kept his hands conspicuously to himself as he guided her through the temple. Beauty had been there before and ignored the fine Amazonian wood and dwarven cut granite of the walls. Her boots clicked across the marble floor of the great hall, and they passed through the congregation kneeling at the location of Ero's arrival. More guards lined the hall, but they parted for the abbot, who guided her through the doors and up the stairs. Passing through the outer rings, they came to the white and gold circle of the high abbot, to the high abbot's personal receiving room. She stepped inside to find Ero with a young woman and a maimed child.

He glanced at Beauty as she entered. Arresting in its intensity, his gaze seemed to bore into her soul. The startlingly clear blue eyes were framed in an ancient face. Snow white hair wafted over his head like wisps of clouds. Then he smiled, and the woman he was speaking to wilted.

"My dear woman," he said. "I cannot remove his ailment without removing the blessing that comes with it. However, I can give you what you need to bring your own aid."

He lifted the lid on a chest sitting on the table and retrieved a pouch. It clinked as he passed it to her, indicating it carried coin. He placed a hand on the boy's head.

"Go to the Sheleiam," he said, "the southern guild of healers. This will cover the cost of his healing."

"How can we show our gratitude?" the woman said, falling to her knees.

He caught her hand and helped her up. "By reserving your coin for your family. There is no need for you to donate to the church again."

99

She burst into tears and helped her son from the room. The moment she left, Alidon entered dressed in gold robes and spoke in a pained whisper. Curious, Beauty enhanced her hearing.

"You are giving gold to every patron that walks through the door," the high abbot said.

"The offerings were made to beseech healing," Ero said calmly. "Now the gold pays for it."

The high abbot forced a smile and tried another tactic. Beauty managed to keep the smile from her face as she watched the high abbot struggle. The man had no idea who Ero really was. Tall and straight-backed, Ero really did look like a god, especially dressed in the flowing white robe with shining yellow trim. Expensive trimmings were noticeably absent from his garb, contrasting sharply with the high abbot's own robe.

"As you will," the high abbot said, bowing before departing.

The moment he turned away there was a scowl on his face. He forced it from his features before Beauty got a good look. When the door shut Ero smiled at Beauty.

"He does not care for my generosity to the church's patrons."

"He's been taking gold from the people for ages," Beauty said. "He may become suspicious of your real identity."

"I suspect he will strike at me soon," Ero said with a nod, "and attempt to prove I am not a god."

"What will you do?"

Ero smiled. "Isn't that why you're here? To replace the other thief guards your guildmaster has set around me?"

"I'm here because Jack feels I betrayed him," Beauty said sourly, wondering why she was revealing the truth.

"Did you?"

"Perhaps," she admitted. "But I did it to protect him."

"Lying rarely protects another," Ero said. "But then again, I'm lying right now."

She laughed in chagrin. "I don't know why I'm telling you so much. I'm usually quite guarded."

"I have that affect on mankind," Ero said in amusement. "But it's obvious what you feel for Jack."

She looked away. "I'm here to stop Skorn," she said. "And once he's dead I'm leaving the guild."

"What if Jack loves you?" Ero asked.

She met his gaze. "I don't know if he's capable of loving a single woman."

"Do you love him?" Ero pressed.

Shaking her head, she changed the subject. "Jack has been strangely reserved about his plan. Care to elaborate on where we go from here?"

"Many of the people still believe me an imposter," Ero said. "And Skorn won't come into the open for one."

"You want *more* people to believe in you?" she asked. "The street is already packed."

He smiled, his eyes twinkling with sudden mischief. "We both know this church is a sham. In the end I will be proven false, and the entire church will crumble."

"Which is why you are emptying the coffers," she said.

"I'll be giving the remainder to Jack before Skorn appears," Ero said. "It will look like a legendary thief impersonated a god and plundered the church's vaults."

The idea had merit. If Skorn killed or kidnapped Ero, the truth would come to light. The church would blame the Thieves Guild but be bankrupt and disgraced. It would wilt like a flower tossed to the flames.

"I always thought Jack's talents were inciting anger and stealing," she mused, "but I've come to realize his strength lies in his cunning."

101

"There is no defense for a crafty mind," Ero said with a nod.

"So how do you plan on garnering more attention?"

"I convince a single soul of my identity," Ero said. "And many will follow."

"The queen?" Beauty asked. "I doubt even you can convince her."

Ero shook his head. "I was thinking of one with greater reach than the elven monarch."

Beauty shook her head. "Who has more reach than a queen?"

"One all the peoples of Lumineia respect," he said, his eyes twinkling again. "Le Runtáriel."

Chapter 12: Ero's Gambit

"That's not wise," Beauty said. "The great tree is as intelligent as you or I. Thousands attempt to speak with her and are left wanting."

"She is known to speak to the queen," Ero said, "and the oracle."

"Only rarely," Beauty said. "You want her to respond to you—*and* provide a show of support?" She jerked her head. "She's as likely to ignore you as punish you for your impudence."

"I'm confident she will speak to me," Ero said, stepping to the door and ringing the bell on the wall.

"You've already claimed you will," she accused.

"It was Jack's idea," Ero said. "I thought you'd like it."

"You don't have Jack's audacity," she said. "This is a fool's plan."

His gaze settled upon her. "Do you trust your guildmaster?"

She opened her mouth to deny it, but the words caught in her throat. "I can't deny he has a way of coming out on top—but that talent doesn't extend to you."

"Perhaps you are right," Ero said with a smile. "But I have my own tricks."

Beauty released an explosive breath. Ero was an ancient being that had lived for over forty thousand years, but could he convince a tree known for its integrity to support a lie? She reached out and caught Ero's arm, forcing him to look at her.

"End this plan," she said, lowering her voice as the door swung open. "Before it ends you."

"Have faith in Jack's plan," Ero said.

Beauty clenched her teeth but fell into step beside him. A pair of guards and another abbot led them into the bowels of the temple, passing the great hall that dominated its center. Since Ero's auspicious arrival the remains of the statue had been removed, leaving an empty column of light to bathe the stage at the center of the hall.

Several times guards raised their hands to Ero and he smiled at each before passing them by. The reverence in their eyes sent a knot into Beauty's gut. If the tree ignored him it would be bad enough, but she might decide to punish Ero. If it caused Ero to bleed, the people would know he was a false god. Then Skorn wouldn't need to kill Ero. The people would tear him to pieces.

They exited the base of the temple and entered the labyrinth of tunnels secreted beneath the city. Stark and empty, the stone corridors stretched away with ensconced doors and side tunnels. Plain light orbs lit the hall at regular intervals, brightening as their charms noticed movement.

Although many of the tunnels were open to the people, most of the elves within them were soldiers, and many of the rooms were guarded. The wealthier families owned rooms in the tunnels and used them to hide their more nefarious dealings.

Beauty cast a charm to enhance her hearing and listened for threats, but kept most of her attention on the route. She took her time memorizing turns in case she needed to use them to escape later.

She smiled wryly as she realized how much she now thought like a thief. Jack had taken to the guild with ease and relished the craft, but it had been much more difficult for her. To her, the assignments seemed empty, with most benefactors just wealthy nobles squabbling over coin.

She thought of her homeland and her heart twinged with regret. She yearned to rejoin her brother and her people—especially with what Golic was doing—but when she'd fled her homeland, it had been a betrayal. Her father had given a blood oath to kill her, and as chieftain of their tribe, Oragon always upheld tradition.

She hadn't seen Golic in months and missed her brother. She fleetingly wondered if Jack missed anything, or was it the thrill of stealing that was his home? She pondered her feelings for Jack as they descended to the base of the city and the Céius Gardens. Then the abbot turned down a side path that brought them to a strongdoor with light streaming under the lip.

Out of habit she mentally listed her inventory of weapons and gear, preparing in case they had to flee. It was too light out to use her shadowhook, leaving her with just her magic and weapons. She'd taken to carrying a collapsible sword along with her dagger and knives, as well as her thief crossbow and other guild equipment.

In addition to her gear she had her magic. Like most barbarians, she could manipulate any aspect of her physical form, temporarily enhancing speed, strength, hearing, or other attributes. She'd trained extensively as a youth and knew the limits of her power. Then they stepped into the open and she realized one thing.

It was not enough.

Thousands of people had gathered in the gardens and surrounded the tree, all talking in hushed tones. The winding paths of the garden were packed with various races. Streams gurgled their way under bridges and between trails until they merged into a pond. The water extended from the great tree all the way to the edge of the city, where the forest stretched to the southern horizon.

When Ero stepped out of the tunnel those nearest reached out to him, their voices joining in cries of worship. They parted, making a path for Ero to reach Le Runtáriel. Then some dropped to their knees and others followed suit, the entire crowd sinking in a wave of movement. Many remained standing, and one began to shout.

"False prophet!" the man shrieked. "You are not the god of light!"

Others joined his cries, and the anger quickly escalated. Acolytes of Ero rose in defense while the antagonists continued to scream obscenities. Beauty tensed and put a hand on the hilt of her dagger, tightening her grip until the blade squeaked in protest.

The crowd turned violent, with screams and shouts spilling into blows. Evidently prepared for a conflict, soldiers in the city guard shoved their way to the disputes. It was like tossing a handful of water on a forest fire. Keiko Ker'Isse, captain of the Home Guard, appeared at Ero's side.

"You should return to the temple before this turns into a riot."

"I appreciate your efforts to protect me, Captain," Ero said, "but that will not be necessary."

As Ero neared the tree the spectators began to quiet, with even the most ardent dissenters craning to get a look. The tension spiked in the silence as the gathering pressed closer, eager to see Ero's divinity proven—or proven false.

Ero kept his focus on the tree as he approached, but Beauty kept her attention on the crowd. Some betrayed a murderous intent with every motion, edging their way toward the tree as if seeking an opportunity to strike. She spotted two in the crowd that looked familiar, and recalled seeing them in Skorn's ranks. On the balcony of a higher level she spotted the queen herself stepping into view. Then Ero reached the tree and all fell silent.

Despite her concerns, Beauty held her breath as Ero reached out to touch the trunk. Ero placed a hand on the rough bark and lifted his gaze to the canopy, closing his eyes as he sought to communicate with the tree.

The seconds stretched into a minute, and still Ero stood rigid. The more impatient began to fidget and whisper, sending a current of doubt among spectators and soldiers alike. Still Ero grasped the tree, as immovable as the being he sought to speak to.

Beauty swallowed and cast about for threats, mentally cursing Ero as she sought an escape route. She could snatch him and go for the lake, but elven arrows would kill them before they could swim to the cliff.

106

Attempting to escape through the crowd would earn a swift death at the hands of enraged acolytes.

The whispers grew, swelling around her, seeping with doubt. Someone shouted in triumph, but a Talinorian acolyte stepped in and smashed a meaty fist into the man, knocking him from view. But others continued to murmur.

One of the Skorn cult members suddenly stood and leveled a crossbow at Ero. The elven guards raised their bows and released in unison, but the man had already fired. Beauty cast a speed spell and the world seemed to slow. Darting forward, she reached out, straining her fingers to reach the bolt as it streaked by. Then her fingers closed around the wood and she yanked it from the air, spinning from the momentum of the bolt.

She caught herself as the man fell, his features twisted in dismay at his failure. Then the crowd surged up, the man's strike bringing acolytes and dissenters to their feet. Shouts rang out and steel was drawn. Soldiers bellowed for order, their cries falling on deaf ears, the crowd dissolving into a mob. As Beauty retreated to Ero's side, another sound touched her ears.

The rustle of branches.

She looked to the enormous canopy of Le Runtáriel, shocked to see the branches twisting and bending. The sound sent a renewed hush among the crowd and the whole congregation lifted their eyes to the great tree. Shock and disbelief spread among them, turning to alarm when one of the great branches shifted.

At thirty feet thick, the enormous limb could have crushed a house, and it curved down to Ero. Beauty sucked in her breath and flipped her sword into her hand, knowing the effort would be futile. The limb reached down and enveloped Ero, bending into what was unmistakably an embrace. Then it lifted Ero out of the gardens and held him aloft.

Other trees in the garden began to move, bending to Ero, bowing before him. Tree and shrub, flower and bush, all paid homage to the man Le Runtáriel had anointed. Men followed their example, dropping to their knees together. Even the soldiers knelt.

Ero smiled at them. "The Church of Light will accept no more offerings," he called, his voice washing over the crowd. "For now, the church and I are here to serve the needs of the people, and to root out the evil that has risen in this land."

He turned to the limbs adjacent to him, which shaped into the form of a woman. Ero bowed to her and stepped close, kissing her hand. The leaves of the tree shimmered a distinct shade of pink before returning to normal. Then she lowered Ero to the earth. Without a word he made his way through the path to the tunnel that would take him to temple. Beauty fell into step behind him.

As she trailed him she could not shake the disturbing sight of thousands on their knees, all reaching for Ero. If they didn't believe before, they certainly believed now. But how would they react when they learned the truth?

She stepped into the tunnel but paused on the threshold, looking back at the great tree. Le Runtáriel was returning to its previous shape, its branches rustling and relaxing. Then she caught up to Ero and they stepped into the tunnel, the strongdoor closing behind them. He glanced her way but gave a tiny shake of his head, motioning the guards to give them space. When they were out of earshot she spoke.

"How?" she whispered.

Ero smiled. "Every woman has her secrets."

"You've been talking to Jack too much," she said.

"He's the one that said I should treat her like a woman, not like a tree," Ero said.

"How did Jack enlist your aid?" Beauty abruptly asked. "When he returned from the Vault of the Eternals the first time he said you refused to help. What changed your mind?"

Ero came to a halt and turned to face her. "I learned what Skorn intended, and what Jack had done in the Vault."

She folded her arms. "What did he take?"

"Something that cannot remain on Lumineia," he said.

108

"He blackmailed you into helping? I didn't realize Jack could be so manipulative."

Ero's lips tightened, betraying a hint of anger. "Jack convinced me of what needed to be done, and I chose my own course."

He turned and strode away, leaving Beauty to her confusion. She looked back down the tunnel, where light was still visible beneath the door. Jack had obviously planned Ero's appearance in great detail, but had he gone too far? Would Jack's arrogance finally be his undoing? For the first time, Beauty wondered if making him guildmaster had been the right choice.

Or if it would doom them all.

Chapter 13: A Woman Scorned

Jack crashed through the Gate in Woodhaven and tumbled to the floor in a splash of seawater. He landed with a grunt but managed to retain a grip on Inna. The impact and the water began to rouse her and she began to stir. Jack slid the pocket mirror into its secret pouch and caught her up, striding to the doorway.

He passed through the illusion that hid the Gate and stepped onto the balcony, leaping into the giant trees of the elven city. Casting his shadowhook, he descended to the base of the city and alighted in a small garden. As he deposited Inna against a tree trunk she groaned.

"What happened?"

"We escaped," Jack said.

"How?" she asked, shaking her head to clear it.

Jack thought back to the moment before he'd released the crossbeam of the *Hullbreaker*. He'd realized that with Inna unconscious he could use the pocket Gate to escape, but doing so without a distraction would be risky. He could not afford word of the pocket Gate reaching Skorn.

He could have portaled to one of the other Gates, but in the moment of decision he'd thought Woodhaven would be the safest. The guildhall in the elven city was reserved for high level thieves, making it the least traveled. If any of the thieves caught him exiting a Gate questions would be asked, and Jack would not have been able to keep the pocket Gate a

110

secret. If he was fortunate, none would suspect he'd used the Gate to reach Woodhaven.

"I took an alternate route to Woodhaven," he said.

She blinked and her eyes widened. She stumbled to her feet and looked around. "We were in the middle of the ocean. Just how long was I unconscious?"

"A while," Jack said with a smile. "But I took care of you."

"I bet you did," she said with a snort.

She cast about as if she didn't believe him, her eyes lifting to the enormous trees of Woodhaven. Homes were nestled among the branches, their walls woven from thousands of smaller branches. Some of the greater limbs lifted platforms up and down like graceful arms. Light twinkled among the trees and buildings, filling the enchanted forest with glowing illumination. In the distance the elven mage guild shimmered in the night, its great arches graced by fluttering birds of pure light.

"How did we get here?" she demanded, whirling to face him.

"Every relationship needs its secrets," he admonished.

She laughed, the sound tinged with anger. "You really expect me to believe you escaped from the worst pirate Talinor has seen in a century, sailed us to an elven haven, and carried me through its streets—all while I was unconscious?"

He shrugged and stepped onto a path that led south. "An answer will cost you a kiss," he said, and flashed a grin. "If you're inclined to know."

She blew out her breath and caught up to him. "Then why not go to Keese?" she demanded. "That's where Skorn's caravan is passing through."

"The route I took came here," he said. "And I got suspicious looks when I carried a beautiful woman on my shoulder."

She flushed and poked him in the ribs. "Don't change the subject."

"Why?" he asked. "We're here."

"Where?" she demanded.

He pointed to a spiral staircase ascending to a large home held aloft by three great trees. Several levels tall, the large structure would have housed dozens elves. It resembled the homes scattered about but was located on the extreme eastern edge of the city. At the summit lay the chamber that contained the Gate. Beyond the guildhall, the trees grew smaller and smaller the further they were from the enchantments of the city.

"What is this place?" she asked.

"Our elven guildhall," he replied. "I wager you could use a rest after our journey."

"Apparently all I've been doing is resting," she said tersely, but followed him up the steps.

They ascended to the lowest level of the structure and entered the alcove for the front door. Jack passed a hand over the rune that permitted entry, and the enchantment recognized him. He swung the door open and led her inside.

"Are you this forthcoming with the location of your guildhall with all your women?"

He grinned and motioned her inside. "Only those I trust."

She grunted and followed him in, her eyes widening at the view. The floor was made of aquaglass, allowing a transparent view of the forest floor below. Comfortable chairs and tables dotted the space, also made from the solid water charm. The space was empty, but the sound of their entry drew an elf from a small office adjacent to the main receiving room.

Urin's features blossomed into a smile when he spotted Jack. "Guildmaster," he said, exiting his office to greet them. "I was not expecting you."

"Our arrival was not anticipated," Jack replied. "Can you find Inna a room and a change of clothes?"

"Of course," Urin said, sidling up to her with a broad smile. "And anything else you require . . ."

"She's an assassin," Jack said. "And quicker than you with a sword."

"How intriguing," he said, his eyes sparkling with curiosity.

Without taking his eyes from her, the thief spun his fingers, casting a fox out of light which darted toward the stairs. Urin motioned Inna after the animal, but she cast Jack an uneasy look. Jack nodded to her and she reluctantly followed the animal from the room.

"We'll depart at first light," Jack called to her.

"Don't let me oversleep again," she said.

Urin's expression turned wounded. "You're supposed to warn me when a girl's already taken," he said to Jack.

"I'm *not* taken," Inna snapped.

"Don't worry," Jack said, his voice conciliatory, "our affection need not be a secret."

Inna growled in exasperation and followed the fox from the room. When she was gone Urin turned to Jack, his smile fading.

"You brought an assassin?" he asked. "Have you forgotten about the bounty on your head?"

"She's not here for the coin," Jack replied. "Gallow killed her father to take over the Assassin's Guild."

"An ally," Urin said with a smile. "We can certainly use that right now."

"Because of the bounty on me?" Jack asked. "Or because someone stole the Gate?"

"That wasn't my fault," Urin said, raising his hands. "I don't know how they got in."

113

"We're the Thieves Guild," Jack said. "People don't steal from us, we steal from them."

"I'm sorry, Guildmaster," Urin said. "Thalidon and Roarthin delivered your personal Gate four days ago. I'll make certain it's back in your office within a month."

"I know you will," Jack said, and smiled to let him know he wasn't angry. "I'm sure it will turn up by then."

"We will continue our search."

"Excellent," Jack said, and clapped him on the shoulder. "Now, how about we share a mug of ale and you tell me what you know."

"I'm two hundred years old," Urin said, his lips twitching with amusement. "It would take decades to tell you everything I know."

Jack laughed. "Then let's settle on what you've learned about Skorn."

The meal hall sprawled across the third level of the guildhall. Banners adorned the walls with images of past guildmasters. Two spaces were conspicuously absent—the last two. Lorelia had ordered Skorn's image removed, and shortly after betrayed the guild to him. Jack had ordered her image taken down as well, but instead of destroying it, the banner hung in his office in the Evermist.

His gut tightened as he looked to the empty wall, wishing it could have been different. Lorelia had betrayed the guild because Skorn promised what she most desired. Jack had kept her secret, and none knew about the ugly features she hid beneath her mask charm.

He reached up and touched the amulet on his throat, wishing he'd had the opportunity to know her better. He turned away from the spot and took a seat, forcing a smile as a mug was placed before him.

"What have you learned?" he asked, taking a sip of the herbal brew.

"They've been recruiting for months," Urin said, "but lately they have become more aggressive. Talinor has taken notice, and several arrests have been made."

114

Jack leaned back in his chair, mulling that over. The cult of Skorn had always operated outside the knowledge of governments, fearing punishment for their perverse practices. For them to act in the open implied a sense of urgency, indicating Skorn was getting impatient.

"How many have been arrested?"

"Two score," Urin replied. "Mostly in Talinor, but some in Griffin and the elven kingdom. I understand Herosian has sentenced four to execution."

Jack peaked an eyebrow. Talinor rarely performed executions, and only in the cases of the most severe crimes. Anticipating his question, Urin smirked.

"Apparently the Keese guard managed to capture Carvia, one of the highest ranking members of Skorn's cult. She and three of her companions were torturing a soldier that had infiltrated their ranks."

"Will Skorn attempt to get her out?"

Urin jerked his head. "He hasn't yet, and their execution is approaching. I got the impression she has been overzealous, and I suspect Skorn is going to let her hang."

"Perhaps we can find another use for her," Jack mused.

"Carvia?" Inna took a seat beside them. She'd changed clothes and placed a bandage over the welt on her head.

"You know her?" Jack asked.

Inna wrinkled her nose and took Jack's cup, draining it. "She led the cult until Skorn showed up and replaced her with Gallow."

Jack grunted in realization. "I suspect she was trying to regain his favor, and failed."

Urin leaned in. "What do you have in mind?"

"A vengeful woman has no allegiance," Jack said.

"You want to turn her to our side," Inna said, catching onto what Jack was insinuating. "But how?"

115

"She's not going to ally with the Thieves Guild," Urin said. "You left Skorn with scars and nearly killed him—twice. She might turn away from him, but she won't turn to us."

"Then we send another," Jack said.

"Who would she listen to?" Inna asked.

"She was betrayed by a devil," Jack said, and smiled. "Perhaps she'll listen to a god."

"Ero?" Inna's eyebrows shot up. "The imposter in Azertorn?"

Urin scowled at her words. "He's real," he said.

"A believer?" Jack asked in surprise.

"I wasn't until I met him," Urin said defensively. "He's . . . different. I can't say if he's a god, but he's more than human."

"He's just a clever man," Inna said with a derisive snort. "He's no more deity than Skorn is."

Jack enjoyed their argument for a moment and then swept a hand. "You are both right. But right now the only thing that matters is that Ero is an ally."

Inna folded her arms. "You expect me to believe that Ero—the supposed god come down to lead the Church of Light—is an ally of the Thieves Guild?"

"It's true," a voice called from the doorway.

Jack turned to find Beauty striding into the room. Jack smiled at Beauty and inclined his head to her. She returned the gesture and took a seat.

Urin shook his head. "How can you know that Ero is an ally?" he scoffed.

Jack's gaze swept the room. It was late and they were the only ones in the meal hall. Then he smiled and turned to them. "Because we summoned him."

116

Chapter 14: Thinning the Herd

Inna stared at him before bursting into a laugh. "I don't believe you."

"Believe what you will," Jack said, turning his attention to Beauty. "What brings you back to Woodhaven?"

Beauty stood and stepped to the bar, filling a mug from the keg. Then she returned to a seat across from him. "I wanted to send a report of his actions back to you. I still don't know how, but he convinced Le Runtáriel to support him."

"They will flock to him, now," Jack said.

"It was a dangerous attempt," Beauty said with a wry smile, "but once again, your plan somehow comes together. But your idea to enlist Carvia is equally as difficult, and will require Ero to leave the relative safety of the temple in Azertorn."

"Ero is old," Jack said, realizing Beauty had overheard his plan for Carvia, "not frail."

She laughed at that. "You really think he can turn her?" Beauty asked. "She was one of Skorn's most ardent supporters."

"If anyone can, Ero will," Jack said. "But you'll need to provide the opportunity. Who can we use in the Talinorian government?"

"Duke Gorwall," she replied. "He has the authority and the means to arrange a meeting before her execution, but I wouldn't call him an ally."

"Tell him we won't accept assignments against his estate for a year. After what we've taken from him lately, the reprieve will be all we need to offer."

She grinned and took a sip from her mug. "I'll send him a message, but aren't you worried it will draw too much attention from Skorn?"

"I'm counting on it," Jack said. "If Ero can draw Skorn out, we won't need to find him. He'll come to us."

Inna and Urin looked between Jack and Beauty, their expressions wide in astonishment. Inna seemed torn between humor and disbelief. Urin released a low whistle.

"How did you do it? Ero is more than human."

"He is," Jack said with a smile. "He's an ancient, just like Skorn."

Inna snorted in disbelief. "The ancient race has been extinct since the Dawn of Magic."

"When Ero and Skorn lived," Jack said, folding his arms.

The disbelief on her features remained and she shook her head. "It cannot be true."

Jack smirked at the doubt in her voice and turned to Urin. "What we have said here cannot leave this room. Rumors already abound regarding Ero's identity. We cannot afford to add to them."

The elf seemed dazed, as if his entire world had been destroyed. Jack wondered if the elf had been a true believer, and meeting Ero had confirmed his faith. Jack called his name and the elven master looked at him.

"There may still be a god," he said, "but Ero is not it."

Urin nodded in agreement but he still seemed shaken. "I'll keep the truth to myself."

"Then you have your assignment," Jack said. "And I have mine."

"Keese?" Inna asked, and stood with him.

"What's in Keese?" Beauty asked.

Jack shared what they had learned on Kulldye Dreg, but glossed over the details of their return. Inna might not know what happened, but Beauty had seen the pocket Gate once, even though she thought it had been destroyed. She was shrewd enough to figure it out if given enough clues.

"Skorn is being cautious," Beauty said. "Talinorian mercenaries are lethal."

"I'll take Gordon and Ursana," Jack said.

"What about the dark elf?" Inna asked.

Beauty raised an eyebrow. "Dark elf?"

"Aranis," Jack said. "Do you remember when we met her in Elsurund?"

Beauty's features darkened. "The one with the cloak? She's worse than Gallow."

"Only if she catches me," Jack said.

"They aren't the only assassins seeking the bounty," Urin said. "In the last week alone we've seen a score of attempts to locate you."

"We'll leave in the morning," Jack said. "And spread the word that I'm seeking refuge among the dwarves. Let the hunters badger them for me. They tend to deal harshly with unreasonable demands."

"As you order," Urin said, grinning broadly.

Inna yawned. "I should be awake after sleeping so long, but apparently I'm still tired." She shot Jack a scathing look and then exited with Urin. When they were gone, Beauty threw Jack a curious look.

"What was that about?"

"Nothing," Jack said, and rose to his feet. He strode to the hall but she followed him, causing him to raise an eyebrow. "Is there something else?"

"I'm sorry," Beauty said.

He turned back to her. "For what?"

"I shouldn't have manipulated you into staying in the guildhall."

He regarded her and then shrugged. "Sometimes you lie to protect those you care about."

"What are you lying about?" she asked, folding her arms.

He met her gaze but shook his head. "You either trust me or you don't," he said. "But I can't tell you the truth."

He turned and left, leaving her to consider his challenge. Instead of ascending to one of the many temporary bedchambers at the top of the guildhall, he made his way to the Gate and portaled to the Evermist guildhall, making his way to his office. He methodically restocked his crossbow with bolts and replaced his spent gear. Then he reclined on his bed and slept.

He rose early and departed, passing Forlana in the hall. Accustomed to his goings and comings, she merely inclined her head to him and yawned. He smiled and passed by her before using the Gate to get back to Woodhaven. He stepped out to find Inna, Gordon, and Ursana waiting for him.

"You're late," Ursana said.

"I'm the guildmaster," Jack retorted. "I choose when it's late."

"Jack," Gordon began. "We shouldn't have—"

Jack cut him off with a wave of dismissal. "Not now," he said, and turned to Inna. "Did you find a ship?"

"I did," Inna said. "But we received word of a dark elf in Woodhaven. We need to leave before Aranis finds you."

Jack considered the news and an idea came to mind. "Split up and meet me at the docks."

Inna wrinkled her nose. "I've had enough of sailing for now."

121

Jack laughed. "It will be harder for her to follow on a ship. I'll meet you there."

"What do you plan on doing?" Gordon asked.

Jack grinned. "Thinning the herd."

He exited the Gate room and stepped to the balcony. Then he levered himself over the railing and dropped toward the forest below. Casting his shadowhook, he swung himself onto a treeway balcony that connected to the upper streets of Woodhaven. Then he slowed his pace and advanced with more caution.

The treeways of Woodhaven curved in graceful streets through the canopies of massive trees. Pathways of intertwining branches ascended and descended, connecting to the thousands of homes clinging to tree trunks. Jack spotted a tavern bustling with elves catching a morning meal before their daily labors. It was one known for a less savory crowd, so he made his way to it.

Jack stepped onto a floating platform and the great limb that held it lowered him to the ground. Stepping off, he strode to the tavern and leapt onto a table. With a flick of his wrist he dropped his crossbow into his palm. Thumbing the explosive rune, he aimed at the ceiling. The detonation blasted a hole through the wood, eliciting cries of shock as the crowd stilled, instinctively turning to him. Jack smiled at the attention and gestured an invitation.

"I am Jack Myst, guildmaster of the Thieves Guild," he proclaimed, "And I have a message for those who want to collect the bounty on my head." He paused and his smile widened. "Come and get me."

He stepped off the table and departed among an explosion of whispers. Several of those present slipped away, their faces gleaming with anticipation. Jack smirked and turned his attention to choosing a battlefield.

Quickening his pace, Jack made his way through the city. He wasn't surprised to see the rumors moving faster than he did, and spotted many glances cast in his direction. As he approached the waterfront the crowd parted, withdrawing to the treeways above.

Jack glanced up to see a growing crowd following out of morbid curiosity. Then a patrol of elven guard appeared, racing for Jack. He smirked and accelerated into a sprint. Weaving between the trees, he outstripped the soldiers and reached the docks. Then he turned north, rushing through the crowds of sailors.

Shouts filled the docks as soldiers and aspiring assassins pursued him. Others fled before the brewing conflict, escaping to the balconies that overlooked the waterfront. Ahead Jack spotted a small elven vessel with its sailors rushing to disembark, and Inna standing at the rail. Jack turned toward it but a voice called out to him.

"Hello, pet."

Jack came to a halt at the edge of a dock and turned to face her. As if she were wreathed in smoke, Aranis's eager smile was the only thing visible. Ring daggers appeared and swirled through the cloak, but it was impossible to discern if they were held by her cloak or her hands.

"Aranis," Jack said with a bow. "I hope you are enjoying the surface."

"It's too bright for my taste," she said.

The dark elf's smile was almost childlike, the innocence contrasting with the menace of her appearance. Another ring dagger appeared, and then another. The others spun in hands of darkness extending from her cloak. In seconds a dozen daggers were spinning around her.

"Are you sure you can handle what you desire?" Jack asked.

She smiled faintly and drifted forward, but a score of elven guards appeared from the south, coming to a halt and forming ranks. Their leader drew his sword and pointed it at Jack, his eyes on the dark elf.

"This is not your concern," he said. "This man has an execution order for crimes against the elven people."

Before the dark elf could respond, a motley collection of elves, humans, and dwarves appeared on the left. Their ragged clothes and dark eyes marked them as brutes, killers, and criminals. They bared their teeth and drew weapons, eyeing Aranis and the suddenly nervous elven soldiers.

123

"His head is ours," a bearded man snarled, pointing a sword at Jack.

"Yinto," the captain said, shifting his sword to point at the speaker. "You have your own execution order."

The man cursed and spit. "Do you see our numbers? You can't stop us."

"Other patrols have been summoned," the captain said, but his eyes flicked between the members of Yinto's mob.

"I'd sit this one out, Captain," Jack said to the elf. "I promise you can shackle anyone left standing at the end."

The elven captain looked between Jack, the dark elf, and the bounty hunters. His wariness tightened his features and Jack could see the internal struggle in his eyes. Fight and die? Or wait and arrest the survivors? Then he glanced at the lieutenant at his side.

"Stay your blades unless attacked," he said, and then flashed Jack a grim smile. "We'll take his body when they kill him."

A man smirked in triumph and turned to Aranis. Backed by fifty pirates and thugs, he swelled in his chest and brandished a saber at Aranis. "And you. Go back to the hole you crawled out—"

He swallowed a ring dagger and went down, the killing so fast that none could react. There was an audible intake of breath and for an instant everyone froze. Then a pair of elves rushed Aranis, dying before they could swing a blade. The others stared between Jack and the dark elf assassin, fear and greed warring on their faces.

"What a choice," Jack drawled. "Come for me and she kills you from behind. Attack her and die with a view of beauty."

Aranis smiled and shook her head. "Flattery will not save your life, Jack."

A knot of bounty hunters turned on Aranis, rallying for a charge. Sensing their odds increasing, others joined them, swelling to surround Aranis. Unperturbed, she turned to face them and stood her ground.

The street exploded into violence. Shouting and screaming, the bounty hunters struck from all sides, but Aranis punished the disorganized attack, cutting them down as quickly as they appeared.

The hands of her cloak doubled in number, each grasping a ring dagger. Like threads of ink the arms streaked out, parrying weapons and plunging into throats and hearts. Aranis spun around a pirate with curved swords and drove a dagger into his back. She ducked and spun with shocking speed, parrying a saber and cutting its wielder across the gut. As the body hit the ground a ring dagger spun, plunging into a man attempting to sneak up behind her. Then a thread caught a man by the throat and lifted him off the ground, tossing him into the elven soldiers.

Bounty hunters began to flee, bleeding away from the crowd as the overzealous leaders were cut asunder. Aranis decimated the stragglers until only a pile of dead surrounded her. When Yinto's lifeless body slumped to the dock she turned to the elven soldiers.

"I'll take my prize now," Aranis said.

The elven captain swallowed and glanced about for support, but the other elves shifted in fear. More than thirty lay dead in the street and the elves were clearly reluctant to join them. Aranis smirked at their hesitation and turned to Jack.

"Come, my pet," she said, striding toward him. "You're mine now."

She reached out to Jack—and her hand passed through his form. Her smile evaporated as his face flickered, and the mirage began to fade. His body turned translucent and then disappeared, leaving the dark elf empty handed.

Chapter 15: Loyalty

From the rail of the ship gliding out to sea, Jack watched the fury on Aranis's face. He smiled and resisted the urge to taunt her. They were still close enough for a pursuit to be mounted, and he had no desire for a second sea chase. Inna, Gordon, and Ursana joined him to watch the assassin slip away, leaving the elven guard to clean up the mess. Inna shook her head and smiled wryly.

"If I didn't see it," she said, "I wouldn't have believed it."

Jack grinned. When the attention had turned on the conflict, Jack had casually removed a ring and dropped it on the ground, the contact casting a mirage charm upon his body. Then he'd slipped off the dock and landed on the water. As the battle intensified he strolled across the gap and scaled the ship to join his friends.

"You get used to it," Ursana said. "Jack has a way with escape."

Gordon grunted in disapproval. "You may not have wielded the blade, but you led many to their deaths."

Jack shook his head. "You heard the elven guards. The bounty hunters that came for me were more criminal as I am. If anything, I saved the guards the hassle of carrying out an execution order—and ensured the bounty hunters will be more cautious."

Inna nodded in agreement. "They may not fear you, but they will certainly fear Aranis."

"Don't be arrogant," Gordon said. "There is still an abundance of assassins and you have only one head."

"Then we stay on the move," Jack said. "When we get to Keese we don't waste time. We find Skorn's transport and steal it."

Gordon's eyes flicked over Jack's shoulder, and out of the corner of his eye Jack spotted the captain motioning to them.

"I suspect he'll want a higher payment," Gordon said sourly. "He wanted two gold each for the passage to Keese."

"That's ten times a fair rate," Jack protested.

"You wanted a fast ship without questions," Ursana said, stepping away from the rail. "I'll go talk to him and teach him that greed has a price."

She strode away and began to speak to captain at the helm. A moment later the man cried out and Gordon sighed.

"I'd better intervene before she breaks his arm."

"Since when does she do the negotiating?" Jack asked.

Gordon smiled as he walked past. "Since we discovered she's better at it."

When he was gone, Inna leaned against the rail and watched Woodhaven recede into the distance.

"I didn't expect it."

"Didn't expect what?" Jack asked, his eyes on Gordon and Ursana.

"I didn't expect your thieves to be so loyal."

"Don't sound so surprised," Jack said indignantly.

She met his gaze. "You have a king's bounty on your head, but not one of your thieves has betrayed you. Why?"

He wanted to make light of the query but found he couldn't. He'd never considered the thought that the Thieves Guild would betray *him*.

127

Now that she'd put the idea in his head he found he had no answer, but Inna seemed to understand anyway.

"They would die for you," Inna said quietly. "So don't get them killed."

She turned and strode away, leaving Jack to his confusion. After all his plans and designs, he'd always assumed the thieves in the guild would support him. But were they loyal because they loved Jack? Or hated Skorn?

The thought remained on his mind throughout the four-day journey. When the others slept in their bunks he used his pocket Gate to escape the ship and the stifling question. He knew Inna had made her comment for his benefit, but he realized he didn't care for the additional pressure.

As they sailed into Keese his eyes settled on Ursana. She'd grown into a young woman, and was nearly as tall as he was, her presently dark hair hanging free down her back. Confident and strong, she knew her abilities and displayed a fearlessness that was inspiring.

But Aranis would kill her without thought or mercy. Like the bounty hunters in Woodhaven, Ursana would be left bleeding in a street for the guards to cart away. Unable to endure the image, Jack looked away.

"Why so somber?" Gordon asked as the boat slid into the port at Keese.

"Just thinking about the Talinorian mercenaries," Jack lied. "They're guarding the shipment we want to steal."

"I've never encountered them," Ursana said, overhearing the exchange and approaching.

"Then count yourself lucky," Gordon said sourly. Jack raised an eyebrow, prompting him to add. "I had the displeasure of encountering them while I was in the Griffin army. They were always searching for the best soldiers, the most gifted with a sword—and they actively sought men without morals. I've even seen a rock troll among their ranks."

"They keep their numbers small," Inna said, joining them, "and invite those skilled but dissatisfied. Then they sell their services to whoever has the coin. Their soldiers may be the best, but they only employ the worst."

"Encountered them before?" Jack asked.

"My father frequently went against them when he was the Assassin Guildmaster, and more than one of his assassins were killed. When Gallow took over he allied himself with the Talinor Mercenary Guild, but it appears they have taken a more active role in Skorn's plans."

"We don't have much time," Jack said as the ship was tied off. "Be discreet. If they know we are coming we'll lose the advantage. Inna, you and Ursana search north. You're close enough in age to pass as sisters. Gordon and I will see what we can learn on the southern side of the city."

"You're splitting us up?" Ursana asked, glancing at Gordon.

"You've worked as partners for long enough they might recognize you," Jack said.

"As you order," they said, but Jack noticed a trace of uncertainty in Ursana's eyes.

They stepped away from the rail and descended the gangplank. He pointed to the nearest tavern, *The Crusty Keel*. "We'll meet at midnight."

They separated and Jack headed south with Gordon. When they were out of earshot Gordon turned to him.

"Is there a reason you sent Ursana and Inna away?"

Jack did not respond. He'd wrestled with Inna's comments but had been unable to explain them. Gordon was one of the few he trusted within the guild, but he still found it difficult to voice it.

"Why do you risk your life for me?" he finally asked.

He shrugged in confusion. "We have faith in you."

"Faith drove you to trick me?"

129

"We shouldn't have done that," Gordon sighed. "But don't blame us for our desire to keep you alive."

"Doing so put more risk on you," Jack said. "So why risk your life for me?"

He frowned. "You've kept us alive against Skorn—twice. We follow you because we believe you can do it again."

"I wasn't asking about the others."

"Yes you were."

Jack looked away, irritated that Gordon had seen through his question. The man's response had only reinforced Inna's thought, making Jack regret voicing his concern. He'd led them successfully, but if they were killed because of him . . .

He shied away from the topic. "How is your family?"

"How did this get turned around on me?"

Caught, Jack grinned. "Have you seen them?"

"They don't want to see me."

"How do you know?" he asked. "You're not the same man they walked out on."

"I tried to find them after we fought Skorn at Margauth," he said. "But I found no trace of them. Wherever they went, they don't want to be found—or maybe they're dead."

"What were they like?"

Gordon had always avoided speaking about his family, and until now Jack had never asked. For several minutes there was only the sound of the gulls and shouts of sailors. Then Gordon released a sigh.

"My wife was from north Griffin, and was visiting Terros with her father when we met. I was in officer training and she first saw me in my formal uniform." He smiled. "She couldn't resist, and we were married a few months later. Gwen came along a year after. She would be Ursana's age now."

130

"When did they leave?"

"Gwen was nine," Gordon said, his voice turning empty. "But it had been coming for a while. I fought in too many battles and saw too many friends die. I hadn't fallen into a bottle, but I didn't want to get out of bed. I was reprimanded, and then again. Shortly after I was dismissed and it got worse."

Now that he was talking he didn't seem inclined to stop, and Gordon shared the tale of his wife's departure in all the bitter details. When Gordon finally fell silent Jack came to a halt and turned to his friend.

"I wager you need a mug."

"I've never told anyone, not even Ursana."

"Then why me?"

Gordon regarded him for several moments. "Ursana healed me, Jack, but she didn't do it alone. I count myself lucky to call you friend."

"I thought you said I have a talent for inciting anger."

He smirked. "You do, but it's actually fun to watch you use that ability on others." Gordon then looked about. "Where are we?"

They had turned off the waterfront an hour ago and made their way into the southern stretch of the city. The city guard maintained a small castle a short distance from the waterfront, and the structure housed the reigning duke that governed the province.

"This is where Duke Orbon lives," Jack said. "His tax collectors are bound to have a manifest for Skorn's shipment. The cargo will obviously be false, but the day and time of arrival will be accurate. Just look for one that is signed by the Talinor Mercenary Guild."

"Me?"

"It's a simple paper grab," he said. "I have another assignment to attend to. I'll meet you in the Crusty Keel tonight."

"You've been disappearing a lot lately," Gordon said, frowning. "And you hardly left your room on the ship—even at mealtimes."

"Just tired," Jack said. "Being chased by assassins is exhausting."

"You're loving that," Gordon said with a grin. "So what aren't you telling me?"

"Nothing you need to know," Jack said with a disarming smile. "Good luck on your assignment."

Gordon reluctantly nodded and strode away, and Jack found an empty alley. Once he was certain he was alone, he used his pocket Gate and disappeared from view. Several hours later, the Gate appeared in the same spot, startling a vagrant wandering by. Jack appeared and strode past him, making his way back north to the tavern. The sun had set in his absence, and the workmen and sailors now sought relief from their labors.

He reached the tavern and stepped inside, spotting Inna with Ursana in the corner. As he took a seat at their table Gordon joined them. Gordon slid a parchment onto the table and Jack bent to examine it.

"It's the only shipment guarded by them in the next week," he said. "And it gets here in three days' time."

Inna's eyebrows shot up. "It's guarded by a full company—a hundred men. What could be so valuable?"

"I'll tell you when we open it," Jack said, leaning back in his seat.

"We can't possibly get past so many," Gordon said, "especially Talinorian mercenaries."

"They will take the open streets," Inna said. "They will not want to get caught in a narrow one. But we cannot assault them directly, and once they get their cargo into a warehouse it will be impossible to retrieve."

Ursana cracked a smile. "We're thieves," she said. "We do not assault. We steal."

Jack grinned and gestured to her. "You have an idea."

"We know the warehouse they are going to," she said. "And we have three days to prepare." Then she laid out her plan. When it was finished Jack nodded in approval.

"She's smarter than you, Gordon."

Gordon laughed lightly. "A fact I already knew."

"Have you lost your wits?" Inna asked, her expression incredulous. "You cannot possibly believe he would fall for that."

Jack smirked and flipped the parchment over. Withdrawing a quill, he began to make a list. With each item he gave them specific instructions. When Jack was finished he looked to each of them, adding to Ursana's plan until they all agreed. Then he tore the parchment into four pieces and distributed them to his friends.

"You want me to be a thief?" Inna shook her head. "I don't know if I can do this."

Ursana laughed and took her list from Jack. "Welcome to the fun side of villainy."

Jack and Gordon laughed and they split up. For the next three days they prepared for the theft. Although the paperwork they had stolen had no details on the structure or its protections, it did list one of the builders. Gordon managed to track him down and get what they needed over a mug of ale. The man had seen mages implementing their work while he'd fortified the walls, and his insights allowed the thieves to piece together the rest. The night before the arrival, the four of them gathered in a thief refuge on the east side of Keese.

Unlike the standard guildhalls, the refuge was small. Located in a wealthier neighborhood of Keese, the house stood two floors high but contained a secret cellar accessible by tracing a rune with one's shadowhook onto a mirror. Jack descended the stairs to find the other three already present, and accepted the plate of food from the caretaker of the home. The aging thief inclined his head to Jack and then departed.

The cellar contained a quartet of sleeping rooms and a small armory, as well as a spacious map room with large maps of the region in tubes in the wall. A new map lay on the table and Ursana and Inna pored over it. Light from bracketed light orbs provided soft illumination in the secret chamber.

"What do we have?" Jack asked, taking a seat and beginning to eat.

Still nursing a headache from his conversation with the builder, Gordon rubbed his eyes. "There aren't very many curses," he said. "But what it lacks in magic it makes up for in ingenuity." He pointed to the parchment on the table.

"The entire warehouse is a strongroom," he said, "and contains two smaller buildings inside." He pointed to the square at the center of the space. "You have to pass through the outer structure and a secondary building to reach the smallest, the one that houses the cargo. The doors are designed so only one of the strongrooms can be opened at any one time."

"No way to open all three at once?" Inna asked.

"The dwarf who designed them built them on a gear system," Gordon said. "And the gears are connected to each door. Given time, I suspect Thalidon and Roarthin could break through, but we don't have the time."

"What about when they bring it out?" Ursana asked.

"There's no way we can get past a hundred Talinorian mercenaries," Inna said. "They are smart and well trained. And they keep the cargo on a wagon at all times in case it needs to be rushed out."

"Will our plan work?" Jack asked.

Gordon cast Ursana an apologetic look. "No. The walls, the roof, and even the floor have been fortified against a breach."

"Then we have nothing," Ursana said, her voice tinged with disappointment.

"Perhaps not," Jack said. "If I can get inside, we can still use Ursana's plan."

"It looks like a warehouse," Inna said, her expression doubtful, "but it's a fortress—and watched by the standard garrison in addition to the company bringing the cargo. I doubt even you can get past them."

"Challenge accepted," Jack said, and grinned.

Chapter 16: Talinorian Mercenaries

The next day the caravan entered Keese through the eastern gate. A full company of Talinorian mercenaries rode before and behind, their hands on their swords, their eyes sharp and wary. In their midst ambled a wagon drawn by a quartet of horses. Lashed to the wooden platform, a steel crate jostled as it passed over the threshold of the city.

A city official stopped them and asked for their papers, which the lead rider provided, along with a sack of coin. The man browsed the papers and stepped on the tongue of the wagon, ascending to the crate. He did a cursory inspection without asking for the crate to be opened and then descended to the street with a smile.

"Workmen are repairing the main road, Captain Herrick," he said. "It will be slow going."

Tall and bearing a jagged scar from nose to cheek, the bald man sneered at the official before accepting the papers and mounting his big roan stallion. As he took his place the other soldiers smoothly fell into a circle around the wagon.

Dressed in grey uniforms, the Talinorian mercenaries wore the insignia of a sword plunged into a skull. The scars and tattoos on the hardened men were deterrent enough, and the crowd parted without a word being spoken.

The soldiers closest to the wagon carried loaded crossbows, the barbed tips reflecting the evening light. The timing of their arrival was planned, avoiding the afternoon rush of workers returning home from work. With the sun low on the horizon, red and gold light cast the city in long shadows.

When the caravan reached a fork in the road, Captain Herrick spotted the workers toiling in the main street, repairing a damaged section of the cobblestone. The work forced the pedestrians to one side of the road, narrowing it so a wagon could barely fit. His eyes narrowed and he stabbed a hand to the side, directing the caravan to the northern throughway. From the roof adjacent to the crossroads Jack smiled, watching them drive the wagon around the work.

"Welcome to Keese, Captain," he said to himself, and turned away before he was spotted.

Striding to the alley across from the building, he leapt it and advanced parallel to the caravan. He would have liked to keep them in view, but the Talinorians were experts, and were likely to spot a man in a cloak on the roofs. He reached one of the mercenaries that had arrived earlier that day and knelt before him. Tussled and gagged like a pig for dinner, he glared at Jack.

"I'm grateful for your assistance," Jack said. The man growled through the gag and shook his head, but Jack merely smiled. "I'm afraid you'll have to escape on your own. No one will be looking for you."

Jack reached up and passed his hand over the amulet on his neck, and his face shimmered. His dark hair lightened, his eyes changed color, and his features widened. The bound man stared in shock as Jack's features changed to match his.

"Good luck getting free," Jack said, in the voice of the bound mercenary.

Jack left the roof behind and descended to the street below. Then he followed the wagon to the warehouse the Talinorian mercenaries owned, keeping his distance. From down the street Jack watched the door open wide enough for the wagon train to enter with ease. Through the opening, he spotted the second door.

The exterior of the building was just a shell, and housed a smaller warehouse inside. Forty feet separated the two, providing a gap between the outer warehouse and the inner one. An abundance of light orbs

137

illuminated the space, erasing every speck of shadow. Jack smirked as he saw it, recognizing the pattern of light orbs as one intended to prevent thieves from using shadowhooks.

"You prepare for what you know," Jack murmured. "But how do you stop what you don't anticipate?"

As much as Jack wanted to walk through the door with the cargo, he had a schedule to keep, and he waited until the door had ground its way shut. When the guards resumed their positions, Jack strode across the street in a bold stride, aiming for the small door adjacent to the cargo door.

"Yorth?" one asked. "Why aren't you—"

"Captain Herrick summoned me," Jack said, breezing past the guards and grasping the door handle.

The guards made no effort to stop him and Jack swung the door open. He entered and slowed, marveling at the defenses arrayed against him. As he made his way to the second building, he kept his eye on the crossbows trained on him.

The second strongroom was fifty feet tall, with a mounted crossbow on each of the four top corners. Soldiers sat behind the huge weapons on swiveling seats, and kept the large bolts trained on the forty-foot gap between them and the exterior of the warehouse.

Jack advanced around the interior structure until he came to a door leading through it. The doorway was flanked by two soldiers with naked swords in hand, their shadowed eyes suggesting a propensity for violence. When he reached the opening, the first guard stepped into his path.

"Yorth," he said. "You are not permitted here."

"Captain Herrick summoned me," Jack said.

"Where's the writ of consent?"

Jack stepped in, ignoring the blade that appeared on his throat. "He told me to come immediately," he said. "Do you want to be the one to disappoint him?"

138

The man scowled, and after a moment retreated. "I'll lead you to him."

Jack saw the suspicion in his gaze but stabbed a finger at the door. "Captain's waiting."

He pushed the door open and gestured for Jack to go first. Jack did as requested and made his way into the second warehouse to find the interior much like the first, except this one contained a quartet of guards patrolling the space around the smallest warehouse.

Jack listened to the guard's footsteps behind him and glanced back to see his blade low but pointed at him. Jack wanted to taunt him but guessed the guard's caution was part of the mercenary training, meaning his persona, Yorth, would know that. With an effort, Jack managed to hold his tongue.

"What's Captain Herrick's favorite cheese?" the man abruptly asked.

Jack looked back. "He doesn't like cheese."

The man sniffed but did not respond, or take his gaze from Jack. Jack hid a smile, glad that he'd researched Herrick before the assignment. With the blade still at his back, Jack strode around the smallest structure to the final door and made his way to it. His companion signaled the guards and the soldiers opened the door for him.

Through the opening Jack spotted stables on one wall, as well as a number of offices and an armory. Soldiers were in abundance, and in the midst of them sat the wagon that had just come in. A driver sat on the driving bench, his hands still on the reins, while another soldier tied feed bags onto the steeds.

As Jack passed through the opening, he felt a tug at his throat, and the magic of Lorelia's amulet evaporated. Realizing his persona was gone, Jack leapt forward—into a ring of blades. The swords extended to his throat on all sides, bringing him to a halt. Then Captain Herrick himself appeared in front of him.

"I don't care for thieves in my home," he said, folding his arms.

"My apologies, Captain," Jack called. "But I must relieve you of your cargo." Amid a ring of steel, he smiled.

His words elicited a smattering of laughter, but Captain Herrick did not smile. "Jack Myst," he drawled, signaling to his archers that were placed about the room. "I was hoping I'd get a chance to kill you myself."

Thirty crossbows took aim at Jack. "I'm curious," Jack called. "Do you have to pay for what you lose? Or will Skorn take your head as payment?"

Herrick scowled. "Blade and bolt stand ready to cut you apart, yet you still cannot hold your tongue?"

"No," Jack said, and grinned.

"You expect to challenge two hundred men and survive unscathed?" He issued a mocking laugh. "You'll be dead before you can touch the wagon."

"Or I steal what you have while you choke on dust."

The man's eyes narrowed and he raised a hand to his crossbowmen, "I hope you enjoy your death, thief."

"Tell me," Jack said. "Do you know the master you serve?"

"Skorn is just like any other benefactor," Captain Herrick said. "He pays and I deliver."

"What if I paid more?"

"Once a contract is set, I never deviate," Captain Herrick said. "Unlike thieves, I have morals."

Jack burst into a laugh. "Says the man serving a devil."

Captain Herrick sneered. "His coin is as good as yours. Too bad you didn't think to contract me earlier. I could have been allied with you."

"I would never contract with you," Jack said. "Because I don't work with men as dirty as the sewers of Terros."

140

"Says the guildmaster of the *Thieves Guild*," Captain Herrick snarled. "Any last requests?"

"What time is it?"

Captain Herrick shook his head in confusion and glanced to his men. One shrugged and offered, "Nightfall."

"That's what I thought," Jack said with a satisfied nod.

Captain Herrick's features turned suspicious. "Why does the time matter to you—"

"Shhh," Jack interrupted. "I'm trying to listen . . ."

Fury lanced across Captain Herrick's expression at the interruption, but he hesitated. The rest of his men followed his example. For an interminable second the silence filled the warehouse, and even the horses fell silent.

From directly beneath the warehouse Ursana aimed her large crossbow at the ceiling of the sewer. She triggered a single bolt, which splintered into needles of steel that slammed into the ceiling, the sound audible to Jack as a muffled thudding. Men twisted to look at the floor, and Jack used the distraction to flip his crossbow into his hand and fire his own splinter bolt.

The bolt shattered into a score of needles, which curved and spread into a circle around the wagon, all except one. The single needle plunged into the rune placed on the wagon tongue by Gordon, who'd donned the persona of the guard at the city entrance. Then the remainder sank into the floor, burying deep into the stone and detonating those beneath.

Gouts of fire exploded in a circle around the wagon, sending horses and men scrambling away. Swordsmen instinctively retreated as the wagon disappeared behind a wall of flame. Dust and smoke blossomed into the trembling warehouse. Horses screamed, men shouted, and the entire wagon dropped into a hole of smoke and dust.

Chapter 17: Talinorian Fury

Knocked to the dirt by the explosion, Herrick dragged himself to his feet and peered into the gaping hole in his floor. Coughing orders, his eyes widened when he saw the wagon sitting in the sewer below and Inna attaching a pair of horses to it.

With the room in chaos Jack swung his cloak in a circle and dived into the mercenaries. Distracted by the sudden detonation, their swords were swept aside and Jack breached their line. Knocking the last to the floor, he dived past Captain Herrick and dropped into the smoke, alighting on the crate. As men stumbled to their feet in the warehouse above, Jack jumped to the driving bench, catching the reins Inna threw him. He looked up to the captain on the edge of the hole above.

"Enjoy the dust, Captain!"

"Blasted thief!" Captain Herrick shouted. "*I'll cut you to pieces!*"

"You can't kill what you can't catch!"

Jack flicked the reins and the horses leapt forward, sending the wagon careening down the sewer. He threw a look back and caught a glimpse of Ursana disappearing in the opposite direction. Then he had to devote his whole attention to controlling the wagon. Confined to the narrow tunnel, the sounds of the charred wagon and the horses' hooves beat against his ears. Foul water splashed against the walls as the wheels bounced through the stream.

"I can't believe it worked!" Inna shouted.

"You never think my plans will succeed!"

"Do you plan the fun?" she asked, and grinned. "Or does that come naturally?"

He grinned in turn—and spotted a steel grate protruding from the ceiling. "Get down!" he shouted.

They ducked, narrowly missing losing their heads as the access grate streaked by. When they sat up she glanced back. Jack followed her gaze and spotted soldiers dropping into view, leveling crossbows after them. They crouched as bolts filled the tunnel, the volley clattering off the stones and digging into the blackened wood of the wagon. One bolt slammed into a wheel and the already damaged wood cracked. Another streaked over Inna's shoulder, creasing a line through her tunic and drawing blood.

"I liked this tunic," she growled.

"I'll buy you a new one," he replied.

Still crouching, he pulled on the reins, turning the wagon down a side tunnel. The bend gave them a momentary reprieve from the crossbow bolts, but the damaged wheel struck a hole and cracked again.

"I don't think we'll make it to the waterfront," Inna said.

"I know!" Jack said.

The tunnel had been built for rains and sewage, but the stonework had begun to crumble. The shallow curve to the floor lay pockmarked with holes and cracks, making the cart's wheels bounce and tremble.

"We're almost to Gordon," Jack said, pulling the reins again. "We should—"

The wheel disintegrated, shredding into bits of wood and shards of steel. The axle crashed into the sewer floor and the other wheel cracked in two. Dislodged by the impact, Jack tumbled off the side, but Inna caught his cloak and yanked him back onto the bench. The flat of the cart bounced and scraped across the floor of the tunnel, sending sparks into the air as the axle ground across the stones. The two horses strained to pull the dead weight as the wagon slowed to a stop and Jack reined

143

them in. The sudden silence allowed Jack to hear the echo of boots thudding behind them. Apparently hearing the crash, Gordon appeared ahead of them. His face turned to ash when he saw the devastated cart and he sprinted to them.

"Take the crate," Jack said, darting to the crate and slashing the ropes holding it to the bed.

Inna cut the opposite side and they bent to lift it. They grunted as they lifted the metal crate and struggled to maneuver it past the horses to Gordon, who caught the other side and helped.

"What happened?"

"Wagon was damaged from the blast," Jack said. "We need to hurry before—"

"Too late," Inna said.

She stepped away from the crate and drew her sword as two mercenaries appeared around the broken cart. She blocked the first blow and kicked him in the groin, causing all four men in the tunnel to wince.

"She fights dirty," Gordon said, his voice strained from the effort of carrying the crate.

"She fights to win," Jack said as Inna engaged the second mercenary.

They reached the side tunnel and heaved the crate onto a much smaller cart and Gordon lashed it down. Together they gave it a shove, sending it sliding down the steep sewer. It careened out of view and disappeared. Then Jack darted back to Inna to find her fighting four mercenaries at once.

"Time to go!" Jack shouted.

He and Gordon raised their crossbows and fired, sending ice bolts into the mercenaries. The first was caught and bound to the wall, but the other three adapted, dodging and twisting to avoid being struck. Inna used the distraction to escape the conflict and joined Jack and Gordon. Together they sprinted down the sewer to a ladder. Ascending to the street, they exited on the waterfront, slamming the opening shut and threading a length of wood through the brace. Muffled shouts came from below and the opening shuddered from a blow.

Jack turned away from the sewer grate and hurried down the street toward the waterfront. The sun had set and the glow from the horizon cast a reddish hue on the city of Keese. Distant shouts came from higher in the city, and a plume of smoke rose into the dark sky.

"They won't be far behind," Inna panted.

"It doesn't matter," Jack said, motioning to the ship below them.

Thundering hooves caused them to whirl and draw their blades, and a trio of riders burst into view. Captain Herrick dropped from his steed and leapt to them, his sword in hand. With blood trickling down his face and his clothing blackened by soot, he stabbed his sword at Jack.

"Did you really think I didn't know where the sewers went?" he sneered, and stalked forward with his mercenaries, forcing Jack to retreat to the edge of the road.

Jack's heels slipped over the edge and he glanced into the darkened water of the sea. With nowhere else to go, he turned and faced the captain, raising his hand to him.

"I suspected you might know," Jack said. "Which is why I led you here. Your cargo isn't the only thing I came to steal."

"There are just three of you," Herrick said, scowling. "You cannot be so arrogant as to think you can best us."

"I don't," Jack said with a smile, and pointed beyond him. "I mean to trap you." He looked over the captain's shoulder to the roof beyond.

Herrick spun, his eyes lifting to Ursana, who was standing on the roof of a warehouse. She aimed the warship ballistae they had stolen two days ago and smiled. She pulled the trigger and the massive bolt exploded from the weapon, bursting into ropes designed to entangle a ship's rigging. Herrick cried out and took one step before the netting crashed to the street around him, the barbs digging into the stone. The netting was huge, falling over the two riders and knocking both to the street. The horses whinnied in fear and kicked, but the netting tangled their legs and held them bound.

145

Jack saluted to Ursana, and she grinned before slipping away. Then Jack strode to Herrick and reached through the net to dig into the mercenary's pockets. The man struggled and bellowed profanities, but Jack found the sealed documents and pulled them into view. Waving them at Herrick, Jack pocketed them.

"Many thanks, Captain," Jack said, striding away, "but I fear I must take my leave. We have a boat to catch." He gestured to the ship where a steel crate was being lashed onto the deck.

"I'll kill you, thief!" Herrick roared.

Jack merely laughed and slipped into the crowd as the Keese guard and Talinorian mercenaries swarmed the area. It took several minutes before ropes were cut and Herrick stepped free. Barking orders, he sprinted to his own warship. An hour later the mercenaries pulled alongside the ship with the crate. When the steel crate was opened it proved to be empty, and the ship held no sign of the thieves. The perplexed captain had no answers. As Captain Herrick frothed at the mouth, his soldiers were helpless.

On the opposite side of town a small wagon departed Keese through the eastern gate. Two men sat on the driving board while two women hid within the wagon. Invisible beneath a pile of blankets, the steel crate was not noticed by the city guards.

The sun dipped below the horizon and the wagon bounced across the ruts in the road. Alone, it ascended a hill and reached the summit, disappearing from view. While Captain Herrick demanded answers aboard an empty ship, the thieves slipped into the night. Gordon was the first to laugh, and the humor quickly spread to the others.

"I enjoyed that more than I thought I would," Inna said.

"We don't get to see Herrick's confusion," Ursana lamented, "but I can imagine it."

"He'll come after you with a vengeance," Inna said.

"Then I look forward to humbling him a second time," Jack said.

His comment elicited another round of laughter, and even Inna joined in. The levity faded when a *bang* echoed from within the wagon. All four turned and stared at the crate, and a moment later it repeated.

Jack pulled back on the reins and brought the wagon to a halt. Jack exchanged a look with Inna before the sound echoed again. Then the quartet climbed into the wagon around the crate. Gordon reached for the clasp but Inna caught his arm.

"It could be dangerous."

Jack shrugged and reached for his gorgon key. "We won't know until we open it."

"Wait—" Ursana said, but it was too late.

The universal key flowed into the lock and pressed against the pins, and the lock snapped open with a *click*. Inna drew her sword as Jack pulled out the rod and lifted the lid. He grunted in surprise at what lay inside and swung it fully open. The group gasped as the dim light revealed the occupant.

A woman.

She blinked and looked up, squinting at them. Her clothes were disheveled but not unclean, suggesting the mercenaries had periodically allowed her to exit her crate. Then she lowered her hand and Gordon went rigid.

"Gwen?"

She looked at him and her eyes widened. "Father?"

"You know her?" Ursana asked.

"Of course," Gordon said, and turned to Jack. "She's my daughter."

Chapter 18: Reunion

Gordon reached down and helped her out. She moved with care and winced as she eased out of the crate. Gordon helped settle her on the side of the wagon and retrieved a water skin. She drank deeply but cradled her arm.

"Are you hurt?" Gordon asked.

"Not by them," she said. "But the last two hours have been painful."

Jack leaned into the view. "That would be my fault," he said in chagrin. "We didn't expect Skorn's cargo to be a person."

Inna's eyes flicked to Jack. "Perhaps we can travel and talk? We're only a few miles from Keese, and once Captain Herrick discovers our ruse, he'll be out for blood."

Jack nodded and she stepped to the bench at the front of the wagon, flicking the reins to get the horses moving again. Casting a look at Gwen, Ursana followed her. Gordon took her vacated seat without noticing the tightness to Ursana's features. His eyes remained fixed on Gwen as the wagon bounced along the road.

"How did you end up here?" he asked. He reached out but his hand came to a stop, and then withdrew.

"I was walking home after my last lesson and they rode up beside me," Gwen said. "The soldiers responded normally, but something about them made me suspicious. Then I grew drowsy and couldn't keep my eyes open. The next thing I knew I was inside that thing." She pointed at the crate.

As the two talked Jack studied her. She was slight of frame and wore a brown dress with the insignia of a raindrop on the shoulder. She looked to be about seventeen, with long brown hair hanging down her back.

"Why did they want you?" Jack asked.

"I heard them talking about why they took me," she said. "It appears I have a talent they wanted."

"She's been through enough," Gordon said. "She needs to rest."

Gwen shook her head and her jaw tightened. "I don't need protection, Father."

Gordon looked away, uncertainty and guilt washing over his face. Gwen pointedly turned to Jack.

"I wasn't the first to be taken."

"There were others?" Jack asked.

"A few from our guild, a few from the other guildhalls. At first we thought they had withdrawn from the guild, but the numbers began to warrant suspicion. The Masters began to investigate but there was nothing to find."

"What guild?" Gordon asked.

She fidgeted for a moment and cast about, fear appearing on her features. Jack realized the girl knew why she'd been taken, but she was reluctant to speak it aloud. Suspecting she was afraid of him, he flashed a disarming smile.

"We aren't going to turn you over to them," he said. "For any price."

"I know," Gwen said with a dismissive gesture.

"Then what is your concern?" Gordon asked. "You can trust us . . . and me. Why did they take you?"

149

Abruptly the girl squared her shoulders and met her father's gaze. "Because I'm a water mage."

"That's not possible," Gordon said. "Humans rarely have elven magic and I have no history of it. Neither did your mother."

"She lied," Gwen said quietly, "to protect you."

"I don't understand," Gordon said. "What was she trying to protect me from?"

Gwen swallowed and her features tightened. "Her family," Gwen said. "Her bloodline carries the gift for magic, but they believe magic is an abomination. Any that showed the talent were slain—and anyone that knew the secret."

"They murdered their own kindred because of magic?" Gordon asked, his eyes widening.

Gwen nodded. "Grandmother was killed because she refused to reveal that mother was a mage."

Gordon turned to Jack. "I thought she had been killed by bandits on a journey to Herosian."

"She was dragged from her bed and given a last chance to speak the name of the mage in our home," Gwen said. "When she refused, she was cut apart and buried in the woods."

"I would have protected you," Gordon said.

"They would have killed us—and you, just for knowing her secret."

Gordon's face turned ashen. "That's why you left," he accused.

She winced. "Once mother realized I had magic, she knew I would never be safe. Grandmother died to protect her secret. She didn't want you to die for mine."

Gordon stumbled back, retreating to the furthest spot in the wagon. "It cannot be. She said she hated me. *You* said you hated me."

Tears appeared in Gwen's eyes. "I'm sorry, Father."

Jack had faced reavers, kings, assassins, Talinorian mercenaries, rock trolls, and ancients—but for the first time of his life, he wanted to flee. He mumbled an excuse and retreated, grateful that they hardly noticed his exit. He slipped out of the wagon to the driver's bench at the front, joining Ursana and Inna. Gordon's conversation was still audible, but at least Jack didn't have to see it. For a few miles he listened to Gordon and Gwen until he could bear it no longer.

"What do you think Herrick will do when he realizes our deception?" Jack asked.

"He'll come for us," Inna said, as if eager for the conversation. "You can be certain of that. He's not the type of man that swallows defeat."

Jack shrugged. "Add him to the list of hunters searching for me."

"Where are we going now?" Ursana asked. "That wasn't the cargo we expected to find."

"Perhaps this has an answer," Jack said. He withdrew the shipping manifest he'd taken from Herrick and unfolded the parchment. Scanning it, he found the destination listed on the bottom, and read aloud.

"The Necrolith."

Inna shook her head. "I've never heard of such a place."

"At least we have a name," Ursana said. "Which is more than we had yesterday."

"We should return Gwen to her guild," Jack said. "Perhaps they will have more answers. Skorn spent a fortune for a single mage, and I'd like to know why."

"How will they know anything?" Ursana asked.

Jack looked at Ursana, but the girl looked away.

"He's taking mages," Jack said, "They might know why he wants them—and why he's taking mages from other guilds."

151

"You think to deduce what he's building from what he's taking," Inna said. "Clever."

"We should have Forlana track other shipments and search for a pattern," Jack said.

Inna chuckled under her breath. "You may not have magic, but you have a gift for misdirection."

Jack grinned. "Misdirection *is* magic."

"But misdirection won't help us when we find the Necrolith. He has Gallow, the cult, and now Talinorian mercenaries. He's building an army. How do you expect to get past it?"

"Walk through the front door," Jack said with a smile.

Inna raised an eyebrow. "How exactly will you manage that?"

"Misdirection," Jack said with a laugh.

She laughed with him and asked for details, but Jack rebuffed her questions. As the conversation shifted to speculation regarding the Necrolith, Jack continued to listen to Gordon and Gwen until the two fell into an uneasy silence.

It took several days of travel to reach Herosian. Uncomfortable with the silence between Ursana, Gordon, and Gwen, Jack claimed to have other duties and said he would meet them in Wedge. They dumped the wagon behind a village inn and then split up. As soon as he was out of sight, Jack used his pocket Gate to escape.

He stopped in the Evermist guildhall and left a message for Forlana to track the Talinorian mercenaries, especially the connections to missing mages. Then he Gated to observe his other plans, which required delicate timing, forgery, and personas.

Before returning to Wedge he passed through Azertorn, indulging in time to observe Beauty. Then he Gated back to the Evermist guildhall and slipped out of the fortress, threading his way through the swamp to Talinor. Renting a steed from a village, he turned east and made his way to the southern tip of Talinor, and the city of Wedge.

The southeastern corner of the kingdom was shaped like a dagger's tip, culminating in a pointed butte that overlooked a river. A large castle sat on the end with an unparalleled view of the surrounding region, a Talinor village filling the breadth of the narrow plateau.

The castle's position bordered Griffin, Barbarian, and Amazonian lands, as well as a sliver of the Evermist. The other nations had built their own villages on the unique border, and over time they had grown until it resembled a single city. Like pieces of different pies on a single plate, the city of Wedge contained districts from each kingdom.

To the north, the Griffin Wedge sat between the plateau and a river, while on the opposite side of the river, the Barbarian Wedge dominated the base of a hill. Adjacent to the hill the ground sloped into the northern edge of the Amazonian jungles, and the powerful women maintained a village at the juncture. Between the Amazons and the plateau, a strip of the Evermist pressed against the south side butte that contained the Talinorian Wedge.

Originally intended as a fortress to prevent attack from its neighbors, the city of Wedge had grown to incorporate each of the five sections. The oddly disparate city was governed by four different sets of laws, and unwary travelers were known to unintentionally break them. Despite the divided nature of the city, Wedge had become a haven for merchants from the region and rarely saw conflict escalate into bloodshed.

Jack had timed his return well, and only had to wait for a few hours before he spotted Inna and the others appear on the road. Turning his steed, he made his way to join them. Inna smiled at his return, the relief palpable on her features.

"I wasn't sure you were going to make it," she said.

Gordon, too, looked relieved, and Jack noticed the distance between him, Gwen, and Ursana. Gwen threw Ursana a look, but she did not return it. The silence between them was telling, and uncomfortable.

"It feels like I never left," Jack said dryly, and Gordon forced a laugh.

Jack pulled the reins, bringing his horse in line with Inna. Then he lowered his voice. "I thought they would have worked it out by now."

"Is that why you escaped?" Inna asked sourly.

"I did not escape," Jack said, indignant. "I had work to do."

She grunted, the sound tinged with disbelief. "Next time, I get to be the one to leave."

"That bad?"

"Ten days with hardly a word spoken," she said, looking back over her shoulder. "Gordon keeps trying, but I've never seen a man sweat so much at the prospect of conversation."

Jack groaned and wheeled his horse around. Gordon, Ursana, and Gwen reined their steeds in, their expressions confused at the abrupt halt. Jack stabbed a finger at each of them.

"Whatever you must deal with, bury it before it gets you killed. We have assassins tracking us and yet the dissension between you three will be the death of me."

Ursana coughed. "There's no dissension—"

Jack glared at Ursana. "Do I have to put you in the stocks?"

The absurdity of the suggestion made her laugh. "As you order, Guildmaster."

Gordon echoed the sentiment, and Jack turned on Gwen.

"Why are assassins tracking you?" she asked uncertainly.

"None of your concern," Jack said, and sniffed. "Now tell us about your guild, and I want to know what made them place so many guards around you."

She shrugged. "I suspect it's due to my recent mastery of the convergence spell."

"That's very high level," Inna said in surprise.

154

"It's very impressive," Gordon said. "Especially for one so—"

"Gordon," Jack said. "Stop talking. It's time for the adults to speak."

Gordon was twice Jack's age, and he guffawed at the statement. Before he could respond Jack turned his horse back onto the road and motioned for Gwen to join him. After a moment's hesitation, she did.

"What does this spell do?"

"It allows mages to combine their energies with other types of magic. When we do, we come close to what the oracle can accomplish in terms of raw power."

"Why hasn't Skorn just taken the oracle?" Gordon asked. "I would think she would be the first he would attempt to capture."

Gwen flashed a wry smile. "I think they tried a few weeks ago, but Siarra tore them asunder."

"Sounds like my kind of woman," Jack said with a laugh.

When the humor subsided, Jack was left with a lingering doubt. Inna had said that Skorn took the remains of the beacon after the battle of Margauth. If Skorn intended to rebuild it, the beacon would need power. A few hundred mages would be a massive source, and would only require a handful with a convergence spell to merge the magics into one. When he voiced his thoughts, Inna's expression darkened.

"If that's true," she said, "he wouldn't need someone with Gwen's skills until the end."

"What does that mean?" Gwen asked.

Jack met her gaze. "It means he's almost finished."

Chapter 19: Wedge

Jack guided his horse down the slope to the Talinorian gate. A great wall curved across the end, preventing access to the village on the plateau. Jack reined in his mount at the gate and raised a hand to the guards in greeting.

"Griffin merchants seeking entry."

The man looked between the four riders. "I don't see goods."

The other guard snorted in agreement. "Unless you have goods for trade, you can go to the Griffin district."

Jack made to retort but Inna smiled at them, drawing their gaze. She flipped her long red hair over her shoulder.

"Our apologies," she said with a smile. "Our goods were delivered in advance of our arrival. We intend to inspect the shipment before they are sold to merchants in the city."

The first guard thawed at her words. "You must present your papers . . ." he caught sight of Gwen and blanched. "Gwen? I thought you were taken."

Gwen swept a hand at Jack. "I was rescued."

The guard stepped to the portcullis and called, "Let them through!"

The portcullis began to grind upward and the two guards ushered them in. "I'll send word to your mother," the guard said.

Gwen smiled at him. "You have my gratitude."

When they had passed into the city Gordon turned to his daughter. "A friend?"

She nodded. "The guards rotate through posts at the academy, and many are close in age to the senior students. We get to know each other."

"Is anyone more than a friend?" Gordon asked.

He tried to keep his voice casual, but Gwen glared at him. "Not the time, father."

Jack laughed. "That means yes, my friend."

Inna joined in his mirth, but when it subsided the silence persisted among them. Irritated at their continued tension, Jack turned his attention on the city. The Talinorian Wedge was shaped like an arrowhead that pointed to the castle. The city had grown far beyond its original intentions and space was at a premium. With nowhere to grow outward, enterprising artisans had grown upward.

Fashioned of stone mined from the south of Griffin, the buildings rose several floors. In such a confined space the crowd should have been packed shoulder to shoulder, but the upper levels of the city boasted bridges and paths that connected the buildings. The upper roads allowed shoppers, tradesmen, and workers a path to walk, avoiding the wagons, carts, and horses on the ground. As soon as they were inside the gates, they left their steeds and Gwen led them to a set of stairs winding up a building. Reaching the roof, she took them across the highest paths.

The vantage point allowed glimpses of the Griffin Wedge to the north. Sprawling and disorganized, the Griffin section of the city abutted the arrow-shaped plateau. Thatch-roofed homes were scattered at the base, while shops and wealthier homes lined the upper steppes of a nearby hill. A large fort straddled the top of the slope, its fortifications facing the castle on the Talinor Wedge. Jack examined the Talinor castle, and spotted the tip of a trebuchet behind the wall and several ballistae mounted on the battlements. Inna followed his gaze and gestured to the castle.

"Griffin and Talinor might be allies," she said, "but they both prepare for war."

"What about the gate?" Inna asked, pointing north.

Through a gap in the buildings Jack spotted a large gate in the exterior wall. The portal led to a roadway that descended to the Griffin Wedge, allowing merchants and travelers easy passage between the two city sections.

"That section of road is held aloft by a long bridge," Gordon said. "Its dwarven made and built to collapse."

"Why do the dwarves have to rig everything to self-destroy?" Jack asked. "You'd think they hate their own handiwork."

Gwen laughed at that. "We have a couple of dwarves that teach at the academy. They teach a class on detonation that all the students enjoy."

Gordon raised an eyebrow. "You have instructors from other races?"

"Several, in fact," Gwen said. "We even have a rock troll."

"Sirani?" Ursana asked, speaking for the first time.

"You know her?" Gwen asked.

Ursana reached up and flicked the crossbow slung across her back, causing it to emit a dull whine. "She's the one that added the wind charm."

"I've heard of her," Inna said. "She was cast out by the rock trolls of Astaroth a century ago. When Tryton became their king she was permitted to return, but she's a born wanderer."

"She has a way of setting you at ease," Gwen said.

"For a rock troll," Ursana added.

Gwen and Ursana shared a tentative smile. Gordon had told Gwen about his occupation, and his partner, but the information had only

158

served to distance the two girls further. Not wanting to strain the positive moment, Jack changed the subject to the academy.

Gwen launched into a description of the academy, its classes, and her studies on magic. Jack listened with only half an ear and kept his focus on the people. Several times he spotted someone staring at him and wondered if assassins lurked in the city. Wedge bordered the Evermist, making it one of the closest cities to the thief guildhall. Tales of guild-trained thieves were abundant, and news of the bounty on Jack's head would be well known. Apparently thinking the same thing, Inna accelerated her pace.

"We should get inside," she said. "Before the crowds learn Jack's identity."

Gwen looked to him. "I'm sorry, I still don't understand your role in all this."

Jack grinned and bowed to her. "Jack Myst, Guildmaster of Thieves."

Her eyes widened and she glanced about in sudden fear. "But there's a bounty on your head."

He sighed. "Everyone wants me."

Inna snorted and turned down the path leading to the guildhall. "They don't want you, they want the coin."

"Same thing," Jack said with a smile.

They reached the guildhall and Gwen nervously spoke to the guards. Jack's eyes lifted to the academy, surprised to find it resembled a spired castle. Smaller than the Talinor castle at the end of the plateau, the academy boasted six towers in a semi-circle, each rising in height to the last, which abutted the city wall. Spiral staircases wrapped around the turrets, allowing students to ascend to the classrooms on each level. An arena sat in the center of the spires, its benches enclosing the turrets.

The guards allowed them through the gate and Jack descended to the arena floor. He lifted his gaze to the great turrets around the arena, wondering if anything of value lay in its halls. Then he spotted the varied spheres sitting atop pedestals around the arena. The balls of energy represented each of the types of magic, and were sources of power for mages.

"How many types of magic does the academy teach?" Jack asked.

"I'm one of four students with water magic," Gwen said. "Most are earth students, but there is a smattering of other energies taught here. The elves and dwarves have their own guilds, and specialize in the magics common for their respective races."

"So why display all the sources of magic?" Gordon asked.

"They're just for show," Gwen said.

As they approached the gates to the largest of the turrets, the door burst open and a woman sprinted into view. She engulfed Gwen in a crushing embrace, her words inaudible through her tears. Jack looked to Gordon, but the man seemed like he'd taken a blow to the skull.

"Rista?" he breathed.

She finally noticed Gwen's companions and straightened. She froze as she caught sight of Gordon, her relief turning to shock. The seconds passed and Jack shifted his feet, wondering if it would be rude to escape again. Inna cast him a warning look that answered his unspoken question.

"Mother," Gwen said, "Father saved me."

Rista tore her gaze from Gordon and looked down at her daughter, then back at Gordon. Abruptly she wiped at her tears and sought to fix her hair.

"I'm sorry," she said hastily. "I look terrible."

"No," Gordon breathed. "You don't."

Rista flushed and turned to Jack and Inna. "Please come in. I'm sure you could use a rest after your journey."

She led them inside and Jack looked about with interest. The main hall of the central turret contained several offices. Unlike the other turrets, this one contained an interior staircase that disappeared to the upper floors.

As they began their ascent a bell chimed, and the hallway flooded with chattering students in colored robes. They cast curious looks at Jack and his companions but passed them by. They fell to whispering, and Jack heard notes of curiosity in their voices.

Gordon and Rista said nothing, but their posture speaking volumes. Although they strode together, waves of tension seemed to pass between Gordon and Rista, prompting Jack to step to Rista's side.

"I know you have a great deal to discuss, but we don't have much time. We'd like to know more about Gwen's captors."

"You aren't the only one," she replied, her features darkening. "But we don't know who took her. She was taken from the city when she went to visit a friend."

"Surely one of you knows something," Jack said, and noticed the woman had not released Gwen's arm since their embrace in the arena.

"Speak to Sirani," Rista said. "She always seems to know more than the headmaster or the professors—if you can understand her."

"Why don't you enjoy a meal in private," Jack said. "Inna and I will talk to Sirani and join you after."

"I'll come with you," Ursana said quickly, stepping to Jack's side.

Rista's eyes flicked to Gordon and her features twisted as if in pain. "Sirani's classroom is on the top level of the white turret," she said. "We'll join you after we eat."

Jack met Gordon's gaze and raised an eyebrow. Gordon offered a slight nod in return, and although he looked like he was about to enter battle, he nodded to Rista and forced a smile. Then he followed her and Gwen higher into the tower. When they were gone, Ursana released an explosive breath.

"Let's find Sirani and get some answers," she said.

Turning on her heel, she strode down the stairs and back into the arena. Students milled about but they parted ways for them. Many of the young women eyed Jack with thinly veiled desire, prompting Inna to grunt in irritation.

"Can you not look so smug?"

Jack smiled, sending a group of girls into fits. "I'm just walking."

Ursana blew out her breath in disgust. "You're smug-walking."

"It's almost a saunter," Inna agreed, "but not quite so arrogant."

"A swagger, perhaps?" Ursana asked.

Jack sniffed. "I don't like the two of you together."

They laughed and then ascended the tower which bore white banners. As they neared the top they passed through a group of students laughing and chattering about their lesson with Sirani. Their hair was plastered to their faces, driven to the side as if they had been through a storm.

Jack reached the topmost floor of the turret and entered to find a spacious classroom. Windows on opposite sides had once held glass, but bore evidence of countless repairs. Apparently giving up on windows, someone had fastened steel bars into the stone.

Jack glanced out the northern window and saw the Griffin Wedge almost directly below them. Through the window on the opposite side, the high paths of the Talinor Wedge were just visible.

The space lacked desks, and aside from a handful of chairs facing a giant stool, the room was mostly empty. A handful of magical sources were bracketed in the walls, the suppressed magics swirling in place. A private section of the room was walled off, and through the open door Jack spotted a female rock troll bent over a desk.

"Sirani?" Ursana called.

The troll perked up and rose to her feet before squeezing through the door. With white and grey hair, she was the oldest troll Jack had met, and wore simple clothing of brown and deep red. As she exited the door, Jack spotted a large greatsword hanging in her office and recognized it as made by the same dwarven smith who had made his dagger.

"Hello, little dove," Sirani said. She smiled at Ursana and leaned down to embrace her.

"This is Jack and Inna," Ursana said. "They're friends of mine."

Sirani loomed over Jack, her eyes twinkling with delight. "I'd like *him* to be my friend," she said, and giggled. Then she reached down and caught his shoulders. Before he could react, the troll picked him up and held him aloft.

"*Hello, handsome,*" she crooned.

And kissed him.

Chapter 20: Sirani

Sirani placed him back on the ground and he stumbled back, sputtering. The rock troll released a cackle of laughter.

"An excellent kisser—but I expect nothing less from the guildmaster of thieves."

"You'd think my office would afford me some respect," Jack said sourly, casting a scathing look at Ursana and Inna, who were beside themselves with laughter.

"Thieves and wastrels," Sirani said, and her smile turned eager. "I smell an adventure in the wind, with all the scents of steel and lightning."

She cackled in anticipation and stepped to her office. She exited with her greatsword in hand and twirled it before sheathing it on her back. Then she clapped her hands together.

"When do we depart?"

"We came here for answers," Jack said, finally recovering from kissing the rock troll. "*Just* answers."

"You would deny me?" Sirani asked, pouting.

Jack stabbed a finger at her. "Don't pretend you're going to cry."

Caught, Sirani gave another cackle. "It was worth a try."

"Have you lost your wits?" Jack demanded. "You don't even know us, but want to join our assignment?"

"I can always smell adventure," Sirani said, and sniffed expansively. "And you reek of it."

"Let's start with what you know," Inna said. "We managed to rescue Gwen, but how many students have been taken?"

Sirani's features darkened and her smile disappeared. The tinge of madness in her eyes remained, making her fury all the more frightening. She growled like a beast standing over its prey.

"Too many," she said. "They spirit them away and none return."

"All students?" Ursana asked.

She shook her head. "Anyone with magic. He wants them all."

"Skorn?"

Sirani turned to face Jack and cocked her head to the side. "Why did you say that name?"

"That is our adversary," Jack said.

"Is he a devil or a man?" she asked, staring at Jack without seeing him. "Or a remnant of a forgotten race . . ."

Jack peaked an eyebrow and exchanged a look with Ursana. Only those in the Thieves Guild understood Skorn's true identity, so how did Sirani know the truth? Jack folded his arms and leaned against a pillar.

"He's taking the mages to a place called the Necrolith. Ever heard of it?"

Her eyes abruptly focused. "Another word from a dead language."

"Do you know its meaning?" Ursana asked.

"The beacon of ending."

"You speak the language of the ancients?" Inna asked in surprise.

165

"I dabble," Sirani said, her eyes twinkling with mischief. "Languages are a passion of mine—but when you get to my age, they tend to blend together into a language of love." She winked at Jack and cackled again.

"Why would he need mages?"

"To build the Necrolith," Sirani said, as if it were obvious.

She twined her fingers together and twirled them, sending a burst of wind spinning into the center of the classroom. It curved and bent, turning white like smoke as it condensed into a pyramid of swirling air. Patterns of symbols appeared on the sides of the pyramid and a long obelisk extended from the peak.

Jack and Inna exchanged a look and Jack ground his teeth in irritation. The shape bore a striking resemblance to the very beacon he'd thought destroyed. Realizing he'd been arrogant to think that Skorn would not retrieve the pieces, he strode to the swirling magic and circled it.

"I've seen one," Jack said, "But it fit into the palm of my hand."

Sirani laughed so hard the magic trembled and briefly lost its shape. "You beautiful little man," she said. "A Necrolith is the size of a fortress. It would take hundreds of mages a year to complete."

"So he's taking mages to build the Necrolith," Jack said. "But how do we stop it?"

"How should I know?" Sirani shrugged. "I'm not the Mind Vault."

"The what?" Ursana asked, but there was no answer.

Jack turned to find Sirani absent. Shocked that she could move so fast, Jack leaned so he could see into the office and spotted her at her desk, chewing on a loaf of bread. He called out to her and she turned. She rose from her seat and strode toward Jack.

"Hello, handsome," she crooned, reaching for his shoulders.

"Woah!" he said, taking a step back. "We're not doing that again."

She blinked in confusion and then smiled. "No need to repeat perfection."

"You were saying something about the Mind Vault?"

"It's a reservoir that contains all of the ancient's knowledge," she said, and then folded her arms. "Don't you ever study history?"

Inna laughed dryly. "Little remains after forty thousand years."

"The one who sees is the one who looks," Sirani chided. "You have but to examine the threads to see the tapestry."

"Where is the Mind Vault?" Jack asked with a sigh.

"Lost," Sirani said, resuming her meal.

"Then why mention it?" Jack demanded.

"Because I think it can be found."

Jack rubbed his forehead, irritated that a headache was beginning to form. Even when he was stealing from them, he liked rock trolls. They were skilled, disciplined, and loyal. Sirani seemed unbalanced and he began to wonder if anything she said was true.

"Where do we find it?" Inna asked.

"In the City of Dawn."

"Is that in Griffin?" Ursana asked.

Inna shrugged. "I've never heard of it."

"I have," Jack said. "It's in the southern sea."

"You know of it?" Ursana asked.

Jack recalled the map of the ancients he'd stolen for Skorn before he'd known the man's identity. On the map had been a location in the southern sea, an island all by itself. The script beneath it had been in ancient text, but someone had scrawled *City of Dawn* beneath it. He turned to Sirani with grudging respect.

167

"It's a real place," Jack said. "I think it was the ancients' capitol before their civil war."

"Surely a city of the ancients would be sought after by treasure seekers," Ursana said. "Why are there no tales of such a place?"

"Because no one survives to tell them," Sirani said, the gleam of excitement re-emerging in her eyes.

"Something guards it," Jack guessed.

"Very clever, my good thief," Sirani said. "Does your intelligence come from your hair?" She patted him on the head like a dog.

Indignant, he slapped her hand away. "Will you keep your hands to yourself, woman?"

She giggled and stepped to the pyramid shape, dismissing the magic with a flick of her hand. Then she turned back to Jack, her expression fierce enough to make all three of them retreat.

"I'm coming with you."

"You aren't one of my thieves," Jack said, reaching to his back to palm the hilt of his dagger.

For the first time Sirani looked like a rock troll. Her black eyes were as hard as granite, her form tense and ready for battle. She'd gone from a light summer breeze to a hurricane in an instant, the change shocking and disturbing.

"I'm coming with you," she repeated, her voice turning harsh.

"You have a place here," Ursana said uneasily, her smile forced.

"Not this time, little dove," Sirani said, not taking her eyes from Jack.

As the seconds passed, Jack measured the seething rage in her features, trying to examine if it was directed at him, or someone from her past. He was confident he could escape, but he wouldn't leave Ursana and Inna behind. The tension mounted until the door suddenly swung open and Gordon entered with his family in tow.

168

He smiled and placed the tray of food he'd brought onto a table. "Who's hungry?" Then he noticed the tension and came to a halt.

"Are we interrupting?" Rista asked.

Sirani burst into a laugh and sidled up to Jack. "A lover's quarrel," she said.

Jack strode to the bread and sliced it with his dagger. He flinched when Sirani's greatsword swung past his body. It sliced through the bread and withdrew, and a gust of wind carried the slice to Sirani's hand. Gwen and Rista laughed while the others stared at Sirani. When she noticed their attention Sirani shrugged.

"*He* sliced it with his blade," she said. "Why can't I?"

Jack began to chuckle, and his humor built into a roaring laugh. Sirani may have been mad, but she sliced the bread without making a dent in the table. Skilled with blade and magic, she was far more formidable—and dangerous—than she appeared.

"Did you learn anything?" Rista asked.

"We knew who was taking the mages and where," Ursana said. "Sirani helped us piece together the rest."

They settled in to eat, and talk shifted to other topics. Jack caught Gordon's eye and raised an eyebrow, to which Gordon smiled and nodded, glancing at Rista. They still kept their distance, but there was a softness to Gordon's gaze that had been absent before. Ursana seemed to notice it as well, and withdrew to a bench at the window. She chewed on her bread and cheese as she looked out over the Griffin Wedge.

When Jack finished the meal, he took a seat at the other end of the bench. He leaned against the wall and watched Gordon laugh with Rista and Gwen. He didn't speak, and after a few minutes Ursana sighed.

"Should I be happy for him?"

"You expect me to know?" he asked, throwing her a wry smile. "I'm not exactly the best at managing friendships."

She smiled at that. "You really are terrible."

He grinned. "He's still your partner."

"Is he?" Ursana asked. "He became a thief because he'd lost everything. If he has his family back, why would he stay in the guild?"

"For you, of course."

As Jack said it, he thought of Beauty. She'd made her position clear. As soon as Skorn and her father were dead, she would return to her homeland. When it was over, would she stay for him? He looked out the window at the setting sun, uncertain of the answer.

"You really believe that?" Ursana asked, not seeing his shift in mood.

"Gwen may be his daughter," Jack said, "but you're his family, too."

She smiled at that, but the expression carried a twinge of sadness. "But can he have both?"

Jack had no answer, and for several moments they sat in silence. Jack's gaze settled on Inna, who was laughing at Sirani's tale of how she'd gained a particular scar. Inna glanced at him and grinned, motioning him to join her. He smiled in turn and shook his head, for once not wanting to speak to a beautiful woman.

"What do you suppose that is?" Ursana asked.

Jack turned and gazed down the cliff to the Griffin district, where a crowd of men were gathering. There were no merchants in their midst, nor entertainers. Then they drew crossbows and aimed them up the cliff, firing in unison. The bolts streaked up the cliff with ropes trailing behind them, and exploded into barbs that dug into the stone turrets of the academy.

"Blasted bounty," Jack muttered, as they began to climb.

Hearing his words, Inna strode to them and looked down. Her smile evaporated when she saw the men scaling the cliff. "We must depart. Now."

"Too late," Gwen said.

Jack crossed the tower to the window and looked down at the courtyard, where two score Talinorian guards were striding across the stone. Their boots clicked on the ground as they spread out, drawing swords. Students cried out and fled, while professors rushed to intervene. The upper roads of Talinor were lined with soldiers bearing crossbows, all pointed at the academy.

"We're cut off," Inna said, her voice tense. "What do we do?"

Sirani began to cackle, the sound laced with anticipation. "And the herald of steel and storm has come to take me to my next adventure."

Jack turned to face her and saw the wild eagerness in her eyes. The emotion was the same he felt before every thief assignment, and to see it in a half-crazed rock troll caused a slow smile to spread on his features. As the soldiers turned toward the white turret Jack spoke.

"Let the adventure begin . . ."

Chapter 21: Thief's Flight

"Can you be calm?" Jack asked.

Sirani was bouncing up and down in excitement, and wind had swirled around her hands, knocking chairs to the floor. She pulled her greatsword and spun it about, causing everyone to retreat. Jack sighed and rubbed the back of his neck.

"We need to split up," he said. "Gordon, you and Ursana get Rista and Gwen out of here."

Rista wrung her hands in fear. "You cannot mean to fight the guards. They are the king's soldiers."

"What exactly do you think we do?" Ursana snapped, loading her crossbow.

Rista swallowed and shook her head, squaring her shoulders. "You may flee, but Gwen and I will remain here. They will not harm us."

"But the Talinorian mercenaries will," Inna said. She peered out the window and drew her sword. "Less than a minute, Jack. Whatever we're going to do, we need to do it fast."

"Inna's right," Gordon said, his tone placating. "When Herrick learns you are here, he'll come back for you."

"Who *are* you?" Rista said to Inna.

"A friend," Gordon said hastily.

"An assassin," Inna corrected.

Rista recoiled and put an arm in front of Gwen, who pushed it away. "She helped save me, Mother. We can trust her."

"We can't trust any of them," Rista said, attempting to pull her daughter away from the thieves.

"And me?" Gordon asked.

Rista's expression turned pained. "Now that you know the truth, you don't have to be part of them."

"You expect me to quit?" Gordon asked.

"I'm no thief," Rista said, and shuddered in revulsion. "And you're a soldier."

"Not anymore," Ursana snapped, striding into the confrontation. "He's a thief, and a blasted good one."

"Mother," Gwen began, but Rista turned on Ursana.

"Thieves inevitably end up in a noose," Rista said. "And I don't desire that for either of you. Your guildmaster and the killer will pay for their own crimes, but if you turn on them, I'm sure the guards will be lenient."

Ursana exploded with laughter, causing the woman to flush with anger. "You expect me to betray friends and watch them die," Ursana said. "What sort of woman are you?"

"The kind that cares for her family," Gwen said. "Do you even have one?"

"No family is better than having a family like yours," Ursana growled.

"Ursana!" Gordon said as Gwen stepped between them, raising a hand to Ursana.

"You need to apologize," Gwen said.

"Or what?"

"Or I make you apologize."

She cast her magic, water flowed out of the glasses and reached for Ursana's feet. Ursana skipped free and darted at Gwen, and the girl raised her hands, calling up a shield from the liquid. Ursana flipped over it and came down at her back, putting a dagger at Gwen's throat. Gwen went still and the water splashed to the floor.

"Don't threaten what you can't deliver," Ursana said coldly.

"*Ursana!*" Gordon snapped, "*Stay your hand.*"

"Would you betray Jack for them?" Ursana asked, rounding on him.

"No," Gordon said. "But they are my family."

Ursana glared at him before abruptly withdrawing the blade and shoving Gwen to him. "You deserve each other."

Jack sighed and strode to them. "Gordon and Ursana, take Rista and Gwen to the guildhall in the Evermist."

"Gordon can take them," Ursana said, moving to the window. "I'm staying with you."

Gordon shook his head. "But we always complete assignments together."

"Not anymore," Ursana said, and Gordon recoiled in surprise.

Rista shook her head. "I'm not going to—"

"We're going," Gwen said, and turned to Gordon. "It appears we have no choice."

"*Gwen!*" Rista cried.

"The mercenaries will come for me," Gwen said, turning to face her. "The city guard won't keep me safe. They will."

"But they're just thieves," Rista said.

"Can we *please* go?" Sirani whined.

Jack looked out the window, gauging the distance. He and the other thieves could use their shadowhooks to escape, but doing so would leave Inna and the others behind. Jack jerked his head, deciding they would have to go through the guards on the stairs and fight their way out in the arena. It was risky and would likely get someone killed—especially when the Griffin bounty hunters joined the fray. He glanced at Sirani and an idea formed in his mind. She was a wind mage, so why not use her talents? A smile spread on his face and he turned to the others.

"Gordon, when we draw them away, get your family out of the city and into the Evermist. Ursana, thin the Griffin pack and slow them down. Then join us in the arena. Inna, you're with me."

"And me?" Sirani asked, fidgeting like an eight-foot child.

"Clear the way," Jack said, pointing to the door where footsteps echoed on the steps beyond.

"With pleasure," she said gleefully.

With surprising agility she leapt out the door onto the landing of the stairs. Men cried out at her sudden appearance and formed ranks, but she pointed her massive sword at them and charged, shrieking like a crazed banshee.

Jack leapt to the landing in time to see her sprint down the curve of the stairs. Wind exploded from her sword, splitting the men apart like a farmer's plow. Soldiers slammed into the wall and the railing, their bodies tumbling to the steps as weapons and helmets clattered about them.

"She's crazy," Inna said.

"I know," Jack said with a laugh.

"I like her," Ursana said.

She placed her crossbow on the railing and aimed at the men below her. The bolt burst from the weapon and curved, arcing around the green turret to sever one of the climbing ropes. The man was several feet off the ground when it gave way, and he shouted in dismay before falling to the dirt. More crossbow bolts followed the first, all severing ropes holding men aloft. Then she took aim at the men higher on the cliff. The crossbow bolts slammed into the rock inches from their heads, causing them to flinch and hesitate. They shouted to each other and pulled the shields from their backs, squinting into the Griffin Wedge as they sought to pinpoint the shooter.

"Well done," Jack said.

"How many did you kill?" Rista said from the classroom door, her features contorted with loathing.

"None," Ursana said acidly. "We're thieves, not killers. Except for Inna, of course."

Inna laughed. "I only kill those who deserve it."

"Good luck, Gordon," Jack called, already turning down the path Sirani had made for them.

Ursana avoided Gordon's gaze as she shouldered her crossbow and darted after Jack. Throwing Gordon an apologetic look, Inna joined them. Jack took the steps four at a time as he raced to the academy's arena, but was forced to pick his way through the groaning men. Some had sought to flee, but the rampaging rock troll had knocked them all to the stones without shedding a drop of blood.

They reached the arena to find Sirani fighting another group of soldiers. Evidently more prepared than the first command, the soldiers in the lead held an anti-magic shield, blocking the furious blasts of wind while his companions edged closer.

"Professor Sirani!" the captain pleaded. "Listen to reason. He's the Guildmaster of the Thieves Guild—a criminal! You are a respected professor!"

"I've resigned," Sirani said. "I've been teaching for too long."

Jack leapt the last steps and darted to the soldiers, who turned in his direction. Using his momentum as a weapon, Jack wrapped his arm around a soldier's arm and twisted, coming to a halt and hurling the man into his companions. Then he drew his dagger and blocked a hasty strike.

"He's here!" someone shouted.

"Surround him!" the captain shouted, turning away from Sirani.

Jack swirled his cloak, using the distraction to approach another soldier. Deflecting her attack, he kicked her in the stomach and knocked her sprawling. Another soldier appeared and Jack stepped inside his guard, smashing his forehead into the man's skull. As he crumpled, Jack stepped over him and engaged the captain.

Inna dove into the battle, putting the vaunted swordcraft of Talinorian soldiers to shame as she decimated their attempts to disarm her. They cried out in dismay as their weapons tumbled from numb fingers. Still on the stairs, Ursana aimed her crossbow with punishing precision, sending bolts deep into legs and shoulders.

"We've wanted the Thieves Guild for ages," the captain snarled, striking at Jack. "I'm not about to let you escape my grasp."

"You're not here for the bounty?" Jack asked, parrying and striking back with his dagger.

"I don't care about the coin," the captain said. "You have pillaged without justice for far too long."

"Killing me won't stop the guild," Jack said, leaping into a flip over his flashing blade.

"But a hanging will discourage others from joining you."

Jack laughed and deflected the captain's strike. "I'd love to escape your prison, but I don't have time to humble you."

"Arrogant little thief," the man snarled. "Don't you see you're already caught?"

The captain retreated from the duel to join those of his men still standing. Jack looked up to see soldiers lining the arena, blocking off every exit. At their captain's order they drew their swords but kept their distance. Several mages were prominent, and they drew on the dirt of the arena to cast golems that lined up with the soldiers. Ursana vacated the steps and joined Jack, and soldiers closed off the steps to the white tower.

177

Students lined the balconies above, whispering and shouting to the men below. Professors struggled to quiet them and usher them inside but their efforts were in vain. Surrounded and alone, Jack smiled at the captain.

"So many soldiers just for me?" Jack smirked. "I'm flattered."

"You should have retained the high ground," the captain said with a triumphant sneer. "You allowed yourself to be surrounded."

"On the contrary," Jack said and sheathed his dagger. "I gave my new friend space to work her magic. Sirani, I've always wanted to fly. Think you can indulge me?"

Sirani issued a cackling laugh and the sky abruptly began to darken. The soldiers shifted nervously as the wind picked up, howling into the arena. The captain's shouts were lost in the rising shriek as wind tightened into four funnels. Compressing and shrieking, the wind wrapped around them until Jack could hardly see the soldiers. The captain stared at him with disbelief marring his features. Their eyes met and Jack raised his hand in salute.

The soldiers struggled to draw close but the gale was too much. They raised their hands to shield their faces, their boots sliding across the stones. One went down and the wind rolled him across the arena floor, slamming him into a turret wall. In the center of a forming tornado, Sirani released a mad laugh and clenched her fists. Jack's clothing sucked upward, his cloak billowing above his head. The tornado wailed. . .

And his boots lifted off the stones.

He grinned as he came free, and climbed into the rapidly intensifying cyclone. Through the churning black wind he watched soldiers fight to keep themselves on the ground, with several clinging to the benches to avoid tumbling away. Huddling behind a soldier with an anti-magic shield, the captain glared up at him.

"BLASTED THIEVES!" he roared.

Jack's smile widened as the tornado ripped him from the arena and launched him skyward. Sirani's tornado carried her through a gap between the towers and into the Griffin Wedge, the other three cyclones following close behind. Laughing in sheer pleasure, Jack relished the sensation of weightlessness and turned his gaze skyward. Then Sirani flipped, and the tornado followed suit. The giant cyclone rolled over, bringing her feet toward the ground at the base of the cliff. Jack's tornado did the same, flipping him over and bringing him to the ground in an explosion of dust. Used to agile maneuvers, Jack landed in a crouch and rose to his feet as his tornado dissipated.

Inna dropped to the earth, clinging to the soil as her cyclone disintegrated. Ursana stumbled and fell, vomiting into the street. As they recovered, Jack turned to Sirani with a broad smile on his face.

"You have my gratitude for the flight," he said.

She grinned wildly, but her features were drawn and weak, suggesting she'd used much of her magic. Jack stepped to Ursana and helped her up. As she stood, Ursana pointed up the cliff, where the Griffin bounty hunters had begun to descend toward them.

"We are not free yet," she said, wiping her mouth.

"Inna?" Jack asked.

"I'm alright," the assassin said, stumbling to her feet. "Just don't do that again."

"I shouldn't have done that in the first place," Sirani said with a sheepish giggle. "One mistake and my magic would have ripped you to pieces."

"You should have said that before you tried it!" Inna growled.

Jack helped Ursana toward the road, where a crowd of onlookers had gathered. "Are you mad?" he asked. "That was more exhilarating than stealing the godship."

"Not if it gets you killed."

Jack laughed as they slipped through the crowd. "That's what makes it fun."

Chapter 22: The Exiled

Jack hurried his companions through the city, but word of their presence traveled faster. Shouts came from all directions, and soldiers appeared in the distance at the Griffin fort. Jack's features tightened in irritation and he picked up the pace. Then he noticed that Ursana was limping and struggling to keep up. She had an arm around Inna's shoulders but they maintained Jack's pace. Sirani ambled along, listing to the side like a sinking ship. The sheen of sweat on her features made it clear that her magic had cost her dearly.

Abruptly Jack shifted directions, turning away from the city exit and threading his way deeper into the Griffin Wedge. As they crossed a city square he tossed an object into the bushes and kept walking. Townsfolk retreated from them and doors slammed shut.

"Where are we going?" Inna asked, her voice strained. "All the exits are back that way."

"Wouldn't matter," Jack said. "Even if we left the city, we wouldn't be able to stay ahead of pursuit."

"Then where can we go?"

"A refuge," Jack said.

He darted down an alley and hurried to the end. Bound by walls on three sides, the alley afforded no place of egress. Jack leapt to the grate on the end and lifted it, ushering them into the sewers below. Inna helped Ursana inside, but Sirani eyed the opening skeptically.

"This pig won't fit through that porthole."

Jack laughed and climbed in. "Suit yourself. But I thought you wanted adventure."

"Your cleverness is not appreciated," she said, sniffing as she climbed into the gap and squeezed through the opening. Jack was quick to follow, and used the ladder to join them below. As he gingerly shut the grate a thudding of footsteps echoed from above. The distinct echo of shouted orders resounded in the street, swelling and then fading as soldiers rushed by.

Jack grinned and turned to the others, motioning them down the sewer tunnel. "This will take us to the river," he murmured. "We can cross to the Barbarian Wedge from there."

"You couldn't pick a better smelling exit?" Inna asked, flashing a pained smile.

"I will next time," Jack said, stifling a laugh.

He stepped into the lead and guided them down the tunnel. Like much of Griffin construction the tunnel was old, and many of the ceiling stones had fallen. Roots protruded from the gaps, the gnarled wood clinging to the underside of the ceiling.

Foul liquid trickled down the base of the drain, but Jack used the fallen stones to keep his fine boots from getting stained. A grunt and a curse caused him to turn and find the hulking rock troll rubbing her head. Muttering more curses, she crouched lower and struggled to keep up.

Several times they heard muffled yells, the sounds filtering through the occasional grates they passed. He grinned at their urgency and frustration, but he did not slow. The soldiers were bound to think of the sewers eventually, and he wanted to be gone when they did.

They came to a junction and Jack chose the southern tunnel. The air grew fetid as they descended closer to the river, the liquid filling the base of the sewer. Then the tunnel came to an abrupt end above the river's surface.

Jack came to a halt at the edge of shadow. The river stretched for a hundred feet before rising on the opposite bank, where a sprawling collection of buildings represented the Barbarian Wedge of the city.

Inna leaned Ursana against the wall of the tunnel and peered out. "There are hundreds of homes that can see the river. How do we get across without being spotted?"

Jack peeked around the edge of the tunnel and saw her words were true. Women cleaned laundry in the river upstream, and children splashed in the shallows. Despite the sewers, the river was remarkably clean, and Jack spotted fish in the depths.

"With a distraction," Jack said.

"Who's going to distract the entire city?" she asked.

He turned to Ursana. "Can you make it across?'

She bobbed her head. "I can swim."

Jack pulled his crossbow into view and aimed it toward the sky. "Then get ready," he said, and fired.

The bolt streaked upward, before banking to the side and aiming for a spot further up in the city. Drawn to the beacon rune Jack had dropped into the bushes, the bolt dug into the rune—detonating the banshee curse.

The piercing wail exploded throughout the city, rising to a deafening shriek. Jack clamped his hands over his ears and saw Ursana's mouth moving as if she was shouting at him. He laughed and dove into the river away from the dark liquid below the sewer. Plunging beneath the surface brought a welcome relief from the wail and he struck out for the opposite shore.

He would have liked to use his boots and stride across the river but the townsfolk were bound to notice him walking on water. When his lungs burned he came up for air, wincing as the wail pierced his ears. He looked back and spotted his friends in the water, with Sirani using a flicker of wind to coast across the surface.

Children that had been running along the bank of the river sat huddled, their eyes clenched shut as they covered their ears. Women held their laundry around their heads, desperately trying to shut out the wail. No one had eyes on the river.

He reached the opposite bank as the wail diminished, leaving a ringing in Jack's ears. He waited for Ursana and helped her from the water, Inna catching Ursana's other arm. Together, they threaded into the trees. A moment later Sirani stumbled out of the water and joined them, disappearing from sight as the people in Griffin Wedge recovered and looked about.

"How much did that bit of magic cost you?" Inna asked.

Jack barely heard the question through the ringing. He put a finger to his ear and pressed in a vain effort to ease the sound.

"Too much," Jack said loudly. "But it was worth it."

"Not if it gets us killed," Ursana shouted.

Jack followed her gaze, and turned to find a quartet of blades extended toward them. Evidently drawn to the sound, the barbarians glowered at them, except for the one in the center. The barbarian was a veritable giant, and carried an enormous double-bladed axe on his back. Although his stature was imposing, his smile was warm.

"Jack Myst," he said. "It's good to see you again."

"You *know* him?" Ursana asked.

"This is Golic," Jack said with a smile, "Beauty's brother."

"We should get out of sight," one of the barbarians said, and they lowered their swords. "The humans will be seeking retribution."

"Come," Golic said. "You can join us at our camp."

Ursana limped a step forward but a barbarian youth reached down and scooped her up. She squeaked in surprise and drew a knife, putting it to his throat. The barbarian merely looked down and smiled at her.

"So little yet so strong," he said. "And so beautiful."

183

She turned pink but kept her knife at his throat. "Put. Me. Down."

"But you are injured."

"You can carry me when I'm dead."

He laughed and gingerly placed her on the ground. She turned away from him and limped to Jack's side, ignoring the barbarian as they wound their way through the trees. Jack leaned down as they turned a corner and murmured to her.

"He's Golic's friend, Balor," he said.

"You say that like I should care."

He shrugged. "I thought you'd like to know his name before you fall for him."

Ursana scowled but Jack merely laughed and sped up to Golic. "The soldiers may come for us."

"They won't," Golic said. "They fear our kind."

"I thought the Barbarian Wedge didn't have a chief."

"No chief claims this land as his own," Golic said. "But those who call this village home stand together in times of strife. The humans cross the river to trade, but soldiers are not welcome."

They reached the village and Jack gazed about in interest. He'd traveled through Wedge a number of times, but never had cause to visit the barbarian section. The settlement did not resemble a village and had no order to its streets and buildings. Forges were as abundant as homes, with blacksmiths busy crafting weapons and armor.

The buildings were a ramshackle collection of structures, appearing like trees sprouting up at random places. Built of rough-hewn logs and covered in thatch, they were simple but clean. Without exception, the barbarians in the street wore armor and carried weapons, and even the children wielded blades. Many of the youths—both girls and boys— fought in clearings under the watchful eyes of trainers.

"Why are you here?" Jack asked. "Shouldn't you be with your tribe in the high mountains?"

Golic cast him a look but did not respond. Instead he motioned to Balor. "Find them a place to stay and have a healer visit them. I'd like to speak to the guildmaster alone."

"As you order," Balor said, and guided the others away.

Inna exchanged an uncertain look with Jack before departing. Jack remained in place until they entered a tavern. Then Golic motioned Jack to follow him, and turned toward the hill that ascended beyond the village.

As they strode through the streets the other barbarians nodded to Golic, their eyes tinged with respect, almost reverence. Jack noted the expressions, his curiosity rising. When they left the village and had risen above it, Jack spoke.

"What's going on?"

Golic came to a halt on a ledge overlooking the village, and spread his hand to it. "This place has been a trading outpost for centuries," he said.

Jack looked to the village and saw an abundance of homes, many of which were under construction. The sound of axes striking wood resounded through the trees, and saws bit into the fresh logs.

"It's not a trading post anymore," Jack said.

"The barbarian clans have waged war for longer than recorded history," he said, "but in recent generations it has taken a turn for the ruthless. Chieftains lead their armies to war while their people starve."

"So what brought so many of your people here?" Jack asked, sweeping a hand to the budding village.

"They stood up against the chieftains in defiance of tradition," Golic said. "Some were killed but many were cast out. They belong to no tribe now."

185

"Except yours," Jack said. "I saw the way they looked at you. By name or deed, they look to you for leadership."

Golic sighed and grasped the handle of his axe. "I tried to speak wisdom to my father but he refused to listen. Now I too have been cast out."

"You don't have to stay in these mountains," Jack said with a shrug. "The world has many wonders to see."

Golic turned and raised his gaze to the mountains in the southeast. "It is our homeland," he said quietly. "The streams, the trees, even the snow are all we know. We will fight for the place we call home."

Suddenly Jack understood. "You're building an army."

Golic nodded. "A great many from all the tribes are undecided. If our figurehead returns, they will join us. She was the first to defy a chieftain, and we all follow her example."

"Who was the first?" Jack asked, a trickle of foreboding creeping into his gut.

"Thera," Golic said, turning to him. "She left for the sake of family, and the tale spread among our people. We wish to fight for a home, not destroy another. When Thera returns, they will flock to our banner."

Jack growled and turned away. "Why has she not told me?"

"She cares about you," Golic said. "And does not want to depart the Thieves Guild. She also fears retribution from our father. If he learned Thera was among us, he would descend upon us in his wrath. Unless our numbers grow, we would not survive."

Jack fell silent, his anger warring with his frustration. How could Beauty have kept this from him? Or perhaps she hadn't. She'd made abundantly clear that she intended on returning to her homeland when her father was dead, and Skorn had been vanquished.

"What do you want from me?" Jack asked.

Golic held his gaze. "Convince her to come home."

"I don't know if I can do that."

Golic sighed. "You're the only one who can."

Chapter 23: Betrayer

Beauty mounted Axe and flicked the reins, leading her horse to the head of the caravan. Many of the abbots had wanted a public departure, allowing the thousands of new acolytes to join Ero on his journey to Herosian. Their excitement had waned in the face of Beauty's answer.

"No."

Although the support of Le Runtáriel had swayed many to believe in Ero, an undercurrent of resentment had risen among the dissenters, many of which were not in Azertorn. The easiest place to strike against Ero would be on the journey to Herosian, so Beauty had planned a secret departure.

With just Ero, four guards, and a wagon for supplies, they left Azertorn behind and made their way through the forest of Numenessee. They entered the forest before sunrise and light gradually brightened the trees, illuminating graceful trunks and lush greenery. Beauty only had eyes for the shadows, and set a blistering pace.

"Why the rush?" Ero said from beside her.

"The high abbot was a little too eager to have us leave," she said.

"Is that why we left early?"

"It's my job to keep you safe," she said. "And your notoriety is going to bring fanaticism."

"It won't be long now," he said. "Skorn will come for me soon."

188

"What then?" Beauty asked. "What do we do when he comes for you?"

She cast a look back at the guards, but they were out of earshot. They had taken up position around the wagon, implying that Ero was inside. Dressed in guard's clothing, Ero resembled the rest of them—except for his eyes, which were impossible to hide.

"Nothing," Ero replied.

She raised an eyebrow. "You intend to let him take you? I don't think that's what Jack is planning."

Ero sighed. "The followers of Skorn are becoming more numerous than I anticipated. Even if Skorn is dealt with, the leaders of his cult will not stop their actions."

"You want to kill his cult," Beauty said.

"Will you help me?"

"Skorn will kill you."

"Possibly," Ero said. "But I cannot let his legacy endure in this world."

A movement in the shadows drew her gaze, but it proved to be a deer slipping away from the road. As she continued to survey the trees she mulled his idea over, considering the possibilities. She didn't want to go against Jack, but Ero was right. Just as people were flocking to Ero, they were also gathering around Skorn. A line had been drawn and people were picking sides. Even if god and devil were killed, the movements would endure. Jack had made plans to end the Church of Light by leaving it penniless and Ero discredited, but what would destroy the Cult of Skorn?

"If Skorn took you, how would that help?" she asked.

"Once I know his location, I can summon you to him."

"You want to use yourself as bait?"

"We both know he wants me," he said. "That gives us an advantage."

"Can I ask you a question?"

"You haven't answered mine."

She smiled and gestured to him. "Jack told me about the construct at your vault, and described it as the most dangerous vault guardian he'd ever faced. Why not bring her to punish Skorn?"

Ero was silent for long enough that she cast him a look. Then he sighed. "Our abilities may be far superior to your own, but they still have limits, just like your magic, I presume."

"What has Jack told you about my magic?" she asked.

"You are a barbarian with magic of the body," Ero said, his eyes sparkling with interest.

"I can enhance any element of my form," Beauty said. "Eyesight, strength, agility, speed, hearing, and so on."

"Why not all of them?"

"Magic always has a cost," she replied. "Using more than one charm at a time has a devastating impact on one's body. Doing so to excess is fatal."

"That must require a great deal of discipline," he said. "Is that why you are so reserved with Jack?"

She laughed lightly. "Is that really what you want to know?"

"Do you love him?"

She thought of his rakish smile and shook her head. "Same question, same answer. I don't know if he's capable of loving one woman."

"I wager he wants to know what you feel."

"Then why doesn't he ask?"

190

"Perhaps he has tried," Ero said with a smile. "But words of affection do not come easily to men."

She laughed again but did not respond, and Ero did not press the issue. For reasons she could not fathom, he seemed sad. As the conversation returned to the tactic of destroying Skorn's Cult, Beauty thought about Jack, wondering what she felt toward him.

The road wound its way through the forest until it reached the great bridge to the kingdom of Talinor. They turned east but Beauty kept them off the highways. After several days on the road they reached the capitol city of Herosian.

With the fortress at the heart of the city, Herosian sprawled across the flatlands, surrounded by the Sea of Grass. The grass swayed in the breeze, bending in various shades of green that reflected the wind.

They entered the city from the western gate and made their way to its heart. Beauty shielded her eyes and gauged the height of the sun, estimating they had less than an hour until sunset. She wanted to be in and out by nightfall, before word spread that Ero had come to the city.

As they passed through the city Beauty examined the fortress in the distance. Built of stone drawn from quarries in Griffin, the fortress rose an impressive three hundred feet. At the center of the courtyard, the keep's turrets reached even higher, their surfaces polished to reflect the sun. Whereas the king's castle in Griffin had a more artistic design, the castle in Herosian was purely utilitarian, the walls and battlements fortified and thick.

They reached the castle as the sun touched the Sea of Grass, and Beauty passed into the courtyard. Dismounting and stretching, she nodded to the approaching captain and withdrew a letter. The man's eyes widened and he nodded.

"You are expected," he said, his eyes flicking to Ero. "The king has prepared quarters for you. We'll have the prisoner brought there."

"You have our gratitude," Ero said.

The man dropped his gaze. "You have ours for visiting our city."

The captain motioned to the guards and led Beauty and Ero inside the castle. They ascended a turret and proceeded down a corridor until they came to an arched doorway. The captain swung the door open to reveal a comfortable receiving room with adjoining bedchambers. A crackling fire warmed the room, while elven light orbs were placed between Talinorian banners. Comfortable chairs and a couch sat in a circle around the room, while tables with decorative porcelain vases lined the walls.

"Duke Gorwall will be here in a moment," the captain said.

"Thank you captain," Ero said.

When he was gone, Ero removed his guard uniform, revealing his customary white robe beneath. When Beauty raised an eyebrow, Ero merely smiled and finished changing. Then he tossed the guard uniform to her.

"We need Carvia to respect us," Ero said. "And appearance is everything."

The statement reminded Beauty of Lorelia, and she turned away, her heart tightening. She'd thought Lorelia was her friend, but had never known the thief's true past. Then Lorelia had betrayed them to Skorn, and it had cost Lorelia her life.

Her thoughts were interrupted when the door swung open and a rotund man stepped in with a guard in tow. Duke Gorwall scowled at Beauty and kept his distance. Dressed in regal red and purple, the duke ranked just below the king, and led the Duke's Council.

"Beauty," he said. "Your guildmaster had better uphold his end of our agreement."

"Always," she said with a smile. "Did you bring her?"

The duke stepped aside and gestured to the guard, who exited and returned a moment later with a woman bound in shackles. She caught sight of Beauty and scowled, and then she noticed Ero.

"Ero," she spit the word like it was a curse. "Come to gloat?"

192

"Your master abandoned you," Ero said. "And I am sorry for your plight."

"I would die for him," Carvia said, straightening in her chains.

"And so you shall," Duke Gorwall said. "A noose waits you in four days' time."

Carvia sneered at him and looked to Beauty. "If you thought bringing this imposter would get me to betray Skorn, you are mistaken."

"Skorn is as much an imposter as I am," Ero said. "Yet you believe in him."

"He is our god," Carvia said.

As they spoke Beauty examined her. Dressed in prisoner grey she didn't look like much, but a sharpness to her gaze gave her an imposing presence. Her hair was short and disheveled, and her hands were worn from the shackles that bound her. Despite her appearance, she retained the regality of her former position as a viscount's wife.

"If I were not in shackles I would kill you," Carvia said.

"You assume you could," Beauty said, and Carvia turned on her.

"You think to stop me?" she sneered. "My master told me much about you, and your talents. But beneath that beauty you are just a worthless thief. I wonder what a certain barbarian chief would say if he knew you were alive . . ."

Ero regarded Carvia with pity and a trace of irritation. Surprisingly, he pulled a knife from a fold of his cloak and stepped to Carvia, placing it against her throat. At the appearance of steel the duke moved to intervene.

"I'd like to kill her myself," the duke said, "but she is still in my stewardship."

Ero cast him a look that made him retreat. Then Ero stared at her. "Do you believe so strongly in Skorn that you would die for him—even when he has betrayed you? He does not deserve your loyalty, but I will oblige your desire."

193

The knife pressed against her throat and Carvia swallowed, the threat of death carried home by the startling blue eyes. As blood trickled down her neck she released a strangled sound.

"He will come for me."

Ero smiled and withdrew the knife. "You still have your faith," he said. "A pity. I wager it will not last the night."

Her eyes narrowed but it was the duke that scowled. "What do you plan on doing to her?"

"I don't need to do anything," Ero said. "I have placed myself—the most hated enemy of the cult of Skorn—with a former head of the same cult, who has become an overzealous thorn in his ambitions. How long before the cult comes for us both?"

The duke snorted at the statement. "We stand in the strongest fortress of Talinor. They cannot breach its walls."

"I suspect they already have," Beauty said.

She'd enhanced her hearing when she'd realized what Ero insinuated, and now heard the meaty *thump* of a body striking a castle floor. Realizing they had only seconds, she caught the duke's arm and pulled him away from the door. Noticing the motion, Ero shook his head.

"The cult will not risk inciting Talinor against them," Ero said. "They are here for Carvia and me."

"In here," Beauty said, all but shoving the duke into one of the bedchambers adjacent to the receiving room. "And barricade the door."

"I will not hide like a rat," the duke said, straightening.

"Then you will die like one," she said acidly, and slammed the door in his face.

The duke's guard pointed to the hall. "Can we not flee before they arrive?"

"No time," Beauty said, listening to the approaching boots.

194

"They will not touch the duke," Ero said as Beauty moved to the center of the room.

"You should have told me your plan," Beauty said, drawing her sword and stepping to the door.

"I thought you would have figured it out," Ero said in chagrin.

Beauty scowled but did not respond. Ero was right, but she had been so focused on an ambush that she had not considered what might happen once they were inside the castle. The duke's guard retreated from the door and drew his blade, and a moment later a man appeared in the hall. Dressed in his customary golden robe, Alidon, the high abbot of the Church of Light, stepped into view with a score of soldiers at his back. In their midst, the leader of the assassin's guild strode into the light.

"Hello Beauty," Gallow said.

Chapter 24: Ero's Staff

"Alidon," Ero said. "I admit I did not expect you."

"You walked into a trap," the high abbot said. "I should thank you for making it so easy."

The high abbot flashed a smug smile as soldiers filed into the receiving room. Her sword and crossbow in her hands, Beauty retreated, measuring the men. They were not common thugs, and she saw the scars and tattoos of combat littered on their flesh. They were Talinorian mercenaries, the best of the mercenary guilds. Marked by the silver bar above the sword and skull, the lieutenant smirked at Beauty's worry.

Beauty's eyes flicked to him but returned to Gallow. Although the mercenary lieutenant would undoubtedly be dangerous, it was Gallow she feared. Slim of build and young, Gallow didn't look like an assassin, but a legacy of murders reflected in his black eyes. He was a predator, one that relished the kill.

"Captain Herrick's soldiers," Beauty said to Gallow. "Jack mentioned they'd contracted to Skorn. Did they bring you here?"

"Actually, no," Gallow smirked. "It was the esteemed high abbot that informed me of Ero's visit to Carvia."

"You allied with *him*?" Beauty demanded, turning to the high priest.

Alidon's smile widened at her fury. "Ero has perverted our ways, and Skorn generously offered to return the church to my leadership."

196

"How benevolent of a devil," Ero said dryly.

Carvia sneered at Ero. "I told you they would come for me."

Gallow's chuckle sent a chill through the room, draining the triumph from Carvia's expression.

"You misunderstand," he said. "We weren't sent to free you . . . we were sent to silence you."

Carvia looked like she'd been struck a physical blow, and she recoiled. Alidon laughed at her dismay and turned to Ero.

"They assured me it would be cleaner without my presence," Alidon said to Ero. "But I insisted. I wanted to see your face, to watch you die."

Beauty eased closer to the duke's guard, measuring the soldiers, gauging how many she could take before they killed her. With no room and no way out, escape was not an option. In her peripheral vision she spotted the duke's guard, his face laced with fear.

"The king's guards patrol this corridor every hour," the man said, recovering from the sudden entry of the mercenaries. "They will kill you for your impudence."

Gallow jerked his head. "A mistake in their paperwork means the guards that operate this shift were mistakenly sent home. No one is coming, soldier. But as much as I would like to kill you, that is not what we are here for. The thief, on the other hand, we are more than happy to gut."

Ero began to laugh, the sound sending a current of tension through the room. "You think to best her?" he asked. "You have no idea the adversary you face."

Beauty spared Ero a glance but he remained unafraid, excited even. Did Ero expect her to fight a score of proficient killers and emerge unscathed? The guard's fidgeting indicated his lack of skill, and she couldn't handle so many on her own. She tightened her grip on her sword and forced a smile, counting on the bluff.

"How many do I kill before you flee?" she asked.

197

"You mean to fight us alone?" Gallow said, and a smattering of smiles appeared on the mercenaries. Gallow held Beauty's gaze, his sneer widening as he leaned forward.

"Who said she was alone?" Ero asked.

The sudden anger in his voice caused Beauty to glance his way—and saw light flowing from his hand, forming into a glowing staff. The Talinorian mercenaries shifted at the appearance of the weapon. Ero began to stride forward, the sheer power of his gaze causing some of the men to retreat.

"What are you waiting for?" Ero asked. "I thought you were supposed to be fearless."

Gallow growled and leapt forward, driving his sword toward Beauty's neck. The motion shattered the calm and the mercenaries charged. Facing so many foes, Beauty opted for a speed charm over strength, and magic surged into her limbs. Her reflexes spiked, her legs trembling with the yearning to move.

Giving in to the desire, she twisted as Gallow's sword arced toward her, whipping her own blade up to parry. Then she ducked inside his guard, driving a fist into his chest, dropping her speed charm for strength. Her body slowed but her fist struck the assassin with the force of a rock troll hammer. The air exploded from his lungs and he tumbled backward, crashing into his men and bouncing off the wall, dropping to the floor.

She released her strength spell and recast her speed, ducking a trio of strikes and whirling to the couch. Rolling her momentum into a flip, she leapt over and alighted on the other side. The soldiers stepped on the couch and came for her, but she sliced the legs off the couch, and all three went down. She drove her sword into one and then aimed her crossbow at the second, sending a bolt into his chest. They cried out and collapsed and she kicked the third in the face, breaking his nose and sending him backward.

She dropped speed and cast agility, leaping to the table and darting across its surface. A sword swung at her legs and shattered the vase, sending bits of porcelain toward her feet. She leapt high and threaded the gap between a bracketed light orb and the wall, coming down behind a group of mercenaries.

Releasing agility, she cast speed and whipped her sword among them. They were Talinorian soldiers, trained by elite weapons masters, but they were no match for Beauty's sheer speed. Swords tumbled to the floor and the men cried out in dismay and pain. A mercenary clutched his wounded arm and shouted for aid, his cry ending abruptly as Beauty's boot smashed into his teeth. Then Beauty spotted Ero.

The ancient twirled his staff, striking the mercenaries as fast as they appeared. Light exploded from each contact, launching men into walls, chairs, and into each other. The smile on his face was almost eager as he twisted to strike at a man attempting to flank him, sending him crashing into a light orb. Glass shattered, raining down on the soldier's back as he slumped to the floor. Gallow rose and stabbed a finger at Beauty.

"Kill her!" he barked.

He drew the idalia from his back and threw it. In the packed confines of the room the triangular blade was as dangerous to the mercenaries as it was to Ero and Beauty. The lieutenant shouted in anger as the blade spun past his skull, narrowly missing his scalp. Then it sliced across the duke's guard, cutting his throat before returning to the assassin's hand. He sheathed it and darted to Ero.

The assassin evaded the staff with expert precision, striking at Ero's back. In the midst of a furious battle Beauty leapt high, caught the bracket of a light orb, and fired her crossbow at Gallow. The bolt exploded into ropes but the assassin leapt back, sweeping his sword to shred the ropes. Then he struck again, nicking Ero's shoulder and drawing blood.

"He's mortal!" Alidon shouted from the hallway. "The truth has been revealed!"

With surprising agility Ero leapt a chair and flipped over a swinging sword, coming down at the doorway. The high abbot squeaked in surprise and attempted to flee but Ero caught his robe and spun, throwing him into the room.

"You really are a fool," Ero said, using his staff to strike at the mercenaries fighting Beauty.

One went down and Beauty leveraged the gap to strike at another. Then she reached out and caught a man's tunic, dropping speed to cast strength. With a surge of power she heaved him bodily across the room. Gallow ducked as the man crashed into a table. Beauty spun and released the strength, using speed again to weave between the remaining blades, her sword and crossbow working in tandem to cut them down.

She lunged for the final soldiers but six remained on their feet, and they converged upon her as Gallow flanked Ero. Swords darted in, cutting Beauty's tunic, drawing blood. She winced, the blood staining her clothing and trickling down her arm.

Evidently learning from their predecessors, they worked as a unit, flanking and striking at her, herding her to the wall. Six swords attacked as if wielded by a single mind, and even with her speed spell she could not keep up.

She growled and snatched a banner from the wall, tossing it over the men on her left. A soldier cut it apart, but the momentary pause allowed her to aim her crossbow and fire at their feet, freezing one to the floor. Before she could finish him the lieutenant on her right lunged for her, forcing her to turn and parry their attacks.

Abruptly fury engulfed her, and she fed it into a strength spell. Reaching up, she grasped a bracketed light orb and yanked it from the wall, hurling the heavy steel at the mercenaries. It crashed into one man and knocked him down, pinning him to the floor. His companion sought to lift it but the effort failed, and he rose to find a crossbow bolt sinking into his gut. He cried out and went down on top of the bracket, crushing the man beneath even more.

Beauty whirled to face the remainder but the lieutenant swung his sword into her crossbow, catching the curve of the weapon and yanking it from her hands. Beauty stepped on a discarded sword and it flipped upward. She caught the hilt and swung both blades, striking at the last three mercenaries.

Out of the corner of her eye she saw Ero surprisingly holding his own against Gallow, his enchanted staff keeping the skilled swordsman

200

at bay. In the distance the pounding of boots echoed, indicating soldiers were rushing to investigate.

"You're out of time," Ero said.

Ero spun and threw a knife, sinking the blade into the high abbot's leg as he sought to flee. The man tumbled to the ground with a shriek of pain, grasping the wound. Gallow scowled and pressed harder, but Ero managed to deflect the strike and land one of his own, knocking the assassin into a table with a blast of light.

"You're just a man," Gallow snarled, rising to his feet.

"And you're a devil's lapdog," Ero said.

He swung his staff in a full circle, the weapon hurtling at Gallow. The assassin raised his sword to block it—but Ero extinguished the staff. Gallow's sword passed through the staff, causing the assassin to stumble. Ero reversed the motion of the staff and cast it again, striking Gallow on the back of the skull. The blast of light sent him tumbling forward, smashing through a table against the wall.

Beauty engaged the last two mercenaries, using her speed to overwhelm their defenses and disarm them. As they scrambled for a weapon she stalked forward, releasing her speed charm and activating strength. They caught up weapons but she picked up the broken couch and shattered it upon them, and then drove her sword through the lieutenant's body. He stared at her, his eyes wide with shock as he died.

"You're just thieves . . ."

"I wasn't always a thief," she said coldly.

She joined Ero at the door and turned to face Gallow, who stood beside the whimpering high abbot. The assassin warily twisted between them, pointing his sword at Beauty and then Ero.

"Next time you won't see me coming," Gallow said.

"Perhaps," Ero said. "But you will fail again because you underestimate your adversary."

201

Gallow sneered at them but did not lower his blade. "Skorn will come for you all. He cannot be defeated."

Ero smiled. "How many times has he tried to kill Jack Myst?"

Gallow's features rippled with fury but he didn't answer. Boots thudded in the hall, the sound mounting with distant shouts. Beauty stepped to the bedchamber door and swung it open, allowing the duke to exit. She stabbed a finger toward the hall and the man nodded, threading his way to it, tripping over wood, glass, and bodies.

"Well done," the duke said to Beauty, glancing at Gallow. "If you want a career change, I have an opening in my guard."

Beauty didn't answer, and kept her gaze on Gallow as the castle guard flooded the hall. The duke raised his voice and his barked orders brought the soldiers into the room, where they moved to flank the assassin. Gallow's eyes darted left and right, and the soldiers came to a halt when he spoke.

"Before I depart," Gallow said, "I have a message from Skorn."

He leapt forward and plunged his sword into Carvia where she huddled behind a couch. She cried out as the weapon pierced her chest and she fell to the floor, grasping the mortal wound in a vain effort to stop the blood.

Gallow leapt to the ring of guards, smashing through them to reach the bedchamber beyond. With a speed charm active Beauty was just a step behind, but Gallow crossed the room and dove out the window. Beauty reached the opening and growled, coming to a halt. Fighting Gallow in a trapped room was one thing, but in the open? Reluctantly she returned to find Ero and Duke Gorwall kneeling at Carvia's side.

"Healers have been summoned," the duke said.

Beauty saw the extent of her wound and shook her head. "It won't matter."

Carvia gasped in pain, her eyes falling upon Ero and lighting with rage. "Will you kill him?"

Ero grasped her hand. "I swear it," he murmured.

202

"The Necrolith lies northwest of Azertorn," she said, her voice growing faint. "And he has another ally."

"Who?" Ero asked.

To Beauty's surprise Carvia looked to her. "Your father."

Chapter 25: The Guildmaster's Mantle

Jack rode into Herosian and wearily dismounted in front of the stables. It had taken them four days of dodging pursuers before an opportune rainstorm had washed out their tracks. But it had left them all sodden and sullen.

The stable boy appeared and reached for his reins, and then noticed Sirani. "What can I . . . *whoa.*"

Sirani grinned down at him. "Hello, child."

Jack ignored the interchange and made his way to the nearest inn. "Two days," he said. "No more. And don't disturb me unless an assassin shows up."

Inna made to ask a question but Jack turned away. Striding up the steps, he paid for a room and made his way to the bed, collapsing into welcome slumber. He spent the next two days in his room, rising only to use the pocket Gate to escape and return several times. When he finally emerged he descended to the tavern, where Ursana was eating with Inna.

"Good morning," Inna said. "I was beginning to think you'd escaped again."

Jack rubbed his shoulder and sat down. "It's been a long few weeks. We needed to rest."

"You like to sleep as much as Gordon," Ursana said with a laugh. Then her smile faded and she looked away.

"What happened to your arm?" Inna asked.

"Tweaked it fighting the guards in Wedge," he said. "What did you learn?"

"Ero arrived in the city last night," Ursana said. "He came to speak to Carvia."

"And?" Jack asked with a yawn.

"Gallow attacked him with a score of Talinorian mercenaries."

Jack straightened. "And Ero?"

"Alive," a voice said.

Jack turned to find Beauty sliding into a seat at the table. He smiled at her and received one in turn. Then he noticed the litany of bandages on her body and his smile faded.

"Gallow?"

She shrugged, but the motion elicited a wince. "Who else? We managed to stop him, but the incident has gone public."

"We?" Inna asked, catching the shift.

"Ero fought well," Beauty said. "Gallow expected an easy kill but Ero had a hidden staff."

"I didn't realize he was a fighter," Jack said.

"He held his own against Gallow," Beauty said. "And few can claim that."

"I wonder what else Ero can do," Ursana mused.

"Gallow will strike from the shadows next time," Jack said. "Where is he?"

"Gone," Beauty said. "My face and those of our caravan are known, so we are departing Herosian today. The crowds will follow us while he travels to Azertorn on a separate route."

205

"You left him alone?" Jack asked, an edge creeping into his voice.

Beauty laughed. "It wasn't my choice. He's as stubborn as you are. Besides, I think he felt bad that I was injured. Trust me, he can take care of himself."

"I still don't like it," Jack said, folding his arms. "He doesn't know the region, and could easily get noticed and killed." He lowered his tone. "I'm not the only one Skorn is hunting now."

"Relax," Beauty said. "I sent Thalidon and Roarthin to follow him. Ero may be cagey, but there's no way he can escape them. Besides, Skorn will not expect us to let him go alone, so he's as safe as he can be."

Jack stared at her and then chuckled in admiration. "When will I learn not to doubt you?"

She sniffed. "I'd think you'd have learned that lesson by now."

He grinned and asked, "Where's Sirani?"

"Out," Inna said. "She said she needed new attire for our adventure."

"Who's Sirani?" Beauty asked.

As Ursana filled Beauty in on their past few weeks, Jack signaled the barmaid for a meal. When it came he dug in with enthusiasm, and finished by the time Beauty had completed her own tale, and revealed the news about her father. As he relished the last morsel, he sank back into his seat.

"What will Oragon do?" he asked.

Beauty's features tightened. "Abandoning a barbarian tribe is a death sentence. He is blood-bound to carry out the execution."

"But he's your father," Inna protested.

"I was raised to kill the enemies of my tribe," Beauty said. "When I left, I became one. If Skorn has told him that I'm alive, he will hunt me down and tear me apart."

206

"Can you defeat him?" Ursana asked.

Beauty's expression became doubtful. "We share the same magic, but he has two decades of experience and skill on his side."

"We met Golic when we escaped Wedge," Ursana said.

Beauty turned to him, her eyes filled with surprise. "I didn't realize he was in Wedge."

"He was," Ursana said, her expression lighting with a smile. "But he's very attractive."

Beauty laughed. "Don't get too smitten," she said. "My brother has one he's favored for a long time."

Ursana sighed. "A girl can dream. But there was another that caught my eye." She flushed and looked away.

Beauty's eyes flicked to Jack, and he saw the question reflected in them. He gave a tiny shake of his head, his gaze drifting to Inna and Ursana. She caught the hint and nodded, recognizing that Jack knew more, but didn't want to share in front of the others.

Jack watched Beauty as she talked to Ursana. Beauty feigned a casual air but Jack recognized worry in the lines about her mouth. After what Jack had learned, Beauty's fears were valid. Still, Jack hated having to share what Golic had requested.

Inwardly he forced his thoughts away from Beauty. Everything he'd prepared was finally coming to fruition and he could not afford to get distracted—even if he wanted to. Jack considered his options, weighing what he knew against what he could guess. Then he gestured to Ursana.

"You should join her in protecting Ero."

Ursana frowned. "You're going to an island no one returns from, and want to leave me out?"

"When you put it that way," he said, "yes."

She laughed at his honesty and Beauty leaned in. "She can stay with you. I'll have Thalidon and Roarthin with me."

Jack didn't want to say the truth, that he was concerned about Ursana without Gordon. The girl had spent her entire time as a thief in a partnership, and taking her to an island known to be lethal would not be wise if she was not in top form.

"I'll have Inna and Sirani," Jack said easily. "Besides. We can't lose Ero."

"We can't lose *you*," Beauty pointed out.

Jack burst into a wry laugh that drew the gaze of other patrons in the tavern. "I'll be fine," he said. "Inna has proven she can handle herself on a boat."

Inna snorted and looked up. "I got knocked unconscious and Jack saved my life. I don't call that handling anything. I still want to know what happened . . ." She looked to Jack and folded her arms.

"Before that you were fine," Jack said dismissively.

"Don't patronize me," Inna said.

"I wouldn't dream of it," Jack replied with a smile.

Inna grunted and returned her attention to repairing the cut in her jerkin. Just then Sirani ducked through the door and entered. Her sudden appearance caused two women to shriek and scramble away in fear. Apparently not noticing their terror, Sirani squeezed through the chairs and sat on the floor, sending a shudder through the wood.

"The ghosts are coming and they want their dinner," she sang.

"Am I the dinner?" Jack asked.

"The most savory kind," Sirani crowed.

Beauty threw Jack a look as they all rose to their feet. "Did I miss something?"

Sirani giggled. "He's a good kisser."

Beauty laughed. "She *kissed* you?"

"And it was *good*," Sirani crowed.

"You don't need to laugh so hard," Jack said, but Beauty's humor spread to Ursana.

They made their way to the street and Jack pointed east. "Split up. Ursana can take the eastern gate and Beauty will meet you outside. Sirani, Inna, I'll meet you outside the northern gate. Make certain no one follows you."

Wiping tears of laughter from her eyes, Ursana nodded and left. Inna and Sirani slipped away as well. But Jack caught Beauty's arm.

"Will you walk with me for a moment?"

Her levity faded and she nodded, and Jack led them through an alley to an adjoining side street. Neither of them spoke as they walked through a market. Merchants called out their wares, attempting to lure buyers from the crowd. Jack paid them no mind as he passed through the street.

"Which horse do you have with you?" Jack asked.

"Axe," she replied.

"He's a good one," Jack said.

"You say that because he likes you."

He smiled. "True."

"Are you going to tell me what's wrong?"

"I wish you were going with me," Jack finally said.

"It was your order to give," Beauty said with a small laugh.

He blew out his breath in disgust. "Yet another aspect to my wonderful occupation."

She arched an eyebrow at his sarcasm. "You don't like being guildmaster?"

"No."

His blunt answer caused her to smile. "It appears you are quite good at it."

"I thought I would enjoy it," Jack said, wiping a hand across his face in sudden weariness. "But I feel as trapped as if I was in a cell."

"It can't be that bad," she protested.

Jack withdrew a coin and tossed it to a baker standing behind a cart. Then he picked up a loaf and held it up to her, wafting the scent of warm bread between them.

"Becoming a thief was like tasting warm bread," he said, "delicious and savory. But being guildmaster has so much . . . weight."

He clenched his fingers, crushing the bread in his hands. Crumbs cascaded into the street as he continued to tighten his fist, the bread breaking apart until it became unrecognizable chunks of waste. He tossed the remainder into the gutter.

"You've kept us alive," she said. "Perhaps the only one that could."

"Is that what is required of me?" Jack asked. "Give up myself for the guild?"

"It's a heroic act."

He laughed but the sound was laced with rancor. "That's not who I am."

"Apparently it is now."

Jack met her gaze. "Do you know how much I have to lie—even to you? No one knows the truth of our war against Skorn."

"You can tell me."

"I can't," he said. "Because anyone that knows the truth will not do their part."

"What are you planning, Jack?"

He came to a halt and turned to her, all his plans resting on the tip of his tongue. But he couldn't bring himself to voice them.

"Does this have to do with Ero?" she asked. "Do you not trust him?"

He grinned. "I trust him because we want the same thing."

"An ally of circumstance never lasts," she said.

"It will last long enough," Jack replied.

"He wants to betray you," she said. "He wants Skorn to take him so he can destroy the cult of Skorn from the inside."

Jack shrugged. "If he chooses to die to kill his brother, it's his choice."

"You don't care?" she asked.

"They're from a dead race," Jack said. "Perhaps they need to join their kind."

"You *want* Ero to be taken?"

"Why not?" Jack asked. "We plan to decimate the Church of Light so it cannot harm anyone else. If Ero leads us to Skorn, we can destroy the cult at its source."

"They might kill him," Beauty said.

"It's his life to lose," Jack said.

"I thought you'd want to save him," she said, a trace of disappointment in her voice.

Jack should have been offended, but the comment made him smile. "You just said he was going to betray us."

"I've never known you to let someone die."

His smile faded. "I told you being guildmaster is heavy."

"You don't have to carry it alone," she said quietly, stepping close to him. "I still don't understand why you won't tell me the truth. What are you planning?"

Jack resumed walking and she fell into step beside him. Apparently content to let him ponder his answer, she remained silent. Jack looked about the city without seeing it, yearning to tell her and yet knowing he couldn't.

"Do you trust me?" he finally asked.

She stared at him, her expression hurt. "Yes," she finally said. "But sometimes I wish I didn't."

"Thera," he said. He reached out to her but she pulled away.

"Goodbye, Jack. I'll let you know when they come for Ero."

"Golic has been exiled."

His words brought Beauty to a halt. She turned back to face him. "I know. My father planned to sneak into a rival village at night, and kill the families as they slept. Golic defied him and refused to carry out the murders. My father beat him and cast him out."

"Golic needs you," Jack said, and managed to keep the regret from his voice. "You are the figurehead they wait for."

"My father is coming after me, now," she said. "If I survive, I can aid my people."

"And if you die?"

She passed a hand over her face. "Then my father will destroy my brother, and my people's war will consume them."

Beauty turned and trudged away, leaving Jack in the street. Jack watched her go with regret in his heart. For the thousandth time he considered the prospect of revealing the truth, but in his gut he couldn't do it. Once a secret was shared it lost its power, and Skorn had proven adept at using secrets to manipulate. He'd learned Lorelia's secret and used it to destroy her.

Jack turned away, wrestling with the guilt and anger of what he was doing. It needed to be done, but he wished there was someone else—anyone else. Trudging through the city, he reached the northern gate and exited to find Sirani and Inna already present with Inna astride a horse. At eight feet tall, Sirani had no need for a steed. Jack rented a mount from the stables at the gate and mounted, flicking the reins to join them.

"Are you well?" Inna asked.

Jack sidestepped the question. "We should hasten our journey," he said. "Time is running out and we have a Mind Vault to find."

Chapter 26: The Sea Dancer

Jack pondered Beauty but his gloom lasted exactly one mile. Then Sirani began to play with wind, tossing miniature tornados into the Sea of Grass, giggling as they spun the grass in artistic patterns. Normally Jack would have smiled, but his irritation caused him to scowl.

"What happened to you?" Jack asked the rock troll. "What drove you to madness?"

Sirani cast a new cyclone and sent it spinning among the others. "A deep question for a shallow friendship."

"Does that mean you won't answer it?" Jack asked.

Sirani laughed. "Few have dared to ask." Then her smile faded and her expression darkened. "Losing a child breaks more than a heart . . . when you are the killer."

"You killed your own child?" Accusation seeped into his voice.

The playful cyclones disintegrated and Sirani whirled to Jack, her greatsword suddenly at his throat. He reined in his steed and sat motionless, staring into the eyes of a crazed rock troll. She breathed hard, her hand and sword trembling.

"I killed her to save her," she spat.

"From what?" Jack asked quietly.

"Will you stop antagonizing her?" Inna hissed, but Sirani ignored her.

214

"From what she was becoming," Sirani said. "She was a killer—one who slew her father, brother, and almost her infant sister."

"How many have you told?" Jack asked.

The greatsword quivered at his throat. "None."

"Then why tell me?" Jack asked.

She blinked and shifted her feet. "I don't know."

Jack felt the steel on his neck and knew his life hung by a thread. If he said the wrong thing she would kill him, and her fractured mind would probably never think of him again.

"I *do* know," Jack said.

"Then tell me," she said.

"Because women always trust me."

Inna and Sirani snorted in unison, and Sirani said, "That's the most arrogant statement I've ever heard."

"You think I like the ability?" Jack asked, anger seeping into his voice. "It's as much a curse as it is a blessing."

The greatsword abruptly lowered and she sheathed it on her back. "Tell another soul, and I'll kill you."

She whirled and strode away. Disinclined to invite another confrontation with the volatile rock troll, Jack gave her several moments to pull ahead before nudging his horse forward. Inna joined him and shook her head.

"I thought I was going see a decapitation," Inna said quietly.

"She's not mad," Jack said. "She's tortured. It's fractured her mind."

"And you choose to antagonize her?"

"She wants peace," Jack said. "I don't think he would have killed me."

215

"Women may talk to you—but that doesn't mean one won't slit your throat."

"Is that a warning?"

She grinned. "Perhaps."

"Does that mean you have secrets to tell?"

She snorted a laugh. "I'm afraid I already shared mine. You know what Gallow did to my father, and know why I'm here."

"Is that your only secret?" he asked, his lips twitching.

"The only one you'll get from me."

He laughed, the conversation with Sirani and Inna dispelling his irritation. "You think she's calmed down?"

Sirani suddenly cast another tornado, this time at her feet. It bent and arched, shaping into a giant horse and lifting her off the ground. She glided across the ground and picked up speed, and her high laughter echoed back to them.

"I think that means yes," Inna said with a smile.

Jack dug his heels into his horse and the mount surged forward. As they followed the laughing Sirani he couldn't help but smile. Sirani may have lost her wits, but her very madness was what made her fun.

For the next several days they crossed the northern stretch of Talinor until they came to a village north of Keese. It took several attempts before Jack managed to procure a ship willing to sail into the southern sea without a destination—and willing to take a rock troll. The *Sea Dancer* rocked when Sirani stepped aboard but the sailors did not seem bothered by her presence.

"Captain Erix," Jack said. "Thank you for being willing to take us."

The man approached with his first mate. "Race has no meaning for my crew," Erix said, a smile playing across his features as he looked up at Sirani.

216

"As long as they keep their blades to themselves," the second man said.

"This is Rezko," the captain said. "My first mate. You said you would tell us our destination once we're on open water?"

"I'm surprised you agreed," Inna said.

Rezko grinned. "We enjoy a good adventure."

Jack heard it coming and raised his hand to stop his statement. "I wouldn't use that word—"

"*Adventure!*" Sirani roared, skipping across the deck and ascending to the prow of the ship, her movement causing the boat to rock.

Erix raised an eyebrow but Inna shook her head. "Don't ask."

The captain shrugged and pointed to the helm. "Rez, get us underway."

"Aye, captain," he said, and began barking orders to the crew.

Within a minute they were gliding out to sea, the sleek ship exploding through the waves, wind filling the sails. Jack had been on many ships, but Erix's vessel outstripped them all. Thirty minutes after leaving Talinor Erix appeared at his side and smiled.

"You strike me as a man with many tales to share."

Jack thought of battling Skorn, meeting Ero, and stealing from the Vault of the Eternals. He laughed lightly.

"A few," he said.

"I'm sure my crew would love to hear them," he said. "I suspect our other passenger will be equally as intriguing."

"I didn't realize you had another passenger," Jack said.

"Only one," he replied. "She wants to visit a fishing village off the coast. We can drop her off on the way to your destination. She's odd, but I never turn away a dark elf . . ."

Jack didn't hear the rest of the statement as he turned to face the forecastle, where a dark elf stood in the doorway. Her shadow cloak billowed about her in the wind, and a quartet of daggers appeared in hands of darkness.

Erix followed his gaze. "Her name is—"

"Aranis," Jack finished for him. "We've met."

Chapter 27: Humbled

"Jack," she drawled. "You've been difficult to track of late."

He smirked. "You expect me to make it easy for you?"

"You could submit," she said, her lips twitching. "But I'd prefer if you didn't."

"Then you're in luck," Jack said, reaching to his back and pulling the dagger free.

Aranis darted forward, unleashing all four ring daggers at once. Jack grabbed the captain and heaved him out of harm's way, twisting to avoid the first three blades. The fourth came at an angle, so Jack reached out and picked it from the air. Continuing his spin, he sent it hurtling back at Aranis.

The knife dug into the mast as the dark elf leapt upward. She kicked off the mast and flipped over a rope, coming down near the prow. Jack drew his crossbow and leapt onto the rail, sprinting along it as the ship dropped into a trough between waves. Aranis shifted direction and came after him, threads of her cloak reaching out for him, forming tiny hands that sought to catch his form.

"*Stay your hand, woman!*" Erix roared, and pulled a thin sword from his side.

She barely spared him a glance, and whipped a ring dagger in his direction. Jack leapt off the rail and fired his crossbow, the bolt passing through the ring part of the dagger and digging into the wood beyond.

"You think to save their lives?" Aranis asked, her smile visible beneath the shadow cowl.

"They aren't part of this," Jack said. He sliced his dagger through a pair of the shadow hands, causing them to disintegrate and withdraw.

"You have nowhere to flee this time," Aranis said. "And they will be dead in minutes."

Sailors drew swords and converged upon her but she spun, her cloak whipped wide and formed arms and fists, smashing into the sailors and sending them sprawling. Drawn to the commotion, Inna appeared in the doorway to the forecastle. She yanked her sword free and darted into the fray, striking at Aranis's flank.

"You cannot stop me, pet," Aranis said. "I told you before, you are mine."

"What do you intend for him?" Inna asked.

The dark elf's smile tilted with desire. "The same thing you do with every pet. You play."

A ring dagger came for Jack on the end of a shadow thread. He leaned to the side but reached up and caught it, wrapping his hand around the thread of darkness and yanking her off balance.

"That wasn't nice," Aranis said, her voice gaining an edge.

She dismissed the threads and came at him herself. Shadows streamed off her back and formed four hands, each with ring daggers that struck at Inna, driving her back. Aranis stalked toward Jack, a ring dagger in each hand.

Jack fired a pair of crossbow bolts but she kicked off the rail and flipped over them, coming down adjacent to him. He deflected her strikes with his dagger but she forced him back with shocking skill. Jack retreated until his back hit the forecastle, and ducked a swipe that came for his throat, nicking his flesh.

"Do you want a dead pet?" Jack asked.

"Come now," she said, pressing her advantage. "The danger is what makes it exciting."

"I agree," Jack said with a grin.

He caught her wrist and pulled, twisting to smash her into the forecastle. The cloak wrapped around him, engulfing them in darkness. He attempted to leap free but her arm snaked around his neck, drawing him in for a bruising kiss. Then she tossed him out of the cloak and the shadows pulled her up onto the forecastle. She laughed as the cloak flowed out behind her.

"A memorable first kiss," she said. Her eyes gleamed beneath the cowl.

"I prefer to lead in such matters," Jack said.

"I'm sure you do," Inna said with a snort, stepping to his side.

"Who's she?" Aranis asked, her features turning hard.

"A friend," Jack said.

"I don't believe you," she said, and her jaw tightened with frightening hatred. "She must die so we can be together."

"HOLD!" the captain roared. "This is *my* ship!"

"Only until I kill you and your crew," Aranis said. "Perhaps Jack can be my first mate."

She smirked and withdrew a handful of ring daggers into each hand. With a deft twist she tossed them into the air where hands from her cloak caught them and set them spinning, the whirling steel sparking a whine as they cleaved through the air.

Sirani suddenly exited the forecastle door, humming to herself as she playing with a ball of wind. Her sudden appearance caused Aranis to hesitate, her eyes narrowing as she watched Sirani stride into view.

"Jack," Sirani asked, her lips pulling into a pout, "I'm getting bored. Think the ship can handle doubling its speed?"

Jack watched Aranis warily retreat and realized the truth. "You didn't know we had a rock troll in our party," he said.

"Her presence changes nothing," Aranis said, but her posture betrayed her tension.

Sirani looked up and noticed Aranis. An eager smile spread across her features and she strode toward her.

"A dark elf!" she cried gleefully. "I've always wanted to meet one."

Aranis whipped a dagger at Sirani's unprotected chest, the blade streaking through the air with brutal force. It struck Sirani's thick flesh—but stopped cold. Unable to find enough purchase, it tilted down and tumbled to the deck. A single drop of blood escaped the wound and the excitement drained from Sirani's face, turning into rage.

"That was not a kind introduction."

She swept her hands wide and took a step forward, bringing them together into a deafening clap. Wind exploded from the contact and smashed into Aranis, driving her to the railing and ripping chunks of wood apart. The hurricane of air sent sailors crying out and scrambling for distance, while Aranis dug her daggers into the wood and struggled to hold on.

She screamed in helpless fury as she clung to her daggers, her entire body flapping in the wind like a banner in a storm. More of the railing was torn away and bits of wood tumbled into the ocean. Grasping the railing in the hurricane, Jack watched Aranis's shadow cloak stream out behind her. It ripped her cowl off, revealing striking features with eyes like glints of obsidian. She shrieked in fury as her fingers finally gave, and her body was launched into the sea.

Sirani extinguished her magic and the wind faded to reveal the devastation. A gaping hole had been torn in the railing and sections of the deck were gone. Ropes dangled freely, the ends frayed from where they'd snapped in two. The corner of the sail flapped free in the breeze.

"Sorry about your ship, captain," Sirani said, her voice suddenly small.

Erix surprised Jack by laughing. "A price well paid for our lives."

222

Jack stepped to the rail and watched Aranis gradually fall behind. She splashed in the water and her cloak kept her afloat, but they were far enough out to sea to suggest she wouldn't survive. He sighed and turned to the captain, raising an eyebrow.

"I know," the captain said with a sigh.

He barked orders for them to come about, and shortly after they pulled alongside the struggling dark elf. Jack looked down at her furious expression and smiled. Aranis didn't smile back.

"If we let you aboard, will you behave?"

"You're *my* pet," she snarled.

"Don't be a fool," Inna said. "It's ten miles to shore. You won't make it."

"I'd rather die."

"As you order," Jack said, signaling the captain. "Let her swim home."

The sail was unfurled again and the ship gradually picked up speed. As they began to pull away Jack held the dark elf's gaze. "Am I really worth your life?"

"Yes," she spat the word at him.

Inna blew out her breath in disgust and muttered to Jack. "Don't look so smug, Jack."

He laughed and called out to Aranis. "A life without a pet is still a life worth living."

Aranis scowled at the statement and finally relented. "I won't pursue you."

"And us?" Inna asked.

Aranis ground her teeth together. "I won't kill them."

"How can I be certain?" Captain Erix asked, stepping to the rail to look down at her.

"You have my oath as an assassin," Aranis said.

Erix held her gaze for a moment before nodding to Rezko, who tossed a rope to her. She caught the end and the momentum from the ship dragged her until the sailors hauled her from the water. She rolled over the rail and collapsed onto the deck. The shadow cloak had absorbed the water and hung limp, making the dark elf resemble a drowned cat.

The sailor hastily retreated but she made no move to strike. She sat up and leaned against the rail, wringing out her shadow cloak like it was made of cloth. The sodden material dripped onto the deck. Rezko appeared with a pair of shackles and tossed them to her, causing her to scowl.

"I gave you my oath."

"I trust steel over your oath," Rezko said.

She grumbled and placed the shackles on her wrists, her eyes on Sirani looming behind Jack and Inna. When she was done she rose to her feet, but Captain Erix raised a hand and motioned to her cloak.

"That as well."

She reached up and undid an unseen clasp. Then she passed the cloak to Jack. "Don't lose it," she said. "It's unique."

"As are you," Jack said.

"Don't tease me."

He stepped forward and began to remove ring daggers from her body. Metal fell to the deck, piling high as Jack found more blades. She smiled at the intimate search and made no move to stop him. Several sailors began to chuckle at the sheer volume of weaponry. When Jack was certain she had been disarmed, he stepped back.

Bereft of weapon or cloak, Aranis seemed small. She wore a tunic that left her arms bare, and pants that matched the darkness of her cloak. Empty sheaths littered her body where the abundance of ring daggers had been. She smirked at the scrutiny.

"I feel almost naked, pet. Care to finish the job?"

"Tempting," Jack said with a smile.

"Take her below," Captain Erix said. "And shackle her feet."

Sailors led the dark elf below and the captain turned to Jack. "I want an explanation. Why did she attack you?"

Jack briefly considered lying but suspected that could backfire. Captain Erix was intelligent and forceful, and if he suspected Jack had withheld the truth, he could refuse to take them to the City of Dawn. But telling him the truth might cause the captain or his crew to attempt to collect the bounty on their own.

"I'm Jack Myst," he said, on impulse speaking the truth. "Guildmaster of the Thieves Guild."

The captain sucked in his breath. "The one with the bounty."

"The same," Jack said.

Rezko whistled in appreciation. "Your head is worth ten ships."

"And many have died in the attempt to take it," Inna said.

Sirani began to laugh, the eager sound causing the surrounding soldiers to retreat from her. "They may want his head—but they'll get my hand." She clenched it into a fist and wind swirled around her fingers.

Captain Erix glanced her way and then his eyes returned to Jack. Then he shrugged. "I admit I am tempted, but I prefer honest coin. Rez?"

The first mate folded his arms. "I have no desire to sail a ship bought by blood."

The other men on the boat nodded their agreement, but Jack swept his gaze among them. None betrayed a hint of deception, leading Jack to raise his opinion of the captain. He'd chosen his crew well, and they reflected his innate sense of honor.

"You have my gratitude," Jack said.

225

The captain grunted. "I'm beginning to suspect I will not like our destination."

"It's a city from which the ancient race departed," Jack said. "Then it was called the City of Dawn. I don't know what it's called now."

"I do," Erix said, his expression darkening. "We call it the Shattered Isle."

Chapter 28: The Shattered Isle

"You can't seriously be considering this," Rezko said. "Thousands of ships have journeyed to the shattered isle and none return."

"You know where it is?" Jack asked.

"All sailors do," Erix said. "We are taught early to avoid its shores."

"What makes it so dangerous?" Inna asked.

"No one knows," Erix replied. "But I suspect it was something left by the ancients."

"Why do you want to go there?" Rezko asked.

"We seek an item called the Mind Vault," Jack said. "And we've learned it lies there."

"Who told you that?" a sailor asked, snorting in disbelief.

"I did," Sirani said, looming over him. "Do you doubt my knowledge?"

"Of course not," he said hastily.

Sirani smiled and patted the man on the back, knocking him to the deck. "The artifact lies on the island," she said.

"Will you take us?" Jack asked the captain.

Erix regarded him for several moments while the crew seemed to hold their breath. Then he shrugged and gestured to them.

"I won't risk their lives on a whim. But if they decide to go, I'll lead them."

Rezko grinned and swept a hand at Sirani, Inna, and Jack. "The first ones to return from the Shattered Isle will be audacious, skilled, and powerful. Perhaps our passengers have such attributes."

Rezko's smile spread to the others, and one by one the other sailors gave their assent.

"Aye."

"It will be a tale for the ages."

"If we survive."

The last statement came from a wiry young sailor, but he bore a smile on his face. Then he inclined his head to the captain.

"I trust the captain. I'm with him."

Captain Erix didn't seem pleased with his crew's faith, but he nodded. "So be it. Rezko, turn us northwest. The rest of you, get this ship repaired and underway. If we must flee, I want us in top condition."

The sailors obeyed his orders with a sense of excitement and a trace of fear. As the ship accelerated northwest Sirani added her magic, powering the ship through the waves with frightening force, the momentum adding to the tension among the sailors. Captain Erix kept rigid control of his crew, keeping their fear in check with a casual smile.

In the following days Jack kept to his room. To ensure privacy he used one of his new tools on the door, casting a mild curse that would prevent entry. The next day Inna commented on the shock she received when she attempted to open the door, and he laughed it off. Her expression remained suspicious, but Jack changed the subject. Five days after the battle with Aranis they reached the Shattered Isle.

The moment it was spotted Jack sprinted to the prow of the ship. The sun hung low on the horizon, illuminating a volcano rising from the sea. As they approached, the sleek boat curved into a wide circle around the island, keeping its distance. Jack ascended to the crow's nest and found Inna already present.

"What do you see?" he asked.

"Are you certain about this course?" she asked.

He picked up the spyglass and put it to his eye. "Afraid of getting killed?"

"Afraid of killing them," Inna said.

He turned to her and raised an eyebrow. "An assassin worried about lives?"

"My father taught me that every life is precious," she said, a smile crossing her face as she spoke of Jaron. "That we take life to better the world, not harm it. These are good men that do not deserve to die."

"I know they are," Jack said. "Which is why I think we need an ally."

It took her a moment to realize what he meant. Then her eyes widened. "You mean *Aranis*?"

"Why not?" Jack asked. "She's a formidable assassin."

"She tried to take you into her own private dungeon and have her way with you."

"Everyone has their flaws."

She laughed wryly. "You really think we can trust her?"

"No," Jack said. "But I think she'll listen to you."

"Why me?"

"You share the same occupation," Jack said.

"But not the same methods," Inna said. "She kills without cause. She's just like Gallow."

Jack gestured to the boat. "She's a ship without a compass."

She grunted in disagreement but did not argue. As she fell silent Jack returned the spyglass to his eye, examining the city in the light of the setting sun. Crystalline spires reflected the light, casting rays of red and yellow upon the city.

Set against the base of the volcano, the city was not large, yet the glow from the white material made it appear larger. Smaller buildings were equally as bright, while the streets were a deep shade of blue. Everything was devoid of life, the emptiness disturbing in such a pristine setting. Then he lowered the glass to the coastline.

Docks extended into the water, the material as white as the city. One of the jetties contained a shimmering boat, the hull pure silver and narrow. The ship lacked a sail or mast, and the deck was as empty as the streets. Then Jack spotted a dark smudge in the water and lowered the spyglass. Other ships lined the waterfront, but they were not above the water.

They were below it.

Masts and hulls extended from the water, protruding like bodies on a battlefield. One ship was twice the size of the *Sea Dancer*, yet the mast was snapped in two, its hull shattered into several pieces. Jack then spotted the rest of the vessel, the prow inside the city, the wood snapped, the beams crushed.

A slow smile spread on his face as he examined the carnage. Thousands had sought the island's secrets and their curiosity had cost their lives. He couldn't deny the trickle of fear, but the excitement burned it from his veins. Great warriors had failed to conquer the truth of the island, so perhaps it required a thief to steal it. Besides, he had two lethal assassins and a crazy rock troll as allies. What could go wrong? The sun dipped beneath the water so Jack removed the spyglass and looked to Inna.

"The captain is going to keep his distance throughout the night."

"A sound plan," Inna replied. "I don't think we want to face the island in the dark."

"Let's go talk to Aranis," Jack said.

"If you insist," she said reluctantly.

They descended the ropes to the deck and made their way into the small cargo hold. Although the Sea Dancer usually booked passengers, it would occasionally take cargo upon request. The sailor guard nodded to them when they appeared and Jack ducked under the beam to enter the room.

One wall curved with the hull, the beams stained to prevent rot. The other walls were equally as bare, with just the slats and the beams showing. Ropes were in abundance, as well as anchors to fasten them to, and both had been used to secure the dangerous dark elf. She rose at their appearance, the chains clinking at her ankles.

"Hello, pet," Aranis said. "You've been suspiciously absent. Come to see me in shackles?" She smirked and lifted her hands.

"We want your help," Jack said.

"I'm not the helping type."

Jack took a step toward her. "Our goal is the—"

"City of Dawn," Aranis said, and gestured to her pointed elven ears. "Sailors gossip as much as dark elf men. They are afraid of what comes."

"They are brave men," Inna said.

"Men are usually brave . . . before the battle."

"You have such a low opinion of the race of man," Jack said and then raised an eyebrow. "Who betrayed you?"

Aranis stared at him. "I will not help you."

"Is that why you became an assassin?" Inna asked.

She lunged to the extent of her chains. "You know nothing about me.

Inna didn't flinch before Aranis's sudden savagery. "My father taught me to be an assassin, before he was betrayed by someone he trusted."

Jack leaned against the wall. "Gallow killed her father."

Aranis raised an eyebrow at Inna. "I underestimated you, but I shouldn't have. You show promise. But why didn't you go after Gallow directly?"

"I tried," she said. "I donned a persona named Tronis and tried to get an invitation to the Assassin's Guild. He discovered my ruse and brought another assassin. That's where I got this." She lifted her sleeve to reveal an ugly scar running up her arm. "I realized I needed an ally and sought Jack."

Jack wanted to comment but held his tongue, unwilling to dispel the sudden curiosity in the dark elf's gaze. Aranis stared at Inna with a spark of interest in her black eyes. Jack folded his arms and waited, but the women did not notice him.

"My cloak is my ally," Aranis said. "And it never fails me."

"Why are you an assassin?" Inna repeated.

Aranis regarded her for several moments. Then she said, "My sister was killed by someone I trusted, and I responded in kind. I was very young but my people sentenced me to thirty years in the Pit, where another assassin took me in. He saw my potential and taught me the craft."

"He protected you," Inna said.

Jack recalled the Pit at the base of the dark elf city. He'd spent only six days in the dark elf prison, but it was enough. A youth spent there would have been horrific, and would have left scars well into adulthood.

"He taught me that the first kill for an assassin is their own heart," Aranis said. "So they don't feel the loss when they kill the second."

"A bleak life to live," Inna said.

"I didn't choose it."

232

"Then choose another," Inna said.

Aranis laughed bitterly. "I cannot be what I am not."

"You can if you help us," Inna said. "Use your talents to serve, rather than harm."

"I won't discard my life on the Shattered Isle," Aranis said. "Not for anyone."

The harshness to her gaze left no room for argument, and Jack sighed, realizing she would not be persuaded. Inna recognized the same thing and turned away. As Jack stepped to the door he looked over his shoulder.

"If we fail the ship will likely sink, with you in it."

Aranis regarded him with a cold gaze. Then abruptly she smiled. "Perhaps I will join you—for a price."

"What do you desire?" Jack asked.

"A favor," she said. "One I will ask in the future and it cannot be refused."

"I won't be your pet," Jack said.

"The favor I ask will not be from you," Aranis said, and turned to Inna. "It will be from her."

"Me?" Inna asked. "What do you want from me?"

"A favor in the future for a favor of now," Aranis said. "That's the offer."

Inna glanced at Jack but he shrugged. "It's your choice," he said.

"I won't betray someone I care about—and I don't kill the innocent."

Aranis dismissed her concerns with a wave of her hand. "I don't need you to kill innocents for me," she said. "And I care little for intrigue."

233

Inna hesitated, and then relented with a nod. "One favor," she said.

Aranis smiled and slipped her hands free of the shackles. "Then let's go."

Jack laughed at her easy escape and stepped to the door—but the ship heaved to the side, sending all three of them into the hull. He caught a beam and righted himself as the ship straightened—but the ship heaved again. This time he held his grip and kept from falling. Jack exchanged a look with the two assassins and they darted to the door. They reached the deck as the ship tilted again, and this time Jack realized the ship was turning.

"What's happening?" Jack asked, grasping the door as the ship banked toward the island.

Erix and Rezko stood at the helm, straining to keep it from turning. "There's something in the water," he growled. "And it's turning us toward the island." Erix's eyes flicked to Aranis. "Why is she out of her cell?"

"She agreed to join our assignment," Jack said.

Jack stumbled to the prow as the front of the ship was struck again, veering the boat toward the island. He scanned the water but the light from the moon was not enough to pierce the surface. Then the unseen struck again, turning the ship a final time to place the island directly in their path.

Jack's gaze lifted to the mountain visible in the moonlight, and a smile spread on his features. "It appears we've been invited."

Chapter 29: The City of Dawn

Erix and Rezko fought the helm until the unseen attacker snapped the rudder from the ship. They stumbled and went down and the wheel spun freely. The captain barked orders for the men to gather weapons and stand ready.

"Are you smiling?" Aranis asked.

Jack glanced her way. "Aren't you?"

Aranis sniffed. "I'm damaged, not crazy."

"I'm crazy, not damaged," Sirani said, appearing behind them. Her cackling laugher caused the rushing sailors to veer away from her.

"I'm not much good without my weapons," Aranis said.

Jack threw Inna a look and she nodded. "I'll get her gear."

"Make it quick," Jack said.

They nodded and darted away. Moments later Aranis returned in her shadow cloak and twirling a ring dagger in her hand. The contrast to the slim dark elf and the formidable assassin was stark, prompting Jack to gesture to her.

"Feel better?"

"A sharp blade is always comforting," she said, her smile visible beneath her cowl.

"I couldn't agree more," Jack said.

They fell silent as the *Sea Dancer* sailed toward the island. The captain ordered the sail furled as they neared the island and they coasted across the still waters. Sailors lined the docks, their sabers reflecting the moonlight as they stood silent. The captain and his first mate joined Jack at the prow.

"We're in Ero's hands now," Erix murmured.

Something bumped the boat again, directing them to a dock jutting out from the island. The *Sea Dancer* scraped against an overturned hull on its way in, and Erix hissed an order. Sailors jumped across and tied them to the dock. Then they leapt back to the uncertain safety of the ship. For several long moments they stood in tense silence until Jack began to laugh.

"Are you mad?" Rezko demanded.

Jack stepped to the railing of the ship and leapt to the dock below, advancing toward the city with bold strides. Behind him the sailors cursed him and tightened their hands on their swords. Sirani giggled and leapt after him, her eight-foot form crashing onto the dock and causing them all to flinch. Then Jack called up to them.

"It could have destroyed us already," Jack said.

"That doesn't mean it won't destroy us now," Inna hissed.

"Look at the ships," Jack said, pointing to the devastated fleet. "They're pointed *out* to sea."

All eyes turned to the broken hulls and masts protruding from the sea. Some lay on their sides, their hulls caved. But most of them had their prows pointed out to sea, their sterns to the island. Their placement suggested they had been dragged back to the island after their destruction.

"How does that matter?" Rezko growled.

"They were destroyed when they sought to flee," Aranis said, a ghost of a smile appearing beneath her cowl.

236

She leapt to the dock and followed Jack toward the city, and Inna followed suit. A moment later Erix ordered a group of his men to find a replacement rudder and repair their ship. Then he gathered a group of ten and dropped to the dock, hurrying to catch up.

"Why would it bring us to the city?" Erix asked.

"More importantly, *what* brought us?" Rezko asked.

In the distance, the sea exploded into a geyser and a massive form burst into view. The group whirled to face it, but the darkness permitted only a glimpse as it rose into the sky, a glimpse of great wings and a tapered body. Its haunting growl reverberated throughout the city, echoing like a predator that had cornered its prey. The distinctly metallic sound resembled a steel sword scraping across glass.

"Dragon?" Inna asked, shuddering as the growl faded.

"Dragons don't sound like that," Aranis said.

"Rez," Captain Erix said. "Find us a place to stay for the night. I don't think the *Sea Dancer* is safe. Make sure it's close to the ship."

"Aye," Rezko said, and peeled away with five of the men.

As they disappeared down a side street Jack examined the city. As he'd seen from a distance, the City of Dawn was a city of spires. Crystal and glass rose to tremendous heights, with some of the towers half the height of the great volcano.

Smaller structures dominated the coastline of the city but were equally as bright. Clouded glass and crystal formed the roofs, making each structure look like a prism. The walls were pristine, as if time itself was afraid to linger.

At first glance the city was flawless, but as they crept through the shadows cast by the spires, Jack noticed the signs of conflict. Doors hung askew, and windows were shattered. One house had a gaping hole rent in the ceiling and wall, as if a fire had chewed through the material.

They turned a corner but found the road blocked by the upper half of a spire. The lower half remained intact, but a titanic force had shorn the spire in half, sending the top crashing onto the homes below. Houses

237

and shops were crushed beneath its bulk, flattened into oblivion by its fall.

Jack walked up to the fallen spire and peered through a crack in the wall. Inside he spotted strange machines and drawings set against the walls. The force of the landing had damaged some, but surprisingly others remained intact. On the opposite side another crack provided a glimpse of the road beyond.

"We should wait until dawn to explore the city," Erix said uneasily.

Jack nodded, and the group cautiously retreated the way they had come. The disturbing silence of the city permeated every street, and their steps echoed against the walls like they were intruders in a graveyard. They reached the ship and found Rezko gathering the men.

"There's a house just up the road," he whispered. "It's got an upstairs window that provides a view of the ship."

Erix nodded. "Get everyone to it."

"Sir," one of the sailors said. "I'll volunteer to stay with the *Sea Dancer*."

"A brave suggestion," Erix said, "but you'll come with us. Take the first watch at the upstairs window."

The sailor nodded and disappeared. After several tense minutes Erix brought the rest of the crew to the house Rezko had found. Once they were inside the men shuddered in relief, evidently grateful to be off the streets.

The three-story house sat close to the docks, and was higher than those around it. The main floor lay empty, with even the furnishings absent. The walls were empty and perfectly smooth, with nary a painting on them.

"It's like no one ever lived here," Aranis said.

Inna ran a finger against the wall, but her hand came away clean. "No dust," she said. "How is that possible? This city hasn't been used for forty thousand years."

238

"You think someone has been cleaning it?" Erix asked.

Sirani laughed lightly and cast a simple charm. Wind swirled around the room, scrubbing the walls and carrying motes of dust out the open door.

"It was *made* to stay clean," Sirani said. She yawned and then said brightly, "I get the top floor!" Then she frowned as she cast about for the stairs. "How do I get up there?"

Rezko pointed to a disc on the floor in the corner. "Stand on that."

Sirani did as requested and stepped onto the circular space. She squealed in delight as it lifted her to the floor above. Jack grinned and followed her, pleased at the smooth transition to the floor above. A moment later Aranis and Inna joined him.

"The ancients had wondrous magic," Aranis said.

Jack shook his head. "Ero told me that the ancients were not capable of magic."

"Then how did they do all this?" Inna asked, sweeping a hand at the city.

"Perhaps he was lying," Sirani said.

She darted to the other corner and disappeared. Jack made to follow but Erix caught his arm.

"I'm ordering my men to sleep in shifts," he said. "We still have a few hours until dawn and I don't want to risk a fatigued crew tomorrow."

"Then I'll see you then," Jack said.

"You're not staying?" Erix asked.

"I'm in an ancient city that hasn't seen a survivor in eons," Jack said. "I'm too excited to sleep."

Erix snorted a laugh and turned away, muttering about a mad thief. Jack stepped to the second disc and ascended to the top floor. The small

239

space had two windows, one of which pointed to the sea. He stepped to it and gazed down on the *Sea Dancer* where it bobbed against the dock.

"What's your plan?" Inna asked from his side.

"You and Sirani get some sleep," he said. "I'm going to explore on my own."

"You think that's wise?" she asked.

He grinned. "I'll return when the sun rises."

A muffled snore drew their gaze and Jack turned to find Sirani sprawled out in the corner of the space. Without bed or blanket, she lay on the floor, sound asleep. Her snore rumbled like a lion, causing Jack to grin.

"At least she's happy," Inna said sourly.

Jack stepped to the window—but a shadow caused him to pull back. Everyone in the room fell silent, the absence of sound augmenting the growl that rent the air. The sailors flinched as the scraping echo reverberated into silence, and Jack stepped to the side of the window. From the shadows of the room he gazed up, scanning the sky for signs of movement. Aranis, Inna, and Captain Erix joined him, and in hushed silence they searched for the sentry.

A great shape soared above them, banking to the side and curving north. The beast was larger than the Sea Dancer, its wings reflecting the dim light. Powerful forearms extended from the narrow body, the claws snapping as it soared into a cloud. It passed into a column of moonlight, allowing a look of the creature. The arms were silver and metallic, as were the nearly translucent wings. A crimson sheen cascaded off the sentry before it faded from sight.

"It appears we know what brought us," Jack murmured.

"A dragon," the captain muttered. "I hate dragons."

"I've never seen a dragon like that," Aranis said.

"Then what is it?" Inna asked.

240

Aranis shrugged. "It looks like a machine. Perhaps dwarven made."

"It's not dwarven," Jack breathed, realizing what it was.

"You know what it is," Inna accused.

Jack turned away and smiled. "The ancients built creatures of pure energy as guardians," he said. "It's a construct."

"You've seen one before?" Erix asked, incredulous.

"I've fought one," Jack corrected, and thought of Myra, the construct that had guarded the Vault of the Eternals. "It was a woman made of pure lightning."

"That isn't a woman," Inna said.

"I know," Jack replied, a smile widening on his face. "It's a *dragon* construct."

Chapter 30: Ancient Secrets

"Are you *excited*?" Inna demanded.

"Of course," Jack said.

"It's killed thousands that came to the island," Erix said. "I do not think excitement is the correct emotion."

"How do we kill it?" Aranis asked.

"If it can be killed," Jack said. "I don't know how. Still, we don't need to kill it. We just need to steal from it."

"You really are mad," Erix said.

Jack laughed and stepped to the window, "I'll be back by sunrise."

"You're still going out there?" Erix asked. "Alone?"

Jack looked out the window again but saw no sign of the guardian. "The night is an ally," he said. "And I like to work alone."

He grinned and dropped from view. The rush of the wind was short lived and he landed on the roof below. Excitement and caution warred within him as he leapt to an adjoining roof and raced across the disturbing city. By the time he crossed the second street he heard a faint footstep. He turned to find Aranis at his side.

"You should be sleeping," he said.

"You think I'd let you go alone?" Aranis asked.

He came to a halt and turned to face her. "Are you not afraid?"

"Death has no mystery to me," she said. "I do not fear it."

"Even from an ancient construct?" he asked.

Her lips twitched into a smile. "Perhaps I am more curious than I care to admit."

"About me or the city?" Jack asked.

"Both," she replied.

He stepped close so he could see her eyes through the smoke of her cowl. "I usually like to look a girl in the eyes when I speak to them."

"Eyes give away too much," she said, but stood her ground. "And anonymity is better armor than steel."

"Your assassin trainer taught you that?"

Her lips hardened in a thin line and she turned away. "Not by intention."

Jack stared at her, confused by the enigma of the dark elf. Aranis seemed focused and driven, capable of nearly anything, yet lacking direction and purpose. Whatever she'd endured as a youth had caused her to shield herself from everyone around her.

Jack realized that as much as she resembled Gallow in talent and inclination to kill, there was a vulnerability to her eyes that set her apart. Jack had taken an instant dislike for Gallow, but not for Aranis. She had just as much blood on her hands as Gallow—more even because she'd lived longer. For the first time he wondered why she'd really come to the surface.

Abruptly a harsh growl erupted from nearby, sending them both into the shadows on a nearby roof. Their vantage point allowed them a disturbingly close view of the dragon construct as it landed on a building nearby.

The daggerlike head swiveled about, its eyes whirring and spinning. Its claws scraped across the roof as it dropped onto the street and

243

padded toward the water. In a burst of speed it leapt into the sea, snapping through a mast that was in its way. The beam was thick, but it sheared in two and splashed into the water.

Jack admired the sleek form as it disappeared, but the dragon exploded from the water an instant later. Flapping for altitude, it banked to the side and aimed for the spires. It weaved through them and disappeared, releasing a final haunting growl. After several moments Jack stepped out of the shadows and dropped into the street. In a whisper of movement Aranis alighted next to him.

"The resemblance to a dragon is striking," Jack murmured.

"But which came first, the dragon or the construct?"

Jack threw her a sharp look. "You think the ancients *made* dragons?"

She swept a hand at the city. "Our people have other records of the ancient race, and their disturbing attempts at creating life."

"Let's not get caught, shall we?" Jack said, uncertain of the implications of her words.

"I never get caught," she replied.

"Except by me."

Her lips tightened. "I permitted the capture."

Jack grinned and crossed the street. For the next few hours they worked their way through the city. Jack kept his senses tuned above but the dragon did not reappear. As they advanced through the city the clouds drifted away, allowing moonlight to bathe the city.

The buildings of the city proved to be frustratingly empty. Jack had hoped to find an abundance of relics from the ancients, but most of the structures didn't even have furniture. The sheer emptiness of the City of Dawn was both curious and haunting, but as Jack continued to find nothing he grew frustrated. Then they found the prison.

The building sat on the upper side of the city. Unlike those around it, the walls were fortified and high, suggesting it was meant to keep

244

something inside. Jack and Aranis exchanged a look, and by tacit agreement slipped through the open door.

The interior was a sprawling collection of structures. Jack entered the largest and found the interior to be lined with strange equipment, some of which glowed with faint magic. Jack peeked into a smaller room and saw a window on the opposite side which looked upon a cell.

"They observed prisoners?" Aranis asked.

Jack moved down the line and saw that each of the cells was different, with the coloring and writing suggesting distinct occupants. He frowned as he spotted the text on one of the doors. The lettering was in ancient script, and he brushed the rune. A flicker of light flowed from the lettering, turning into the image of a gnome with the words *Specimen 7* glowing above it.

"What were they doing here?" Aranis asked. She stepped to the next one and brushed the rune, her lips tightening when the image of a dark elf appeared.

"It appears you are Specimen 13," he said, stepping to her side.

"I'm glad the ancients are dead," she said, her tone dark.

They exited and Jack motioned to the other buildings. "Perhaps the Mind Vault lies in one of them."

"This was a prison for the living," she said. "I doubt they kept anything of value here."

"There is nothing here," Jack said, irritation coloring his tone. "I was hoping for more than empty buildings."

Abruptly she turned to face him. "Is Skorn an ancient?"

His lips twitched into a smile. "Why would you ask that?"

"I'm not a fool," she said. "You seek to stop an adversary by learning about the ancient race, and Ero's appearance in Azertorn cannot be coincidence."

Jack grinned. "Skorn wants to summon his people, and is building a beacon for that purpose."

"The Necrolith."

"You really have been listening."

She glanced back at the disturbing building. "I find I've gained a desire to kill him."

"You and me both," Jack said.

They slipped out of the prison and made their way into the streets of the city. Light touched the horizon, heralding the coming sunrise. Aranis paused in the shadow cast by a statue in a square.

"Dawn approaches."

"I think we should climb a spire," he said, pointing the towers at the center of the city.

"Why?"

"Sometimes the best view is the one from above."

"And the most dangerous when a dragon is about."

He grinned. "Think you can keep up?"

"Don't worry, pet," she said. "I'll slow down for you."

He laughed and sprinted away. Dodging buildings and leaping to roofs, he raced through the city to one of the spires. Although his pace was fast, he kept his senses focused on his surroundings, and listening for the city's guardian.

He reached the spires and paused to examine them. Six of the spires were placed in a circle with a seventh at the center, its height exceeding the others. Jack scanned the darkness for the dragon and then darted to the center spire, slowing to circle the exterior. To his surprise it lacked doors or windows, the surface as smooth as glass. Aranis fell into step beside him and gestured to one of the other spires.

"Care to choose another?"

"No," Jack said.

He aimed his shadowhook up the wall and sent the thread of darkness as high as it would go. He twisted his body and raced up the wall, sprinting to the end of the shadowhook. When he reached the apex he released and fired again, his momentum slowing until the thread of shadow caught in the gloom above.

Movement caught his eye and he glanced at Aranis. Hands from her cloak rose and caught the wall, fusing to the shadow and scaling the wall for her. She smirked at him.

"Don't get too tired," she said. "You might need your strength later."

He grinned and accelerated, and together they scaled the exterior of the towering spire. Higher and higher they climbed and Jack looked back at the receding ground. They were hundreds of feet above the city but the spire continued to reach for the heavens. They passed the tops of the lower spires and still they climbed, ascending beyond the taller ones until finally the summit came into view. Rising to a point, the spire resembled a spear that pierced the night sky. Jack scaled to the top and grasped the point, breathing hard. Aranis joined him, also out of breath from the ascent.

"And why did we come up here?" she panted.

"For the view," Jack said.

She muttered under breath. "What do you expect to find?"

"I'm not sure," Jack said. "But I wanted to see the breadth of the city."

The predawn glow had begun to light the horizon, and as it brightened Jack examined the Shattered Isle. From his vantage point he realized the city was actually rather small, its streets sufficient only for a few thousand to live. The seven spires made the city appear much larger.

As the light continued to brighten he scanned the city, searching for anything that resembled a vault. The city appeared to be separated into three distinct sections. The outmost ring contained smaller structures and homes. He'd passed through the inner ring on his way to the spires, and Jack recalled that they resembled shops.

The center of the city contained the seven spires, including the broken base of the southernmost spire. Jack had chosen to climb the one at the very heart of the city. He frowned, his gaze falling to the spire at his feet.

The entire city pointed to the center spire, suggesting that anything of value would be contained inside. But on the ascent he had not spotted any place of ingress. Perhaps the entrance lay beneath the ground? He shook his head, dismissing that idea. He'd seen nothing in the city that descended beneath the earth.

"Jack?" she asked in a rising tone.

"Do you see the dragon?" he asked, casting about for movement.

"See for yourself," she said, gesturing to the eastern spire.

He turned to find Aranis leaning out, her gaze on the spire nearby. The sun had yet to breach the horizon but the light was sufficient for him to see a bump on the side of the spire that had been absent before.

He frowned and peered into the gloom, surprised to see the bump was growing. Swelling and stretching against the side of the spire, the protrusion moved like liquid rather than stone. It stretched to the side, turning into wings, a tapered body, and an arrowlike head. The liquid condensed and the body hardened, the claws stretching away from the spire. In spite of himself, Jack's gut tightened with fear as he watched the dragon coalesce into shape.

Movement shifted in his peripheral vision and Jack's eyes flicked to a different spire. He sucked in his breath as he spotted the second dragon taking shape. At the top of the center spire Jack twisted, spotting the other dragons bound to the spires.

"The island doesn't contain a dragon," Aranis breathed.

Jack met her gaze and completed the thought. "It contains a nest."

Chapter 31: The Vault Guardian

"How many do you see?" Jack asked.

"Five," Aranis replied, her voice tense.

Jack looked down at the great dragons clinging to the spires, their bodies wrapped around them. Wings of silver curved about the spires, the material as flawless as the structures they clung to. Their bodies reflected a distinctly metallic sheen. Then Jack looked down—and spotted another dragon clinging to the spire they stood on.

"Make that six," Jack said, easing out of its view.

Aranis followed his gaze and then retreated with him to the peak of the spire. Surrounded by six dragon constructs, his gaze was drawn to the seventh spire, the broken one. Aranis noticed it as well.

"The spires are the source of magic for the beasts," she whispered.

"And someone destroyed one," Jack said.

"Why are they coming out now?" Aranis whispered.

Jack shook his head, his gaze still on the beast below them. The huge head was less than fifty feet from the apex, and Jack examined the tapered skull with its thousands of needlelike teeth. Its eyes were closed. The strange dragon seemed not to breathe, its body as still as the spire it used as a bed.

The proximity allowed Jack to see red veins just beneath its skin. The lines were faint, but pulsed with power. The air around it radiated with heat, indicating the construct was one of fire and steel rather than lightning.

"I've never seen a machine so complex," Aranis said.

"The dwarves would like it," Jack said.

Aranis snorted a laugh and whispered, "They would be killed trying to take it apart."

"I'm sure some have been," Jack said, gesturing to the ring of broken ships that lined the beachfront of the island, some of which were distinctly dwarven.

Light touched the horizon, and the spires seemed to suck in the glow, growing brighter by the second and filling the city with light. Aranis leaned back from the drop and turned to Jack.

"Time to go."

Jack leaned out for one last peek at the beast. "We'd better hurry."

"Why?"

He watched the eyes snap open and felt a chill as they focused on him. Multifaceted and containing various shades of red and orange, the eyes reflected his expression. He turned and stepped to the edge, diving off.

"Because it just woke up," Jack shouted.

He plummeted down the side of the spire with Aranis in his wake. The dragon construct released an unholy growl and surged to the top of the spire, wrapping its claws around the top and angling its head down at them.

The growl was answered by another construct, and then another. In seconds the entire nest had woken, and their collective growls sent a shudder throughout the city. Then they leapt into the air.

Jack cast his shadowhook at the spire and yanked against the rope, launching himself to the side as the first dragon dove for him. Aranis went in the opposite direction, using her cloak to shift directions. She threw her arms wide and the cloak fanned out, allowing her to glide between the spires.

Jack cast his shadowhook again, splitting the gap between two spires and wrapping around to the right. Then he released his magic and fell again. Wind shrieked in his ears as he accelerated and his cloak streamed out behind him. A rumble of warning came from behind and he cast his shadowhook at a nearby spire—but a dragon construct exploded into view.

Jack's body tumbled along the creature's back and bounced off the wing. He grunted in pain as he slammed into the hard surface of the spire and released his shadowhook, plummeting again toward the street below.

Dragons flapped their wings above him, their growls shredding the air as they sought the intruders. He caught the shadow on the wall and held on, sliding down the spire at shocking speed. At the last second he tightened his grip and slowed, landing hard in the street. He rolled to absorb the impact and sprinted away.

A dragon came down in front of him, its jaws opening to unleash a stream of fire. Jack dodged into a broken house but the dragon turned its breath upon him, the flames filling the house and bursting through the windows. Jack leapt through the opposite window and came up running in another street.

The dragon in his wake growled and pounced upon the roof, tearing it apart as it sought for Jack inside. Before it spotted him, he leapt to a building and sprinted alongside it, using the eave of the roof to block the dragon's view.

A second dragon came down in front of him, the impact nearly knocking him from his feet. He lunged through a window, sprinting back to the first street as he sought for an escape. Then he spotted Aranis. The dark elf raced along a rooftop before diving from view, a trio of dragons streaking toward her.

Jack veered toward Aranis, crossing the street and sprinting through a house. Dodging down an alley, he used an adjoining alley to reach her. He slid to a stop at the corner and spotted Aranis racing down the street—as a fourth dragon dived into her path, cutting her off.

251

Trapped, she slid to a stop and spun, launching a trio of daggers into the dragon's face. One bounced off, while another sank into the dragon's eye. The third managed to pierce the flesh and sink all the way to the hilt. The dragon released a bellowing roar and leaned down. Air hissed and built into a shrieking wail—and flames burst from the construct's maw, blasting a current of fire at the dark elf.

Jack cast his shadowhook on the dark elf and it fused to her cloak. Then he leaned back and heaved her across the gap, yanking her out of the way as the fire engulfed the street, scorching the white material with a feathering of dust. Jack caught Aranis in his arms.

"Hello, pet," Jack said with a smile.

She scowled at his words and twisted out of his grip. They raced down the alley, dodging into a building. Behind them, the fire faded to reveal an empty street, and the dragons leapt about like enraged cats, searching for them. Jack watched them from the darkness within a house, but the dragons did not spot them. Growling in fury, they moved on and Jack leaned against the wall, breathing hard.

"That was more fun than I thought," he said with a grin.

"They are faster than dragons," Aranis said.

"They're constructs," Jack said, sliding to the floor. "But they are worse than the female construct I fought in the Vault of the Eternals."

Aranis snorted "Why is it always women with you?"

Jack grinned. "Captain Erix will keep his men inside until the dragons calm down. Looks like we're stuck here."

She sank into a seat across from him. For several moments they stared at each other, and Jack wondered again about her past. On impulse he decided to voice his thoughts and gestured to her.

"How many have you killed?"

She stared at him and then shrugged. "Over a thousand."

"How many have you failed to kill?"

"You."

Jack chuckled dryly. "Is that frustrating?"

"Yes."

"But you didn't come to the surface for the bounty."

She remained silent, confirming his guess. Then she asked, "Do you choose what you steal?"

"I do now," he replied. "But not when I first became a thief."

She looked away. "Every one of my targets was chosen by another."

"You're a weapon," Jack said.

She peeled back her cowl and pointed to her cheek, to a small tattoo of a dagger embedded into a heart. "This was given to me when I left the Pit," she said. "If I failed to eliminate a target, my master would activate his, and kill me. Then I was sent to murder an infant child, but instead I killed my master."

"When?"

She stared at him and then shrugged. "Right before I came to the surface."

Pain and rage reflected in her dark eyes, and Jack realized why she looked different than Gallow. Aranis hadn't killed out of choice, and ultimately she'd killed her master rather than continue being his pawn. She'd escaped to the surface and latched onto Jack, most likely because he represented what she'd never known, freedom.

"Until now you have killed for another," Jack said. "But now you have a choice. Will you be like Gallow and kill for pleasure? Or Inna and kill for justice?"

Aranis didn't respond, and after a moment she returned her cowl over her face. Jack let conversation lapse and stood, moving to a window. In the distance he could see the hunting constructs. After several minutes Aranis joined him, all trace of her vulnerability gone.

253

"Did you see the smallest dragon?" she asked.

Jack shook his head. "They looked the same size to me."

"It stayed behind the others," Aranis said. "When the others attacked us it was to protect the smallest of their number."

Jack peeking out at the rampaging dragons. Although they all looked similar, he spotted one that was indeed smaller than its companions.

"Why would the pack protect one?" Jack asked.

Aranis tossed him a spyglass. Jack recognized it as the personal spyglass of Captain Erix, and threw her a questioning look. The dark elf shrugged.

"I'm an assassin," she said. "Doesn't mean I'm not a thief."

Jack stifled a laugh and used the spyglass to examine the dragons. They rushed about, occasionally pulling a roof off and tossing it aside. Then he spotted the smallest of the dragons up on the mountain. It paced back and forth and snarled, its features more dynamic than the others.

It roared, the sound deeper than the others, more grating. The threads of power beneath its skin pulsed and fire exploded on its back. The flames cascaded behind it before it leapt into the air, winging for the waterfront.

"Is it the queen?" Aranis asked.

"Perhaps," Jack said. "They keep looking its way."

"But why is it smaller?" Aranis asked.

Jack returned to his examination of the small dragon. He retreated into the gloom as one of the dragons soared above, dropping into the adjacent street to begin the search anew. Jack and Aranis waited for it to pass on before returning to the window.

The sun continued to rise, reflecting off the spires and flooding the city with light. Jack shielded his eyes from the glow and continued to watch the dragons. Shortly after, the queen hissed and the others obeyed

254

the order. They leapt to the spires and wrapped about them, their hides glowing with power as they returned to their former position. A trio of the constructs glided about the city, their pattern suggesting a patrol.

"You think one of them brought us here?" Aranis asked.

"Has to be."

"But why?" she asked. "Why not sink us when we were on the ship?"

Jack tried to puzzle out the mystery, his eyes drawn to the small dragon. The construct clung to the spire in the center, strategically the most guarded from the others. But why? The entire city seemed empty, devoid of any sign of life. But if the spires were the lairs of the dragons, where was the Mind Vault?

He dropped his gaze to the city, considering where they had searched and where it might be. Nothing was out of place, and the only thing the dragons protected was the smallest of their number . . .

His eyes snapped to the small dragon and he used the spyglass to examine it anew. The more he looked the more he noticed what set it apart. The others were more liquid, with more fire in their bodies. The one in the center seemed more solid, with sharp protrusions extending at uniform locations.

Was it possible?

He shifted to watch the others, noting their posture and propensity to look to the small dragon—in perfect unison, as if the small dragon was the mind of all of them. A smile spread on Jack's face as he realized the truth. The dragons didn't protect it because it was the queen. They protected it because they were part of it. The smallest dragon didn't guard the Mind Vault.

It *was* the Mind Vault.

Chapter 32: A Daring Plan

Jack and Aranis tried several times to escape their hiding place, but each time they were nearly spotted. Resigned to waiting, they stayed until darkness fell and all but one dragon returned to the spires. Then they slipped into the eerily silent streets of the city and made their way back to Erix and his crew. The moment they stepped through the door, Erix and Inna demanded answers. Jack briefly shared the tale and his suspicions, and when he finished the captain shook his head.

"If what you say is true," he said. "Why would they force us to come to the island? Why not just destroy us?"

"Perhaps guarding the island is not their only function," Sirani mused, her gaze on the dragon of air she was crafting.

"What does that mean?" Inna asked.

"The ancient race is a mystery because they did not want to be seen," she said, "The constructs do not just protect the island, they protect the region."

Inna nodded at that. "Perhaps they bring nearby visitors to their masters."

"But there are no masters to tell them we are friend or foe," Erix said.

"Which is why they are hunting us," Aranis said.

"So they serve the same functions they did thousands of years ago?" Jack considered the ramifications of that idea. "Perhaps the Mind Vault is the only thing left that controls them."

"If that's true," Inna said, "they will never let us escape."

"That explains why the other ships are pointed outward," Erix said. "They fought the dragons in the city until they realized it was empty, but when they fled the dragons tore them asunder."

"We know what *they* do," Rezko said, joining them. "What do *we* do?"

"We can't fight and we can't flee," Erix said. "We need a third option."

"We steal the one that controls them," Jack said. They all turned to face him, and he grinned at their astonishment. "I suspect the central construct is the Mind Vault we came to retrieve."

Sirani burst into a wild laugh. "A vault that protects itself. How ingenious."

"Now that we know what it is," Jack said. "We can steal it."

They stared at him until Inna said, "You want to *steal* a dragon construct?"

"It's what we came for," Jack said. "And I know how to trap it."

"This is madness," Rezko exclaimed. "You don't even know if the dragon is the Mind Vault you seek."

"Are you afraid, human?" Aranis asked.

"I'm not a fool," he said heatedly. "So yes, I'm afraid."

"It's better than our other options," Erix said.

"You support his plan?" Rezko rounded on him.

"You don't?" Sirani asked.

"Enough," Erix said. "Rez, get the rudder fixed. Strip whatever you can from the other ships and add sail to ours. When the time comes, Sirani can use her magic to give us the boost we need to escape. And don't let those blasted constructs see you."

"It'll take us a few days," Rezko said.

"Then that's how long we have to come up with a plan," Erix said, and turned on Jack. "You'd better be as good a thief as I hear, because stealing from a nest of ancient dragons is outside my skill set."

"Don't worry, captain," Jack said with a grin. "It's within mine."

Sirani chose that moment to yawn. "Dragons will spot me if I wander about the city, so let me know when you have a plan. I'm going back to sleep."

"How can you sleep in this place?" a sailor growled.

Sirani shrugged. "It's the most peaceful place I've ever visited. Very quiet."

She ambled to the ascender and departed to a higher level. Jack laughed in her absence and several of the others joined in his mirth. Sirani had lost much of her wits, but she seemed to truly enjoy the disturbing island. When his humor subsided Jack motioned outside.

"Inna, Aranis, and I will see what we can find when they're asleep at night. I'd suggest you split your men up among a few houses so it's harder for the dragons to locate you."

"I'll do that," the captain said.

Jack stepped into the street with Inna and Aranis. Once they were out of earshot he stabbed a finger at the spires rising above them.

"Anyone have an idea?" Jack asked.

Inna scowled at him. "You made it sound like you knew what to do."

"I've never trapped a dragon," he said. "Let alone one built by the ancients."

258

Aranis chuckled at his admission. "Do you always lie to your allies?"

"I only lie on assignment," Jack said, quoting a thief saying. "But we have plenty to work with."

"Like what?" Inna's features darkened with fury. "Rope and arrows?"

"A rock troll and a dark elf," Jack said with a smile.

"How can they help?" Inna snapped.

"I like being called an asset," Aranis purred, "but I don't know how to kill these creatures."

Jack came to a halt and pointed to the downed spire. "Someone defeated one of the constructs. Let's find out how."

Inna growled at him but did not argue, and Jack led the way to the fallen spire. When they reached it Jack leapt up and caught a wide crack, levering himself through. He slid down the curve of the wall to the interior. A moment later Aranis and Inna joined him.

"The spires do not have windows," she said.

"But why?" Jack asked.

"Perhaps they are not for living," Inna said.

Jack looked about the chamber, tilting his head sideways to imagine what it would have appeared like when vertical. Strange machinery lined the walls with pillars extending from floor to ceiling. Jack spotted a disc on the floor and made his way to it. It evidently connected this level to the one below, but it did not activate when Jack touched it.

"There's nothing here," Inna said.

"Perhaps we are looking in the wrong place." Jack pointed to the base of the spire. "When this was upright, the most likely place for the ancients to access it would not have been above."

"It would be below," Aranis said.

259

They climbed out of the fallen turret and worked their way through the darkness to what remained of the base. The spire was over forty feet thick and two hundred feet tall. Its fall had flattened homes and shops, crumpling roofs and blocking streets, cracking the smooth exterior.

The proximity to the other towers required caution, and they avoided the moonlit streets. The construct flew above them once and they stilled until the dragon had passed on. Then Jack worked his way to the broken base of the spire.

"No windows," Inna said.

"At least we know how they broke it." Aranis stooped to pick up a large triangular shard on the ground. Black and as hard as steel, the object did not match the architecture of the city.

A dragon's scale.

"Someone brought their own dragon," Jack said.

Inna grunted in recognition. "My father's history books told of a pirate that enslaved dragons. He used them like an army and no one could stop him. Then he disappeared."

"The Shattered Isle claimed another victim," Aranis said.

Inna motioned to the point where the spire had broken off. Jack noticed the pockmarked texture to the white material where the dragon's acid had eaten through, weakening it. Like an ax cutting into the side of a tree, the black dragon had cut a wedge in the spire, and it had fallen under its own weight.

"*He* had a dragon and failed," Inna said. "What can we do?"

Jack ignored her. "Let's see what's inside."

He cast his shadowhook at the darkened wall of the broken spire and ascended until he could peek into the interior. He scanned the dragons clinging to the spires nearby, and then pulled himself up and over, dropping into the darkness below.

He landed on his feet and rose, twisting to look at the walls. As in the higher level in the spire, the room contained strange machinery and

260

thin columns. Moonlight filtered into the space, providing enough illumination to examine the space. Then Jack turned and noticed a pedestal at the center.

A small dragon sat atop the pedestal, limp and lifeless. He reached out and touched it, unsurprised to find it metallic. Inna and Aranis joined him and the dark elf bent to examine the beast.

"It looks like the constructs outside," Inna said in surprise.

"I suspect the beast was controlled by this," Aranis said, gesturing to the dead creature. "Remember how they flowed out of the tower? They gain power from the spire, but their mind resides here."

Jack noticed a thread of faint light coming from the side of the spire. The conduit passed across the floor and came to an abrupt halt where a fragment of the spire had plunged into the floor. On the other side the lifeless thread continued to the pedestal, connecting to the dragon.

An idea began to form in Jack's mind and he paused to consider it. As he thought through the possibilities a smile appeared on his face. Noticing it, Inna raised an eyebrow. Jack swept a hand at her unanswered question.

"I have an idea now."

"Let's hope it's a good one," Inna said sourly.

"It is," Jack said. "But it won't work without the black dragon."

"The *dead* one?" Inna asked. "How are we supposed to find it?"

"Follow the trail of destruction," Jack replied. "It would have died fighting."

"And what do we do with a dragon's corpse?" Aranis asked, folding her arms.

"Cut it open and gather the acid from its stomach." Jack said it like it was obvious and then turned away.

"You want us to cut open a rotting dragon?" Inna asked.

261

"I'm a killer," Aranis said. "I don't do carrion."

"Get Rezko and the sailors to help," Jack said with a shrug. "You can supervise."

"And while we do the disgusting part, what will you be doing?"

"The hard part," Jack said. A faint chime echoed in his ear and he abruptly walked away. "I'll meet you back with the others."

He cast his shadowhook and departed the spire. As soon as he was out of sight he used the pocket Gate and left, returning a few hours later with a pack of supplies. Stashing the pack near the prison he'd discovered with Aranis, he returned to the refuge.

"They told us about the black dragon," Erix said. "What are you planning?"

"Do you want me to explain it? Or do it?"

"Both," Erix said.

"Later," Jack said. "I need to set something in motion first."

Erix scowled at the lack of information and swept a hand at the sailors packed in the room. "What would you have us do?"

"Oh, it's not you I need," Jack said, catching sight of Sirani playing dice with a group of sailors. "It's her."

Jack strode up to her and said, "Ready to fight?"

Sirani giggled when she rolled all sixes, causing the men to growl in disgust and throw their money onto the floor. Sweeping up the coin, she stood and faced him, a twinkle in her eye. Behind her, one of the dice wobbled as the wind caressed its corner.

"Ready for duty and debauchery," she said.

"This way," Jack replied, guiding her into the dark street.

He led her through the streets, staying clear of open areas. Several times the dragon sentries soared above them and Jack was grateful the unpredictable troll held her tongue. She settled on making a rude gesture at the dragons as they soared away. They reached the prison and Jack retrieved the pack, opening it to reveal a collection of whitish discs.

"My dear thief," Sirani said, "wherever did you acquire those?"

"You can find nearly anything in Griffin," Jack said, "if you know the right merchants."

"I doubt our good captain had these aboard his ship."

"I acquired them by other means," Jack said evasively.

She winked at him. "I'm sure you did. But just what do you intend for me?"

"Did you know that the druids are led by a man bonded to a phoenix?"

"Newhawk," she said with a low whistle. "He's as delicious as you are."

"I once saw him astride his firebird," Jack said. "They were trying to land in a storm but the gusts of wind kept driving into the bird's wings, keeping it aloft."

"Anything with wings can be turned aside with wind," Sirani said, her expression lighting with anticipation. "Even an almighty dragon."

"Can you keep the constructs occupied without getting killed?"

"Alone?"

Jack handed her the pack. "You'll have these."

She laughed and accepted the pouch. "I can give you a few minutes."

"Don't die for it," Jack said.

"You may be delicious," she said, "but I only die for family."

"Good," Jack said, and swept his hand at the prison. "Here's your playground. Go play."

263

Sirani grinned and hurried away. Stopping in an open area, she cast a charm that dug a hole into the ground. Like planting a seed, she dropped one of the discs into the hole and then covered it up. Satisfied, Jack turned and left.

"Let's steal a dragon," he said.

Chapter 33: Stealing a Dragon

Two days later Jack put his plan into motion. With dawn on the horizon he watched the spires for any sign of the slumbering constructs. A lone dragon remained on patrol, sweeping around the island on its great wings.

A gout of fire abruptly exploded next to the prison, causing the beast to fold its wings and dive. Its haunting snarl reverberated throughout the city as it flew through the smoke rising from the explosion. Then Sirani stepped into its path and shouted up to it.

"This pig is more bite than bacon!"

The dragon snarled and dropped—but a gust of wind caught one wing and sent it spiraling away. Unable to withstand the blow, the dragon crashed through an ancient home, crumpling the roof and collapsing the walls. Fire lanced from its jaws as it scrambled to its feet and darted back, but again Sirani punched its wing and sent it careening away. Deep in the shadows near the fallen tower, Jack spotted two dragons flowing out of their spires.

"They're taking the bait," he murmured.

"I still can't believe you asked her to fight dragon constructs . . . alone," Inna said, her voice worried as the two dragons descended upon the prison.

"She's loving every minute," Jack replied.

Sirani's cackling laughter echoed back to them as she ignited one of the cyclone hexes buried in the ground. Wind exploded forth, churning and twisting, forcing both dragons to bank to the side. They unleashed their fire breath upon the building, but it just grazed the roof.

Another dragon exited its lair and flew to the battle, and then another. Titanic growls and snarls punctuated the morning, accompanied by bursts of fire and a shrieking blast of air. Cyclones blossomed up, turning the entire prison into a deadly battleground of fire and wind. Sirani darted through the charred buildings, adding her magic to the wind, knocking the enraged dragons away, preventing them from landing. The last of the dragons left its spire, the one from the center, the Mind Vault. It unleashed an unholy scream and streaked for the battle, flames igniting across its back.

"No one likes to be wakened from slumber," Jack said, stifling a laugh.

"Let's just get this done," Inna said.

"Before it comes back and burns us to ash," Aranis agreed.

The three of them bent and picked up a bowl fashioned out of black dragon scales. With great care they worked their way out of the shadows and through the spires, aiming for the one at the center. Drops of acid seeped through, dripping to the ground and leaving wisps of foul smoke in their wake. They reached the center pillar and positioned themselves against the wall.

"Don't let it splash on you," Jack said.

"It's dragon vomit that can melt flesh from bone," Inna hissed. "I'm not going to let it touch me."

They nodded in unison, and swung the bowl, sending a splash of dragon acid into the wall. Acrid smoke blossomed from the contact, rising into the air. The white stone, impervious to blade or blow, began to bubble and steam. It dripped to the ground as if reluctant to relinquish its shape, great globs sinking into an expanding puddle.

The smoke increased, forcing them to retreat as the acid ate through the wall. Then a thundering roar caused them to whirl and face the

266

prison in the distance—to see the small dragon and three others streaking for them.

"Go!" Jack barked. "Try to lead them away and then get to the ship."

"What about you?" Inna asked.

"The acid is working," he said. "I'll find a way inside."

"You can't expect to fight them," Aranis said.

"I'm not stupid," Jack snapped. "I intend to run."

He turned and sprinted away, casting his shadowhook at one of the spires, using it to launch himself into the city. The four constructs closed fast, winging toward him, fire exploding from their jaws. One darted after Aranis, while another went for Inna. A third came for Jack, and he raced through a destroyed section of the city.

Jack swung to the side and dived through a building, leaping out a window on the opposite side. The dragons ripped the house apart in an almost desperate fury, rending it to shreds and coming for him. He caught a glimpse of the small dragon landing at the base of its spire, bending its neck to inspect the hole in the wall.

A burst of fire forced Jack aside, sending light into the dim street. Jack cast his shadowhook at a roof and yanked himself upward, kicking off the roof and dropping into an alley. The dragon tore both buildings apart, leveling every inch with searing flames.

Jack twisted and leapt, fighting to stay clear of the construct. He turned and fired his crossbow and ice exploded over its face. The dragon swung its head against a structure, shattering the ice and flattening the wall.

Jack kept his path in a wide arc, keeping the spire in view. When he saw the last of the material eaten away, Jack veered toward it. He activated his speedstone and sprinted down the street, inches from the fire reaching for his back. In his peripheral vision he spotted the two constructs following Aranis and Inna abandon their pursuit and come for him, fire lancing from their jaws.

The small dragon spotted him and whirled, barricading the opening. It lowered its head and roared its fury, sending a current of fire into Jack's path. He fired a frost bolt into the flames but the bolt disintegrated, unable to endure the tremendous heat. Caught between three dragons behind and one ahead, Jack pulled out a lightstone and threw it on the ground. It shattered, turning into a miniature sun that flooded the spires in blinding light.

He dove to the ground and fired his shadowhook underneath the dragon, where it passed through the acid-created doorway and fused to the shadows inside the spire. Skidding and sliding, he streaked across the ground with flames arcing above him, the blinded dragons blasting everything in an effort to find him. The light subsided as Jack passed beneath the small dragon. It snapped at him and the jaws tore a chunk out of the ground. Then Jack slipped into the darkened interior of the spire.

He rolled to his feet and leapt to the pedestal, snatching the small dragon and recasting his shadowhook high above him. His cloak billowed around him as he flew upward, evading the explosion of flames as the dragon shoved its jaws into the hole and unleashed its might.

From high within the spire Jack paused to catch his breath, coughing as the temperature spiked. Then the flame cut off and claws ripped into the opening, making room for snapping jaws and an angular body. Jack winced when the tiny dragon in his hand bit him, and he looked down at the struggling creature.

The dragon snapped at his arm, its claws tearing into his tunic. Tightening his grip, Jack peered at the beast, examining the markings placed along its back. His grip on the wall shuddered as the dragons rent a chunk from the wall below. Then he heard a snarl that didn't come from beneath.

He snapped to look up, and spotted the small dragon melding through the wall above, its body twisted to point down. Just then a construct at the base of the spire smashed through the opening, crashing into the interior. Two more followed suit, and the trio clawed and snapped at each other as they pointed their jaws upward.

Jack pointed his pocket gate at the wall. The silver Gate flowed into shape and he dove through the portal. He landed in the Griffin Gateroom, and retreated to the wall as fires trickled through the Gate, the heat sufficient to scorch the walls and ceiling. While he waited he pulled a thread from his torn sleeve and used it to bind the miniature dragon in his hands, noticing as he did that the dragon's body did not look like the one in the broken spire. Its arms angled down, curving like it wanted to grasp a spherical object. The tail too wrapped down, bending as if following the curve of a neck.

The fire subsided and Jack slung the bound Mind Vault over his shoulder. Then he stepped to the Gate and leaned far enough through to examine the opposite side. The dragons clawed their way up the interior of the spire, the queen hissing at them from above. Jack caught a glimpse of the opening below and leapt through the portal, falling into the mass of constructs.

The dragons spotted him but he was too close for fire, so they reached for him with claws and teeth. Jack used his shadowhook, casting it at the wall and swinging to the side, alighting on the back of a construct. Leaping and sliding, he slipped between them, rolling onto the back of another before finding a gap against the wall. He squeezed through and fell, and used his shadowhook at the top of the gaping hole, swinging himself into the open.

He landed in the rubble from the side of the spire and whirled, throwing a disk into the gap. Then he aimed his crossbow and fired, detonating the cyclone and filling the doorway with a wall of wind.

Leaving the constructs trapped inside the spire, Jack turned and fled, racing for the ocean. In the distance he spotted the *Sea Dancer*, the sleek ship already pulling into open water. Erix had left on schedule, using Jack's distraction to flee the Shattered Isle. On its deck Sirani used her magic to turn aside the remaining two dragons, keeping them from blasting the ship. One dove into the ocean but Sirani sent a hurricane into the water, forcing it away. Jack veered another direction and aimed for the only other boat floating against a dock.

The ancient vessel.

He sprinted down the street, reaching the dock as a deafening crack resounded in the City of Dawn. Succumbing to the damage of the dragons and the hole at its base, the center spire cracked from base to peak, and four dragons burst into the open. Jack leapt aboard to find Inna and Aranis already present.

"Did you get it?" Aranis asked.

"Of course," Jack said.

"I doubt they'll let us keep it," Aranis said, stabbing a finger at the *Sea Dancer*.

Jack turned to see the other two constructs abandoning the ship and banking toward them. With six enraged constructs bearing down on them, Aranis darted to the back of the ship and leaned out, slapping the rune Sirani had placed on the stern.

The ship punched forward, slamming them all to the deck. Skipping across the water, it rocketed away from the island. The dragons surged after them, closing the gap as the ancient vessel raced for the unseen barrier that marked the border of the ancient's territory.

"You think they'll stop?" Inna shouted.

"We can only hope!" Jack shouted.

They turned back and watched the dragons close the gap, their great metallic wings churning the air, driving them forward. Even with Sirani's charm they could not outrun the constructs. Their only hope lay in an assumption that the constructs were leashed to the city, and could not go beyond its borders.

The dragons did not stop.

Six dragon constructs reared back in unison and bellowed a challenge. They gradually closed the distance, until their wings buffeted the boat and fire sparked in their jaws. The queen shrieked its fury, the sound rattling Jack's teeth.

"You were wrong," Aranis said, her voice tinged with surprise.

"And now we're dead," Inna said.

Both women drew their weapons, the gesture one of futility. As fire exploded toward them Jack did the only thing he could think to do. He yanked the Mind Vault from his shoulder and ripped the bindings, slamming it onto his head. The legs wrapped around his skull, clamping tight, the tail feathering down the back of his neck.

And the world froze.

Chapter 34: The Mind Vault

Jack stared at the flames that were just feet from his face but they were frozen solid. The dragons in the air remained fixed, their wings unmoving, their multi-faceted eyes staring at him. He turned and found Inna and Aranis equally as frozen, with both assassins standing tall, unflinching in the face of death.

He stepped to the edge of the boat and looked at the water, but found it equally as rigid. Water had splashed away from the hull, the droplets of white hovering in midair. He reached out and touched it, his fingers coming back dry.

"This is unexpected," he said.

To his surprise someone answered.

"Specimen zero is not permitted to use this archive."

Jack turned to find a slender man standing behind him on the boat. Shorter than Jack, the man was translucent, and the sunrise was visible through his body. His clothing was sleek and grey, with flecks of green that made it shine.

"Who are you?" Jack asked.

"I am Archive," he replied.

Jack gestured to the frozen dragons. "Did you stop time?"

The man regarded him with a haughty expression. "Time is constant. While you are linked to me you are merely tuned to my sight. I

272

think faster than you can perceive, so the halting of time is merely an illusion to you."

"Can you rein them in?" Jack asked, gesturing to the dragons.

"I will not," Archive said. "They serve to protect the installation built by Ero and Skorn—and if I am not mistaken, you are stealing from it."

"Your constructs have killed thousands," Jack said.

"They fulfill the purpose of their creation," Archive said.

"Their purpose is to kill?"

"Constructs were created to punish criminals," the man said, his expression flickering with disdain. "And thieves."

"Is that what the ancients did?" Jack asked. "Kill criminals?"

"Is that what humans do?" Archive countered. "Steal?"

Jack laughed. "Only the good ones."

The man cocked his head to the side and regarded him with curiosity in his eyes. "Who are you?"

"Jack Myst," he said, and bowed. "Guildmaster of Thieves."

"I am surprised you survived this long against the constructs," he said. "Do you possess a powerful magic?"

Jack folded his arms. "Why would I tell you?"

"You don't have to answer for me to know the truth," he said.

Archive passed a hand between them and light flashed across Jack's body. The light did no harm as it scanned his torso, its touch warm but brief before it was extinguished. Archive didn't seem to notice Jack's irritation.

"Interesting," Archive said. "Animal magic, bonded to a panther. The animal's power now resides within you, an as yet unseen ability,

273

but not overly powerful. Your chances of survival against a construct are negligible."

Indignant, Jack stabbed a finger at the man. "I'll have you know, I've fought a construct before."

"Boasting is a common trait for your kind."

Jack scowled and described Myra, the lightning construct he'd battled in the Vault of the Eternals. By the time he finished, Archive's expression had turned curious. Abruptly he stepped forward and peered into Jack's eyes.

"You should not be alive."

"Death is like a spoiled child," Jack said. "He always thinks he gets his way."

"I believe Ero would be pleased with you," Archive said. "As would Skorn."

"I've stolen from both," Jack said wryly. "I don't think either is pleased with me."

"So why come to the City of Dawn?" Archive asked.

"I came for answers."

"My purpose is to record and answer queries," Archive said.

"Even if it comes from specimen zero?" Jack asked.

The man's lips tightened. "From anyone."

"What is the Necrolith?"

Archive swept his hands apart and the entire vista went white. The dragons, the assassins, the boat, even the sea, all were gone in an instant. In its place an obelisk appeared. Extending from the top of a pyramid, the structure rose hundreds of feet high. A burst of light exploded from the top, piercing the sky and illuminating the stars.

"The beacon of ending," Archive said.

"What does it do?"

"Summon the krey to the harvest."

"What are the krey?"

The scene changed again. As if they stood on the deck of a flying ship, they soared above an unending city that resembled the City of Dawn. Towering spires and white structures were interspersed with blue waterways and purple vegetation. Boats soared through the sky, their hulls shaped like swords.

Millions of people lined the streets below. At first glance they appeared human, but their eyes were bright, their luster as striking as Ero's. Other eyes were purple or gold, the coloring vibrant and sharp, matching the shine to their skin.

Some were hulking, their bodies layered in bone armor. They resembled rock trolls but were smaller, their skin hardly visible beneath the bone. Sword hilts extended from their shoulders, suggesting they were warriors of some kind.

Humans were also in abundance, most carrying heavy loads as they strode between the krey. Jack then spotted a construct, and then another. The glowing figures were made of different magics, their coloring varied.

A flicker of silver drew his gaze, and he spotted a krey activate a pocket Gate. He aimed above a building and cast it again, and strode through, appearing on the roof of the building. A human bearing a load followed him and the Gates closed.

"Where is this?"

"You would call it another realm."

"How many realms are there?"

The scene changed to another city, this one with a green glow in the sky. Then the vista shifted gain, this time to a city with an abundance of glowing blue plants. Again and again the vista changed until Jack jerked his head.

"Stop," he said. "Give me a number."

"Your system of measurement does not contain that answer."

Jack wiped a hand over his face, his confusion mounting. Then he turned back to Archive. "You said that when the Necrolith is activated, the krey come for the harvest. What do they harvest?"

Archive regarded him for some time. "You."

"Me?"

"Humans."

Jack recalled the prison he and Aranis had discovered. "And the other specimens?"

"The other specimens are not known to the krey, just as Lumineia is unknown."

"And if the beacon is activated, the krey will know?"

"And they come for the harvest."

"Where is Skorn's Necrolith?" Jack said.

"My knowledge is limited to what is given to me, and no krey has returned to the City of Dawn for four senteniums."

Jack had hoped for a different answer, but supposed that it was to be expected. "If Skorn's Necrolith is destroyed, can he build another?"

"Not without a beacon's core," Archive said.

He lifted a hand and an ethereal pyramid appeared. Jack recognized it as the beacon he'd thought he destroyed at Margauth. He scowled, wishing he'd ensured its destruction then.

"Is there another Necrolith on Lumineia?"

"Not one he can access."

Jack folded his arms, considering whether he'd gotten all his questions answered. Archive waited, his expression patient. At Jack's

276

request the vista returned to reality, and the dragons hovered nearby, their fire reaching to him.

"Will you stop your constructs?" Jack asked.

Archive seemed amused at the answer. "I will not defy my purpose. The moment you remove the link, you will be killed."

"Can I persuade you to assist me?"

"I cannot be persuaded. And as intriguing as you are, I have no directive to save your life."

Jack sighed and reached up to his head. "Then you leave me no choice."

He wrenched the small dragon free. All at once the fire came at him, the sound of Inna's defiant scream and the rush of wind exploding in his ears. Then Jack twisted and hurled the Mind Vault into the dragon's fire.

The Mind Vault shattered, the pieces disintegrating in the flames. At the exact moment the Mind Vault died, the constructs shattered, their fires cutting off. The pieces rained into the sea and sank to the depths. In the distance the spires of the Shattered Isle trembled and crumbled to the earth. Every wall, roof, and fragment of the city went with it, and the entire City of Dawn turned to dust. Then the boat they were standing on dissolved, plunging Aranis and Inna into the ocean. Jack landed on the surface of the water, his boots keeping him dry.

Shocked by the sudden change, Inna managed to sheath her sword. She wiped water from her face and stared at the destroyed city. Then she turned to Jack. "What just happened?"

Jack shrugged. "I destroyed the Mind Vault."

"You *destroyed* it?"

"It was that or we all die."

"I'll take living," Aranis said.

277

"I always end up drenched around you," Inna said. She splashed at Jack but he skipped out of reach.

"Get your own boots."

"Then it was all for naught?" Aranis asked.

"No," Jack said, and shared what he'd learned about the Necrolith.

Deciding it best not to reveal everything he'd witnessed, he held his tongue regarding the krey. He didn't understand it, and had no desire to voice the implications of krey realms until he did. Turning to the *Sea Dancer* in the distance, he waved and watched the ship bank in their direction. Thirty minutes later they were climbing onto the deck and Jack was forced to explain anew. When he finished Erix issued a bark of laughter.

"You destroyed an ancient city that has endured for forty thousand years."

"Not by intention," Jack said defensively. "I figured the Mind Vault controlled the constructs, so destroying it would destroy them."

"At least the Shattered Isle will claim no more victims," Rezko said.

Aranis wrung the water from her cloak, muttering about how long it took to dry. "I hate the ocean."

Jack grinned and sank into a seat on the rail. "It's always full of—"

"ADVENTURE!" boomed Sirani, and the rock troll bounded to a position behind the mast. Slapping her hands together, she sent a gust of air into the sails, propelling the ship to even greater speeds.

"I think she's ready for another one," Inna said, a smile on her face.

"We barely survived the last one," Rezko said.

"I'm ready for a nap," Jack said, and yawned. "Wake me when we get to Woodhaven."

With that he left and descended to his small bunkroom. He shut the door and stared at the bed, yearning for its warmth. With a reluctant sigh he cast his pocket Gate and left the ship behind.

Chapter 35: Ero's Intrigue

Beauty arrived in Azertorn and left Axe in the same stables she had before. Dismounting next to Ursana, she stretched her back to ease the strain and removed the saddle. Then she grabbed a brush and wearily rubbed the horse down. Ursana leaned against the stall.

"It's so much easier to rent a steed," Ursana said. "Why keep them yourself?"

Axe tossed his head and whinnied, causing Beauty to grin. "I agree. You can't rent loyalty."

Ursana laughed and turned away. "I want to visit a friend. Can I meet you at the temple?"

"Friend?" Beauty asked. "Does he have a name?"

"How do you know it's a he?"

"Am I wrong?"

"No."

Ursana grinned and turned away, and Beauty watched her go. Ursana had joined the guild as a fifteen-year-old child, but now she was a young woman with the skills of a veteran. Tall and slender, she carried herself with grace and intelligence, and Beauty guessed a large part of her confidence had come from Gordon.

But that confidence had been shaken with the appearance of Gordon's family. On the journey to Azertorn, Beauty had tried to coax her into talking, but the girl had dismissed the topic. Still, Beauty could see the worry in the young woman's gaze.

When she was finished with Axe, Beauty ascended to the city and made her way to the Temple of Ero. To her irritation the crowds were twice what they were before, and throngs of potential patrons clogged the streets. Elven soldiers were in abundance, their presence maintaining order.

Beauty threaded her way through the crowd until she reached an entrance, and found the same abbot she'd encountered on her first visit. The man swallowed as he caught sight of Beauty and motioned her through, giving her a wide berth. Beauty climbed the stairs and strode through the nine circles of the upper offices until she reached the high abbot's private quarters, where she found Thalidon standing in the hall with his brother. They turned at her appearance.

"When did Ero get back?" she asked.

"Three days ago," Thalidon said, and scowled. "At least that's what we've been told."

She raised an eyebrow. "You didn't follow him?"

"We never found him," Roarthin said. "We tracked him as you asked, but he disappeared in a village outside of Herosian."

Thalidon grunted in irritation. "We searched all the way to Azertorn, where we discovered he'd already arrived."

"You lost him?" Beauty asked.

Roarthin scowled. "He's an ancient being walking in a strange land. We thought he'd be easy to track."

"He disappeared," Thalidon insisted.

"Where would he go?" Beauty asked. "The only reason he's here is to stop Skorn."

"Unless he has another agenda," Thalidon said, lowering his tone as an abbot strode by.

Beauty mulled that over. Thalidon and Roarthin were both skilled mages, warriors, and trackers. If that wasn't sufficient, their suspicions added to her own.

But what did Ero want? Ero had carved out nearly a fortnight on his own, but where would he have gone? Then a thought crossed her mind that made her jaw tighten. She'd assumed Ero was an ally, but what if he was an ally of Skorn? They were brothers, after all.

"Why don't we ask him?"

Thalidon rumbled a laugh. "Thieves don't usually choose the direct approach."

"Barbarians do," Beauty said, striding to Ero's quarters. She caught the handle but found it locked, so she struck the door.

"Just a moment," came the reply.

The seconds passed but still he did not come. Just as Beauty was considering bashing the door in, Ero called again. This time the handle gave and she strode in. Dressed in his ceremonial white robes, Ero stood on a balcony overlooking the crowd and Le Runtáriel in the distance. He turned at their entrance and smiled.

"My guardian returns," he said. "Was your journey pleasant?"

"Where did you go?" she demanded.

He gestured to the table, where food had been set. "Care to join me for a meal? I'm sure you're hungry."

Beauty jerked her head. "No more delays. I want the truth."

"Of course you do," Ero said, his piercing gaze turning shrewd. "But what you ask I cannot give."

"Did you meet with your brother?" she asked.

Ero burst into a laugh. "You really have begun to doubt me, if you believe that."

Beauty read the truth in his expression. Ero might have his own agenda, but he was no friend to Skorn.

282

Thalidon grunted. "You disappeared for two weeks. Why?"

Ero shifted to face him. "You dwarves are always so blunt. Well I shall be blunt in turn. What do you know of the Eternals?"

"Jack mentioned it," Roarthin said. "Seems you are one of them."

"We protect Lumineia against threats," Ero said.

"Like Skorn?" Beauty asked.

"No," Ero said quietly. "We protect it from threats outside Lumineia."

"What is that supposed to mean?" Thalidon asked.

Ero cocked his head to the side. "There are many realms," he said. "And we protect Lumineia from them."

"What do the Eternals have to do with your absence?"

"My presence here leaves other duties unattended," Ero said. "I completed them and then returned. I cannot abandon the Eternals, even for Skorn."

"You're hiding something," Roarthin said, his tone doubtful.

"You wanted the truth," Ero said. "Now you have it."

"You expect us to believe you?" Thalidon asked.

Ero kept his gaze on Beauty. "You'll just have to trust me."

"I don't," she said.

"Your guildmaster trusts me," Ero said, his tone gaining an edge. "Is that not sufficient?"

Beauty held his gaze but did not respond. Without a word she turned and left, and the dwarves followed her out. Once they were in the hall, Roarthin shut the door and the trio strode to the eighth circle, out of earshot.

"I don't believe him," Thalidon said.

"I don't either," Beauty said.

Roarthin grunted. "I don't like being lied to—especially by an ancient. It's all too familiar."

"Keep your eyes open," Beauty said. "Skorn is going to come for him and we need to be ready. I'll be at his side while you cover the main entrances."

Ursana appeared at the end of the hall and strode to join them. The lightness to her step faltered as she caught sight of Beauty's expression. She frowned as she approached and came to a halt before her.

"What happened?"

"We can't trust Ero," Beauty said.

She nodded. "What's the plan?"

"I want you on the roof of the temple," Beauty said. "Keep an eye on the crowd, but I suspect that when Skorn comes, he'll come at night."

"As you order," she said, pulling the large crossbow from her back. "How soon do you expect him to come?"

"Any day now," Beauty said. "After what happened in Herosian, Gallow will come—soon."

"Because they failed to kill Ero?" Ursana asked.

"That was not his only goal," Beauty said. "Skorn wanted to ascertain if Ero was his brother and not an imposter."

"And by now he knows the truth," Thalidon said.

Roarthin scowled. "He'll come for Ero—before Ero comes for him."

The dwarves nodded and strode toward the end of the corridor. "We'll watch the entrances," Thalidon said.

"It appears Jack's plan is working flawlessly," Beauty said. "Skorn is playing into our hands."

"You sound disappointed," Ursana said with a smile.

Beauty laughed sourly and turned to her, suddenly realizing that they were almost the same height now.

"Every time I think I know Jack, he surprises me," Beauty said.

"Isn't that what makes love interesting?"

"You think I love him?" she asked.

"Don't you?"

The honest question made her sigh with regret. "What do you know about love?"

"A recent acquisition," Ursana said blithely.

Beauty smiled shrewdly. "And I take it he's in Azertorn. An elf, perhaps?"

Ursana's smile widened. "Barbarian, actually, and he's just passing through. But don't change the subject. You should tell Jack how you feel."

"I will—when you tell Gordon how you feel about his family."

Ursana muttered to herself and turned away. "An unfinished conversation, then."

She strode to the end of the corridor and ascended, leaving Beauty to sigh and rotate back to Ero's quarters. To her surprise he stood in the doorway, calm as a summer nightingale. He smiled at her expression and motioned to Ursana's retreating back.

"It appears she is more honest than you are."

"She has yet to learn the cost of honesty," Beauty said.

"Honesty with the one you love costs little."

"Does your kind even love?" Beauty asked.

He smiled. "We are not so different from you."

"So who do you love?" she demanded.

His smile was sad and fleeting. "One who withheld her heart."

"And did you voice your favor?"

"I should have," Ero said, his features somber. "But I lacked the courage."

"Perhaps we are not so different," she said after a moment's silence.

He flashed a sad smile but the sudden appearance of an abbot interrupted them. "The patrons are getting anxious, your grace."

Ero turned to the abbot, all trace of his vulnerability gone. "Bring them in," he said.

For the rest of the day Beauty stayed by his side as he spoke to adoring admirers, throngs of patrons, and the occasional skeptic. Ero spoke to all with equal grace, flawlessly dealing with conflicts and doling out coin with shocking excess.

As she watched Ero she listened to the monks. They were rife with tension and anger, especially about the high abbot's involvement in Herosian. The bulk of the clergy harbored a seething resentment toward Ero, their hatred growing with every coin he poured into the hands of patrons.

Over the subsequent days Beauty noticed that not all of the clergy felt the same. Visible in the approving looks cast at Ero, and the scorn on their expressions when they overheard others muttering about him, a handful of the abbots sided with Ero.

Led by a woman named Paro, the loyal segment of the church began surreptitiously watching over Ero, inserting themselves into mutinous conversations, attempting to disrupt the growing tide of anger. As the unseen power struggle heightened, the patrons continued to flood the city, compelled to worship or to request coin from the benevolent Ero.

As the gold reserves of the powerful Church of Light reached a critical low, Beauty took to watching her charge with increasing vigilance. Within a week of their return she began to fear another strike from within, and ordered the dwarves to retreat from the entrance to guard his chambers. Throughout day and night the four thieves watched Ero, and frequently changed personas in case anyone was watching them.

Tensions continued to rise, and Beauty reached out to Paro, meeting with her in secret to plan. Ero noticed the rising concerns and requested hours of solitude, locking the doors and going unseen for hours. Rather than relieve the pressure, his times of absence served to heighten it. Realizing the time had come, Beauty managed to convince the city guards to dispel the crowds at night, creating an opening for Skorn to appear.

She sent several messages to Jack but didn't hear back. Each night she went to sleep with her sword under her pillow, and woke at the slightest sound. Each day she watched the abbots for betrayal, and the patrons for Gallow or her father. When the pressure was too much, she ascended to the roof and spoke to Ursana, who had mounted her crossbow and lay beside it. With the bow's magic she could bend a bolt to strike anywhere around the building—including inside. Her chosen spot by the opening in the roof allowed her to see the breadth of the great hall and the hundreds of patrons waiting inside.

Three weeks after her return to Azertorn, Beauty sank into bed exhausted—and woke when a crossbow bolt streaked into her room. She snapped up and watched it quivering in the wall, reading the message as if it was painted on the wall.

They are here.

Chapter 36: Ancient Enmity

Beauty leapt out of bed and yanked her boots onto her feet. She'd taken to sleeping in her clothes and was now grateful she had. Her sword slid into its sheath with a comforting rasp and she darted to the door. When she stepped into the hall Thalidon stumbled through the door on the opposite side.

"What time is it?" the dwarf growled, rubbing his eyes as he pulled his cloak about his shoulders.

"After midnight," she said. "Where's Roarthin?"

"Guarding Ero," he said. "I was about to trade him on watch."

Another bolt streaked through Beauty's open window, thudding into the door. This one came with a parchment around the shaft. She reached up and removed it, unrolling to read it aloud.

"Two score. East Gate. The guards let them in."

Thalidon cursed. "The abbots are helping them."

"Get to Paro," Beauty said. "Have her gather the loyal and meet me at the great hall."

The dwarf darted down the hall and disappeared, and Beauty sprinted to Ero's chambers. When she turned the corner Roarthin raised his axe to her. He scowled and pointed the weapon at the crossbow bolt embedded in the wall next to him.

"What's going on?"

"They're here," she said, glancing down the dim corridor.

She opened the door but Ero was already dressed and striding to her. Instead of fear it was anticipation in his blue eyes. He flicked his hand and the glowing staff blossomed from his palm, extending in both directions, shimmering into solid form.

"We'll need to put on a show," he said. "Or they'll think I want to be taken."

"They might just kill you here."

"Kidnap or killing, the wait will be over."

She couldn't argue with that. The past few weeks had built her tension to the breaking point and her hand virtually trembled with the desire to fight. She turned on her heel and led Ero into the hall, where Roarthin fell into step behind them. Together, they hurried down the hall and descended the curving stairs, where Beauty noticed a disturbing lack of guards. At the base of the stairs Thalidon appeared with Paro.

The woman had traded her abbot's robe for soldier's garb. She cinched a scabbard to her belt and tied her hair back. Ero smiled at her shift in appearance.

"You are much more attractive as yourself."

"I wasn't always an acolyte of Ero," the woman said.

"I fear there is something you should know before it begins," Ero said.

"That you aren't Ero?" Paro smiled. "I guessed as much when you gave away the entirety of the church's fortune."

"I am indeed Ero," he replied. "But I am no god."

Paro raised an eyebrow but Beauty stepped in. "Answers come later."

She stepped to the arched opening that led to the great hall and the others filed in behind her. The giant star-shaped chamber contained hundreds of pews facing the stage where Ero had first appeared. The

289

night sky was visible through the opening, and Beauty caught a glimpse of Ursana on the lip, her crossbow aimed toward the figure standing on the stage.

Skorn.

"New staff, brother?" he asked.

"I hear a rock troll broke your blade," Ero replied, stepping past Beauty.

"Specimen fourteen has surpassed our expectations," Skorn replied. "But I suppose you know that."

"You took longer than I expected," Ero said.

"I had difficulty believing it was really you," Skorn said. "After all you said about not interfering in the affairs of Lumineia, you came for me."

"You look worse for wear," Ero said.

Skorn's lips curled with hatred and he reached up to touch his scarred features. Four claws had raked his face, tearing ragged lines in his flesh. Other exposed flesh was mottled and white, the legacy of severe burns.

"Jack Myst," Skorn drawled. "It's disturbing how one human can be so vexing."

"At times he seems more than human," Ero said, taking another step forward. "But he convinced me that I needed to step in."

"You broke your oath for him," Skorn said. "And now you think to haul me back to your cage?"

"Perhaps it's time I just kill you," Ero said.

A flicker of motion drew Beauty's gaze to the other entrances of the star chamber. Talinorian mercenaries glided through one door, and were led by Captain Herrick himself. Another door opened and Gallow strode in, a score of cult members at his back. Then a third door crashed open

290

and a massive figure ducked to enter. Beauty's heart sank as she met his gaze.

Oragon.

A score of barbarians stood with the barbarian chieftain. His black hair hung to his shoulders, obscuring the litany of scars lining his face and neck. The man's eyes glittered with hatred as he caught sight of Beauty and he raised his massive spiked maul, pointing to her.

She hadn't seen her father in years, but the sight still terrified her. He was a brute of a man, grizzled and scarred from thousands of duels, battles, and wars. For one to flee a barbarian clan was akin to betrayal, and fathers were known to hunt their children for decades in order to mete out the requisite death.

"Is that your father?" Thalidon murmured.

She nodded without looking away from her father. "Chief Oragon of the Bearkiller tribe."

Thalidon sniffed. "Do you really think he'll kill you?"

"Like he would a mosquito—and with equal distaste."

Another movement drew Beauty's gaze to the last point of the star, where dozens of abbots and Church of Light guards appeared—with Alidon at their head. The former high abbot had lost weight from his time in prison and Beauty could not guess how he'd gotten out. He locked eyes with Paro and sneered.

Beauty liked the odds less and less. She had the dwarves, Ursana, Paro, and a handful of loyal acolytes at her back. Arrayed against them were the head of the assassin's guild, captain of the Talinorian mercenaries, slighted clergy from the church, and her own father. Twenty against two hundred.

Ero seemed to be aware of the threat, and as he spoke to Skorn he glanced about, his gaze measuring. The four groups began to drift forward, sensing Skorn's conversation approaching its end. Beauty locked eyes with her father and saw death there.

"You hold the reins of an assassin," Ero said, gesturing to Gallow. "And I understand he prefers subterfuge for his work. Why not send him for me?"

"You think I want to kill you?" Skorn laughed. "I will let you die—after you see your experiments destroyed."

"Jack Myst has defeated you twice," Ero said. "And I don't think you have room for any more scars."

Skorn snarled at that. "You dare to mock me?"

"You think your allies will bring you victory?' Ero asked. "You always use pawns, and they will never be anything more."

Ero's words elicited scowls from Skorn's captains, and Skorn glanced their way. "They are lethal enough to kill you . . . and your friends."

"Perhaps," Ero said. "But if I die here, Jack will still defeat you."

"You have faith in a thief?" Skorn said, his features darkening. "You were always so superior, and it's time you were humbled."

He signaled his forces and they advanced between the pews, the sound of steel being drawn reverberating throughout the hall. Paro barked an order and the loyal acolytes spread out, while Beauty shifted to face her father's approach. As Skorn's followers passed the stage he smiled.

"I have a prison prepared for you, Ero," Skorn said. "I hope you enjoy it as much as I enjoyed mine."

Oragon advanced at the head of the barbarians, his gaze fixed upon Beauty. His scarred lip curled in a sneer as he approached and he raised his spiked maul. Embedded with steel spikes and animal fangs, the weapon was ugly and brutal, an instrument to maim as much as kill.

"I know you will fight," Oragon said, his voice a raspy growl. "And I look forward to it. It's been years since another offered a challenge."

Beauty stood her ground. "Our traditions are perverse and yet you still uphold them."

"You sound like your brother," he growled.

"A compliment before I die?" she asked. "How unexpected."

"It wasn't a compliment," he growled. "Golic tried to prevent me from going after you, and now he's an outcast."

She pointed her own sword at him. "You exiled him because he defied you? Or because he could defeat you?"

He scowled but did not respond, and swished his maul as he stalked forward. Approaching on the right flank, Gallow scowled at the barbarian chief and drew his idalia from his back.

"Just kill her already and be done with it."

"Don't speak to me, assassin," her father snapped. "I wouldn't need a blood oath to kill you."

"Careful, barbarian," Gallow said. "I'd hate for you to wake up with a knife in your throat."

"Do you intend to talk them to death?" Captain Herrick snapped, drawing his sword.

Standing behind the abbots and guards, the high abbot called out to Ero, "Whoever you are, Ero, you cannot survive this."

"Dissension among the ranks?" Ero asked and they slowed, raising their blades to him. "I expected better from your followers."

"They are loyal enough," Skorn said, and raised his voice. "Kill them all, but I want Ero alive."

"If I come willingly," Ero said, "will you grant the others their lives?"

"A willing sacrifice?" Skorn said in surprise. "You care for them so much?"

"Do you care about your followers so little?" Ero asked. "They may stand triumphant, but how many will die here today?"

293

Skorn regarded him for several moments and then shrugged. "I'd rather watch them die in front of you."

Gallow chuckled at that answer but Ero stabbed a finger toward the roof. "Even if it costs your life?"

Skorn turned and looked up to see Ursana's crossbow leveled at him. He scowled and glanced at Gallow.

"I told you they would have someone on the roof."

"I sent three to deal with her," Gallow snapped.

Three swords tumbled through the opening and clattered on the floor. "You should have sent more," Ursana called down.

Skorn laughed at her comment. "You've grown a great deal, Ursana, but you would not be able to hit me with your toy."

Ursana pulled the trigger and a bolt streaked for Skorn. He dodged with inhuman speed—but the bolt dodged in the air, plunging into Skorn's shoulder. He growled and reached up, yanking the bolt free.

"It doesn't like to be called a toy," Ursana called down. "And the next one goes for your heart."

"Where's Gordon?" Skorn asked, his voice seething with pain and rage. "I thought the two of you were inseparable. Or did he find his old family and abandon you?"

Ursana's features tightened. "Says the man here to kill his brother."

Ero burst into a laugh at her statement. "It appears she's lost her fear of you, Skorn."

Skorn sneered at him. "Have it your way. Come to your prison, brother, and I'll let them live."

"*No!*" Oragon snarled, striding toward Beauty. "I came to fulfill a blood oath and that is what I shall do."

He surged into a sprint and raised his maul. Beauty cast a strength spell and raised her blade, swinging it to intercept. To her surprise Ero stepped between them. He jammed his staff into the ground, sending a

294

massive blast of energy into the giant barbarian. The force of the blow sent him careening over the heads of the other barbarians. Wood snapped beneath his bulk as he crashed into the pews and he struck the floor. Ero stood with his staff blazing, the weapon matching the fury in his eyes. When he spoke, it was the coldest Beauty had ever heard.

"You vile, putrid excuse of a father. You will get your chance for her to crush you—but it will not be this day."

Beauty blinked in surprise as he turned to her and inclined his head. Then he whirled and strode to Skorn. As Ero threaded through Skorn's army the others slowly retreated, and in minutes the only ones that remained were Alidon and the other abbots. The high abbot looked between Beauty and the departing followers of Skorn. His eyes flicked to Ursana and the dwarves before settling on Paro.

"Enjoy your leadership of the church while you can, Paro," the high abbot said. "Once Ero is dealt with I will return for what's mine." Then he turned and followed Gallow and the cult members.

When their footfalls echoed into silence Thalidon stepped to Beauty. "Did we win? Or lose?"

Beauty shook her head. "I do not know."

Chapter 37: Jack's Secret

Jack stood on the prow of the ship, watching the city of Woodhaven approach in the distance. After everything that had happened in the City of Dawn, he should have been considering what he'd learned, but he couldn't stop thinking about Beauty.

"Are you feeling better?" Inna asked, stepping to his side. "I've hardly seen you out of your cabin in a week."

"I managed to keep my lunch down," Jack said with a smile. "That's an improvement."

"That's an accomplishment for us all," Inna said, lowering her tone. "I respect the captain, but his choice of cook leaves a lot to be desired."

Jack's laugh attracted Aranis, who was sitting on the rail nearby, her legs dangling over the water. After the battle with the dragon constructs he'd expected her mood to lighten, but she'd been as reserved and taciturn as ever.

"His food tastes like tar," she muttered.

"Someone's excited to be on solid ground again," Jack said.

"Ships are unnatural," Aranis said. "You surface races have a madness for exploration that will lead to ruin."

"You're just jealous there are no oceans in the Deep."

"Actually, there are," Aranis said. "But we aren't fools enough to sail them."

Jack and Inna shared a look, and Jack grinned. "The mysteries of the Deep never cease," he said.

"Do you plan on returning once we land?" Inna asked.

"I have nothing to return to," Aranis said.

Inna peaked an eyebrow but the dark elf did not elaborate.

"Where will you go?" he asked.

Aranis didn't answer, and after a while Jack shrugged and turned back to the approaching city. After a while Inna left him to his thoughts, but when she did Aranis slid off the rail and glided to his side.

"I've never seen you so somber, pet. Perhaps you need a kiss to cheer you?"

He grinned at the offer. "You're relentless."

"I know," she said, her lips twitching into a smile. "So have you given up?"

He turned to face her. "You are beautiful, lethal, and mysterious."

She pressed against him, leaning up to brush her lips against him. "I don't mind being your pet—"

"But my heart belongs to another," Jack said.

She retreated, her features hardening. "If I kill her, your affection will have no anchor."

Jack laughed quietly. "You cannot hide anymore, not from me."

"You presume to know me?" Aranis asked, her voice taking a dangerous edge.

"I do—and if I'm wrong, you'll get your kiss."

She folded her arms. "You have yourself a wager."

He stepped close, and lifted the hood of her cloak so he could see into her eyes. She made no move to stop him or retreat, and stared at

297

him with a touch of suspicion and curiosity. Her body tensed as he leaned in and spoke.

"You have lost your home, your family, and have nothing. You did not choose to be an assassin but were forged into being. You claim to have killed your heart but we both know you failed, and you are terrified that I will see what you want most."

"What is that?" she asked. She attempted a sneer, but her voice trembled.

"A home."

He backed her into the railing but she did not resist. She flinched at the contact, and he put arms on the railing, holding her fast. He leaned against her until his lips brushed against hers, holding with his challenging gaze.

"Am I wrong?"

She swallowed and then shoved him away, striding toward the rear of the ship with enough force that sailors made a path for her. In her absence Jack sighed and returned to his scrutiny of the sea. The ropes creaked above him and a giant form dropped to the deck.

"Will no one leave me alone?" Jack sighed.

"Honesty is like a dagger to the heart," Sirani said. "But it can hurt more than steel."

"She needed to hear it," Jack said.

"Not so harshly," Sirani said.

He rounded on her and stabbed a finger into her stomach. "You think to lecture me on matters of the heart? Your mind is broken because you won't be honest with yourself."

Her features darkened with fury and for a split second Jack wondered if he'd gone too far. Then she released a breath and turned away.

"Your words will not hide your fear," she said.

298

Jack turned back to the sea and this time no one appeared. He should have been relieved, but instead it was regret that seeped into his heart. He remained in place as the *Sea Dancer* banked toward the elven port.

Part of his frustration was directed at Beauty, but most was directed at himself. He'd kept her out of his designs and now regretted that. She was perceptive and knew him well. If Jack had brought Beauty with him, she would certainly have figured him out.

He smiled sourly as he realized it was not Beauty—or even himself—that deserved his ire. It was his office. How could becoming a thief be so freeing, but becoming guildmaster be so stifling? He'd learned far more than he ever wanted to know from the Mind Vault, and wished he could go back to the freedom of ignorance.

"It's almost over," he murmured to himself.

The *Sea Dancer* glided into port and Jack turned, striding to the gangplank. There he met a handful of sailors led by Captain Erix and Rezko. The men inclined their heads in unison and then the captain spoke.

"It's been an interesting voyage," he said.

"It has at that," Jack replied. "I hope your travelers always bring you adventure."

Rezko grinned. "I'm sure few will compare to you, but we'll manage."

Jack clasped their hands and then descended to the dock. Sirani thudded down to join him while Inna appeared at his side. He saw no sign of Aranis and fleetingly wondered if she had taken the opportunity to flee. They strode along the docks before turning inland, making their way to the thief guildhall.

It had been a long journey and Jack was grateful for the feel of dry land under his boots. Rays of green light filtered through the beautiful canopies, illuminating the winding paths of the elven city. The peace and tranquility inherent to the city eased his tension and he made no effort to rush. They crossed the breadth of the city until they reached the

299

thief guildhall. Ascending to the front door, he reached for the handle but a pair of dwarves burst into view.

Surly and unkempt, the two dwarves reeked of sweat and mold. One had a pair of gold teeth, while the other seemed to be missing most of his. They yanked chipped axes into view and pointed them at Jack.

"Aye, it's him," the gold-toothed dwarf barked.

"The bounty is ours," the second replied.

Jack rubbed his forehead. "Any other time, I'd love to strip you of your pride, but I'm weary from the journey. Can we do this tomorrow?"

The gold-toothed dwarf stepped forward and raised his sword. "We've waited for a month. We're done waiting . . ."

His words faded as Sirani climbed into view. Huffing from the ascent, she caught the trunk and gasped for air.

"Why does your hall have to be so high?"

"Be gone, troll!" One dwarf shouted.

Sirani blinked at them and then flicked her hands, swatting them away. They squeaked as they slammed into the trunks on either side and dropped to the steps. Another gust of wind sent their forms tumbling down the stairs, and the sound of them bouncing gradually faded.

"I like having you around," Inna said.

Jack grunted in agreement and reached for the handle, but the door swung open. Apparently drawn to the conflict, a pair of thieves stood on the other side. Jack smiled as he saw Beauty and Thalidon staring back at him.

"About time you got back," Beauty said.

Jack stepped past her to enter the hall. "What happened?"

"Skorn took Ero," she said. "Five days ago."

Inna cursed. "He's probably dead already. Did you try following Skorn?"

300

"We tried," Thalidon said, "But we lost the trail outside of Azertorn."

"Then how do we find the Necrolith?" Beauty asked, her voice trailing off as Sirani ducked to enter the room.

"A thief guildhall," she giggled. "I've always wanted to see one."

She darted to the wall and examined a sword, gushing about it before leaping to the next decoration. Watching an eight-foot troll dance around like a gleeful child caused Jack to grin. Beauty raised an eyebrow and leaned close to him.

"I'm surprised she's still with you."

"She won't leave," he replied.

"She's actually been an asset," Inna said

Sirani squealed in delight and rushed to a thief crossbow hanging on the wall. She turned and unloaded every bolt in the weapon, sending forty bolts streaking about the room. Only Jack and Inna remained standing as the others dived behind couches and chairs. Cackling in wild glee, Sirani cast her magic, sending the crossbow bolts in swirling patterns before returning them to the weapon. With a sigh of regret she placed it on the wall before noticing Beauty and Thalidon on the floor.

"What's wrong with them?"

Jack shrugged. "I don't know."

Beauty came to her feet, her expression a mixture of caution and confusion. "Can we please focus?"

Jack wiped his hand across his forehead. "I'm going to bed. We'll talk in the morning."

"What about her?" Thalidon asked, eyeing Sirani as she rushed about the room, her heavy footfalls causing the room to tremble.

"She's harmless," Jack said with a yawn. "Unless she doesn't like you. Then get out of her way."

301

Leaving Sirani to her excitement, they ascended the guildhall and Beauty pointed Inna to a room. As Jack entered the bedchamber reserved for him, Beauty followed him in and shut the door. Then she turned and folded her arms.

"You expect me to wait until morning?" she demanded. "I want answers."

He yawned and stripped his tunic off, revealing his bare chest. "I want to sleep."

She eyed him as he pulled on a more comfortable shirt. "Why did you let Skorn take Ero?"

"We need someone on the inside," Jack said wearily, sliding into the bed.

"Please, Jack, tell me the truth."

He paused in pulling the blanket up and met her gaze. It was the first time he could recall her speaking with such earnestness, and saying please. He hesitated, measuring the need in her eyes. Then he sighed and gestured to a chair at the small table. When she sank into a seat Jack groaned and collapsed into the seat opposite her, passing a hand over the rune hidden in his gauntlet.

"Skorn has been listening to us."

"How?" she asked, pouncing on the opening.

"The first time I entered the guild vault a charm was activated, and a memory of Lorelia appeared. Apparently Skorn had placed charms throughout the guildhalls, charms to watch everyone in the guild. Lorelia removed them while she was guildmaster."

"He was watching us even after he left?" Beauty asked, and shuddered. "Just when I think he can't get any creepier, he does."

"That's not all," Jack said. "Just before she was killed she discovered that Skorn had also placed listening charms throughout the guild—including on our gear."

Beauty peaked an eyebrow and whipped her hand, dropping her crossbow into her palm. "You mean he could be listening right now?"

Jack nodded and raised his gauntlet, motioning to the yellow rune glowing faintly. "I've suppressed the sound magic nearby, so he's not hearing us now."

Beauty stood and began to pace. "He's been listening to everything? That means he knew about—"

"Ero," Jack said. "I know."

"Why didn't you remove the charms?" she demanded. "Get rid of them so we can be free of Skorn."

"Because," Jack said. "I realized it could be used as a weapon."

She came to a halt and stared at him. "You *wanted* him to listen."

Jack grinned slyly. "So far he's done mostly what I expected him to do."

"But what now?" Beauty asked.

"We gather our forces and go to the Necrolith," Jack said.

"You know where it is?"

Jack grinned. "I do now."

Chapter 38: Last Assignments

"You're going to have to explain that," Beauty said.

Jack shared the tale about the City of Dawn and the battle with the dragon constructs. Then he detailed his partial success in the Mind Vault and what he'd learned about the Necrolith. When he finished, Beauty was shaking her head.

"Before you came along the Thieves Guild dealt with guards and mercenaries, bandits and thugs. What about you attracts ancients, rock trolls, and constructs?"

He shrugged. "Luck."

"Most wouldn't call legendary threats luck."

He yawned. "I'm not most people."

"The truest statement you've ever uttered," she said with a laugh. Then her expression turned pensive. "How did the Mind Vault know the location of the Necrolith? Skorn didn't start building it until a few months ago."

"I didn't learn the location of the Necrolith from the Mind Vault," Jack said. "I learned it from Ero."

"However did you manage that?" she asked.

"We set up a way for him to get a message to me if Skorn took him."

She folded her arms. "Just how many secrets are you keeping from me?"

He sucked in his breath as if in pain. "More than I want to," he said bitterly.

She regarded him for several moments, the irritation melting from her features. Then she sighed and relaxed in her chair.

"I still can't believe you fought a dragon construct," she said.

Jack didn't comment on her shift in topic. "Six, actually."

She laughed lightly. "Jack Myst, liberator of our guild, guildmaster of thieves, destroyer of Margauth, and now dragonslayer."

"It sounds pretentious when you say it like that."

She laughed again, this time with appreciation. "How many titles do you plan on accumulating?"

"I've had enough for a lifetime," Jack said with a smile.

"Because you have earned enough?" she asked shrewdly, "or because there is nothing left to earn?"

"It wasn't the first time I fought a construct," Jack said. "And constructs are more dangerous than anything I've ever faced."

"We still have Skorn to deal with," she said.

"I know," he replied. "But I have a few tricks up my sleeve."

He was tired, but he did his best to keep his smile bland. Beauty was far too adept at reading his expression, and he couldn't afford to reveal any more. Everything he'd put together, every piece he'd painstakingly put into place, would all be at risk if Beauty suspected too much. He hoped that what he'd shared would be enough to satiate her.

She stared over his shoulder as if not seeing. "Skorn will know we're coming. He'll be ready for us."

"It's almost over now," he said. He ran his hands through his hair and stood, signaling their conversation was over.

Her expression turned concerned and she strode to him, reaching up to touch his face. "You know, I've never seen you so tired."

"I've never been so tired," Jack replied, relishing the warmth of the contact.

"I'm sorry," Beauty said. "I didn't know the burden you've been carrying. I can only imagine how much you've planned to bring us to this point."

"You have no idea," he said wryly, and then his voice gained an edge. "From this moment on you'll have to watch every word. If he suspects we know he's listening, he'll guard against us."

"I'll watch my mouth," Beauty said, and then smiled, stepping close in invitation.

He took it, and wrapped his arms around her, kissing her soundly. The contact sent tingles to his toes and warmth into his weary limbs, but just as he tilted she withdrew. She smiled and stepped to the door.

"Beauty?" he called out.

She stopped with her hand on the handle. "Is there something else?"

"I missed you."

"I missed you too, Jack." Then she was gone.

Jack watched her slip from the room. As the door shut he sighed in regret and returned to the bed, sinking into its welcome softness. Unfortunately, sleep did not come easily. He'd told a partial truth to hide the whole truth, and hoped it would be enough to satisfy her. He finally fell asleep and dreamed of Ero and the Necrolith.

He woke when the door creaked open, and he groaned. Rubbing his eyes to clear his vision, he saw a form glide through the dim light and climb onto the bed, straddling him and leaning down over his face.

"Aranis," Jack said. "I thought I made my position clear."

"You did, pet," she whispered.

"Can you just kill me and let me get back to sleep?"

306

She smiled and traced a finger down his chest. "Assassins are preparing to strike," she said. "Apparently the bounty has been increased now that Ero disappeared."

Jack groaned and considered the consequences if he just stayed in bed. "How much time do we have?"

"A few minutes," Aranis said.

"Then it's time for you to choose a side," Jack said. "Kill me. Or join me."

She leaned down and kissed his cheek before pulling a knife into view. It glittered in the soft light of the room and Jack glanced at his weapons nearby, cursing himself for his fatigue. With a flick of her wrist she sent the knife spinning into the darkness.

A grunt of pain came from the blow and a small man tumbled into view, the knife in his throat. He choked as he died and went still, but Aranis never took her eyes off Jack. Then she flashed a disturbing smile.

"No one harms my pet."

Jack rose and she withdrew, allowing him to step to his clothes. She watched him change with a small smile on her lips. "Who was he?" Jack asked.

"Scout," she replied. "He was supposed to confirm you were here so the others could strike."

Jack grabbed his dagger and sheathed it along his spine. "When he doesn't come back, they won't wait for an invitation. I don't suppose you know their plan?"

She grinned as he pulled on his cloak. "They're going to burn you to the ground and search for your head in the ashes."

"They've given up on the subtle approach," he said.

"They've learned to fear you," she said.

307

Jack strode to the stairway, ascending to Beauty's room. He swung her door open without knocking and found Beauty standing beside a rack of weapons, in her nightclothes. She glared at him.

"Just because you're the guildmaster, doesn't mean you don't have to knock."

He laughed. "We have a situation."

She shoved him out the door and spoke through it. "Does this have to do with last night?"

"Last night?" Aranis said, stepping into the doorway and twirling a ring dagger.

Beauty swung the door open, now dressed in her thief blacks. She cinched the strap of her weapon and then caught sight of Aranis. She snatched her sword and pointed it at the dark elf.

"What is she doing here?"

Jack stepped between them before blood could be spilt. "We don't have time for this," he said. "Assassins are at our door."

Beauty slowly lowered her sword, her eyes turning hard. "Good. I could use a fight."

"Then you'll be disappointed," Jack said. "Get everyone up and use the Gate to get them out. Take anything of value, but keep it quiet."

"You want us to abandon the guildhall?" she asked.

"Too many know of its location," Jack said. "It's time we had a new one."

She skewered him with a look. "You ordered Forlana to take the valuables from this hall months ago. How long have you been planning this?"

"A while," Jack said. "Once everyone is gone, take Thalidon, Roarthin, and Ursana, and take the Gate north."

"Where are we going?" Beauty asked.

Jack pulled an envelope from his pocket and handed it to her. "Follow these and I'll use the Gate to get to you."

"You wrote something down?" she asked, incredulous. "Forlana will be shocked."

He grinned at her tone. "Contrary to rumor, my handwriting is readable. I'll meet you there."

"What about Sirani?" Beauty asked.

"She has her own assignment," Jack said, and then his voice gained an edge of warning. "Just make certain you follow my instructions *exactly*. No mistakes." He stabbed a finger at the envelope.

He knew he was asking a lot but she merely nodded and turned away. Smashing a fist on doors as she passed, she roused the other thieves. In seconds the hall was filled with thieves rushing about, many of whom cast curious looks at Aranis.

"They do not seem surprised at my presence," she murmured.

"Is that a smile I hear in your voice?" Jack asked.

"No."

Jack grinned. "Home is found among those you trust."

She grunted in irritation and looked away, so he turned and headed to the top of the guildhall. Aranis followed him as they wound their way through the sudden pandemonium of rushing thieves. When they reached the top floor of the guildhall Jack stepped onto a balcony and scanned the darkened forest.

"Do you have a plan for me?" Aranis asked.

Jack turned to face her. Her features beneath her cowl remained inscrutable, but the question cracked the shield she maintained. She *wanted* an assignment, not because she wanted to be around Jack, but because she needed a target. He considered her request as he searched the dark forest, and then inclined his head.

309

"Actually, there is something you can do," he said. "But it will mean returning to your homeland."

"What could you need from my homeland?"

"A friend," Jack said. "One that will aid us against Skorn."

"Who?"

Instead of answering, Jack withdrew a parchment and scribbled a note onto the paper. Once he was done he added the location of the Necrolith. Then he handed it to her. He couldn't see her eyes beneath her cowl, but her mouth parted in shock.

"Think you can find her?" Jack asked.

She pocketed the parchment. "It will take a few days."

"Hurry," Jack said. "You don't have much time."

The smile on her face betrayed a touch of eagerness. "I look forward to it."

Aranis withdrew into the shadows, evaporating as only a dark elf could. When she was gone Jack aimed at the trees and fired his shadowhook, soaring into the canopy of a nearby tree. Latching onto a branch, he watched the thieves slip away through the Gate.

Beauty left by the front door and descended to the ground, threading through the trees with a casual pace. Her striking features would command attention, and the bold exit undoubtedly drew the gaze of the hidden assassins. Jack noticed a trio of figures carefully lowering a large bound package behind the guildhall. When they reached the ground, the dwarves and Ursana evaporated into the night, taking the Gate with them. Last to go, Sirani strode down the steps and left, her unhurried pace causing a stir in the bushes that marked the assassins' presence.

The silence persisted, and Jack could almost hear the assassins debating their course of action. Wait or strike? Ten minutes went by before they chose the latter. A spark of light ignited on the ground, briefly illuminating a quartet of dwarves and a horde of men, goblins, and elves. The dwarves cast their charm and a streak of fire soared

310

toward the guildhall like a flaming lance. It thudded into the wall above a window, sparking and glowing before detonating.

Half the structure disappeared in a ball of smoke and fire. The trees that held the guildhall recoiled like a fighter struck in the jaw. Shouts erupted beneath the guildhall as men and elves kicked down the front door and filed inside, the elves using their magic to extinguish the flames.

Jack smirked as their shouts of triumph turned to rage. They rushed about in a vain attempt to find anyone, clearly searching for Jack's body. Someone roared in fury as the top floor succumbed to the flames, sending sparks filtering into the canopy, igniting leaves and branches.

Screams rang out from nearby homes and answering shouts echoed. The distant thudding of boots echoed as water mages from the city rushed toward the fire. The assassins abandoned the guildhall, escaping like roaches before a torch. Jack grinned as he watched them go, his gaze lifting to the ruined guildhall. The walls were caved in and flames had consumed the trees, scorching the trunks.

He sighed and pulled his pocket Gate into view. Activating its magic, he waited for the silver liquid to flow into shape. Then he stepped into the mirror and disappeared from view, the Gate closing behind him. In his wake the guildhall continued to burn.

Chapter 39: To War

Beauty ensured the Gate was loaded into a rented wagon, and then strode to her horse. Thalidon climbed onto the driver's bench and flicked the reins, easing the horses onto the northern road. Beauty grabbed Axe's saddle and leapt to his back, but paused to look at the burning guildhall.

Smoke climbed into the distance and fire glowed through the foliage. Elven water mages pulled from a nearby river, sending sprays of water splashing into the devastated guildhall. Steam mingled with the smoke billowing into the sky.

"What are you up to, Jack?" she murmured.

Shaking her head, she pulled the reins, guiding the horse onto the road. The dwarves drove the wagon while Ursana rode a horse behind it. Beauty brought up the rear, her thoughts on what Jack had revealed. He'd trusted her with the truth, but she knew it wasn't the whole truth. Despite his secrecy she was grateful for the revelations, not for what he said, but for what he didn't say.

Jack wasn't withholding the truth out of fear, he was doing it out of foresight. Jack's greatest talent was his cunning, and this time he'd planned months ahead—a surprisingly cautious plan, especially for him. A faint smile crossed her face as she realized how much she'd underestimated him, again.

"What's the smile for?" Ursana asked, slowing her horse to ride beside her.

"Just realizing that in spite of everything I've seen him do, Jack still surprises me."

Ursana laughed lightly. "You'd think a man tracked by assassins and hunted by a devil would be fighting for survival. Instead he manages to think ahead of everyone."

Beauty motioned to the forest around them. "Most trees grow where the soil is soft and easy, while some manage to find purchase on rock. I've never known one that thrives in the tempest and feeds on fire."

"Danger is like food for him," Ursana agreed. "It's the reason he'll triumph over Skorn."

"You really believe that?" she asked. "You saw the army he brought to the Church of Light. He's bound to have far more at the Necrolith—and we just have our guild."

"I have no idea how," Ursana said. "But I don't need to know. I trust Jack"

Beauty raised an eyebrow. "How did you gain such faith in him?"

"The first time he climbed the Machine. Do you remember?"

Beauty grinned. "He climbed a killing wall and made it look easy."

"I looked at the wall and saw an obstacle," Ursana said, "a foe that would test my mettle. But I think Jack saw the Machine like an exotic meal, one to be savored for its spice."

"When did you become so wise?" Beauty asked, casting the girl an appraising look.

"Those were actually Gordon's words." Ursana smiled before looking away.

"I think you should talk to—"

"I'd rather not talk about it," she said.

Beauty threw her a look and saw the emotions written on her face. She thought the girl would speak but the seconds passed into minutes and still Ursana held her tongue. With a sigh Beauty turned her thoughts back to Jack.

They journeyed north until they reached the Giant's Shelf and followed its curve west, away from elven lands. With the great cliff on one side and the sea on the other, the narrow road showed signs of age and disrepair, the ruts from wagon wheels deep and filled with rainwater.

They pressed on until dawn, when they reached a village outside of elven lands. Small and containing a motley assortment of races, the village was not part of any kingdom. Fishermen were already at their boats, unfurling their sails and pulling out to sea. Shopkeepers bustled about, opening doors and placing their wares on counters for display. Several carts ambled down the street with produce from nearby farms. Thalidon brought the horses to a halt beside an inn. With a groan he descended to the street and strode to Beauty. She descended to join him and patted Axe on the neck.

"Boron owns this place," Thalidon said. "He's an old thief contact. We can stay here for a day or two."

"Any chance he'll tell Skorn's followers?"

Thalidon shook his head. "He got out before Skorn took over."

A dwarf appeared in the inn's door and rumbled a laugh. Dressed in a strange combination of armor and apron, the dwarf had his beard and hair braided. Stains flecked his clothing like a meal had exploded as he cooked.

"My two least favorite dwarves," he said with a hearty laugh. "What brings you to my door?"

"Need a place to stay for a few days," Thalidon said.

"It'll cost you a keg of your family's finest," the dwarf replied.

"I thought we were friends," Roarthin said.

"Care to make it two kegs?"

Roarthin laughed and inclined his head. "You'll get your payment."

Boron stabbed a thumb toward the alley adjacent to the inn. "You can stable your wagon and horses in the back. Thalidon, you know where to put them."

Thalidon lowered his voice and leaned close to Beauty. "There's a second stables hidden beneath the ground. The Gate will be safe."

Boron gestured to them. "I'll have four rooms prepared for you."

"Make that two," Beauty called. "My companion and I must press on."

Boron nodded and entered the inn. When he was gone Ursana dismounted and stepped close to Beauty.

"Please tell me we aren't going to keep riding," she said, her words distorted by a yawn.

"No," Beauty said. "You and I are going to the Evermist guildhall."

"Why?" she asked.

Beauty thought of the instructions Jack had given her. "We have work to do."

Thalidon climbed onto the driver's bench of the wagon and flicked the reins, turning the horses down the alley to the rear of the inn. A barn sat at the base of a hill, its bulk sufficient to house several steeds. Thalidon strode inside and went to the workroom, fumbling for a latch. It clicked, and a section of the floor rose to reveal a ramp disappearing into a subterranean level. Roarthin kept his hand on the brake as he eased the wagon down the ramp.

Beauty dismounted and led Axe into a stall. As the dwarves unhitched the horses from the wagon, Beauty wearily cared for Axe. By the time she finished she could barely keep her eyes open. Leaving him behind, she found Ursana sitting on a bench, fast asleep.

"She's exhausted," Thalidon murmured.

"She's not the only one," Beauty said, rubbing her eyes. "Sometimes I envy your dwarven endurance."

315

Thalidon smirked and lowered his voice. "Why do you want to take Ursana with you? She obviously needs to rest, especially if we're going against Skorn."

"We'll be back tomorrow," Beauty said.

"Is this Jack's doing?" Roarthin asked, wiping his hands as he stepped to join them.

"It is," Beauty said, nudging her.

Ursana jerked awake. "Can I go to sleep yet?"

"Not yet," Beauty said with a smile. "But the good news is that you get to sleep in your own bed."

Ursana reluctantly rose to her feet and joined Beauty at the wagon. Climbing into the back, Beauty stepped over the handful of weapons and gear to the large mirror. Then she touched the rune that connected the Gate to the one in the Evermist. The mirror rippled like water before returning to its smooth surface, and Beauty stepped through the portal. She exited into a room packed with crates and gear, the last of the valuables from the Woodhaven guildhall. A moment later Ursana joined her.

Forlana looked up at her appearance. "I wasn't expecting you."

"I'm going to bed," Ursana said, slipping past Forlana and stifling a yawn.

Forlana raised an eyebrow as Ursana left. "Are you up late or early?"

"Late," Beauty said. "But there are some things I need to do."

Forlana swept a hand at the abundance of crates. "I've already got my hands full," she said. "There's an entire guildhall's worth of things to deal with."

Kuraltus suddenly appeared between the piles, his eyes on a hand crossbow that had been in the Woodhaven guildhall. Apparently not noticing Beauty, he strode up to Forlana and set it down. Then he

316

wrapped an arm around Forlana and kissed her. When he pulled away he smiled.

"Now that we're alone . . ."

Beauty coughed, causing Kuraltus to spin and face her. The elf flushed and straightened. "I can explain," he said hastily.

"No need," Beauty said in amusement. "How long has this been going on?"

They exchanged a look. "A few months," Forlana admitted.

"Why keep it secret?" Beauty asked. They shifted uncomfortably and Beauty grinned. "Your secret is safe with me."

"What brought you back?" Kuraltus said, obviously attempting to change the subject.

"Summon every class three to Ember Hall," she said.

Forlana's eyes widened in surprise. "That will take time. Some are out on assignments."

Beauty nodded. "Wake me when they're ready." Then she turned and picked her way through the crates, but Forlana caught her at the door.

"What's going on?" Forlana asked.

Beauty pointed to the Gate. "We found Skorn."

Forlana's features turned determined. "I'll summon them."

Beauty nodded in gratitude and ascended through the fortress, making her way to her room. Stripping her gear and outer clothing, she collapsed into the bed and welcomed unconsciousness. She slept fitfully, her dreams filled with her father and Jack. A knock at the door roused her and she sat up in the bed.

"Come in," she called.

The door swung open and Forlana strode inside. "The last of them just arrived. They're gathering in Ember Hall now."

317

Beauty nodded and rose to her feet. "I'll be there in a moment."

"Where's Jack?" Forlana asked. "They trust you, but they're expecting him."

"I have no idea where he is," Beauty said with a sigh. "But he gave me a message to deliver."

Forlana's smile faded and she reached into a pouch at her side. "Like this message?" she held aloft a scrap of parchment.

Beauty raised an eyebrow and held her own instructions aloft. "I thought Jack hated paperwork."

"He does," Forlana said.

"What does yours say?" Beauty asked.

Forlana hesitated before shaking her head. "He forbade me from sharing it."

"Mine says the same," Beauty said.

"I suspect that soon we'll know everything."

Beauty felt the same note of finality, as if they had entered the final hour before a storm. She stood and began to dress, gathering her gear and checking every weapon. She felt a touch of nervousness, but surprisingly it was faith that dominated her emotions. Jack had a plan, and merely needed her to carry it out. Catching up Jack's instructions, she turned to Forlana.

"I'm ready."

Beauty entered the hall and Forlana fell into step beside her. Together, they strode down the corridor and descended to Ember Hall, exiting onto a balcony overlooking the space. She came to a halt at the rail overlooking the thieves gathered at the base of the hall. They stilled at her appearance and looked up to her.

Beauty felt a chill as she spoke. "Skorn has built the Necrolith, a beacon that will summon the ancient race. He has gathered cult members, Talinorian mercenaries, the Assassins Guild led by Gallow,

318

and a mighty barbarian chief. We are outnumbered and our foe has an army at his command. The threat is more dire than anything the guild has ever faced. But the Guildmaster has us."

Her words echoed into silence and her challenging gaze swept across them. They stared at her without fear or doubt, and several smiled as if eager for the impending battle.

"When do we depart?" someone called.

"We're ready."

"He's our guildmaster," another said.

Beauty smiled at their loyalty, and she spotted Ursana with a grin on her face.

"Where are we going?" Slyver asked, stepping to the front of the group.

Beauty turned to him, her answer sending a chill through the room.

"To war."

Chapter 40: The Necrolith

Beauty left Ember Hall in the hands of the higher ranked thieves and made her way to her bedchamber. She changed into a supple armor and gathered her steel, choosing each blade with great care. Then she grabbed her hand crossbow and loaded every bolt, checking each rune before sliding it into the pocket in her sleeve.

She donned her cloak and looked into the mirror, staring at her reflection. Knives dotted her torso, her dagger sat on her hip, and her sword lay on her back. Armed to the teeth, she was ready for war.

But not her father.

She sighed and turned away, entering the hallway to find it filled with bustling thieves. They rushed about, gathering weapons and supplies, their motions laced with anticipation, even excitement. She wanted to feel the same, but her mind was drawn to Skorn at the Church of Light. He'd amassed a formidable army. Although they hailed from different factions, they were united under his banner. The Thieves Guild numbered a few hundred, and although many were talented in combat, few could match up to the barbarians, cultists trained by Gallow, and Talinorian mercenaries.

The Thieves Guild was walking into a slaughter—yet they did so with excitement in every step. She knew it was because of their faith in Jack, but it seemed hopeless. How could Jack possibly outwit an army?

"Still doubting Jack?" Ursana asked.

Beauty turned to look at her, lowering her voice so the passing thieves would not hear. "You saw what we faced at the Church of Light. He has an army."

"We have a Jack."

"You think that's enough?"

"It's the devil of Lumineia against a master thief," Ursana said with a smile. "Skorn doesn't stand a chance."

Beauty laughed at the confidence in her voice. "Who am I to argue with faith like that?"

"Don't argue with her," Gordon said, appearing beside them. "She has a habit of winning."

"I've got to go," Ursana said, slipping past him.

"Ursana," Gordon said, catching her arm. "Are we going together?"

"There's no together anymore," Ursana said.

He winced and let go, and Ursana strode away.

"Ursana," Beauty called. "You need to talk to him."

She came to a halt and rotated back. "Is that why you insisted I come back? Because you want me to work with him again?"

"You have to," Beauty said.

"Are you *ordering* me?" Ursana demanded.

Beauty thought of the fourth item on her list. "On the contrary," she said, "the order comes from your guildmaster."

Ursana's eyes widened. "Jack?"

"You have faith in him or you don't," Beauty said.

Ursana's eyes flicked to Gordon. "I'll meet you at the Gate." She ground the words out. Then she spun and departed.

In her absence Gordon passed a hand over his face. "Ursana was my family. Now I have two—and they are both angry with me."

"Don't ask me for advice," Beauty said. "My father wants to kill me."

He laughed bitterly. "My wife thinks I should leave the guildhall, my daughter doesn't understand why we're going after Skorn, and Ursana wants nothing to do with me."

"You don't have to come," Beauty said.

"I'm not letting Ursana face Skorn without me at her side."

Beauty grinned at the force to his words. "Then I'll see you soon."

He nodded and strode away, and Beauty turned down the path to the Gate room. The hall was already lined with supplies, and she threaded her way through the mass of bodies and crates to the end of the hall, where Slyver caught her attention. Forlana had wisely moved the Gate to a more accessible location than the chamber at the bottom of the well, and Beauty motioned Slyver inside the new Gateroom. When he joined her, she shut the door and turned to him.

"Any idea what we are going to face on the other side?" Slyver asked. "You were light on the details."

She shook her head. "You know as much as I do."

Slyver frowned and tapped his sword hilt. "I don't care to start a fight without knowing the opponent."

"Neither do I," Beauty said. "But Jack has his reasons for keeping us in the dark."

Slyver shook his head, his expression doubtful. "We'll be ready for your summons."

Beauty nodded in gratitude and then stepped past him to the mirror. Pressing the correct rune, she waited for the glass to ripple and then stepped into the wagon she'd left earlier that day. It was already moving, and she lifted the flap at the back to find her horse trotting behind the wagon. Leaping onto it, she untied the reins and directed her mount past the wagon.

"I thought I heard someone come through," Thalidon said with a grunt.

"The Thieves Guild is preparing for war," she said. "Any idea how much further?"

"According to this," Thalidon fished a scrap of parchment from his pocket, "we've got three days ride."

"You got one of those as well?" Beauty asked.

"His handwriting is terrible," Thalidon said with a laugh, which Roarthin shared.

"It's worse than mine," Roarthin agreed.

Beauty grinned. "I'll scout ahead. The closer we get to the Necrolith, the more likely we are to find sentries."

"Don't get killed," Thalidon said.

"I don't intend to," Beauty replied. "I'll bind any I find and leave them in the road. Send them back through the Gate, would you?"

She flicked the reins, spurring Axe into a trot. The road climbed into the mountains west of elven lands, ascending through a forest of pine and elder trees. Gaps in the foliage provided brief glimpses of the southern sea, its crystalline waters blinding in the afternoon sun.

She cast a listening charm, enhancing her hearing to that of a hound. Her ears tingled as her magic flowed into them and she suddenly heard the rustle of branches, the skittering of rodents, even the distant cough of a panther. With the charm active she would hear a sentry's clothes rub on skin from half a mile away.

It was the first time she had been alone in months, and as the miles passed her tensions eased. The last few months had been a whirlwind of threats and combat, yet the current calm did not bring peace.

She sighed, her thoughts turning to Jack. The man was an enticing enigma, one she harbored strong feelings for, but he was not the sole thread tied to her heart. She missed her brother, Golic, and yearned for her homeland. The warm summers and even the harsh winters called to her, as did her people.

She recalled Valia, a cousin and friend. They had trained together as children, and the girl had privately shared how much she despised their people's traditions. It was the first time Beauty had realized she was not alone. It was a dangerous secret, one that merited a swift death by the clan. Others shared the same sentiment, but as they passed from childhood they all fell silent, denying they had ever voiced it.

But once she'd seen the truth, it could not be unseen. Many of her people felt as she did, but the legacy of tradition was too ingrained, and no one dared defy it. She may have lost her sister, but her clan was her family, and they were shackled to the tradition of battle. Once her father was gone, she could go back and aid Golic's army.

She fleetingly wondered how Jack would fight her father. Oragon had defeated countless mighty foes, and even slain a dragon, yet Jack always seemed to triumph even against the impossible.

She relished the idea of a duel between Oragon and Jack, imagining how Jack would defeat her father, a victor of a thousand battles. She realized it provided insight into how she could defeat him, and she laughed in chagrin. If she admitted that to Jack, he would never let her forget it.

The distinct sound of a boot caught her attention, and she brought Axe to a halt. Dismounting, she cast a speed charm and sprinted through the trees, following a curved path to reach the sentry. She was not surprised to find a pair of cult members hiding adjacent to the trail. She crept up behind them and disarmed them, leaving them bound, hooded, and gagged in the middle of the road. Then she returned to Axe and pressed on.

Throughout the next three days the frequency of sentries increased, and increased in skill. It took all her ability to deal with them quietly, clearing the way for the dwarves and the wagon carrying the precious Gate.

The road paralleled the curve of the sea but the terrain grew increasingly mountainous. Hills topped with trees and brush gave way to cliffs of granite. The road cut into the stone as it switched back to manage the ascent.

At the top of a cliff the road continued west until arriving at the ruins of an ancient castle overlooking the sea. Worn and aged with time, the dilapidated fortress clung to life. The keep was gone, as were most of the walls. Corridors and tunnels crisscrossed their way beneath the ground, some having caved in to leave gaping holes in the earth. The gates were an unrecognizable mass of twisted metal beneath a faded arch. The road continued beyond the citadel, but it dropped to little more than a game trail. There was no sign to indicate the castle's identity, but she knew the name from Jack's instructions.

Seastone.

She spotted a handful of men and women lurking in the ruins. Withdrawing before she was seen, she made her way to the cliff, crouching to peer over the edge. A winding road descended a hundred-foot escarpment to the village on the coast below. Although parts of the village showed the same level of ruin as the fortress, many of the buildings were new. In the setting sun she spotted hundreds of mages laboring under the watchful eye of armed guards.

Her lips tightened as she estimated their numbers. More than five hundred cult members were visible in the village and on the beach, with many working on tubes of pulsing light that disappeared into the water. A pair of newly constructed docks stretched into the water nearby, with a trio of ships lashed to them. She scanned the crowd for her father and spotted several hulking barbarians, but none carried the familiar maul.

She frowned, her eyes flicking between the village and the ruins. Skorn's army had been building the Necrolith for months, yet had little to show for their efforts. Or perhaps Jack was wrong, and this was merely a launching area for a site offshore. But if so, where was the Necrolith?

The sun was setting on the horizon, so she eased away from the cliff and retreated east, searching for a campsite where she could watch the village. She found a curve of stone hidden behind a copse of trees, and led her steed to it. She removed Axe's saddle and tied him to a tree. Then she withdrew a strip of dried beef and took a bite, chewing as she considered what to do. The thieves were geared for war, but without a destination the effort would be futile. Was Jack wrong . . .?

A distant rumbling drew her gaze, and Beauty snapped to look at the sea. Rising to her feet, she glided to the cliff. She drifted into the shadow cast by a great oak and watched the darkening ocean.

Another rumble echoed, sending a shudder through the waves of the sea. Beauty's eyes widened when she spotted an object rising from the depths near the village. It pierced the surface of the water, its metallic surface glistening. It passed twenty feet, then thirty.

And kept rising.

The base of the obelisk suddenly swelled outward, revealing a pyramid base that lifted the obelisk from the sea, its sides reaching all the way to the beach. Seawater cascaded down the walls of the obelisk and black pyramid. Beauty sucked in her breath as it ascended higher than the cliff she stood on, and she had to look up to keep the summit in view. Then abruptly it came to a halt, and the distant clanking of machinery locked into place.

She stared at the structure, shocked by its sheer size. It rivaled the castle in Herosian in height, and could have housed the entire Evermist guildhall. Windows dotted the surface of the obelisk and pyramid, and faint lights glowed from within. A shout rang out from the beach below, a cry of worship from the cult members. The sound caused Beauty to shiver.

The Necrolith had risen.

Chapter 41: Seastone

Beauty watched the Necrolith until a patrol of sentries forced her away. She retreated to Axe and saddled him, hurrying back down the road. Four hours later she spotted a pinprick of light through the trees and exited the road. Before she'd taken ten steps a metallic wolf stepped into her path.

"I see Roarthin posted sentries," she said.

The wolf sniffed her and Axe before padding away, and she dismounted. Leading Axe through the trees, she brought him to the fire and tied him to a tree. Thalidon looked up from the pot he was stirring and motioned her to a seat by the fire. Retrieving a bowl from his pack he filled it and offered it to her.

"Did you find the Necrolith?" he asked.

"I did," she said.

Beauty detailed what she had seen as they shared a meal, and the dwarves gradually lost their smiles. When she finished they sat in silence, their stew cooling in forgotten bowls. Then Roarthin grunted.

"How many in his army?" he asked.

"At least a thousand in the village and the ruins," she replied. "But the Necrolith is large enough to house four times that number."

"We have four hundred," Thalidon said. "At best."

"And they have the defensive position," Roarthin said with a scowl.

"Let's hope Jack has a plan for this," Beauty said.

"Where is he?" Thalidon asked. "We can't exactly assault the Necrolith without our guildmaster."

Beauty had no answer, and as they speculated on Jack's absence she found herself wondering how Jack knew so much about the Necrolith. His list had included detailed directions to its location, and even contained instructions on when the assault should begin.

"We have until tomorrow morning," Beauty finally said.

"To do what?" Roarthin asked.

"We take the ruins at sunrise," she replied. "Then we wait."

Thalidon leaned back against a log. "Even if we take the ruins without discovery, it won't be long before Skorn's army notices our presence. They will retaliate, and even with the Gate we will not be able to escape."

Beauty considered her answer, recognizing the moment as a precipice. If she planned the assault on the ruins it would put the entire Thieves Guild in a dangerous position, risking everything on Jack's mysterious plan. Or she could act contrary to Jack's instructions and the thieves would obey her, potentially saving their lives.

She felt the insane urge to laugh, realizing that the moment had come. She had to trust Jack . . . or forsake him. Doubt assailed her, and abruptly she realized it came from her youth. Every day she'd been trained to live with caution, to trust her instincts. But Jack was asking her to act with an entirely different emotion.

Faith.

She thought of every time he'd snatched victory from defeat, and every time he'd saved her life. And done so with a smile. Everyone in the guild seemed to trust him, and now it was her turn. Despite her instincts, she nodded.

"We'll clear the ruins at dawn," she said. "Then we strike."

Thalidon measured her response. "Are you certain?"

She should have been concerned but instead it was a smile that crossed her face. "I am."

The dwarves exchanged a look and nodded in unison. Then Roarthin gestured outward. "We cast entities to watch our camp. Get some sleep. We're going to need it."

She unrolled her bedroll and lay down with her back to a gnarled oak. It should have been difficult to sleep but she was out in seconds, and woke when Roarthin touched her shoulder. She blinked awake and his bearded features came into focus.

"It's time."

She rose and donned her cloak, accepting the crust of bread and wedge of cheese from Roarthin. They ate in silence, and Beauty looked to the sky to gauge the time. Light had yet to touch the horizon but the constellations indicated sunrise was imminent. She finished the bread and then stood, and the dwarves stood with her.

"Roarthin," she said. "You're with me. Thalidon, bring the guild through and lead them to the ruins."

"As you order," they said, and Roarthin followed Beauty from the camp.

As they left the camp, Beauty looked back. Thalidon stripped the top off the wagon and pressed the rune leading to the Evermist guildhall. A moment later thieves poured into view, stepping onto the wagon before dropping to the ground. Ten became twenty, and then she lost count.

Beauty turned away and returned to Axe, putting the saddle on and climbing onto the steed's back. Roarthin mounted another horse and together they guided their horses to the road. She cast a sound charm, tuning her ears to the darkened forest. She smiled when she heard a padding of metallic footfalls and spotted a flicker of movement.

"Why wolves?" she asked.

"I like wolves," Roarthin said, and smiled. "They remind me of a girl I once knew."

She laughed, suspecting there was more to that tale. They trotted up the road in silence until she cast him a look. "Are you here for Skorn . . . or Jack?"

"I could ask the same of you," he replied with a grunt of amusement. "Skorn killed your sister, after all."

"And Skorn imprisoned you for two decades just to ensure obedience from Thalidon."

"I would love to say that I'm here for Skorn," Roarthin said. "But I find myself inspired by a thief."

She laughed in chagrin. "You aren't the only one."

He grinned and they turned their attention to the road ahead. Beauty had dealt with the sentries and Thalidon had taken the unconscious forms back through the Gate, but the sudden absence of the guards had likely already been noticed.

They left the horses half a mile from Seastone and approached on foot, easing into a vantage point on the hill above the ruins. For several minutes they watched the guards patrolling the ancient fortress.

"Same as yesterday," she murmured. "Only ten left to guard the ruins."

Thalidon's bushy eyebrows were knit in thought. "They should have noticed the sentries were gone."

"He knows we're coming," Beauty realized.

"The question is, did Jack expect this?"

She smiled. "I suspect he did."

He drew his axe and twirled it in his hand. "Don't forget, these aren't hired men simply doing a job. These are cult members committed to the cause of Skorn. If you are not lethal, they will be."

"I'm a barbarian," she said. "Remember? I've probably been in more battles than you."

He grunted in agreement. "I'll slip around the back and come from the north."

"I'll go in through the main gate."

Roarthin nodded and slipped away, his two wolf entities following him out of sight. Beauty stepped from the trees and worked her way down the slope, reaching the gate as one of the cult members stepped into view. Beauty darted in and swung her sword, striking low. Despite her words to Roarthin she hesitated, striking for the man's leg.

"Stay silent," she growled as the man fell.

His face twisted in pain, the man fumbled for a dagger. "Intruder!" he cried, and raised the blade.

Beauty growled to herself and deflected the dagger, plunging her sword into his heart before leaping toward the sounds of running men. Part of being a thief was combat—but not killing—and she realized she'd lost the edge she'd gained as a barbarian. It was disturbing how quickly it came back.

A man turned a corner and raised a sword, howling as he lunged for her. Beauty angled her body, allowing the blade to slide past her as she rotated inside his guard. She swept her sword across his stomach and twirled around him, driving her weapon into the next man that appeared. She leaned into a kick, sending his body into the woman behind him, flicking her crossbow into her palm. She fired a single bolt into the woman's throat and leapt over them, casting speed as a trio of cultists aimed crossbows at her.

Dodging bolts, she leapt to a hole in the ground and dropped into a tunnel, sprinting through the corridor littered by aged stone and moldy beams. She heard someone drop into the tunnel behind her and twisted, firing a bolt at the same time they did. Hers found its mark. His didn't.

The man grunted in surprise and went down, and Beauty dropped speed in favor of strength, leaping through a hole in the ceiling to land in the courtyard. The other crossbowmen turned on her, but she darted to a ruined wall and leapt above it, alighting next to one of cult members. She caught his crossbow and turned it aside, forcing him to fire into his companion on the next wall. Then she sank her sword into his body and hurled him to the courtyard stones below.

She dropped down after him, rolling to absorb the impact. Then she spotted a dwarf striding toward her, fire blossoming in his hands. The flames formed into a shimmering blade as he advanced upon her.

"You have no idea what you are up against," he snarled.

Beauty leapt to a wall, kicking off it and spinning, hurling her sword with lethal precision. The sword plunged into the dwarf's chest and he tumbled backward, his fire blade dissipating into smoke. As he gasped for life she strode to him and pulled her sword free.

"Neither do you," she said.

Roarthin appeared at her side. "You could have left some for me," he said. He wiped the blood from his axe on the dead dwarf's tunic.

She ignored him and strode to the cliff, peering down the winding path to the village below. Shouts echoed off the Necrolith and men rushed about, clearly gathering into ranks. She released an explosive breath and turned to Roarthin.

"They're coming for us," she said.

They both turned when the clopping of a horse sounded on the road. Roarthin smiled, "At least the Thieves Guild is here."

They exited Seastone and stepped onto the road, but came to a halt when they spotted the approaching riders. Roarthin summoned his wolves and twirled his axe.

"Those aren't ours," he said.

"But they're mine," she breathed.

Tears blossomed in her eyes as Golic dismounted and strode to her, engulfing her in a huge embrace. He set her down and grinned, the expression remarkably like when they were children. Now he towered over the barbarians dismounting with him.

"Who brought you here?" she asked.

"Who else?" Golic asked with a shrug, and held aloft a piece of parchment.

She stared at the scrawl of Jack's writing, shocked to realize Jack had stretched beyond the Thieves Guild for aid. Golic grinned at her stunned silence and gestured to the barbarians that formed up behind him.

"Father is here," she said.

"We know," Golic said. "And we are ready for him."

Beauty's gaze swept the group, and saw many faces she knew. Then she spotted Valia, and the girl stepped forward, inclining her head. The girl was now a woman dressed for war. Blue paint marked her flesh like a beast had raked its claws across her features. Her fearsome appearance contrasted sharply with her smile.

"Thera," she said. "I hope you have a good battle for us."

"We are assaulting a superior position and are outnumbered," she said. "Even with your aid."

"What about everyone else?" Golic asked in confusion.

"Who?" Beauty asked.

Golic and Valia turned and pointed back down the road, where others were just appearing at the bend. Beauty's eyes widened when she spotted hundreds of soldiers rounding the curve. Their disparate uniforms marked them as coming from different kingdoms and guilds. There was even a group of rock trolls striding in their midst. Roarthin began to laugh, his entire frame shaking with amusement.

"It appears Jack brought his own army."

Chapter 42: A Thief's Army

The barbarians retreated before the rock trolls, their hands on their swords. The lead rock troll ignored them and strode to Beauty, flicking his hand to his companions. The rock trolls spread out and advanced into the ruins, obviously checking for threats.

"Thorvaldur," the leader said, inclining his head as he identified himself.

"Why are you here?" Beauty asked, staring up at the massive troll.

The rock troll lifted a scrap of parchment and handed it to her. "I received a summons from Jack Myst," he said, a smile playing on his features.

"And you came?"

"Life is always intriguing when he is involved."

"You can say that again," Sirani said, speeding to join them in a gust of wind. "Where is our handsome devil, anyway?"

"Not here," Beauty said, causing Sirani to pout.

"We cannot start the festivities without him."

"We may have to," Beauty said. "I believe he has another assignment."

Another rock troll appeared at Thorvaldur's side. "Skorn's army is on the beach below. They were preparing to charge but are now aware of our presence. They await our advance." She then turned to Beauty and grinned. "Jack's last invitation proved to be interesting. We could not pass up another."

Beauty blinked in sudden understanding. "You were the trolls at Margauth."

"A fine battle," the female troll said.

"I never got the chance to thank you," Beauty said. "I'm sure you don't normally contract with thieves."

The two trolls exchanged a smile. "King Tryton was . . . irritated, but I think he understood. Kythira was another matter."

Beauty laughed wryly, recalling that Jack had infiltrated the king's quarters to steal the contract. Kythira's children had been sleeping in a nearby bedchamber, and she'd responded with the fury of a protective mother. Jack had narrowly escaped.

"I'm grateful you have come," she said, and motioned to Golic. "This is my brother. I suspect the two of you have the most combat experience. May I ask that you lead the battle?"

The rock troll peaked an eyebrow. "You won't take that honor for yourself?"

"I have a different assignment," she said. "But I'm confident that you and Golic will do better than I."

Hearing his name, Golic stepped close. He stood well over six feet tall, his huge body dwarfing the other barbarians. But he had to look up to meet the eyes of Thorvaldur. To his credit he did not flinch.

"I've always wanted to meet one of your kind," Golic said.

Thorvaldur grinned. "I as well. Do you really battle in the snow?"

"Frequently," Golic said with a laugh.

As the two warriors strode toward the ruins of Seastone, Roarthin stepped in and lowered his tone.

"They may hail from different races, but those two bear a striking resemblance."

Beauty grinned and turned to address the next group ascending the road. The force of mercenaries were from Griffin, and apparently had been hired by Jack. The man despised the Talinorian mercenaries and told Jack he would take the contract.

The next group was dwarven, their leader a white-haired smith named Urthor. Brilliant and shimmering in the dawn light, his axe drew the gaze of everyone around. The other dwarves were equally as armed, and she got the impression they were all smiths. The crotchety dwarves hurled insults at Roarthin, who returned them with a smile on his face.

More allies continued to arrive, and from every corner of Lumineia. Val'Trisian appeared with a contingent of dark elves, while Paro and the remaining abbots of the Church of Light came in armor and geared for war. There was even a quartet of librarians from the Library of Worchestan that arrived with staff and sword. The weathered old man leading them was spry for his age, and seemed eager for the impending battle.

A small group of elves came from the elven mage guild, and said they'd come on behalf of an old friend. Shortly afterward Ursana arrived with Gordon—and Rista and Gwen. Beauty raised an eyebrow to Ursana, but the girl would not meet her gaze.

The soldiers of Talinor kept looking at their orders, clearly doubting their veracity. The Griffin army had brought an equally large force, and the two groups cast uncertain glances at each other.

Some came for coin, others for adventure, but most came for Jack. All carried scraps of parchment with Jack's handwriting scrawled across them. Thieves from the guild mingled with the strange army, the conversation laced with laughter and tales of Jack Myst, the atmosphere almost festive.

As their ranks swelled Beauty found it difficult to speak. Jack Myst was a thief renowned for provoking others, yet he'd managed to cobble together an assortment of races and creeds under a single banner.

Thalidon appeared, leading the wagon that held the Gate, the mirror once again hidden under the wagon's covering. He pulled the wagon off the road and dropped to the ground. For a long moment he stood in mute shock, staring at the army swarming the ruins. Then he approached Beauty.

"What happened?"

"They just showed up," she replied. "Came to join the battle."

"Jack?"

She nodded. "Jack."

He released a belly laugh. "He never ceases to surprise, does he."

Inna strode to Beauty, and the assassin's shock matched Beauty's. "I never thought I'd see thousands ready to fight for a thief."

"Least of all one like Jack," Forlana said.

Dressed in armored thief blacks, Forlana and Kuraltus joined Beauty. Both looked ready for combat, and carried additional daggers in various sheaths. Beauty noticed their proximity and suppressed a smile.

"The rock troll and the barbarian have a battle strategy," Kuraltus said. "They just disagree on who should lead the charge."

Abruptly a dark elf stepped from the shadows and came to Beauty's side. Everyone retreated at Aranis's appearance and Inna drew her sword, but the dark elf assassin smiled beneath her cowl.

"I'm a friend," she said. "Today at least."

"Let me guess," Inna said. "You're here for Jack?"

"I am," she said. "But I didn't come alone."

A rumbling snarl came from the trees and Beauty spun to face the threat. Fear lanced through her body as a massive beast stalked into view, its jaws bared to reveal metallic teeth. Beauty swallowed and retreated, drawing her blade in a smooth motion.

"You brought a *black reaver*?" Thalidon growled, fire blossoming in his hands.

I'm here at Jack's request, dwarf.

Beauty flinched as the beast spoke into her mind, surprised at the female voice. Then she noticed the scars across the animal's arms and chips in the steel spikes protruding from its back—and realized why the beast looked familiar. She lowered her sword.

"Triskella?"

How do you know my name? she growled, causing Beauty to retreat a step.

"I was there when Jack freed you from the dark elves," she said, her tone placating.

The reaver cocked her head to the side. *An ally of Jack's is an ally of mine.*

Shouts rang out as the other forces caught sight of the reaver, instinctively closing ranks. Crossbowmen hastily armed their weapons while the rock trolls and barbarians leapt to the front, their weapons pointed at the huge reaver. Triskella sank onto her haunches and swiveled her head to Beauty.

I'm here to kill an army, the reaver said, *I'd rather it not be Jack's.*

Beauty leapt in front of her and raised her hand to the army. "This is Triskella, and she's here for the same reason we are."

The captain from Griffin called out, "It will turn on us. We won't fight beside a devil beast."

The reaver snarled and the man stumbled back. "You fight with her, or you go your own way," Beauty said.

The captain spit on the earth but reluctantly shook his head. "We have our orders."

"Even if Jack forged them," Thalidon murmured, hiding a smile.

Thorvaldur and Golic exchanged a look, and then Golic nodded. "If Triskella is willing, she can lead the charge."

It will be my pleasure, Triskella said.

Thalidon nodded. "It seems we are just waiting on Jack."

"He's not coming," Beauty said.

Thalidon raised an eyebrow. "Where is he?"

A distant shout drew her attention and Beauty strode to the edge of Seastone, leaning over to peer at the army gathered on the beach below. They had begun to shout and smash weapons on shields, clearly itching for the battle to begin. As the light of dawn spilled onto the area Thorvaldur released a chuckle of anticipation.

"It appears they have underestimated Jack's resourcefulness."

Beauty turned to Golic. "Your job is to distract them."

"With what Jack has brought?" Golic swept his hand at the army and grinned. "We'll crush them."

"Just be careful," she said.

"Then where are you going?" he asked.

"I have another assignment," Beauty replied, stepping away from the cliff.

"Alone?" Thalidon asked.

In answer, Beauty turned to Inna and Aranis. "I'm supposed to take Inna and Aranis with me, if they're willing."

"Where to?" Inna asked.

"I cannot say," Beauty replied.

Aranis's shrug was barely visible within her shadow cloak. "My pet calls? I come."

Inna hesitated, but her gaze swept across the army in Seastone. "I suppose I want to see what Jack has planned." She sheathed her sword and stepped to Beauty.

Beauty nodded to Golic and embraced him one last time, murmuring into his ear. "Stay safe, brother."

"You as well, sister," Golic murmured back.

Beauty withdrew and nodded to the others. Then she turned and led Inna and Aranis to the wagon holding the Gate. As she reached it Golic began to call out orders, and one by one the forces fell into line, forming up behind the road that descended to the village. Beyond them the peak of the Necrolith cast a shadow onto Seastone.

"They'll be fine," Inna said.

"I'm not worried for them," Beauty said. "I'm worried for Jack."

At the head of the army, the black reaver released a thundering roar and bounded down the road to the beach. As Triskella dropped onto the road the army filed after her, and Beauty met Golic's eyes before he too descended out of sight.

"Where are we going?" Aranis asked.

Beauty climbed into the wagon and pointed to the mirror. "Through that."

Inna shook her head in confusion. "A mirror?"

"A Gate," Beauty said. "A relic from the ancient race that connects to others of the same make."

"A portal?" Aranis said, her lips twitching. "How intriguing."

Beauty stepped to the mirror and examined the border. Several runes marked the edge of the glass, each bearing a different symbol. One linked to the guildhall in Griffin, another to a guildhall in the Evermist. Other runes marked the edges but they never connected to anything. She pulled out the list of instructions she'd received from Jack and held them aloft, reading the last item again.

341

Use the Gate. Press the rune at the top.

She examined the top border of the mirror, peering at the scrollwork. But no runes adorned the top. She ran her finger along the surface, casting a touch charm to enhance the feeling in her fingers. At the center her fingers brushed across a slight indentation in the gold. She smiled as she pushed it, and a hidden glyph glowed to life. The glass of the mirror rippled and returned to her reflection.

"How many secrets do you have, Jack?" she murmured, but realized she would probably never know.

She exchanged a look with the two assassins and then stepped through the glass. As always, the mirror flowed across her body like water, depositing her on the other side. To her surprise she stood in a cell made of dark stone, one with a window. Through the opening she spotted Seastone from another direction, and realized that she was inside the Necrolith.

And she was not alone.

"Beauty," Skorn said, standing on the other side of the bars. "Your arrival is right on schedule."

Chapter 43: Trapped

Beauty whirled to the Gate but Inna and Aranis were already stepping through. The silver mirror trembled and then disintegrated, leaving the three of them trapped in the cell. Skorn held aloft a small hand mirror and smirked.

"It's a hand Gate," he said. "Apparently Jack stole it when he took the beacon from the Vault of the Eternals. It may not be as powerful as the other Gates, but it has given your guildmaster an advantage—until I captured Ero with it."

Across the corridor a figure stirred and stepped to the bars of a different cell. Still dressed in white robes, Ero appeared disheveled and worn, his clothing rumpled and dirty. His smile was weary as he met Beauty's gaze.

"Hello, Thera," he said. "I wish you had not come."

Skorn laughed at Ero, sweeping his hand at the two cells. "For all Jack's scheming he cannot defeat me. I have his weapon and his greatest allies."

"I don't see Jack," Inna said, folding her arms. "If he's still out there, he's still fighting."

Skorn's smile turned into a sneer. "Don't you see? I have everything. Even if he infiltrates the Necrolith, he would have to fight through a thousand soldiers, and then face Oragon and Gallow."

Beauty's hand tightened on her sword. "Jack's army is greater than yours."

Skorn's features tightened with anger. "I admit I was unprepared for Jack's resourcefulness, but when the Necrolith reaches full power it will unleash its beacon . . . and everything in the vicinity will be obliterated."

"You would kill your own army?" Beauty demanded.

"He cares nothing for their lives," Ero said. "There are all slaves to him."

Skorn turned to him. "They were once slaves to you."

Ero looked away and did not respond. Skorn's smile turned smug and he rotated back to Beauty's cell, his eyes settling on Aranis.

"You are a new ally of Jack," he said. "But I know your name. Aranis, legendary assassin of the Deep, slayer of thousands . . . outcast."

A thread of the dark elf's cloak began to twirl a ring dagger, and abruptly it streaked for a gap between the bars, aimed for Skorn's chest. A wall of light blossomed into view, causing the ring dagger to bounce off and clatter back into the cell. The barrier faded amidst Skorn's chuckle.

"I built this to contain anyone," he said. "You will not escape, not unless you join me."

Aranis folded her arms, her expression inscrutable beneath her cowl. Skorn's voice turned persuasive as he leaned close to the bars, his scarred features twisting with desire.

"You have so little in common with these people," he said to the dark elf. "They will never be the allies you seek, or the family you crave. Join me, and I will show you realms you cannot imagine. Kill them to prove your loyalty, and you will have your freedom."

Inna eased away from Aranis and Beauty took the hint, drifting away from the black fury visible in the dark elf's lips. The shadow cloak picked up on its owner's agitation and began to tremble, twirling ring daggers into view. Then she spit on the floor.

344

"I would not betray my pet."

Beauty released a held breath, realizing she had nearly died. Skorn sighed in regret and turned away.

"A pity," he said. "Enjoy the devastation of your friends. Then I will let Gallow and Oragon have you."

He turned and strode away, his heels clicking on the dark floor as he departed. When he was gone Beauty stepped to the bars and stabbed a finger at Ero, but hesitated, her gaze scanning the room.

"There are no listening charms," Ero said, understanding her caution. "My brother believes these cells keep us impotent."

"Where's Jack?" she demanded.

"He was supposed to be here by now," Ero said, and passed a hand over his face. "He was supposed to free me before you arrived."

"At least we know Skorn hasn't killed him," Inna said, and shrugged when Beauty looked to her. "Skorn is the type to gloat. If he'd killed Jack, he would have told us."

"I hate the ancients," Aranis said.

"We all do," Beauty said without taking her eyes off Ero.

She turned and examined the cell. Although large, its walls and floor were polished smooth. A tiny privy sat ensconced in an alcove at the back, but it afforded no place of egress. She crept around the edge of the cell, tapping her blade and using an amplification charm to listen. To her dismay the dull reverberation suggested the walls to be several feet thick, far beyond what she could damage even with a strength spell. The floor and ceiling were equally as dense.

She stepped to the window and touched it, but the material was not made of glass. Instead the window was fashioned from aquaglass. She dropped her hearing charm and amplified her touch, and felt the tingle that suggested the window carried magic to shield it from breaking. A ring dagger smashed into it, causing her to flinch away.

"It's unbreakable," Beauty said.

345

"Doesn't mean I won't try," Aranis said. Her voice turned tense as she muttered. "I hate being confined."

Beauty returned her attention to the window but her gaze was drawn to the village below. The black reaver reached the final bend in the road and charged, plowing into the portcullis guarding the gate. Steel rent and snapped, and stone shattered as the beast plowed through the barricade. As if through cotton the muffled screams of men echoed up to Beauty, and the black reaver rampaged through Skorn's line.

Golic and the barbarians followed in Triskella's wake, flowing in a mass of armored bodies to widen the breach. The ten rock trolls struck the left flank, their hardened flesh deflecting arrows with ease.

The rest of the ramshackle army charged into the opening, striking at cultists and Talinorian mercenaries with surprising zeal. Although the thief forces were outnumbered, the presence of the reaver, the rock trolls, and the barbarians tipped the scales.

The reaver caught a sword in her paw and wrenched it from its owner. Slicing him in two with his own blade, she hurled the blade into a knot of cultists, the sword cleaving through flesh like a guillotine until it shattered against a shield.

Thorvaldur swung his hammer with tremendous strength, crushing shields, bodies, and bones. He roared, galvanizing his people to action, the group fighting with supreme skill. Beauty had been raised to fight with her people, but the skill of the rock trolls robbed her of breath.

With his twin-headed axe, Golic stood out among the mass of writhing bodies. The weapon plunged through cult members and barbarians, leaving still forms in Golic's wake. Barbarian and beast, ally and foe, all retreated from his might.

But Skorn's army was not alone either.

Mages cast their magic and stones rose from the beach, forming ranks of golems that charged the thief army. Fire blossomed into wolves and lions, and even a lumbering giant. The thief army cried out in dismay and their charge slowed. Then Beauty spotted Gwen and Rista.

The two mages stepped in, casting a giant golem between them. Rista raised it from the beach, the earth rising and formed into shape. Seawater ascended the golem's body as Gwen added her magic, the water hardening into armor and a glimmering sword. The greater golem lumbered toward the lesser golems, cleaving the stone entities in two. Dust exploded from the contact.

Apparently recognizing the thief line could not be breached, archers aimed and fired, sending arrows angling for Gwen and Rista. Sirani stepped into their path, sending a gust of wind that knocked the volley back into Skorn's forces.

Captain Herrick dodged past the giant golem and charged Gwen and Rista, his two companions cutting through a line of Griffin soldiers. He raised his blade to Gwen just as the girl turned, her eyes widening in horror.

Ursana appeared and struck the captain in the throat with a mailed fist. Herrick coughed and stumbled, and Ursana raised her crossbow, firing a single bolt inches from the other mercenary's chest. The force of the bolt sent him skidding across the battlefield, dead before he came to a stop. Ursana rotated to the third but the man was too quick, knocking the crossbow from Ursana's hands. She ducked as it fell, and rose inside the man's guard, driving a knife into his stomach. Then she spun to face Herrick, who sneered at her, darting in with his sword. From within the Necrolith, Beauty smashed her fist against the glass, her helplessness churning into fury.

Ursana appeared tiny before the legendary captain, but she casually flicked a second knife at her feet, where her crossbow lay. The blade struck the rune at the top, firing the weapon at Herrick's leg, nearly tearing it from his body. He went down, hard, and she scooped up her crossbow to fire again, burying a bolt in Herrick's neck. She then turned and took up position beside Gwen, exchanging a determined look with the girl.

Beauty sighed in relief and wiped the sheen of sweat from her forehead. She'd thought she would witness Ursana die, but the girl managed to hold her own. Gordon joined Rista, and the quartet anchored the heart of the thief army.

Anger burned in Beauty's veins as she watched her friends and family battle. Unable to endure the sight, she spun away from the view. She strode to the bars and tested them, searching the enchanted barrier for any hint of weakness.

"We must wait," Ero said.

"I'm not waiting anymore," Beauty snapped back.

"Trust your guildmaster," Ero said. "He will be here."

"But he's not," Beauty growled.

While she searched, Aranis leaned against the wall, cleaning her nails with a ring dagger. The motion was tense, as if she struggled to control herself. Inna searched as well, her motions becoming more urgent as she scanned the cell. Beauty's anger boiled over and she snapped at Aranis.

"Care to help us?"

"Why?" Aranis said.

"Because time is running out," Beauty growled.

Aranis's voice was cold. "Jack will be here."

Beauty turned on her but the retort died on her lips when the floor shuddered. She darted to the wall and craned to see the base of the Necrolith. Threads of light glowed to life inside the pyramid, ascending through the surface of the stone, rising toward the obelisk. The light pulsed with power, and Beauty spotted mages chained to the tubes of energy on the beach.

Cultists snapped whips at the bound mages, forcing them to increasing efforts, and the magic flowed into the Necrolith, the threads of power rising into the beacon, ascending toward the peak.

Beauty retreated as the magic passed their cell, the walls lighting up with threads of power. Pulsing with green light, the threads grew brighter. The cell shuddered again as the Necrolith came to life, and a burst of power exploded from the obelisk, streaking into the sky. The magic drew on the surrounding light, causing the entire beach to darken.

Beauty turned to ask Ero what was happening, but Ero stood at his own window, his expression oddly excited. Then Ero darted to the privy in his cell and withdrew a small package from behind it. He strode to the bars and fastened it onto the metal.

"It appears our time has come," Ero said.

Ero withdrew and Beauty took the hint, retreating to the rear of the cell. Then Ero pulled a hand crossbow from the folds of his robe and took aim, firing at the package on the bars. It plunged into the package, releasing an inky liquid that dripped to the floor. The liquid poured faster and faster, creating a puddle that suddenly lifted up.

And formed a hand.

Beauty's eyes widened as the hand extended from the puddle, grasping a bar, pulling itself off the floor. A head came next, followed by a second arm and a narrow torso. The puddle diminished as the creature formed legs, morphing into a figure of ink holding the bars.

"What is that?" Inna asked.

Ero responded without taking his eyes from it. "An anti-magic entity."

Beauty gasped, shock binding her tongue. Every type of magic could create an entity, but a sentient being of anti-magic was notoriously the most difficult—and expensive. It required dozens of skilled gnome mages and months of time. Ero noticed Beauty's expression and smiled.

"Paid for by the Church of Light," he said.

The entity placed its face on the enchanted barrier and inhaled, drinking the magic like it was fine ale. Built to withstand any strike, the barrier shimmered and darkened, drawn into the anti-magic entity. The being latched onto the magic and devoured it with frightening hunger. The bars disintegrated and the entity stepped free, immediately going for Beauty's cell, devouring its barrier even faster than the first.

The entity seemed to swell, growing an inch before ambling down the corridor, latching onto a conduit of power pulsing in the wall.

Beauty stepped over the steaming remains of her bars and joined Ero in the hall.

"Jack may not be present," Aranis said. "But he makes his presence known."

Ero sprinted down the hall. "We must hasten. Unchecked, the entity will eat through the entire Necrolith. We have to stop Skorn and escape before it does."

"What about Jack?" Beauty asked.

"He'll be here," Ero said.

Ero took the lead and they rushed up the stairs at the end of the hall. Curving and ascending through the structure, Ero seemed to know exactly where to go as he climbed the labyrinthine interior of the Necrolith. They reached the top level and skidded to a halt, gasping from the climb. Then Ero stepped to the wide double doors and shoved them open.

The peak of the Necrolith was a hundred feet across, the ceiling rising to a glowing point. Strange panels set against the exterior walls displayed ancient glyphs, the symbols matching the pedestal at the heart of the room. Beauty spotted the mangled remains of a small, black pyramid floating above the pedestal, purple light flowing through it and coursing to the pointed ceiling above. Gallow, Oragon, and Skorn turned at their appearance, Skorn's expression turning rigid with disbelief and rage.

"It's not possible . . ." Skorn breathed. "No ancient could have escaped that cell."

Ero smiled at him. "But I'm not an ancient."

He reached up and grasped the amulet around his neck, pulling it free. As the chain snapped Ero's features changed, the mirage fading away from his clothing, his flesh, and his face. Beauty gasped in shock when Ero faded from view, and revealed another.

Jack Myst.

Chapter 44: The God Thief

Jack smirked, relieved to finally shed the persona of Ero. The shock on Beauty's face alone was worth the wait, and he winked at her before drawing his dagger and snapping his crossbow into his palm. He knew he should strike while his adversary was stunned, but could not resist basking in the moment.

"Where is Ero?" Skorn asked, confused and stunned.

"He was never here," Jack said, his smile widening. "I never invited him, and he never came to Lumineia."

"But he descended to the temple in Azertorn," Skorn said. "He bore a staff of light, spoke like my brother."

"Me, me, and me again." Jack released a mocking laugh. "It was always me in the persona of Ero. I particularly enjoyed my arrival at the Church of Light."

Skorn twitched, his scarred features laced with disbelief and a trace of fear. "I do not believe you."

"Believe it," Jack replied. "Ero never came to Lumineia, and you never spoke to him. It has always been me."

"But you *knew* things," he said, his jaw working.

"Nothing you didn't tell me," Jack said.

Jack's gaze flicked to Gallow, but the assassin seemed as astonished as Skorn. Even Beauty's father seemed uncertain, and the giant barbarian shifted his feet, his confusion turning to anger. Before they could recover, Jack glanced to his own allies.

"Beauty, take care of your father. Inna and Aranis, you have Gallow. Skorn is mine."

"It was you the whole time?" Inna asked.

"It was," he said.

"*How?*" Beauty asked.

"Does it matter?" Aranis said, her smile brilliant beneath her cowl. "Well done, pet."

Beauty jerked her head. "When this is over, I expect answers."

"I expect one as well," Jack said.

Beauty blinked in surprise, realizing that every time Ero had asked, *Do you love Jack*, he'd been asking for himself. A smile spread on Beauty's face, her expression one of shock, chagrin, and pride.

"As you order," she said, inclining her head.

Jack turned away from them and surged into a sprint. Inna and Aranis leapt for Gallow, while Beauty charged her father, who was the first to recover. The giant barbarian swung his maul, sending a whistling whine through the room.

"You accept your end with dignity," he growled.

"I'm not here to die," Beauty said.

Jack wanted to hear the rest of the conversation, but Skorn's shock turned to rage and he yanked his thin sword into view. Jack activated his speedstone and felt the rush of magic through his limbs. Skorn was still faster, and deflected his strike with ease.

"You will not escape again," Skorn snarled, his scarred features twisted with fury.

Jack struggled to stave off the assault, and retreated to give himself space. Driven by rage, Skorn did not waver or deviate, nicking Jack's clothing and driving for his heart. Jack took advantage of his lethal intent and fired a crossbow bolt at his feet. Anticipating an explosive bolt, Skorn leapt aside, but the bolt detonated into smoke, engulfing the two of them.

Instead of retreating Jack dived toward his adversary, brushing against him and darting out of the smoke, using the contact to pickpocket the hand Gate. Leaping into the open, he pointed it to the ceiling and pressed the first rune—and pointed at the floor to cast the *second* Gate.

Jack dropped through the floor as Skorn exploded from the smoke, swinging his sword where Jack had been standing. Then Skorn spotted the portal on the ground and his eyes widened—and Jack dropped behind him. Jack stabbed a knife into Skorn's leg and rolled away, rising to his feet. Snarling in pain, Skorn yanked the weapon free and stood, rotating to keep Jack in focus.

"How did you learn that ability?" Skorn demanded.

Jack grinned. "The Mind Vault was very informative," Jack replied.

Jack cast the Gate on the wall behind him and fired his crossbow into the Gate on the floor. The bolt came at Skorn's back but Skorn managed to dodge, twisting into Jack's dagger. He growled as the blade cut a shallow line on his arm and Jack retreated again.

Before Skorn could recover Jack fired the Gate twice again, once below Skorn and again on the ceiling. Skorn cried out as he dropped from view, reappearing on the ceiling and falling toward the portal on the floor.

Jack leapt into a kick that smashed Skorn in the chest, sending him tumbling into another Gate. Skorn sailed through the ceiling again. Jack kept up the assault, casting the Gates on walls, the ceiling, and even in the air, using both portals to send throwing knives and crossbow bolts at Skorn's flanks.

He cast a Gate behind himself and ducked, launching Skorn into it and dropping him on top of an exploding bolt. Unable to recover, Skorn struggled to defend the attacks that came from all sides. By bolt, blade, and Gate, Jack fought Skorn, leaving his flesh scored, his clothing torn.

Skorn screamed in rage and pain as he swung his sword, but he was helpless beneath the assault. Then Jack noticed Beauty . . .

Beauty risked adding strength to her speed charm, the power surging through her limbs and making her tremble. She caught the great maul on her sword and turned it aside. The spiked weapon crashed into the floor, pelting Beauty's body with bits of stone.

She growled and charged through the onslaught, slicing her blade across her father's side. Anticipating her move, Oragon twisted and reached down to grab her hair, using it to toss her aside. She cried out but managed to roll when she hit the ground. She came to her knees and caught the maul as it came for her skull.

The impact sent her knee into the floor, the maul grazing her cheek, the spikes cutting next to her eye. Blood dripped into her vision as she forced the maul aside and leapt away, firing a crossbow bolt at her father's chest. The barbarian *caught* the bolt and flicked it aside, where it detonated against the wall.

"You cast two charms at once," he said, his tone disapproving. "It will consume you."

"Not before I kill you."

She threw a lightstone at him but he caught that as well, the burst of light hardly visible in his fist. He sneered at the attempt but she used the slight distraction to fire another bolt, this time going for his foot. The bolt burst into ropes and wrapped around his legs, but Oragon reached down and snapped them free.

"Your thief tricks will not stop me," he growled.

"They're not meant to stop you," she said.

She locked eyes with Jack and he cast one of his Gates at Oragon's feet. He grunted in dismay as he abruptly dropped through the floor, his feet kicking into Skorn across the room, knocking him down.

Beauty leapt forward, driving her sword for Oragon's eye. He twisted his head to the side and clamped his teeth on her sword. Her

354

surprise cost her, and the barbarian ripped the weapon from her grasp with his jaws. Then he dragged himself from the Gate.

"You will yield to defeat," he snarled, stalking toward her.

Beauty looked at Jack but he was hard pressed by Skorn. A glance revealed Inna and Aranis closing in on Gallow. The assassin's idalia streaked through the air, narrowly missing Aranis when she leapt into a flip. The hands of her cloak tried to catch the spinning blade but it cut through them, returning to Gallow's hand.

"Your friends cannot help you," Oragon snarled, raising his maul once more.

"They will always help me," Beauty said.

She twisted as the weapon came down and dived close, plunging a knife into his shoulder. He twisted and struck her with his free hand, the blow sending her tumbling toward Gallow. But that was her intent.

She rolled to her feet at Gallow's side. Holding her stomach, she feigned weakness as Gallow launched the idalia toward her—and she ducked. The blade streaked toward Oragon and the barbarian instinctively smashed his maul into it. The triangular blade wobbled and spun away, burying into a panel of energy.

"Fight your own foe!" Gallow screamed, and sprinted for the embedded idalia

"Little toys for little men," he growled, striding for Beauty.

But Aranis stepped in front of him. Hands streaked from her cloak and spun a dozen ring daggers. With speed active, the giant barbarian struggled to deflect them but there were too many. They nicked and cut, shredding the bearskin armor and leaving bloody furrows on his flesh. He snarled his fury and turned on the dark elf, charging at her.

Aranis withdrew into her cloak—and the weapon fell upon nothing. She reappeared on the side of the cloak and used hands from her cloak to catch the barbarian's feet, causing him to stumble and crash into a panel of glyphs. Beauty nodded her gratitude to Aranis and leapt for her father, and the dark elf surprisingly smiled and joined her. Out of the corner of her eye she spotted Inna.

355

The young assassin dived for the idalia, yanking it free and raising it high. The triangular blade glowed crimson, the light reflecting off Inna's eyes. She stood stunned for a moment and then turned to face Gallow, whose expression was twisted in disbelief.

"That was mine!" he shrieked.

"Not anymore," Inna said. Raising the triangular blade in her hand, she hurled it at him, the weapon slicing across his arm before spinning back to her.

With Aranis at her side, Beauty advanced upon Oragon. Wounded and furious, the great chief turned on them with a vengeance, his body shimmering with power. Beauty realized he'd cast strength, agility, and speed at once. The giant barbarian seemed to swell in size, flickers of brown light sparking across his form.

Beauty called out to Aranis as the dark elf attacked, her ring daggers slicing into the barbarian. He ignored the sting and his hand whipped out, striking her in the face and sending her skidding toward Jack and Skorn. Then he charged at Beauty, his bloody features alight with power.

She added agility to her own magic but her body was already weary. She groaned and sprinted away, leaping onto the panels of glyphs to gain height. Enraged and empowered, her father smashed his maul into the panels, sending sparks and bits of magic exploding throughout the room.

Skorn and Jack ducked away from the blasts, and Skorn shrieked at the barbarian chief. Heedless of Skorn's orders, Oragon swung his maul with lethal abandon, shredding the stone, the aquaglass windows, and the panels of glyphs.

Beauty parried his blows but fought for distance. With magic thundering in her veins she should have felt powerful, but she had never felt so weak. Her father was stronger, faster, and better. Then she spotted Jack casting Gates and battling Skorn, and realized what she needed.

To be smarter.

She curved her path toward Skorn, stabbing a finger toward a wall when Jack spotted her. He grinned and dodged Skorn's weapon, casting a Gate where she indicated. As she leapt toward it she pointed at Skorn.

She dived through, the room shifting in an instant as she exited beside Skorn. She sliced her sword across his shoulder and slipped away. From across the room the barbarian chief swung his maul through the Gate, the weapon raking Skorn's face as he whirled to Beauty.

He cried out and tumbled aside and the barbarian chief stepped through the Gate—and dropped into another cast by Jack. He cried out as his feet slipped through, his own boots clipping his skull as he caught himself on the floor's edge.

Beauty leapt to him and reared back, bringing every speck of power into her fist. She struck him in the face, rocking his head back and dislodging him from his hold. He grunted in surprise and slipped through, his whole body passing through the Gate. Beauty twirled and aimed her sword towards his exit, impaling him as his chest appeared.

Jack dismissed both Gates and the barbarian tumbled to the floor, fighting for breath and staring at the sword in his heart. He managed to reach his knees and meet Beauty's gaze. His jaw worked and he clawed for his maul but she picked it up instead.

"I will fulfill my oath . . ." he snarled.

Beauty swung the maul, smashing it into his head and the helmet tumbled free. His eyes glazed in shock and he teetered before slumping to the floor. As the barbarian chieftain died Beauty stepped over him.

"That was for mother," she said.

Abruptly weary, she dropped the maul.

And the Necrolith shuddered.

Chapter 45: Crumbling

Jack witnessed Beauty defeat her father as he advanced upon Skorn. The ancient's face was a mask of torn flesh, his dark eyes glittering with frightening rage. As Jack aimed his crossbow the Necrolith shuddered, and Skorn's eyes widened.

"What have you done?"

As if in answer the anti-magic entity burst into the room. Now twice its original size, it loomed over all of them and lunged for the sparking glyphs like a rabid mongrel. The light dimmed as it consumed the power and it leapt for the next. Skorn stumbled to the panel at the center, latching onto it as the Necrolith shuddered again.

"It cannot be!" he shrieked. "I need more time!"

Jack appeared behind him and plunged a crossbow bolt into his back. As the ancient cried out the bolt exploded into ropes, binding him to the center pedestal. Wounded and weak, he fought against the bonds but failed to break free. Jack turned to find Inna kneeling over Gallow.

"Why did you have to kill Jaron?" Inna asked, her voice low and harsh.

Gallow gasped for life, the idalia still buried in his chest. "He betrayed me."

"He *loved* you," she hissed.

Gallow flinched. "I know," he mumbled. "But I was not worth loving."

"He wanted you to replace him," Inna said. "Did you know that? But you refused to learn the creed."

Gallow fumbled to press a hand on his wound but the effort was in vain. "I'm sorry," he said, his features twisted with pain. "I failed him."

"I won't," Inna said. She pulled the idalia free and rose to her feet.

"Forgive me . . ." Gallow breathed, his body going still.

Inna straightened her shoulders and turned, her jaw setting in a firm line. Jack inclined his head to her, and she returned the gesture. She'd slain her father's killer, and her expression bore an intense satisfaction. Jack turned to the bound Skorn and the others joined him.

"You're just slaves," Skorn shrieked. "Born unto death without the masters you are meant to serve."

Jack leaned down until Skorn could meet his gaze. "Arrogance will get you killed," Jack said.

Skorn's eyes nearly burst from his skull and the Necrolith shuddered again. Then Skorn's expression turned furious and he yanked his hand free, catching Jack's tunic and pulling him close.

"At least you'll die with me."

Jack pulled his hand free and stepped back—and saw Skorn holding the pocket Gate. With a jerk of his arm Skorn hurled it directly at the anti-magic entity. The inky figure caught and devoured it, causing an explosion of silver sparks from its mouth. Silver liquid splashed outward with several drops landing on Jack's hand.

Jack cried out and wiped them off but they sank into his flesh, burning like coals. He dug his nails into his skin but the liquid disappeared, the pain evaporating as quickly as it had come. Jack cursed as the Necrolith shook, the floor tilting slightly before righting itself.

"There goes our escape route," he growled.

Skorn began to laugh, the sound rising with madness as he struggled against his bonds. "You cannot escape!" he screamed. "The power of the Necrolith has nowhere to go—and it will build until it detonates. Even you are not fast enough to escape."

The anti-magic entity consumed the last of the panels and hunted for more—and spotted the center pedestal. It charged to it, clamping its jaws onto the small black pyramid. The purple light briefly illuminated the entity before the pedestal was extinguished. Then its jaws opened wide and settled on the entire panel—and Skorn's screaming body. It sucked in, consuming all the energy, taking Skorn's life.

Skorn's screaming mounted before abruptly cutting off, and Skorn disappeared along with the remains of the panel. The thread of power was cut to the peak of the room and the Necrolith shook violently, the burst of white that extended from the top of the obelisk reversing, filling the room with light.

"The stairs!" Jack shouted, and the foursome sprinted for the doors.

As they charged from the room, Jack spotted the anti-magic entity raise its hands in an attempt to consume the beacon's power. It trembled in ecstasy before bursting apart, shredded by the monumental power. Fires ignited in the chamber as threads of power exploded.

Jack took the lead, racing down the labyrinth of stairs and corridors. All around them threads of magic detonated, engulfing the halls in fire and smoke. Jack veered away from a corridor filled with flames and dropped down another flight of stairs.

"How do you know where to go?" Inna shouted.

"I snuck out and mapped the place at night," Jack shouted. "This way!"

He glanced back and saw Aranis and Inna right behind him—but no Beauty. He reversed and leapt up the stairs, catching sight of Beauty as she collapsed on the floor. He slid to a stop at her side and scooped her up, shocked by how frail she seemed.

"I used too much magic to fight my father," she mumbled. "It has a cost."

With fires exploding on both sides he sprinted down the corridor. "You never answered my question."

Her smile was faint. "I can't believe it was you all along."

He dodged a blast and dropped down a flight of stairs, sprinting for another staircase. "I wanted to tell you," he said. "But Skorn was listening to everything. I needed him to believe it was Ero."

"Did you even attempt to talk to the real Ero?" she asked.

"No," he said, and grinned.

The floor shook and the side of the corridor crumbled. Inna leapt across and kept running on the other side, while Aranis used her cloak to grab a broken beam on the ceiling and swing herself over.

Threads of magic pulsed and exploded on both sides, shredding the walls as fragments of the ceiling caved in. Jack heard a crash from above, and then another, and guessed the Necrolith had begun to collapse. Realizing they wouldn't make it out in time, he veered to the side.

"Where are you going?" Inna shouted.

"Out!" Jack replied.

Heaving Beauty onto his shoulder, he raised his crossbow to a wall and emptied it, sending a dozen exploding bolts digging into the wall. They exploded violently, the ceiling collapsing halfway into the corridor. When the smoke cleared Jack caught a glimpse of sunlight beyond and dived to the floor, sliding beneath the caved-in corridor and bursting into the open.

Inna followed his example, while Aranis leapt over the beams, threading through the gap in a twisting motion that carried her outside the Necrolith. Inna cried out as she slid into open air and fell.

They plummeted down the side of the Necrolith until they reached the pyramid's base. Jack grunted as he bounced off the curve and slid down the side, accelerating as he streaked for the ground below.

He'd lost his grip on Beauty and she slid nearby, her face white and strained. Jack cast his shadowhook at her side and it managed to bond to her belt. With a yank he drew her to him. Then he sought for a way to slow them down before they slammed into the beach with lethal force.

361

He caught a glimpse of the thief army fleeing up the road to Seastone, carrying wounded and dead on their shoulders. Skorn's army lay on the beach, while the survivors piled onto boats that would take them out to sea. The freed mages sprinted alongside the thief army, rushing to reach Seastone before the Necrolith detonated.

The Necrolith shook again, and a great whistling sound pierced the air. Like a great beast sucking in its breath, the sound mounted until it became a thundering wail. Jack looked up and saw the top of the Necrolith crashing into itself, while the threads of power continued to push power upward. When they collided . . .

"We're not going to make it!" Beauty said.

"I'm not letting Skorn be right!" Jack shouted, and looked up at Aranis. "Can you slow us down?"

"For a kiss!" The dark elf shouted.

"You'll get your payment!" Jack shouted back.

Aranis chuckled to herself and her cloak expanded into hundreds of tiny hands, each digging into cracks in the pyramid's surface. A pair of hands caught Jack's tunic while another pair grasped Inna's hands.

Jack's arms burned from the effort to hold Beauty, their momentum gradually slowing. The beach streaked toward them and Aranis screamed, her cloak sparking as it continued to slow them. But it was not enough.

He cast about for another solution and spotted Sirani on the beach. The rock troll was chasing the survivors, riding a small wind dragon that snapped playfully at their heels. Since his crossbow was empty, Jack grabbed for Beauty's, and fired an unenchanted bolt at Sirani. He cursed when it missed and fired again, and the bolt bounced off her back.

The rock troll came to a halt and looked up, spotting Jack sliding down the side of the pyramid. She crowed in delight and turned her dragon aside, leaping into the air and winging toward them. As Jack neared the ground a gust of wind slammed into him, slowing his momentum so he didn't break his legs when he hit the beach. He grunted in pain and rolled to his feet, helping Beauty to hers as Sirani's wind dragon disintegrated and she landed beside them.

"Hello, handsome," she crooned, stumbling.

"We need to get to Seastone," he shouted, but saw at a glance that Sirani could not do it. Her smile was wild and excited, but her features were drawn and white.

A crash drew his gaze to the ships attempting to flee. Triskella charged a boat loaded with Skorn's army, smashing through the hull like it was made of paper. As cultists cried out and attempted to fight, the reaver exploded through the deck, rampaging through their ranks even as the boat sank.

I hate to interrupt playtime, Jack thought to her. *But I could use some help.*

The black reaver paused and looked over at Jack. She snarled and bounded off the ship, the motion causing it to swing violently to the side, sending a man screaming into the sea. As the reaver sprinted toward them Jack's gaze was drawn to the Necrolith. The shriek from the beacon continued to mount, rising in pitch and volume. The thief army scrambled up the last of the road, retreating into the ruins of Seastone for safety.

Triskella reached Jack and he grasped one of the black reaver's spines. He lifted Beauty to his side and held on. Inna and Aranis caught the other side while Sirani grabbed a spine at the shoulder. Ignoring the weight, the reaver bounded up the road.

Empowered with the blood of its kills, the reaver moved with shocking speed, crossing the battlefield and ascending the road. Sirani's wild laughter reverberated off the cliff as Triskella sprinted up the curves. The wail from the Necrolith approached a breaking point and Jack turned—to see the beacon's power collide with the summit.

The magic detonated in a titanic *boom* that rattled Jack's teeth. The obelisk snapped in half and the explosion expanded outward, shredding the stone of the Necrolith and devouring the pyramid base, shattering the last of Skorn's ships. The explosion slammed into the cliff as Triskella leapt the remaining distance. The black reaver landed in

Seastone outside of the billowing flames and slid to a halt, her flanks heaving from the exertion of the climb.

Stone cracked and rent from the beach to the mountain, the entire region trembling from the monumental blast. Boulders tumbled into the flames and half the cliff collapsed, sinking into the receding flames and crashing onto the inferno raging on the beach.

The explosion devoured it all, swallowing the stones, the Necrolith, the village, and much of the beach in its hunger. Fed by the blast of magic, white-laced fire reached for Seastone, but fell short of the thief army. Its power extinguished, the flames began to recede.

When the earth finally stopped shaking Jack descended from Triskella's back and nodded his gratitude to her. He limped to the cliff's edge and stared down at the devastated beach. A single corner of the Necrolith's pyramid base remained. Its black stone burning like a limb in a dying fire, while the sea roiled around it. Steam and smoke billowed into the sky, already darkening the sun. Jack watched it burn with a smile on his face.

"So dies the devil," he said.

Chapter 46: Jack's Truth

The thief army disintegrated as quickly as it had joined, with the commands of Griffin and Talinor the first to depart. Their captains bore matching expressions of anger, clearly guessing their orders had been forged. Still, Jack had no regrets about conscripting them. They had given his army much needed strength. As if reading his thoughts, Thorvaldur gestured to them.

"You coerced them into joining your force."

Jack turned to the hulking rock troll and noticed a dozen new tattoos on his flesh, each marking a kill.

"They had as much a stake in our victory as we did," Jack said. "Even if they didn't know it."

"You could have requested their aid," Thorvaldur said, his lips twitching in a smile.

"Is that judgment I hear?" Jack asked. "Or jealousy? Yours aren't the only contracts I steal."

Thorvaldur laughed. "You are a clever thief," he said.

Jack grinned and reached up to clasp his hand. "You have my gratitude for coming."

"Don't thank me," he said with a shrug. "King Tryton permitted the contract."

Jack raised his eyebrow. He'd sent the message directly to Thorvaldur in the hopes to avoid Tryton's refusal. "How did Kythira feel about that?"

"I'll let you know when she finds out," Thorvaldur said with a laugh.

Jack laughed with him until he sucked in his breath. A thief healer had managed to repair his wounds but they still hurt. As he watched the rock trolls depart he spotted Paro striding to him.

"Paro," he said.

The abbot inclined her head. "I'd say it's a pleasure to meet you, but it appears I've known you for months."

"You aren't angry at my deception?"

"On the contrary," the abbot said. "The Church of Light had become corrupted and filled with greed. It needed to be cleansed."

"Did Alidon escape?"

"One of the first to flee," Paro said, her expression one of disdain.

"Don't worry," Jack said. "The church doesn't have a single copper left, and all of the buildings have been sold. I left a small cache of coin with a moneychanger in Azertorn under your name. I assume you will distribute it to your loyal."

The abbot laughed, the sound laced with chagrin. "I used to despise thieves," she said. "I never expected one to be our savior."

"Don't tell anyone," Jack replied, lowering his tone. "It will ruin my reputation."

Paro laughed and clasped his hand before departing, and Jack turned to the next in line. He would have preferred to slip away and share a mug with his friends, but he was still the guildmaster, and they had come because of him.

For the next hour he bid farewell to the other factions that had answered his call. Val'Trisian warned him of Aranis before departing, and the dark elves cast the assassin wary looks as they slipped into the trees. Then Triskella padded to him.

"Triskella," he said, his voice fond. "It's always good to see you."

She settled on her haunches and shook her lionlike head, rattling the steel spines. *I was surprised by your invitation.*

"Did you enjoy yourself?"

Tremendously, she said, her mental voice tinged with amusement. *Perhaps next time I'll bring my children.*

Jack imagined the family of black reavers at his side and grinned. "Farewell, Triskella. Happy hunting."

Don't get into too much trouble, Triskella said.

She growled but it sounded more like a laugh. Then the black reaver turned and padded into the trees, the sounds of her passage fading as she departed. Jack shook his head, grateful to have the loyalty of such a powerful creature. With a sigh of regret he turned to Urthor, who'd waited until the black reaver was gone to speak to him.

Jack spotted Beauty standing with her people at the cliff's edge. They spoke throughout the disintegration of Jack's army, and Jack cast several looks their way. He heard snippets of their conversation and realized the barbarians were praising Beauty for her triumph over Oragon. It was also clear that Beauty wanted to return with Golic to the barbarian mountains. From across the gap she met Jack's gaze.

"Not yet," she hedged. "I have unfinished business."

"Don't take too long," Valia said. "Our people need you."

Beauty embraced Golic one last time before the barbarians departed down the road. With them gone it was just the thieves remaining in Seastone, and Jack ordered Thalidon to send them home.

Many were wounded, but only a few had been killed. Although the guild members mourned their losses, the thieves lived a dangerous occupation, and laughed and talked as they passed through the Gate.

By the time the fires on the beach had burned to embers, the last of the thieves had returned to the guild. Only a handful of Jack's closest friends remained with Inna, Aranis, and Sirani. Jack had suspected the aged rock troll would depart with Thorvaldur, but she'd rebuffed his invitation with a smile.

"I have a new occupation," she'd said cheerily, glancing at Inna.

Jack strode to the group gathered around the wagon. Before he could say a word, Aranis stepped to him and wrapped her arms around his shoulders. She smiled beneath her cowl as the cloak flowed around them, plunging them in darkness. Then her lips touched his and he kissed her back. The contact continued until someone coughed in amusement and the dark elf withdrew.

"Payment accepted, pet," she said smugly.

Jack spotted the irritation on Beauty's face and shrugged. "I always pay my debts."

"I bet you do," Sirani said with a giggle.

"Speaking of debts," Aranis said, turning to Inna. "I have one to collect from you."

Inna squared her shoulders. "What would you have of me?"

"To join your Assassins Guild," Aranis said.

Inna smiled at the request, glancing at Jack. "With Gallow gone there are only two left of the seven. I mean to take the leadership of the guild for myself."

"Your father would be proud," Beauty said.

"I look forward to being an assassin," Sirani said, a wide grin spreading on her features. "Can we hunt Griffin berserkers? Or bandits in Talinor? Or maybe pirates in the south sea!" She cackled and fell to muttering about the possibilities.

"I see you have everything in hand," Jack said. "But you can't lead the guild with a name like Inna."

368

"I know," Inna said with a smile. "Which is why I'll use the assassin persona my father gave me. Tronis."

"A name bound for legend," Beauty said, her tone one of approval. "And it appears you have a weapon to match." She pointed to the idalia on Inna's back.

Inna smiled at her words and reached out to clasp Beauty's hand. "You have my gratitude for your aid in defeating Gallow. I could not have done so alone." Her eyes swept to Jack, indicating the words were meant for him as well.

"I enjoyed his defeat as much as you did," Jack replied.

Her red hair bright in the sun, her clothes torn and bloody, Inna stood tall. Jack saw the steel in her gaze and recognized it as a glimpse of things to come. The girl had vanquished her father's killer and become the assassin she was meant to be.

"I don't think I'll ever understand everything you did," Inna said, "But from this day forth you can count the Assassin's Guild as an ally."

Jack clasped her hand and smiled. The thieves said their farewells and the trio of assassins departed down the road. Only Aranis looked back.

"Goodbye, pet," she said. "Don't think I've given up on you."

"I haven't," Jack said with a smile.

Aranis held his gaze, and an unspoken gratitude passed between them. Jack inclined his head to her and she smiled before slipping away. Jack watched them go with a twinge of regret in his heart. The last few months had been riddled with danger, escapes, assassins, and risk. Despite the weight of his office, he'd never had so much fun.

He sighed and turned to find Beauty standing with Thalidon, Roarthin, Gordon, and Ursana. Jack motioned to the wagon and raised an eyebrow, but the five thieves shook their heads in unison.

"Don't think you will escape without answers," Beauty said.

"Can't we do this tomorrow?" Jack asked, gesturing to the billow of smoke still rising from the destroyed Necrolith. "It's been a long day."

"No," Thalidon said with a smile. "We've waited long enough. You can share your tale as we walk back to Woodhaven."

"Walk?" Jack asked, and groaned.

"Yes," Gordon said. "Walk. It will give you plenty of time to explain yourself."

Jack looked between them but saw no hint of an opening. Grunting at their betrayal, he muttered. "I thought *I* was the guildmaster."

Thalidon grinned and climbed onto the driver's bench of the wagon, turning the horses back onto the road. Beauty patted Axe on the flank and then fell into step with Jack. As the group ambled down the road they looked at him expectantly. Resigned to telling the truth, Jack began.

"When I became guildmaster the vault key appeared in my hand," he said. "Then I stepped into the guild vault and learned the truth, that Skorn was listening to everything . . ."

As they made their way back to elven lands Jack shared the full tale of what he'd done in the last few months, including how he'd stolen the Gate from the guildhall in Woodhaven and hidden it in the Church of Light, using it as a terminus so he could access it at any time.

He explained how every time he was absent from the Thieves Guild he became Ero, frequently several times a day. Beauty laughed when he spoke of portaling to the church to keep his persona alive.

He explained how he'd stolen from the Church of Light and used the coin to purchase the entity of anti-magic, storing it within the Thieves Guild vault until after Skorn came for him. He explained that during the weeks he'd disappeared from Thalidon and Roarthin he'd been traveling to the City of Dawn, and when he'd been feigning sickness on the return journey he was with Skorn on the way to the Necrolith, enduring Skorn's endless monologue.

From within the Necrolith cell he'd used the Gate to escape, and continued preparing for the upcoming battle as Jack. He'd retrieved the anti-magic entity and dispatched his final summons, bringing together an army he knew could stop Skorn's forces.

"When did he get the hand Gate from you?" Beauty asked.

"He caught me returning and I had to give it to him," Jack said. "Skorn laughed, thinking Ero had brought the hand Gate as a means of escape. He still had no idea that I had stolen it from the Vault of the Eternals when I took the beacon."

"Is there anything you won't steal?" Ursana asked with a laugh.

Jack grinned. "Everything can be stolen."

"Even Le Runtáriel's affection?" Beauty asked shrewdly. "I still don't know how you managed that. The moment she touched your mind she would have known your identity."

"I'd spoken to her before," Jack admitted, "and knew she liked me. When I told her about Skorn she agreed to help."

"Her integrity will take a hit for supporting a false Ero," Ursana said.

"She didn't seem to mind," Jack said. "Like every woman, she has her mischievous side."

"But *how*?" Gordon asked. "How could you possibly pull off two personas at once?"

"A question I'd like to know as well," Beauty mused. "All it would have taken was one person getting suspicious when you didn't answer a door."

Jack cast her a sly grin. "Just because I wasn't there, doesn't mean I didn't answer the door."

Ursana shook her head in confusion. "However did you manage that?"

Jack reached to his gauntlet and removed a star shaped rune hidden beneath a secret pocket in the leather. Then he tossed it to Beauty. She caught it and held it aloft, and flinched when Jack's voice came from it.

"You never got suspicious," the object said. Jack's spoke on the other side of the fire, his voice carried through the magic to the charm in Beauty's hand.

"You spoke as Ero when you were Jack?" Roarthin asked.

"When you all thought I was going to beseech Ero to join our cause, I was preparing my persona. That," Jack pointed to the disc, "cost me a fortune, but it's what allowed me to be in two places. When Beauty knocked on the door in the Temple of Light I would hear it in Talinor. All I had to do was step away and answer."

Ursana laughed first, and it quickly spread to the others, the sound echoing off the rocky walls around them. They had made camp in an isolated ravine, and their fire cast flickering shadows onto the walls of stone. After a brief meal they urged him to finish the tale, so Jack leaned against a dead tree and spoke of the final battle in the Necrolith. Beauty added several elements, filling in the gaps. Then Jack gestured to them and they shared the tale of the battle on the beach. When the silence fell Ursana stabbed a finger at him.

"We kept you in the guild because we thought it would protect you," she said. "But you were out protecting us."

"Guilty," Jack said.

"I understand your reasons in withholding the truth," Gordon said. "But I still wish I would have known."

Thalidon grunted sourly. "I look forward to destroying each and every listening charm Skorn left at the guild."

Beauty flashed a chagrined smile. "Who knew that Jack Myst, the wayward scoundrel, would be such a good guildmaster?"

"Not I," they chorused together.

Jack did not join the ensuing laughter. The extended duration of the ruse had taken its toll, and Jack had never been so weary. It had almost done the unthinkable, and robbed his occupation of its pleasure. As they quieted he gestured to them.

"I hope your new guildmaster will do as well."

They stared at him, their humor evaporating. Before they could argue Jack yawned.

"I officially resign."

Chapter 47: Parting

"*Why?*" Ursana demanded.

"Because I *hate* it," Jack said fervently.

"But you performed admirably," Thalidon said.

Jack jerked his head. "No. I didn't. We may have defeated Skorn, but I did not inspire, teach, or grow the guild. If anything, I left us in a worse position than before—especially now that the Woodhaven guildhall is destroyed."

"We were at war," Roarthin said. "Without you we would have lost far more than a single guildhall."

"Perhaps," Jack said. "But the guild needs a guildmaster that understands leadership."

"You brought an army together on a whim," Gordon said.

"I *stole* an army," Jack corrected. "Half of those that came received forged orders, and only a handful came at my request."

Thalidon opened his mouth to argue but Beauty cut him off. "You are certain?"

Jack affected a languid pose. "As of this moment, I'm done." He grinned as he said it.

"Are you leaving the guild as well?" Ursana asked.

"Of course not," Jack said, "But I think from now on I'll choose my own assignments."

Gordon released a bark of laughter. "You want to be part of the guild, but do as you please?"

"Yes."

"You think the new guildmaster will allow that?" Thalidon asked.

"I don't really care," Jack said, closing his eyes.

Beauty sighed. "I think it's also time I admit my own departure."

"You as well?" Ursana asked, dismayed.

"My brother is right," she said. "My father is gone and my sister's killer is dead. My oath is fulfilled. It's time I returned to my homeland."

Jack opened his eyes and found Beauty looking at him. "How soon?" he asked.

"A few days," she said. "I'll return to the guildhall and say goodbye."

"Beauty," Thalidon began, but she jerked her head.

"Not anymore," Beauty said. "Skorn gave me that name, and it dies with him. I'm Thera now."

"We won," Ursana said with a scowl, "but this feels like we lost."

With that she stood and reclined on her bedroll, rolling away from the group. The motion signaled an end to the conversation and Jack unrolled his own bedroll. He uncoiled his body on it and was asleep in seconds. For the first time in months he slept without dreams and woke rested.

He scratched the itch on his arm and stood, joining the others as they broke camp. As they made their way back onto the road the others continued to pepper him with questions about his two personas, and he resigned himself to answering.

The journey home was long, but none of them seemed to mind. For the first time in years they had nothing to fear. Word had yet to spread that the bounty on Jack's head was over, but few dared to come for him. Three weeks after the battle at the Necrolith they reached the Evermist and returned to the guildhall.

Jack endured the praise of the thieves but chose the first opportunity to name Forlana as his replacement. With Kuraltus at her side Jack was confident she could handle the fallout from the war with Skorn. The furor of their victory descended into drinking and laughter, and Jack caught Thera's arm, motioning her to follow.

He exited the fortress and entered the Evermist. With the moon high, the mist veritably glowed as it swirled about them. Jack came to a clearing and turned, but for several moments simply regarded her.

"I still cannot believe you stole a god," she said.

Jack smiled. "I'm rescinding my question."

"Why would you do that?" Thera asked. "Are you afraid of the answer?"

"No." he said. "I already know the answer. But your heart is divided, and I know which you will choose."

"You could join me," she asked, her voice soft.

"I can't," Jack said. "I'm not a warrior, and I would just be a distraction in the barbarian revolution."

"Where will you go?" Thera asked, and a knowing smile played across her features. "I suspect you will not be content to steal from normal strongrooms."

"I saw places in the Mind Vault that I want to see," he said. "Other lands, other kingdoms, and even other races."

She released a long breath and stepped in, reaching up to draw him into a kiss. He returned it with passion, but sensed a note of finality in the contact. When she withdrew, Jack knew it was the last time.

"Find someone to love, Jack," she murmured.

She turned and departed, leaving Jack in the Evermist. For several minutes Jack remained rooted in place, staring up at the fortress. Wreathed in light from the celebrating thieves, the guildhall veritably glowed, a beacon in the swamp.

He spotted Ursana and Gwen on a balcony, talking and laughing. The battle at the Necrolith had forged them into friends, and he saw the glimmerings of a sisterhood between them. Whatever course Gordon's family took, the fissure in the group was healed. Jack sighed, grateful he'd managed to repair Ursana's relationship with Gordon, yet regretting he could not do the same with Thera.

He loved Thera, but the fact that he could say goodbye spoke volumes. She was his first love. She was not his last. A smile spread on his face as he turned his thoughts to the future. He'd met many women that appealed to him, and wondered if any were capable of capturing his soul.

His thoughts turned to what he'd learned in the Mind Vault. The world had far more to explore than the five kingdoms knew, and with Skorn and Gallow dead the guild was headed for an era of prosperity and peace. He instinctively jerked his head, disliking that fate. He craved conflict, and after what he'd learned he knew where to find it.

"Let the adventure begin," he said.

Epilogue: The Living Gate

Forty Years Later

Jack hiked through the endless sands of the desert, the bright moon casting the expanse into shades of shadow. He crested a rise and the sand troll village came into view. Nestled beneath a massive ancient barrier, the village slumbered in the depths of night. Jack slipped past the sentries and used his shadowhook to ascend to the Irilian Shield. Alone in the moonlight, he advanced up the curve to the summit of the ancient structure, to the hidden Gate leading to the Vault of the Eternals.

He reached the top and paused, breathing deep of the crisp autumn air. In the forty years since he'd defeated Skorn, Jack had returned to the Irilian shield eight times, but each attempt to enter the Vault of the Eternals had ended in failure.

He considered what he'd learned in the Mind Vault, and his decision to keep it secret. He'd told no one about the krey, their realms, or their power. Jack had even kept the secret from his beloved.

He smiled as he thought of her. After Thera he'd never thought to love another, but his beloved had stolen his soul with a glance, and never relinquished it. Of anyone else, Jack wished he could tell her about the krey.

"Not until I know the truth," he murmured, withdrawing a pair of daggers from his pack.

He'd made the first attempt to enter the Vault a month after Skorn's demise, and taken the original keys that had opened the Gate. To his dismay the keys had failed, leaving him standing on a barren surface. Unable to dismiss the nagging desire to learn about the krey, he'd employed smiths from across Lumineia, each contracted to replicate the daggers. Then Draeken had unleashed his mighty army, plunging the world into The Second Draeken War. In the aftermath Jack had been distracted, and several years had passed before he could make another attempt to enter the Vault.

Jack approached the location of the Gate. The surface of the Irilian Shield began to glow and the daggers brightened, the glow illuminating his features. Jack kept his excitement in check, and reminded himself that it had happened before. He slid the first dagger home and then moved to the second lock, driving the second key into place. The surface between the two keys shimmered silver, and then abruptly darkened.

Jack scowled in disappointment and yanked the daggers free. Shoving them into his pack, he turned and trudged away. He came to an abrupt halt when light blossomed behind him. He whirled, and watched a geyser fall into a shimmering pool of silver.

Jack looked to the keys in his hand and back to the portal, foreboding spiking in his gut. The keys hadn't opened the Gate, indicating someone *within* the Vault had activated the portal. His curiosity overcame his caution, and he strode to the portal and dropped through.

The view shifted to that of a flawless corridor, the wide windows depicting a scene of the stars. Walls curved to an arched ceiling, while the floor contained a subtle texture. The corridor appeared identical to his previous visit to the Vault of the Eternals. Except it was not empty.

Ero stood at the end of the hallway. Dressed in a flowing robe over slacks and a tunic, he hadn't changed. His white hair framed his features, while his startlingly blue eyes settled on Jack. At Ero's side stood Myra, the construct of lightning.

"Jack Myst," Ero said. "Did you enjoy your time carrying my mantle?"

379

"Skorn and then Draeken," Jack said. "How many mistakes will I clean up for you?"

Ero released a pained sigh. "I did not know of Draeken's attempt until the war had already ended."

"I thought you were supposed to protect Lumineia," Jack said, folding his arms. "Your exiled Eternal nearly destroyed it."

"You *dare* to speak so harshly?" Myra growled.

"Myra," Jack said, his eyes shifting to woman. "Has anyone else stolen from you while I was away? I hate to think another has bested you."

Her features darkened and she looked away. Ero smiled at her response and stepped forward, clearly attempting to change the subject.

"I wasn't certain you were going to make another attempt to return."

"You knew I had tried to enter the Vault before?" Jack asked.

"I did," Ero replied. "But I saw no reason to permit your entry."

Jack folded his arms. "I wasn't coming to steal."

"Liar," Myra said, blue lightning arcing up her arms.

"I missed you too," Jack said, winking at her.

Ero raised a hand to forestall Myra's outburst. "Why did you come, Jack?"

Jack regarded Ero for some time. His question had seared into his mind for four decades, but now that he stood before Ero, he found himself uncertain if he wanted the answer. Then he shrugged and stabbed a finger at the ancient.

"I want to know about the krey."

Ero's eyes widened imperceptibly. "Where did you hear that name?"

380

"From the Mind Vault."

Ero stared at him for long enough that Myra began to fidget. Then he gestured to Jack. "I will answer your questions if you answer mine."

"Agreed," Jack said.

"You are human," Ero said. "I am krey."

"What is man to the krey?"

"A slave," Ero admitted, his features tightening with bitterness and regret.

"And the other races of Lumineia?" Jack said. "The Mind Vault called them specimens, and said the krey do not know of their existence."

Ero sidestepped the question and asked his own. "Why have you not aged?"

"Druids age slower than normal men," Jack said.

"Not that slow," Ero said.

Jack noticed the curiosity in Ero's eyes and realized the truth. "You let me through the beacon to ask why I haven't aged?"

Ero's lips twitched, confirming Jack's suspicions. Then he glanced at Myra. "Scan him."

Myra floated forward and raised a hand, sending a current of power into Jack's body. He recoiled but the magic did not hurt, but sent a warm tingle through his torso, expanding into his extremities.

"It appears I cannot protest," Jack said dryly.

"Be glad I'm not shredding your heart," Myra muttered. Then she frowned, her energy focusing on Jack's arm. "It's not possible."

"Myra?" Ero asked.

She extinguished her power and looked to him. "Shards of a portal have embedded into his body, halting the aging of his flesh."

381

"It should have killed him," Ero said, his voice surprised.

"Luck has always been my ally," Jack said, looking between the two of them.

Ero turned to him, regarding Jack with new eyes. "My people have tried many times to create one like you, and you accomplish it by accident. I can only assume it was due to your bond to your panther that helped you survive."

"Create *what* like me?" Jack asked.

"One that can portal without a Gate," Ero said. "With the shards in your flesh, you've become a *living* Gate."

Jack felt a chill and looked at his arm, to the scars left from when the pocket Gate had exploded. Jack touched the white skin but it felt no different than his other scars. Ero then released an irritated sigh, drawing Jack's gaze.

"The element has prevented your aging," Ero said, clearly annoyed, "and you have proven that you protect Lumineia. As much as I am loath to admit it, you have met the qualifications to become an Eternal."

Jack realized what he was saying and smirked. "An Eternal thief. I like the sound of that."

Ero scowled. "I would tell you the rest myself, but in this case there is another you should speak to."

"Who?" Jack asked, but his attention was on his arm. Now that he knew what to look for, he could feel a flicker of power in his hand, and it swelled when he mentally reached for it.

"Your beloved."

Jack snapped to look at him. "How would she know about the Eternals?"

"Because she is one."

Jack stared at him, confused and uncertain. Was it possible? She always had her secrets, but he hadn't realized she carried one of such

382

magnitude. His confusion turned to anger when he considered how much she'd kept from him.

"Before you depart," Ero said, "you must take the oath. If you'll follow me."

Jack met his gaze and shook his head. "Perhaps another day."

Myra realized what he was doing and raised a hand, power arcing on her fingertips, but Jack had already harnessed the energy in his arm. Jack evaporated from view, reappearing an instant later on the Irilian shield.

He stumbled forward before righting himself, his eyes lifting to the moon. A slow smile spread on his face as he considered what he'd just done. He half expected Ero to attempt pursuit but realized it did not matter. No one could catch him now. His smile faded as he thought of his beloved.

"No more secrets," he said, and Gated home.

The wind brushed the empty Irilian shield, its cool touch spreading sand across the smooth material. Abruptly the portal opened anew, and Ero stepped into view with Myra at his side. Ero sighed as he saw that Jack was already gone.

"You should never have permitted him to join the Eternals," Myra demanded. "He's unpredictable, arrogant, and impulsive."

"It was only a matter of time before he realized the truth," Ero said. "And better to watch him as an Eternal than have him act on his own interests."

"That man will not be leashed," Myra said.

"Not by us," Ero agreed. "But his beloved will control him."

Myra scowled. "His newfound power is dangerous."

"As are you," Ero said. "But I count you as an ally."

"Your will be served," Myra said, and reluctantly turned away, passing through the portal.

Ero stared at the empty expanse, wondering if he'd made the right choice. Jack Myst could not be trusted, but he had aided in the defeat of Skorn and Draeken. Now that he could Gate at will, where would he go?

And what would he steal?

The Chronicles of Lumineia

By Ben Hale

—The Master Thief—

Jack of Thieves

Thief in the Myst

The God Thief

—The Second Draeken War—

Elseerian

The Gathering

Seven Days

The List Unseen

—The Warsworn—

The Flesh of War

The Age of War

The Heart of War

—The White Mage Saga—

Assassin's Blade (Short story prequel)

The Last Oracle

The Sword of Elseerian

Descent Unto Dark

Impact of the Fallen

The Forge of Light

Author Bio

Originally from Utah, Ben has grown up with a passion for learning almost everything. Driven particularly to reading caused him to be caught reading by flashlight under the covers at an early age. While still young, he practiced various sports, became an Eagle Scout, and taught himself to play the piano. This thirst for knowledge gained him excellent grades and helped him graduate college with honors, as well as become fluent in three languages after doing volunteer work in Brazil. After school, he started and ran several successful businesses that gave him time to work on his numerous writing projects. His greatest support and inspiration comes from his wonderful wife and five beautiful children. Currently he resides in Missouri while working on his Masters in Professional Writing.

To contact the author, discover more about Lumineia, or find out about the upcoming sequels, check out his website at Lumineia.com. You can also follow the author on twitter @ BenHale8 or Facebook.

76729998R00233

Made in the USA
Columbia, SC
10 September 2017